I0823170

THE RED WINTER

THE RED WINTER

Cameron Sullivan

TOR PUBLISHING GROUP

NEW YORK

This is a work of fiction. All of the characters, organizations, and events portrayed in this novel are either products of the author's imagination or are used fictitiously.

THE RED WINTER

Map by Rhys Davies
Endpaper art by Christina Mrozik

Designed by Omar Chapa

A Tor Book
Published by Tom Doherty Associates / Tor Publishing Group
120 Broadway
New York, NY 10271

www.torpublishinggroup.com

EU Representative: Macmillan Publishers Ireland Ltd, 1st Floor, The Liffey Trust Centre, 117–126 Sheriff Street Upper, Dublin 1, DO1 YC43

The Library of Congress Cataloging-in-Publication Data is available upon request.

ISBN 978-1-250-36276-6 (hardcover)
ISBN 978-1-250-36277-3 (ebook)

First Edition: 2026

Printed in China

10 9 8 7 6 5 4 3 2 1

For Mum and for Meg

Paris
FRANCE
Gévaudan
Mercoeur
Margeride
Mountains
Apcher
St. Chély
Allier
Dayane's pool
Peyre
Randon
Marvejols
Mende
Cenaret
Tournel
Canilhac
Lot
The Bow and Brace
Ocerne
Château d'Ocerne
Saint-Julien-by-the-Stream
St. Germain
GÉVAUDAN

FOREWORD

I decided to write this all down while on a business trip to my European offices in Florence. It was one of those romantically black and violent autumn days when the rain does not fall so much as dash itself against the city. The majority of the tourists were in their hotel rooms, trying like so many before them to come to grips with Italian television.

I should have been working, drawing up contracts for a very large acquisition on behalf of a very old client. But the intimate, empty streets beckoned, so instead I went wandering. I visited my most beloved friends—the wise ghosts of the Duomo; the Boboli Gardens; Laocoön and his sons in their ecstasy of fear—but I found them all cold and listless.

It was on my way back along the Ponte Vecchio, in the fairy-tale light of the goldsmiths, that I chanced on an exquisite brooch. I recognized it immediately—an antique cameo in amber and ivory, depicting a young woman. It was badly damaged and the setting had been stripped of its gemstones, but I paid the dizzying sum on the ticket and tucked it into my coat. In my head, I was already repairing the jewel. I knew somewhere in my archives there was a pouch of tumbled Persian sapphires that would fit perfectly in the antique setting. Manic with inspiration, I rushed immediately back to my offices, a sturdy stone manse in the old artists' quarter. I told Livia to handle my client appointments for the coming week—she's at least as good a lawyer as I am anyway—and headed for the attic. It's one of the things I love most about returning to the Old World: I always come across something unexpected, something I've forgotten.

I never found the sapphires[1] but at the back of the attic was buried an old wooden chest. It tugged at something in my mind; I think it may have been what I was really looking for all along. With some effort, I lifted away the sealed effigy of a long-dead patron and wiped the dust from the carved walnut panels. The chest was a beautiful, if neglected, relic of the French Empire, decorated with scenes of the Revolution.

The French Revolution. The peasant's dream that toppled kings and ignited decades of war across Europe—across the world. The faces carved into the wood were righteous and proud, an army of the downtrodden throwing off their shackles for Liberty, Equality, Fraternity.

I knew better.

The troubled young woman whose likeness was engraved into the cameo—she had known better, too.

A few phrases of eighteenth-century Occitan dissolved the Wards on the chest (still airtight after two hundred years, if you don't mind) and I knew that my gem-cutting plans had been postponed indefinitely.

---

1. I love my European staff, but they are avid little thieves.

I spent the rest of the day turning through volumes of notes and evidence from one of my most infamous and fascinating commissions. My indwelling Spirit, Sarmodel, had been silent for days, but I invited him to enjoy the rediscovered treasure with me—they're his memories too, after all.[2] After a little petulance, Sarmodel came forward in my mind, rousing himself like a drowsy cat, and joined me in reliving what was in retrospect quite a landmark case. We went through the old journals and specimen canisters with a sweet melancholy. A switch of Bombay thorn apple, jars of snowmelt, a pouch of wolf fur, a box of lavender-scented talc—each time I reached into the chest I retrieved another wonder.

I'd forgotten how much I loved that part of my life—the 1700s were a *glorious* time to be in Europe, until they weren't. And I felt truly close to Sarmodel, for the first time since we averted the End of Days the previous year.[3] I have so few friends left and it was reassuring just to have him with me as my companion again, and to remember how well we can work together.

But the reason I decided to write this case down properly was right at the bottom of the chest, buried under a bushel of faded letters. It was a lambskin riding glove, shredded beyond repair and still spotted with bloodstains. Sarmodel and I had been trading happy remarks for hours, but now we both stopped. I felt a longing

---

2. Not that he would be able to read any of my notes—Sarmodel holds the written word as the pinnacle of human vanity, a position it shares with matrimony. Where I have endeavored to learn the myriad languages of humans, demons and angels, my indwelling Spirit wears eight thousand years of illiteracy like a medal.

3. About which I will not go into detail here—we got it done and you can go back to your online shopping. Suffice it to say the Mayan calendar's pinpoint accuracy had nothing to do with astronomy.

that my demonic Guest understood completely, and for once he didn't mock my human frailty as my eyes filled with tears.

Still, Sebastian? he asked quietly in my thoughts.

"Yes. Still," I replied. "How did I forget?"

Antoine's, the glove and the blood both. I was hundreds of years old before I ever met him, but that day we were both young. Danger was nothing to him and his sense of abandon was contagious. It was inevitable that we would end up broken and bleeding in a midden somewhere, given the situation, but it was spectacular fun just the same. I didn't realize how long it had been since I'd remembered Antoine. His innocence. His wild blond hair and ridiculous inability to light a campfire. I had the thought, for the first time in months, that life without death is a miserable gift.

So these pages are for him, one of my dearest ghosts.

For Antoine Avenel d'Ocerne.

Sebastian Grave

Florence

2013

P.S. I take no responsibility for Livia's contribution.

PART ONE

A Contract Unfulfilled and a Terrible Secret

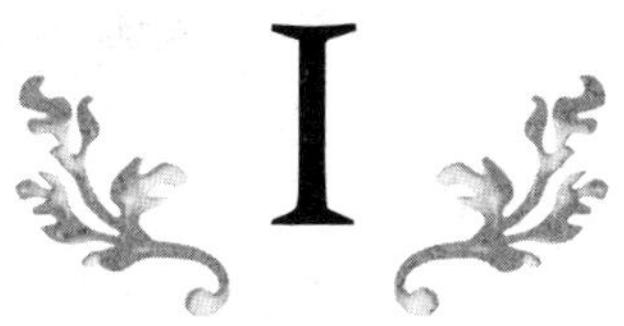

Eastern Piedmont
1785

The girl was surprisingly beautiful in the moonlight.

"Surprisingly" for two reasons. First: she had a reputation for beauty. In my experience, this would usually mean only that she'd managed to keep all her teeth in the long weeks between puberty and pregnancy. And second: she was two days dead, and I have violated enough graves to know that corpses are not, to common tastes, beautiful.

I believe her name was Cristina. Her ghost sat opposite me on a crude tombstone, watching me work. Now, the *ghost* was beautiful, but they often are. This spirit girl's hair was typical of Piedmontese folk, thick and dark and curly, falling just below her shoulders. Her eyes were large and bewitchingly deep with the gravity of the hereafter. Her shade glowed softly, wearing the same white smock I had just cut away from her corpse.

"That was *expensive*," muttered the girl, looking at the ruins of the dress.

"I can tell," I replied. "Aren't you pleased that it's not going to rot in the ground?"

Sarmodel, my indwelling demon, had Projected himself in human form to sit beside her, with the very worst intentions. He appeared as a black-haired boy of about ten years, with a long face and an exquisitely aquiline nose, which I assume was how I looked when we were first joined.[1]

"Aren't *you* pleased, Sebastian, that you can add to your stock of used cerements?" Sarmodel asked me, smiling. "And wasn't this worth leaving home for?"

Among many other things, I have need of good cloth in my line of work, and the dress would not be wasted. But Sarmodel's point was plain; Cristina was a charity case.

"We weren't doing anything else," I replied.

In truth, I had hoped Cristina's late-night visitation might result in more than another evening combing through entrails at the cemetery. I had been, if not quite preoccupied, a little out of sorts over the previous few days. I had experienced a growing sense of *waiting* for something, which I have learned never to ignore. The pretty ghost with her tale of a deadly curse had seemed a promising start.

"I guess it doesn't matter—it's just a dress," Cristina sighed. "Have you finished?"

---

1. We have both agreed that "joined" is the most acceptable term for my/our condition—"possessed," "demoniac" and "abomination" are inaccurate and most offensive. I often call him my demonic "Guest," but he's as embedded in my body as I am. We are in every sense inseparable, a situation unique (to my knowledge) in the history of the occult, not to mention theoretically impossible. He is a male Spirit and has had many aliases over the centuries, among them Nott, M'quet and Lariel, but I generally use the one he gave me: Sarmodel.

I had dissected the girl's body (rather neatly) at her behest and examined it for the cause of her demise.

"Yes, I have, Cristina. But you haven't been completely honest with me."

"What do you mean? I was killed, wasn't I?"

"Well yes, and no," I offered. "You certainly didn't die naturally—"

"*Bastarda!* I *knew*—!"

"—but I don't think White Marta was responsible. Not unless she snuck into your home and strangled you with your own hands."

"My own hands?" She looked at me with her wide, wide eyes.

"I'm afraid so. The bruising and scratches on your neck are a perfect match—see?" I held her corpse's hands up to its throat to demonstrate. "Note also the scraps of skin under your fingernails."

"But that's impossible! I didn't kill *myself*—I swear it!" She crossed herself, scandalized. "The pastor says there's only damnation for *suicides.*" She whispered the last word as though the Almighty might be eavesdropping from the hedgerow.

"I believe you, Cristina, if only because it would, in fact, be impossible to kill yourself this way." I let the dead hands fall once again. "At least not on your own."

"Who was it then?" she persisted. "It had to be White Marta! She's the only one it could be."

"And why is that?"

"I went to her not a week ago, and she turned the evil eye on me, she must have!"

"Went to her for what?" I knew Marta quite well. She was a competent hedge-witch, but the "evil eye" was not really her style (or anyone's, given it is utter nonsense).

Cristina resisted, but she'd made a Contract of Truth,[2] and she was bound to answer. "I asked her for a blessing. I am . . . I was newly married."

I raised my eyebrows. "A 'blessing'? A fertility charm, you mean. Witchcraft."

"No! Well, yes."

"And?"

"I went all the way out to the scree to find her, with a fat hen as payment, and all she gave me was a strange little pouch. She said I was to put a tooth inside and leave it under my pillow and I would dream of my future child." Spectral tears brimmed in her lovely eyes. "Instead, I dreamed of a woman with no face, choking me in my bed, night after night."

"Wait—a tooth? Whose tooth?"

"Mine."

"Are you lying to me, Cristina?" She lowered her eyes and I knew I had the right of it. The mark of my Contract burned brightly on her right palm, and she covered it with her other hand.

"Well . . . Marta said to use one of mine, but I went to the field below the granary instead. They're always digging up bones there." She lowered her gaze. "I knew it wasn't right, but I couldn't cut out my own tooth, I just *couldn't*."

I grimaced. "Cristina, that field is full of bones because it's sitting on a mass grave."

"From the plague?" She looked aghast.

---

2. Contracts are the chief means of interaction between the Spiritual and Mundane realms. Truth is one of the most common, but Contracts can govern the exchange of almost anything, including information, money, services or anima. They're the main way Sarmodel and I put food on the table, often quite literally.

I shook my head. "From the witch hunts. I think you may have unintentionally brought home more than a tooth. Old bones are dangerous, and those ones in particular."

"What do you mean?" She seemed on the verge of tears again.

"I believe you may have collected a witch's bone, containing either her angry spirit or one of her familiars. It doesn't really matter which." I sighed. "It's dreadfully unlucky—very few of the women in that field were actually witches at all. Can you guess how they were executed?"

"They were strangled," she murmured.

"I'm afraid so. And now one has had her revenge, misdirected as it was."

She looked around helplessly. "But . . . but I didn't *know*! I didn't mean to! With my own hands?"

"That's your Truth, Cristina. I am sorry," I said, and I meant it. Death had come unfairly for this one. The burning mark on her hand faded away, signaling the fulfillment of my Contract. The identical mark on my left hand soon followed.

"It doesn't matter anymore, my lovely one," I continued. If I could have dried her tears, I would have.

"Please—*please* don't tell the pastor," she implored. "I don't want to go to Hell."

"There's no fear of that," I said. "It was an accident. God never punishes an accident."[3]

"Truly?"

"Truly."

"So, I can . . . go?"

Sarmodel sat up now, suddenly interested. "Yes! Yes—there's nothing to fear," he said. "You can rest now, take my hand."

---

3. The girl had heard quite enough Truth for one night.

"Sarmodel," I said. "*No.*" I dragged the girl's body back toward the edge of her grave.

He gave me an unfriendly look. "Just get that meat back in the ground," he said. "This is not your concern, Sebastian. How else do you think she's going to pay?"

"She's a *client.*" I leveled the knife at him. "We agreed on this."

Generally speaking, a Contract must be paid for immediately on completion, either in coin[4] or in anima—spiritual energy—proportionate to the Contracted service. Cristina had only herself to offer, but I consider consuming the client as a very last resort, so I had accepted her pretty funeral dress as payment.

"Oh truly," continued Cristina dreamily. "Do you mean it? I can go, and I won't be damned?"

"She's not a client anymore," Sarmodel insisted. He lifted the ghost girl's hand, now clear of the Contract mark. "Look!" She was barely paying us any attention, but her light was beginning to grow; Cristina was getting ready to leave.

"Sarmodel, you cannot possibly be hungry! Only last week—"

"Sebastian Grave of Larnaca?"

A man's voice shocked us all into silence.

Distracted by the business at hand, I hadn't noticed the rider approaching up the grassy slope. He directed his horse slowly toward us.

"I am *Professor* Sebastian Grave of Larnaca, yes. Who goes there?" I demanded through clenched teeth. I was acutely aware that of the three of us, I was the only one visible to the Mundane; to a casual observer I would appear to be arguing with nobody in a cemetery in the middle of the night. I prayed that it was dark enough to

4. Nowadays I will also accept a bank transfer.

hide the mess I had made, never mind the naked, mutilated corpse I was discreetly nudging with my foot.

"I am Monsieur Jacques Avenel d'Ocerne," replied the newcomer, with an accent. He was wearing a broad hat and a scarf that covered the lower half of his face, so I couldn't see much of him other than his eyes. Then he switched into Provençal Occitan and added, "Son of the Baron d'Ocerne."

"Ocerne. Your father—Antoine d'Ocerne is your father, sir?" I finally succeeded in tipping Cristina's body into the grave, where it landed with a wet thump.

Sarmodel—Antoine's son!

Sarmodel had forgotten the ghost girl for the moment and was watching with great interest. I felt a growing excitement, something between joy and trepidation. This was it! *This* was what I'd been waiting for—it had to be.

"He is indeed. I will speak plainly, for the journey here was long and I am weary." He drew himself up. "Sebastian of—Professor Grave, my lord father summons you to return immediately to Gévaudan with me, to complete the contract which he holds unfulfilled, signed by you at Château d'Ocerne and witnessed by the Bishop of Mende in the presence of our Holy Father."

"*Summons* me? Contract unfulfilled?" I repeated, quickly smothering the flutter of fear in my gut. In my mind, I could see the blood on the snow, and the frozen gorge full of roaring white water. "But that was *twenty years* ago!"

"Just so," said the young man grimly. "But we must ask your aid once again. The terror of the Red Winter has returned."

I made a show of packing my tools back into my valise.

It's not possible, I said to Sarmodel. *Is it?*

Oh, Sebastian, he replied. Sarmodel shook his head, half sad, half mocking. His childlike Projection faded into shadow and he receded to his customary position in the back of my mind.

"Sir? Will you return with me and resume your charge?" the young man insisted.

"It seems I have no choice, sir," I replied. "May I go home to set my things in order? I would be honored if you would accept my hospitality tonight. I can be ready to leave at dawn, if it pleases you."

I seldom do anything because "I have no choice, sir," but I needed time to think—away from the graveyard.

"I will accompany you to fetch what your work requires." He looked over the tumbled tombstone to the body in the pit, and then to the shredded skirts half-packed into my valise. "But I will not sleep in the home of a grave robber. My lord father told me your habits were strange, but this is ungodly."

Clearly it was not quite as dark as I'd hoped. "I have *permission,* sir," I replied, which was mostly not a lie. "I am in the business of finding truth, and all too often it is buried in a graveyard."

He was looking at me coldly, but then he softened. "Very well. I would indeed welcome somewhere warm to sleep. It has been a very trying journey."

"No doubt," I agreed. I glanced apologetically at the white corpse and then motioned for Jacques to follow me down the other side of the hill.

"To whom were you speaking?" he asked as we left the tombstones behind. "Just now, when I arrived?"

"Nobody, sir," I said, glancing back. Where Cristina's shade had been, there was now only a soft white gloaming, like the reflection of the moon. Sarmodel's disappointment was like the weight of a stone in the back of my mind. "Nobody at all."

It took less than an hour to reach my home.

Jacques Avenel d'Ocerne offered little conversation as we rode. The young man was in great discomfort, perhaps injured or lame, though he tried bravely to hide it. His left hand barely gripped the reins and when he dismounted at the gate he snatched the arm close to his body with a grunt of pain.

I had a modest, isolated estate not far from the town of Corvano, on the outskirts of Turin. Thankfully my years of living in squalor as a pariah were over by this point in history. It was very comfortable, with solid stone walls and a slate roof, and the grounds were small, tidy and—most importantly—private.

The eighteenth century's growing interest in science and medicine allowed me to earn a respectable living in larger towns as the local doctor, scholar, undertaker and sometime jeweler, as the occasion required. Science at this time was a lot of flashy bunkum, so it was easy enough for me to pass off some of my more exotic work as "physicks." Corvano had been home for nearly ten years, and while I was not quite a pillar of the community, I was well known and well regarded.

Livia, my housekeeper, brightened immediately at the sight of our houseguest. To my relief, she was respectably clothed when we arrived and there was a savory meal of rabbit stew, soft cheese and barley bread ready on the table.[1]

"I apologize for the humble meal," I said as Livia filled our plates. "I was not expecting—"

"Your contract," he said, sliding a rolled sheet of paper across the table to me, "should you require verification. It commits you to my father's service in the hunt for the Beast, does it not?"

"I believe it does, sir." I made a show of removing the ribbon and unrolling the page, which had been removed from a larger volume. "The bounty was also, as I recall, paid out to Monsieur Bauterne."

Well.

My signature was right there near the top of the page, directly under Antoine's. Above our names were the insignias of the king and the baron and the particulars of the bounty—*six hundred livres for the head of the Beast of Gévaudan*—and below were dozens of other signatures belonging to men long dead.

"It was, but my father has promised to restore the bounty to you, should you be successful," Jacques added.

"He—Really? All of it?"

"So he said."

I pretended to read the details of the document, watching Jacques d'Ocerne over the edge of the page. The man was clearly

1. Livia is a succubus I met in Rome at the height of the Empire. We share a deep affection, but it took her nearly five hundred years to learn to cook anything other than naphtha.

starving and he ate like a jackal; he must have pushed himself hard on the journey from Château d'Ocerne.

In the lamplight, he was a thinner, graver version of Antoine. He could have been no older than nineteen and not quite able to produce his father's thick beard, but the dark eyes and blond hair were Antoine's. There were differences I presumed came from his mother: a softer, full mouth and wider jaw. He was pensive and deliberate in his manners as well, which Antoine had never been. I also noted that he ate entirely with his right hand; the left arm he cradled protectively close to his body.

"I am glad that you are still here, Professor," he said, sounding not at all glad. "Your last letter was many years ago, according to Papa."

"He never troubled to reply to my letters," I told him carefully. "I saw no further need for correspondence. And I must admit I am curious how you found me so late at night and so far from town."

"The wise woman by the scree told me I might find you at the cemetery."

"I see," I said. I added "professional discretion" to the list of things I would be discussing with wise White Marta after the night's business was concluded.

A dutiful son, remarked Sarmodel, *to come all this way alone, and in such a hurry.*

Indeed, I thought to him, smiling evenly as I offered the young man some more wine. *And I wonder what sort of baronet sends his son and heir out on a long, dangerous errand with no escort.*

Jacques accepted the wine and watched me silently over a mouthful of cheese. Just as I was growing uncomfortable, he spoke again.

"I expected an older man," he said. "Sebastian Grave of Larnaca was a lettered man of some many accomplishments at the time of the Red Winter. If you are the same man, you have remained remarkably untouched by time."[2]

"Ah," I said with some amusement. "I believe that this question has been troubling you, young sir. And the answer is simple: I lied. I made good pretense with beard and bluster, but I was barely in my twentieth year when I left Gévaudan. No older than you are now." I gave a light laugh. "I suppose I did not wish to appear the untested whelp among the hunters of France."

The smile he returned was weak. "Of course, Professor. You must think me quite rude."

He excused himself to get what sleep he could before our departure, leaving me full of braised rabbit and squirming apprehension. Livia escorted him upstairs to the guest bedroom and I remained there at the table, watching my coffee cool. The succubus returned and cleared the table around me with rather more care than usual, but she knew better than to interrupt my thoughts.

It wasn't until I rose from the table that she struck. Firm hands pulled me into the scullery and closed the door.

"Meatbag,"[3] she whispered sweetly to me, as Jacques moved

---

2. I stopped aging as soon as my body and mind were mature. I am naturally olive-skinned and dark-haired thanks to my staunch Cypriot heritage, and I can usually present myself as anything from twenty-five to thirty-five. Over my years in Corvano I had altered my appearance toward maturity, with slightly longer hair and a studied disdain of young people. It was enough to deflect suspicion, but I would eventually need to move on, as always.

3. A rough translation of the Tartaric term "*v'herrec*," Livia's appellation of choice for human beings. The verb form is *herrequet,* which she uses to describe the process of human living, but it doesn't translate quite so well: "to meatbag."

around in the upstairs guest room. "Did you enjoy your supper? Is your hunger satisfied?" We were in very close quarters and she had me backed up against the door. A troubling amount of heat was emanating from her body. True to her nature,[4] Livia is devastatingly beautiful, with some singular imperfections. I forbade her to show tail, talons or horns in polite company, but even in her shapeless housekeeper's pinafore with her auburn tresses dutifully pinned under a cloth cap, she managed to be utterly heart-stopping. Thankfully, my unexpected guest had paid her little mind as she prowled around the dinner table.

I knew where this was heading. "Yes, Livia, thank you. Supper was delicious. And no, Jacques is not for you," I whispered back.

There was a hissing sound and a cloud of steam as she plunged her hands into the dishwater. "Why must I always *starve*? This one is young and ready to mate. You don't care for him, I can tell. He will come willingly—and I will bring only pleasure to him!"

"I don't disagree. But he would still be dead when you finished. I forbid it."

"Sebastian you are cruel. Why does *he* get to feast while I diminish by the hour?" she demanded, pointing above my head. She meant Sarmodel, of course.

"Feast"? Indeed. You are welcome to join us at the piggery next time I am "feasting," half-breed. I will stuff you both ends with as many swine as you desire, he replied. *But you should think about what she*

4. Not true Spirits, succubi are among the more sophisticated occult half-breeds. Along with a host of other abominations, they're the product of demonic or angelic involvement in mortal reproduction. Unsurprisingly, such a union rarely results in viable offspring, but there are enough to keep me in business. I have written extensively on the subject in my *Occult Compendium*, available for purchase from my website.

offers, Sebastian. The succubus may be the easiest way out of the situation, and this younger Ocerne is quite disagreeable. And he ***was*** *traveling alone on a long and dangerous road.*

Livia turned to me, her luminous green eyes full of tears. She held up her talons, dripping with dishwater. "I work so hard and ask for so little. He wants me, I know, and *I want him.*" Her barbed tail emerged from beneath her skirt and stroked my thigh. "Please, Sebastian. It will be fast and magnificent, and I promise to clean up afterward."

"Livia. No."

A long creaking came from the floor above us as Jacques opened the armoire in the guest quarters. Livia stamped her foot in frustration. "He is *undressing* ready to *mate,*" she insisted.

"He is undressing ready to *sleep.* And he is Antoine's son, no matter what I think of him. I will Shackle you if I must,"[5] I warned her.

"Sometimes, meatbag, I hate you," Livia said darkly, folding her arms. Her tears dried up with a sizzle, and just like that, she was all business again. "Have you packed?"

I spent the remaining hours of darkness collecting everything I would need for the journey. The Gévaudan I remembered was a bleak, hostile place full of bleak, hostile people and I packed accordingly. After some consideration, I included some formal attire in green silk and a short courtly wig. I unraveled the cellar Wards and descended into the basement proper to pack my valise. I checked and packed all of my standard equipment (bandages, surgeon's knives, deer brushes, specimen jars, that kind of thing) and then found myself reaching for the high shelves and locked

---

5. I made a beautiful pair of silver earrings for Livia, inscribed with the sigils of her Contract. They're very elegant, but to Livia each is a leaden anvil.

repositories where I kept my most potent inventory. Two precious globes of quicksilver,[6] an amphisbaena gland, a stick of waxed pyric chalk—I threw them all in with shaking hands.

I had been thinking all the while, hypothesizing on what might be causing the troubles in Gévaudan, without really wanting to believe what Jacques had told me. But the memory was there. Huge and naked and smiling with red teeth, it was there.

Are we storming the Holy See? asked Sarmodel. *What in the name of the Rift are you doing?*

"I know. I know! I need to calm down." I sat down on a stool, pulling off my gloves. "I just don't know what we're going to find," I said.

That's exactly right. We ***don't know*** *what we're going to find.*

"You heard what the boy said—the terror of the Red Winter. The Beast."

He could not have survived, my love.

"Are you sure? Could he have returned somehow?"

So many questions. I felt a shifting in my mind as he thought, like the shuffling of immense coils.[7] *You could always send the boy on*

6. A liquid alloy of mercury, silver, chromium and platinum, with various alchemical salts. Needless to say, it's prohibitively expensive, highly toxic and extremely difficult to make. It will, however, take the pepper out of just about anything: angels, demons, monsters, undead, clergy—*anything.*

7. I get the impression that my Guest is many times larger than I am, or he would be if able to manifest in the Mundane world. I can't see him unless he Projects an image, but Livia looks straight *up* when she speaks to him, which is quite unnerving. I've no desire to know what he really looks like. I have witnessed three powerful Spirits in their Prime Incarnations and suffered in turn blindness, madness and deadly illness for my efforts.

his way, you know. Even if you won't kill him, there are ways to make him forget he was ever here. Or who he is, if it comes to that.

I thought about it. The sensible part of me really didn't want to go back to Gévaudan. I had barely survived my last visit and made some enemies in high places; I was especially loath to put myself back within reach of the French clergy and their Divine counterparts. France was also developing a nasty reputation for lawlessness, with rumors of riots and treasonous uprisings. And Sarmodel was of course correct; I had numerous means within arm's reach to charm, drug or otherwise dispose of Jacques.

But if I did any of those things, I wouldn't see Antoine again.

And I needed to *know*. I needed to be certain.

"No," I said to Sarmodel. "If this is something I've left unfinished, I need to make amends. And six hundred livres will not go astray."

What a terrible bind, he said lightly. *Is twenty years too long to wait to say "I told you so"? I don't think it is.*

"What should I have done, Sarmodel? Left them all to die?"

Do you really want me to answer that?

"No, no." I waved his laughter away. "Just . . . help me. Tell me what I need. I can't think properly."

He turned and turned in my head.

Better take it all. Just in case.

III

Morning found me at the gate, ready with a small loaded wagon and a flatulent draft horse. She was no destrier, but she was sweet-tempered, unflappable and strong enough to carry me and pull the wagon at the same time.

I looked back on the familiar trio of handsome tiled rooftops—manor, stables, storehouse—and wanted nothing more than to change into my robe and sink into the reading chair in the solar. The day was dreary and overcast, the perfect morning to be reading in front of the fire with hot coffee and an almond pastry. Instead, I was bidding farewell to my home as I had so often in the past, more than a little unhappy at leaving at such short notice and on such unpleasant business. I looked wistfully at the orchard behind the main house, just beginning its autumnal transformation. I would miss this year's beautiful display of foliage, as well as the bounty of my kitchen garden and pumpkin patch. I took a moment to dwell on uncharitable thoughts of Monsieur Jacques Avenel d'Ocerne.

I wore black buttoned breeches of soft leather, a cream shirt and a long waistcoat of stormy gray to suit my mood. My boots were knee-length and hardy, ready for the muddy backwaters we would be visiting. As Jacques appeared in the doorway, I pulled on a long coat of fine-spun wool in a deep forest green, handsome enough for the gentleman I was supposed to be, but durable enough for the road as well. I carried a silver flask of strong pomace brandy clipped to my belt. We faced over three weeks of riding to reach the mountains of Gévaudan, and I had a feeling they would not be easy.

"My apologies for keeping you waiting, Professor," said Jacques. "The journey must have tired me more than I knew." I had ensured that Jacques overslept, to give me time to set the appropriate Wards around the estate. I felt it prudent to add some extra precautions to deter burglars, half-breeds and Christians in my absence. They would also help to keep Livia in check. Twice in the past I had been forced into hurried relocations because she lost her self-control while my back was turned.[1]

"Not at all, sir," I replied. "It has been a busy morning. I trust you enjoyed your breakfast?" Jacques's traveling garb had seen more use than mine. He had prudently eschewed the buckles and ridiculous hats that marked a French nobleman of the time. Instead, he had chosen simple brown leather for his boots and breeches, with a black waistcoat and dun cape. I was quite the dandy in comparison.

---

1. To be fair, the last one was not entirely her fault. Livia had attracted a very persistent suitor from the local town despite my best efforts to keep her hidden. I returned from town one day to find her in the kitchen, delirious with satisfaction atop his smiling husk. If I leave one piece of cautionary wisdom for the young men of the world it will be this: do not put your penis inside anything with a tail.

"It was most satisfying. Please thank Mademoiselle Livia for me," he said. "I could not find her."

"I believe she went to town for larder stock."

"Perhaps we shall pass her on the way."

"I rather doubt that, sir." "Mademoiselle" had been kept very busy since her performance in the scullery. She was currently in the root cellar, counting grains of rice with a hairpin. "Shall I bring your horse?"

It began to rain as we rode out, Jacques on his fine gelding and me on my gentle draft horse with the wagon in tow.

Tally-ho, said Sarmodel. *Wake me when we get there.*

Jacques and I barely spoke the first day. After stopping for some basic supplies in Corvano, we headed west, planning to follow the old Roman road to the French border. With some luck we would reach the foothills of the Alps within the week.

Our route was a busy thoroughfare for merchants and travelers from the surrounding lands, most of them braving the rain as we were. Jacques seemed to travel in a half doze for most of the afternoon, swaying lazily in the saddle and muttering to himself. Occasionally he would look sideways at me, as though he thought he had heard me speak.

We stopped for the night at Ferno, a small village tucked in among the forested foothills. I dismounted at the first building with a shingle, a little trattoria with a few rooms available to rent. It was clean, reasonably priced and filled with the smell of warm bread, garlic and pinewood. Jacques seemed to take great exception to the place, however, and barely managed to thank the staff as they took our horses.

I gave the ostler a generous tip and asked him to take extra care with our animals and the wagon. I wasn't worried about thieves; my Wards ensured my goods were well protected. But I had noticed Jacques's gelding flagging badly for the last few hours. The poor creature was too thin and I suspected that it needed new shoes. But most importantly, it needed food and rest, and it seemed that my companion was blind to its condition.

How has he made it this far? I asked. *Antoine would never have let an animal reach this state.*

The young Ocerne is not his father, Sarmodel replied. *But you are right. He is distracted—lost in his own thoughts. Watch him tonight.*

We had a pleasant meal of cabbage and potato stew, with slabs of dense, chewy bread. Again, Jacques ate like a man near starvation. I felt a measure of compassion for the boy and had resolved to be as charming and amiable as I could be.

"Your father must be proud of you, Jacques," I said. "A courageous son who cares about his people and the land he governs."

"Papa will be pleased to see me return" was all he said, though he seemed to brighten a little. He laid a hand over his breast pocket, his mind momentarily elsewhere.

"And do you have a wife waiting for you at Château d'Ocerne?" I pressed on.

"I do. Eloise and I were married not a year ago." A group of German travelers sitting by the fireplace rose up in laughter as one of their number spilled a tray of drinks, and by the time they settled again, Jacques had lost his inclination to converse. He offered nothing more on his wife and was curt to the point of rudeness for the rest of the meal. Defeated, I agreed to his suggestion that we retire early.

We had a small room above the kitchen, a little noisy but warm and dry. As we ascended the stairs, Jacques hunched like an old man, cradling his left arm. And, like his horse, he was much too thin.

The young one is not well, remarked Sarmodel, *in body or spirit. He is certainly nursing an injury of some kind. But what?*

Jacques was weary to the point of collapse after the short climb to our room. He removed his waistcoat, belt and boots before falling onto the narrow bed.

I waited until he was properly asleep and then spoke a Litany[2] of Rest, sealed with a mark of the dawn. He would not wake before the sun, and hopefully he would get some respite from whatever harried him so. I watched him for a few minutes, seeing the boy beneath the ragged blond stubble, and the uncertainty held in check behind the stubborn jaw. Jacques began to breathe more peacefully, no doubt dreaming of his gentle Eloise.

"Rest now, troubled young sir," I murmured.

It only took a few seconds to empty his pockets. His waistcoat yielded a handkerchief and some crumbs of barley cake. On a hunch, I checked his breast pocket, where he had placed his hand so protectively earlier. Inside was a cameo brooch depicting a young woman in amber and ivory, with a jet-studded silver setting. It was a woman's fancy—Jacques likely carried it as a keepsake from his wife. I held it to the light, admiring the craftsmanship (if not the gauche choice of materials), and then returned it to his pocket.

The weapons in his belt were in good condition, as I would have expected. He had brought a short sword, a hunting knife and a flintlock pistol. I found the blades were sharp and oiled, and the

2. A small invocation of power from a patron Spirit, Sarmodel in this case. Think of it like a prayer that works.

gun ready for use.[3] I could feel an anima residue on the knife; he had killed something small with it recently, perhaps a rabbit or scrub fowl.

But the real horror was in his breeches pocket.

"Sarmodel," I whispered. "Do you see this?"

The young man's purse was all but empty. He had enough florins to maybe—*maybe*—cover our night at Ferno. Things were not going to improve on the other side of the Alps. Three French livres huddled miserably in the leather fold at the bottom of the pouch. And that was all.

"Are we to sleep in the mud all the way to Gévaudan?" I muttered, upending the man's saddlebag onto the floor. A pouch of gunpowder tumbled out alongside a handful of lead pellets, a flint and striker and some hardtack. Still no money. "How?" I hissed. "Why?!"

Oh Sebastian, said Sarmodel. *Oh dear.*

"Surely not."

It took me a long, dreadful moment to understand. My companion's disapproval of our lodgings, the condition of his horse and his general shabbiness all aligned on a dismal trajectory.

Jacques did indeed plan for us to sleep in the mud, all the way to Gévaudan.

I took immediate stock of my own coin. I would have enough money in my purse—barely—and certain emergency reserves hidden in my boot heels. With a little haggling and some judicious devilry, we could manage beds most of the way—*cheap* beds.

But it made no sense. The Antoine I knew was a gifted spend-

3. As ready as it could be. It would still take the better part of a minute to prepare and load, or half as long if Jacques was *really* good. Gunfights in the 1700s were a very tedious affair.

thrift. I would have expected a certain allowance for expenses, on his son's behalf if not mine. But the boy was traveling on a pauper's wage.

"Be assured I will be running an *account*!" I declared to nobody. I began to pack Jacques's belongings back into the bag, none too gently. I was tucking the flat, wretched little purse back into his pocket when Sarmodel flinched in my mind.

Sebastian, can you smell that?

"The young lord is none too fresh," I agreed. "But I shan't be financing a trip to the bathhouse."

No. He's . . . contaminated. He directed my attention to Jacques's left arm. *There.*

I would barely have noticed it if not for my Guest. There was a slight bulge below his left shoulder—the binding on the wound I had suspected earlier.

What is it? I asked.[4] I had switched instinctively to mental discourse; it didn't feel right to discuss the young man's health aloud with him lying right there.

How should I know? I'd need to see it properly.

There was an expectant silence.

I can't just take his clothes off, Sarmodel.

He shifted irritably. *I will never understand this! You are quite happy to do it for every passing milkmaid and carpenter.*

That is ***different****. And in this case, I believe it may be unnecessary.* Now that I was closer, I could feel the corruption Sarmodel had

4. Sarmodel will often detect things that escape my notice, though for all practical purposes we share the same set of senses. He tells me it's a matter of focus. My attention only allows me to register a very small amount of what I see, smell and hear at any time, while he assimilates every speck and trace.

mentioned. Frowning, I placed my hand lightly on the wound. Beneath my palm throbbed the young man's troubled anima, so similar to Antoine's in spite of their obvious differences. It glowed through his body, driving his pulse, his warmth and his healing. But there was something else growing in the flesh, poisoning his blood. The sensation was still light, but it was unmistakable. *You're right, the wound is infected. No wonder it's bothering him.*

And he travels with a physician, yet seems determined to keep it concealed, mused my Guest. *The young baronet is quite the tangled knot.*

That's one thing we can agree upon, I replied, standing up stiffly. A full day of riding had begun to work its way into my legs and spine, and I crackled like a bunch of kindling. *But he is carrying burdens much too heavy for such a young man. A little stumble and he will drop them all.*

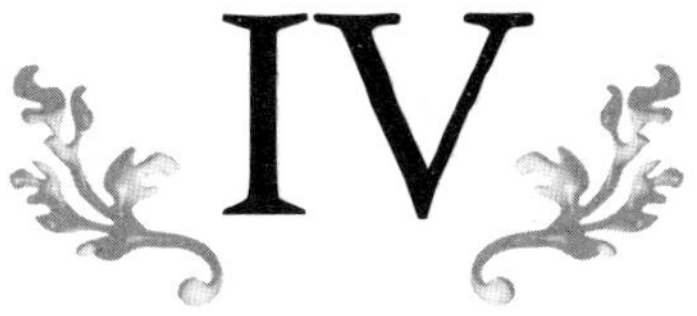

IV

The old Roman road was our most direct route west to the border. Jacques set a punishing pace. He was mounted and ready each morning before dawn and we set camp well after dark.

He was also quite unpleasant company. My concerns about his injured arm were rebuffed with steely courtesy and any attempts at conversation were treated as an imposition.

By the end of the first week, our food supplies were almost gone thanks to the proud and silent game of brinksmanship that had developed between us. I refused on principle to spend my own money on food I would be obliged to share with him, so I endured trail rations and forage with stony fortitude. Jacques, in turn, seemed quite happy to spend no money at all and would have subsisted on bootstrap soup just to spite me.

Is it a game? What is the matter with him? I fumed to Sarmodel.

So Jacques rode and slept and ate in a polite daze while I slowly filled with bile. I would have continued the farce indefinitely (superhuman endurance is a specialty of mine) if it weren't for the terrible state of Jacques's gelding, Aherin.

Claviere was the last major town before the Alps, and our last opportunity to prepare for the difficult mountain passage. I took us along the busy main thoroughfare, which had been trodden into an icy slush by crowds of travelers and townsfolk. Thankfully the rain had stopped, but Jacques and I were both riding with scarves wrapped around our faces against the cold. I had scented mine with lavender and orange, but there was no masking the ripeness of animal yards among the various smells of the town. I turned my horse toward the stench.

A request, my dearest, if you please, said Sarmodel. *I cannot stomach any more rabbits.*[1] *Can we get a cow? There must be cows here.*

I am not buying you a cow. And you are not the only one with an appetite, I replied. *We need food, and it is time the young Ocerne tended to his horse.*

"Where are we going, Professor?" Jacques demanded. "I would prefer to stay on the road and find somewhere dry to camp for the night, away from this place."

"Certainly, sir." A group of filthy children came shrieking down the street and engulfed us briefly. There were a few genuine screams as curious young hands tested the anti-theft Wards on my wagon, and then they were gone.[2] "But I thought we might visit

1. Sarmodel and I both benefit immeasurably when he feeds regularly on anima, which is what the layman might call "life force" or "soul." I had procured a farm near my estate at Corvano to satisfy my Guest between funerals and exorcisms, but on the road, he ate what I could kill.

2. By "gone" I mean the children, not their hands. Sarmodel and I had agreed earlier in the century that it was no longer appropriate to dismember would-be thieves. These urchins would suffer only minor electrical burns and possibly some loss of bladder control.

the farrier before we move on. I feel my horse limping. I will have Aherin seen to as well, if you like."

I tried to say the words lightly, casually, as though it were something he had mentioned earlier. Jacques could hardly disagree with me; his horse was unbalanced and lumbering.

But disagree he did. "I would rather press on," he replied, shaking his head. "There are farriers in France, no doubt of superior skill."

I was momentarily silent, suspecting some sort of miscommunication. "Sir, if you please, it would be but a small gesture on my part to—"

"I do not *please.* And you do not listen. Now let us be gone from this cesspool."

"As you will, sir," I said, snarling behind my scarf. We returned to our original course, with Jacques now leading the way through the throng.

Oh Sebastian, that was masterful, said Sarmodel. *You play the young gentleman like a violin.*

Shall I force him at knifepoint? I demanded. *The beast will not survive the mountains.*

No, but one day you must stop thinking like cattle. He came forward slightly. *Try this.* A triptych of Tartaric symbols appeared in my mind's eye; a Word.[3]

What does it do? It seems awfully complicated.

It **is** *complicated. Can you manage it?*

---

3. Something of a misnomer. A Word is in fact a phrase made of two or more Tartaric or Samadhic ideograms. The ideograms themselves can represent concepts as complex as seasons, chemical formulae and specific individuals, so three of them together can take a lot of concentration. Not to be confused with *Wards,* which originate from human Arcane practice and are entirely different.

I think so.

Then go ahead and say it. Keep a tight focus and don't get it wrong. I promise it won't kill him.

I'm not sure I would mind.

Don't tease me. Sarmodel retreated a little, watching. *Now, concentrate.*

I kept my gaze firmly on Jacques and relaxed the scarf around my mouth slightly. The Word took me several seconds to say and my mouth felt very strange afterward, as though I'd loosened my teeth.

The effect on Jacques was more noticeable.

There was a sound like a dull, iron hammerblow. Aherin stumbled heavily. With his next steps, the gelding left all four of his worn shoes in the mud, the nails red and smoking. Jacques swore as he lurched in the saddle, and then suddenly every strap and fastening slithered apart around him. He reeled as the reins came free in his hands and the rest of the bridle dropped to the ground. He tried vainly to grip with his legs, but the cinch had already come apart and the saddle slid slowly off to the side. Jacques tumbled into the mud alongside my wagon, like the world's most disagreeable pig.[4]

I immediately slumped with the plunging fatigue that follows any of Sarmodel's tricks, but it was a small price for the satisfaction I felt. I was glad the scarf concealed my smile.

You need to work on your triphthongs, said Sarmodel, *but I think he'll agree to see the smith now.*

---

4. This Word has since become known as the Uttered Undoing and it's one of my most prized secrets. With some minor modifications, it can be brought to bear on anything man-made with parts that are joined together—machines, buildings, clothing, etc.

There was a small, serviceable forge rumbling at the back of the farrier's shop, and a quick inspection told me he would be as capable as any of Jacques's Frenchmen of "superior skill."

Jacques was covered in filth and walked in the mud, carrying the gelding's tack. Naked of his saddle and equally soiled, Jacques's mount was haggard and miserable.

"Forgive me, Aherin," the baron's son whispered, stroking the animal's neck. "I've been a poor master to you."

I secured my wagon to the rail beside him. "Might I suggest we find somewhere for you to bathe, sir? The smith will be some time, I fear."

Jacques looked at me directly for what seemed the first time. The fall had humbled him somewhat, and the eyes that now recognized his sorry treatment of the gelding were looking at me differently too. He was for a moment painfully like his father. "Yes, Professor, I would be grateful for somewhere to bathe and wash my clothes. But I fear I have been no friend to my horse, and I will see to his needs first."

"We can get someone to take care of that, if you wish."

He shook his head, flicking droplets of muck from his hair. "No. Mine the fault, mine the fix."

"As you will, sir. I'll find us something to eat."

I returned an hour later with the scant palatable food I could afford. Jacques was brushing Aherin the gelding, murmuring softly. In spite of his injured arm, he had taken time to work out the snarls from the animal's mane and tail. He had also spent what must have been the last of his money on rough oats and a handful of small, hard apples. I found that I could not begrudge him the expense.

Some nobility from the nobleman at last, I remarked.

Quite, replied Sarmodel. *Talk to me when he's riding that horse toward the money.*[5]

Tommaso the farrier was a taciturn little fellow who asked no questions about how the gelding had lost all of his shoes. He worked quickly, and within the hour Aherin had been hot-shoed very neatly. Jacques stiffened as I paid the smith from my own pouch, but said nothing.

We left Claviere in silence, following the course of the fast-flowing river. I loaded Jacques's muddy tack into my wagon and we both walked alongside our horses. I was busily discussing the new Word with Sarmodel, working the ideograms into useful alternative permutations in my mind. I was so used to ignoring Jacques's misery that I didn't notice his discomfort straightaway. His muddy clothes had begun to dry and stiffen, and his teeth were clenched against the pain of his injury.

Sebastian, I do not care if this one lives or dies, said Sarmodel. *But if you would avoid the latter, you will need to see what he's hiding under those clothes. Quickly.*

You have a colorful turn of phrase, but I agree. And it's time for some answers.

5. Like most Spirits, Sarmodel adores money. If you are wondering why, the answer is simple: they love money because *we* love money, and usually for all the worst reasons.

By late afternoon, Jacques's exhaustion had returned. His distracted muttering, which had become almost constant, was now punctuated with pained grunts.

"Pardon me, sir," I said aloud. "There is a place nearby where we can bathe and set up camp for the night." He only nodded and motioned for me to lead the way.

The land sloped away on one side of the road, down to the riverbank. I guided our horses along a run of shallow water and through a screen of thick brush. We emerged on a sheltered, sandy beach. Here the Po skipped and kneaded over smooth stones and the current peeled around a high, white boulder partway across, creating a shallow eddy. We stopped under a stand of willows that appeared to be stepping into the rapids with thick roots. We were hidden from the road, and the far bank was a thorny tangle of blackberry woodland, resplendent in autumn foliage.

Excellent.

Be careful, Sebastian, said Sarmodel. *We're not alone.*

The ghost of a Roman legionnaire stood on the crest of the white boulder, looking down into the river with spear in hand. He had started to forget himself, losing color and definition. His armor glinted in the sun but it was a cold, distant light. Only his tunic was still clear, a slash of vivid red above the white water. He ignored us and I did not acknowledge him.

"A perfect place to bathe," Jacques remarked weakly. A heavy slant of afternoon sunlight hit the surface of the water through the trees. "You were right."

"Take your time, sir," I said. "I will make camp."

Jacques undressed with leaden limbs as I secured the horses and strung up a sheet of oiled sailcloth for shelter. I busied myself among the items on my wagon, retrieving some cheese and smoked pork, as Jacques waded into the water, gasping.

I watched him sidelong. Jacques kept himself turned to one side, attempting to hide the blood-crusted bandage on his shoulder from me. He ducked his head below the water and I took my chance.

I whispered a Litany of the Dusk and drew the shadows into myself like a long, cold breath.

The warm shaft of afternoon light flickered. To Jacques it must have seemed that a cloud had raced across the face of the sun. He looked back to the riverbank. Only the horses moved there now.

"Professor?" Had he looked down, he might have seen my shadow gliding between the roots of the willows. "Professor Grave?"

"I am here, sir."

Jacques turned to find me seated cross-legged on a thick branch, high out above the current. In my hand, I held his cameo brooch. His confusion was almost comical. Jacques looked to the riverbank, then back up at me, then back to the horses, then down to the water, as though he might find some trace of my passage on the surface.

"The pastor was right. You are a man of unnatural gifts." He crossed himself[1] but did not move.

"I have seldom been so abused for climbing a tree, sir, and if I may respond in kind—*you* are a man of unnatural obstinacy." My tone was pleasant, and I began to flip the cameo back and forth across my knuckles like a coin.[2] Jacques's eyes widened and he drew himself up, watching the flickering jewel with palpable concern.

"Return that to me, *now*," Jacques replied, his voice thick with fury. "You are not fit to touch it."

"I will return it as soon as we have had a frank discussion, young sir. I am in the business of Truth, and it seems I've had little of it from you yet."

He looked at me with real malice, the first I had seen from him. "Very well. I am glad that you finally show your true face. I do not fear you, Sebastian Grave, but I do welcome an end to this game of yours."

"You—game of *mine*?"

The young man has some pluck, remarked Sarmodel. I clenched my teeth against his laughter.

"Indeed. You do not charm me with your fine speech and manners," Jacques went on. "You are insolent. For every 'sir' that leaves your mouth there are a dozen baser words unsaid. This I can abide; you are not giving your assistance for love of me." His

---

1. A gesture which, like nose-picking, has endured through the centuries and serves only to lower my regard for mankind.

2. Childish, perhaps. Effective, certainly.

lemon-sucking grimace as he looked at me was most insulting. "But you are unwholesome. You defile the dead. You do not sleep. You *steal.* I do not know how, but I believe you were responsible for unhorsing me. You are not a godly man—or a professor for that matter."

"Then why, *sir,* have you come to me for help? There must be any number of *godly* men in Gévaudan who could better serve you."

"I came to you, *Professor,* because my lord father would accept help from nobody else," replied Jacques grimly. "You are the only one who was able to defeat the Beast during the Red Winter. If we were not in such dire need, I would see you clapped in irons and drowned in the sea. In truth, I expected you to refuse."

"*Refuse?* Your father *summoned* me," I snapped, "and—as you have taken great care to remind me—I made a commitment to your family in this matter, thanks to the contract you hold. I will honor it."[3]

"You do not seem the sort of man who places any meaning on honor." *That* was unfair. I was silent with shock and he continued his barrage. "But I will give you your 'discussion' if I must. I know why you paid the farrier and it will please you to hear that your suspicions are correct—until we reach Gévaudan, I am a pauper in all but name."

"The truth at last! Now tell me how and why your father sent you here with no escort and half a florin. Did he give you no money for the journey? You do not seem the type to spend it all on whores and liquor."

---

3. My own motives aside, it was indeed prudent for me to return and assess the state of affairs in Gévaudan. A powerful Spirit was potentially a very dangerous thing to leave behind—if indeed it still lived—never mind my signature under the king's letterhead.

"No indeed. Though the men of my *escort* are likely doing just that."

That was a surprise.

"You were robbed by your own men?"

Jacques was shivering now. He looked down at his hands, nodding. "In the mountains. I caught them stealing from my saddlebag, and we fought. I woke bloodied with only my horse, the money in my purse and a shot wound." He gestured to the dirty bandage on his shoulder.

"I see. And why didn't they kill you?"

"Because, Professor, we were friends," he said, his voice harsh with pain. "Gévaudan kept its children close after the Red Winter, and Gerard and Henri were the brothers my parents never gave me."

"Brothers who beat you, shot you, robbed you and left you to freeze to death in the Alps?"

"It is bitter, but I understand them. They are commoners and there was only hardship waiting for them back in Ocerne. Even without the recent troubles, it has become a place of misery and fear for the common folk, ever since the Red Winter. And my father—my father does nothing about it. He will not see and he does not listen." Jacques wrapped his arms around himself, and not only for the cold. "They asked me to go with them, to start anew somewhere else with the money, but I refused."

"I see." I studied him, noting the ribs showing through his pale skin, his feverish eyes and the red streaks emerging from beneath his bandages. "And why—for the love of Almighty God—*why* did you not tell me any of this?"

"*Because it does not concern you!*" he almost screamed. "I was sent to retrieve a dubious acquaintance of my lord father's. I made no promise to take him into my confidence. And nor would I, if he were anything but a base charlatan holding me to ransom with my own belongings."

"Even a charlatan likes the truth sometimes," I replied. "And did you expect us to make it to Gévaudan with three livres and a handful of crumbs?"

"I . . . I admit I had avoided the thought. I intended to travel as quickly as possible, through the night if necessary, to return home and be done with you before things grew too desperate."

"You are a man standing naked, shot and I suspect dangerously ill in a very cold river, with nothing but a tired horse and some stale oats to feed it." I tossed the cameo down to him. "Desperate? I would say that fruit has fallen. Now wash yourself properly and I'll prepare something to eat. I'm going to have a look at that wound." I walked easily back along the branch and swung down onto the sand. "And I *am* a professor."[4]

---

4. I lost most of my curriculum vitae in the various fires in the Museum of Alexandria, around the time of the Roman conquest. Julius Caesar was a passable statesman, but he had absolutely no respect for culture.

VI

A short while later we sat by a heartening fire, our bellies full of pork, bread and cheese. Jacques had grudgingly offered to add his trail rations to the meal, which I declined. I had already decided that if we were traveling on my money, we would be traveling on my terms—no more riding in the rain and no hardtack. I anticipated prompt reimbursement when we reached Gévaudan, with a healthy garnish for my trouble.

The Roman ghost on the boulder was watching us now. I had attracted his attention with the Litany and now his face followed my every movement, a glowing white smudge with a deep purple bruise near the temple.

Jacques was wrapped in a blanket, naked to the waist. He spoke as I gently unwound the bandages on his shoulder.

"The wound was no great trouble at first," he said. "I removed the shot and cleaned it with salt. It seemed to be healing. But perhaps a day from Corvano it began to rise with pestilence."

"And then what?" Jacques had wrapped a ridiculous length of cloth around the wound. The bandages had not been changed and the deeper layers were rank with sweat, old blood and pus. I composed my face.

"I know our monks use fire to cleanse the flesh. So, I heated my blade and—ah!"

I added a little warm water to peel away the final strip, but to Jacques it must have felt like acid. "You burned it."

The naked wound was vile. The shot had blasted away a ragged crater about the size of my palm, just below the boy's shoulder. Around it was a shredded mess of flesh and a constellation of smaller shrapnel wounds. I could only guess at the severity of the original injury; it had been completely eclipsed by mortification. The filthy bandage had harbored a reservoir of poison that only thrived on Jacques's inexpert cauterization. The burned skin was tight and seeping, and—perhaps most concerning—an angry red streak marked a pathway of infection into the hollow of his armpit, toward his heart. I was amazed that he had been able to use his arm at all.

"I'm sorry, Professor, I cannot look at it," said Jacques weakly, gasping against the pain. "Please just change the binding and be done. Do . . . do you have any wine?"

"Of course, sir," I replied. "And please, be at ease. It is nothing I can't manage."

Nothing you can't manage with a bone saw, said Sarmodel. *That is killing him, Sebastian. He already knows. Why do you think he's been hiding it?*

You are always so quick to dismember. Just let me think. I sat in silence for a moment, turning the decision this way and that. If Sarmodel was right, I had allowed this young man to deteriorate to the point of deathly illness, for the sake of my pride.

No. I'm sure I can help. I collected some clean bandages and a bottle of paregoric[1] from the wagon.

You're not sure at all, he accused. *I've seen enough of your Mundane quackery to know that.*

Perhaps, I said, handing the tonic to Jacques, *but we didn't help matters by rolling him in the mud. I need to try at least.*

Jacques took a sip as I made a show of measuring out bandages and counting pins. He grimaced. "That's not wine."

"No, but it's what you want. Drink up—slowly. I won't be long."

He was asleep in minutes. I took the bottle from his hand and set the bandages aside. In their place, I rolled out my doctor's instruments. Sarmodel obliged a quick Litany of Rest and I set to work. He watched me like a snake around my shoulders, shifting and coiling.

I drained and cleaned the wound as well as I could; the burns I would treat later with honey and balsam. As I suspected, fragments of shot were still lodged in the muscle. I dug them out and carefully cut away the tissue that was already dead, scraping out the infection beneath. The boy would have a fearsome scar when it healed, but the deeper flesh was thankfully still red and healthy. With a stick of charcoal, I drew an alchemical wheel on the new bandages and marked the points with symbols for sulfur and silver. After a moment's consideration, I added Purgation and Ablution sigils as well.

Do you mind? That is most distracting, I said irritably. In essence, my handiwork was killing millions of bacteria, and Sarmodel was

1. A reasonably common cough remedy formulated by eighteenth-century "scientists." I liked a little extra opium in mine, so I tended to make it myself, and the poppies were quite a picture in the springtime.

busily consuming the mist of anima they released. The effect was like somebody intermittently slurping the foam from a mug of beer.

I'm hungry, he replied. I could feel him scrutinizing the diagram on the bandages. *What does it say?*

Do you really want to know?

I asked.

Very well. It's a series of processes. I explained the Elemental Successions and their attendant alchemical properties, the fruits of centuries of human Arcane practice. My arrangement was quite ingenious.

I see. He regarded my work and consumed another flurry of anima. *Was the bone saw too easy? How unspeakably tedious.*

Sometimes, I hissed, ***you*** *are unspeakably tedious.*

I mixed a balm for the wound and bound it again, ensuring the symbols were facing directly onto the exposed flesh. The charcoal would dissolve with a little time and Jacques would be none the wiser. The old bandages I threw into the fire along with Jacques's miserable hardtack. Then my long watch began.

Jacques descended into a ferocious fever, as I had feared. The moon was a bare sliver, so I stoked the fire high and stayed close by him, checking the wound and his anima regularly. He had done a lot of bleeding in the last few hours, but if he survived the next day he would likely recover. I was determined to keep him alive that long at least.

The night was not to pass without interruption, however.

"Are you an augur, stranger?" The Roman ghost was suddenly standing by the fire, his form shimmering like a curtain of water. I had been meditating, and it took me a few moments to interpret his Latin.

"I am, good soldier," I said slowly. The centuries had worn on this one; he barely knew himself anymore. Aside from the frightful purple bruise, the legionnaire's face was almost completely blank—the barest shadows marked his eyes and mouth. His scarlet tunic was dripping wet beneath a scale cuirass. I was stung a little with memory of the Empire that was, and my life there. "Do you wish to treat with me?"

"I do." He nodded. "I beg knowledge. Will you consult the signs?"

"Knowledge has a price," I replied. "What have you to offer?"

"Salt. My full ration."

"A fair price. I will consult." I raised my left hand to mirror his right, feeling the familiar flush as Truth was written across our palms in otherworldly fire.

A fair price? Salt?

It was a small fortune in his day, Sarmodel.

Well even if he could get it—and let us not fool ourselves on that front—it's worth considerably less now. And he's got something else we can certainly use.

We don't eat the client, Sarmodel.

We don't eat at all! I am tired of your charity cases!

The soldier beheld the burning mark with his featureless face. "Where is my helmet?"

Oh, groaned Sarmodel, *one of* ***these****.*

"I see what the gods have written, in the clouds, in the wind, in the tracks of the heavens," I said, gesturing to the stars. "I will find your answer. But tell me—how did you come to lose it?"

"It was a moment's inattention," he replied. "I was filling my waterskin and my helmet fell into the rapids. My patrolmen are searching for me, and I *must* return to them. I fear we will be surprised by the tribes if we do not move soon."

I threw a bunch of dried herbs[2] onto the fire and took some deep breaths. My eyes rolled back to the whites and I cast my unseeing gaze heavenward. Eventually a meteor flashed through the sky and I stiffened in oracular ecstasy. "A sign has been sent!" I coughed and slumped forward. "You ask in vain; what you seek is yours already."[3]

"Mine?"

"It rests with you," I insisted gently, "where you fell."

"You are mistaken, priest," he answered, though his voice was not as certain as his words. "I have fallen many times in the rapids, but I have never given up the search. It has been . . . so long. I *will* return to my decurion."

"I believe you fell once, good soldier," I said, pointing to his bruised face. "But I do not believe you rose again in life. The body you knew and the thing you search for have both returned to the earth."

He stared at the mark of Truth on his palm. "My patrol. They are not waiting?"

"They have been waiting a very long time."

Among the willows, luminous figures were appearing, drawn by the light of the Contract. Like the legionnaire, they were indistinct. I saw white hands and bloody tunics, the flash of greaves and spattered weapons, but nothing else that spoke of the men they

---

2. My secret *bouquet garni,* no less.

3. The temple theatrics were an act of compassion, not necessity. It is no kindness to thrust self-awareness onto a ghost, especially one as old as this one. I try to do it as gently as possible, in terms that will be understood. If that means I have to twitch and moan a bit, I'll put on a show.

had once been. Leading them was a proud specter, with a crimson cloak and a plumed helmet. He stepped forward into the firelight.

"We have found you at last!" The decurion was the only one of them with a face inside his helmet. His voice was heavy with relief. "It is time to leave, Lucius."

"I . . ." At the sound of his name, the dead legionnaire's features suddenly sharpened, like a foggy mirror wiped clean. He was startlingly young, one of Rome's many lost sons. The side of his head was dark and misshapen like a squashed plum. "Gods, I remember. The rocks. I *did* fall! I couldn't get up and the water was so *cold*. You searched for me?"

The decurion nodded gravely. "Our search was brief. The tribes found us. They were many."

"All of you." The young man looked around the gathered specters, stricken. "You must believe I am sorry!"

The older man raised his hand and the boy fell silent. "We died in service to the Empire. Many, many years ago." He shook his head. "We may both stop searching now."

"Yes, Decurion." The Contract mark grew brighter on the boy's hand, swelling like a tiny star. When it faded, he held a dented helmet, dripping wet.

"The gods do forgive," he said to me, looking at the helmet with wonder. "You have my thanks, Augur."

"Divine service requires no thanks," I replied. The mark of Truth had faded from my palm as well. The young man's ancient ghost began to lose form altogether. His fellow patrolmen were discorporating alongside him, dissolving into bright mist among the willows.

Not so the decurion. He looked at me with black, eyeless hollows.

"I know you, Augur," he said. "You wrought a great deal of good in our Holy City. Tell me, does Rome still stand?"

I will admit I was touched, though I didn't recognize the man. "It does, Decurion. The city has changed, but her glory is undiminished."

"Then we have both served well," he said with a smile. "I can leave gladly, and you have my thanks. Tell me true—are my father's gods waiting for me, or is it the Christ?"

"The gods of Rome have moved on," I replied gravely. "Like the city, they have changed. As for the other, I cannot say."

"Then do me a service, if you will. I am . . . I was Aelius Agrippa of the Third Legion Italica. When next you are able, commend me to my homeland."

"I give you my word, Decurion."

"Again, my thanks." He looked through me for a long moment, his form brightening toward the infinite. "One last thing, Augur: counsel from one who has seen nearly as many years as you have." He pointed over my shoulder with a bloody finger. "Know that you are treating with a dark creature. It deceives you with every word. Be rid of it before it shows its true face."

"Believe me, I have tried, good soldier," I replied. "It is most tenacious."

But the decurion was already leaving. His anima shed its human form, pulled free of its worldly moorings and returned to its purest essence, without sense or identity. He joined his soldiers as a brilliant wisp among the trees, ascending toward the reaches . . .

Finally!

Sarmodel struck like an asp. The decurion's anima was taken in an instant, blazing briefly and silently as it was consumed. It was followed immediately by a dozen of the souls among the willows. In the Arcane light of their demise I had the impression of a hulking, many-armed monster rearing above me. I closed my eyes and waited for it to be over.

Have you no decency? I asked weakly, when the darkness returned. I could already feel new vitality flooding through my mortal tissue. *He* ***knew*** *me!*

Sarmodel's voice was thick with satisfaction.

Not the client was all he said.

ADDENDUM:

On the Origins of Jehanne d'Arc

Domrémy, France
1425

If you've come this far, you're probably crinkling up your little meat face wondering how the succubus was permitted to use the writing machine. Did she hijack it? Will she be Scathed for leaving her sticky fingerprints on the master's things?

No. Sebastian Grave the Midtown Lawyer has asked me to write all this down.[1] *Clearly this is some sort of punishment, but "clerical duties" are in fact a minor clause in my Contract, so I am "delighted to oblige."*

It's quite obvious that I wasn't present for some of these events. I'm going to include them anyway, because I've been told not to leave anything out. I won't apologize for any inconsistencies in the rest—six hundred years is a stretch, even for my powers of recall.

So. We're going to use your imagination. Clear your mind of the

1. As I had nothing better to do in between running his business, his errands and his life.

notifications and the advertising and the incessant bathroom urges, and see this with me.

Imagine a farmer's field, a long time ago (several hundred years before the rest of this unnecessary epic, in fact). The family are groveling away in the sod. Picture the mother in her dress and bonnet, scratching at buried radishes or whatnot. She's holding a plow under one arm and an undersized baby in the other, sucking the life out of her chapped teat. Scratch, scratch, suck, suck. Inside the charming stone house, the father is tallying the accounts and thinking about the local abbess's forbidden pudendum.[2]

Now see their daughter, no more than thirteen. She's a little farther away, where they bury the carrots. Soon she'll be getting married, mating and preparing to die,[3] *but right now she's scratching, scratching, just like her dutiful mother.*

But what's this? The young girl's hoe strikes something hard in the ground. It doesn't yield or break apart, so she kneels down to pull it from the earth. The obstacle is wide and curved like a dish. As she brushes the dirt away, she realizes it is metal, still brightly burnished beneath the sod. Lifting it up, she sees it's an implement of war; an oval-shaped steel shield with two round notches cut away at the sides. It reflects her face like a mirror. Almost as tall as she is, the shield is nonetheless wonderfully light, and it is engraved with a wolf's head.

Her pubescent, mammalian brain does not wonder why the an-

---

2. In fact, let's assume that every man I mention is, somewhere in the dripping caverns of his mind, undressing everyone else.

3. This is not a joke (to you). The medieval debutante will be considered old at forty, if she makes it that far. I suppose it's all academic in this case.

cient thing has not rusted in the ground. Nor can she read the Latin writing around the rim. And she certainly doesn't think twice about the disc of ivory inlaid at the center before she rests her fingertips upon it.

I feel you, supplicant.

The voice is so very faint. It seems to come from the air. In her reflection, she sees a man's hand on her shoulder, though there is nothing there when she checks.

"Lord?" she whispers, her heart pattering away like a woodpecker. She has heard stories about visitations from the Almighty and his angels, and she believes them.

The girl feels something strange. It is as though she is being touched everywhere at once, or perhaps covered in ants. It lasts only a moment.

Yes, Jehanne, *says the voice from the air, stronger now.* ***I am the Messenger. Will you receive the message?***

"Yes!" she whispers fiercely. She leans down and kisses the circle of ivory, which is, after all, only another type of bone.

Will you give yourself to me and carry me in your heart?

"Yes!" Again, she kisses the surface, not knowing why.

Are you mine and only mine?

"Yes! Take me, Lord! I am yours!" A third time her lips brush the ancient bone, and the deal is done.

Now, Jehanne is facing away from the house, so nobody sees her eyes roll back or the drool hang from her mouth. The shield collapses into rust. The disc of bone disintegrates last of all, leaving a smear of sulfurous ash and yellow plasma.

The girl is transfixed there on her knees. In her mind, she witnesses a beautiful puppet show of saints and angels. It doesn't seem strange to her that they look exactly like the images she remembers from the church, or that they speak in her own provincial dialect.

"Jehanne!" The father has tired of his daydreaming and is calling from the window. "Come! It's time to churn the gruel!"[4]

Jehanne rises and walks slowly back to the house, her eyes wide. Her head is full of singing. On the doorstep, she stops and falls to her knees again.

"Father, I have witnessed!" she cries. "The Archangel Michael has come to me with his handmaidens, Santa Cretina and Santa Ignorama!"[5]

This is certainly not what the father was expecting! Does he check young Jehanne for head trauma? Does he administer some head trauma himself and then point her in the direction of the gruel pot? Does he smile paternally and make plans for an earnest discussion with the pastor?

Naturally not.

"Lo!" replies the father, seeing the light of Divine Revelation in Jehanne's small, pink eyes. "My common and unremarkable daughter has been chosen by the Almighty God!"

"What is that you say, husband?" calls the mother from her radish furrow. "How important! Our household has been blessed above all others for absolutely no reason!" The baby soils itself in adoration.

And so it goes, on and on through the countryside, as each new meatbag hears the story of peasant Jehanne and her miraculous visitation in the field. Jehanne herself is hazy on the details; she remembers finding **something** *in the ground that day, but the rest is obscured by the beautiful, leonine face of the Archangel.*

We will leave Jehanne here for now, though she has quite the career ahead of her. Don't get attached.

The most important part of this bucolic tableau unfortunately

4. Or similar.

5. Some names have been changed.

disintegrated with the shield, which in Imperial Rome would have been recognized as an ancile.[6] *The Latin words Jehanne the Virgin couldn't read were both an exhortation and a warning, graven in the surface by acolytes wearing ceremonial blindfolds and protective silver gauntlets.*

MARS VIGILA.[7]

---

6. There were twelve of these shields in Rome. Only one was genuine, containing the anima of the Spirit of Mars himself, and only the *salii* priests knew which one. The Romans believed that the city would fall if the true *ancile* of Mars were ever to pass outside the Servian Wall. I would guess that it was lost in one of the many sackings of Rome in the fourth and fifth centuries—or perhaps it was the loss of the *ancile* that enabled the sackings in the first place. Speculation abounds.

7. I will wait while you run it through Google Translate.

VII

The Western Alps
1785

Jacques's fever lasted for three days. I wrapped him in my warmest clothes and made a padded nest for him in the wagon. My own belongings I loaded onto the draft horse, who only farted in response. I saddled Aherin for myself.

Our pace shifted markedly from Jacques's frantic bolt for the border to a convalescent crawl. My companion had brief periods of wakefulness in which I fed him bread soaked in broth and a little wine.

"Lorette," he said to me between mouthfuls. "Darling Lorette. Thank you."

"You are most welcome, young sir," I responded, shaking my head. "And have a care—your wife's name is Eloise."

The fever made him erratic and I had to watch him at night. He got up occasionally, calling for Henri and Gerard, his faithless companions. Once, as I was inscribing a new set of bandages, I caught him staring at me across the fire with the hunting knife in his hand. And each night he limped slowly from his bedroll to stand by Aherin, whispering close to the horse's ear and weeping softly.

His delirium unsettled me. His illness took away his bristly formality, and sometimes it was not Jacques but his father I saw sweating and shaking in his blankets. His silhouette by the fire. The uneven set of his shoulders. The knot of muscle in his jaw when he drank. I began to see shadows of Antoine in his every movement, and there were times I could barely stand to look at him.

It was only as we climbed higher into the Alps that Jacques began to return to himself.

"Professor?" His voice made me start, weak as it was. I slowed Aherin to walk beside the wagon.

"I am here, sir. Are you warm enough?" By now we were high enough to encounter pockets of snow among the bracken. I had bundled Jacques in as much of our bedding as I could fit in the wagon and he looked out at me like a sickly blond weasel.

"Yes." He strained to sit up. "Where are we?"

"On the road to the pass," I replied. "We are still some way from the mountains. How is your arm?"

"Better. It pains me still, but the fire is gone. Your doing, no doubt."

This was as close to gratitude as he would come. "You are an easy patient, young sir. And you are too proud to die in a charlatan's wagon."

His condition was, in fact, quite worrisome. The burn was healing well, and the deep shot wound was already improving. I had found no more fragments in the flesh and made sure the wound was scrupulously clean, but still Jacques's fever persisted.

Sarmodel had no advice to offer, so I put it down to the boy's general poor health and my inexperience with bullet wounds.[1]

"I expected you to leave me behind," he said after a silence. His voice was distant, as though he were simply thinking aloud.

"My apologies, sir," I replied. "I could find nobody to nurse an ill-tempered Occitan nobleman."[2]

To my surprise, he laughed. It was a thin, panting effort that left him exhausted. "I fear your estimation of me must have improved little, Professor."

"If you seek to earn my esteem, you need only stay alive long enough for me to return you to your lord father," I said. I threw down a piece of cheese from my saddlebag. "Here, eat."

"It is soiled." He sniffed at the cheese, which was dusted in black crumbs. "What is this? Gunpowder?"

"It is indeed. It will do you no harm. Eat."[3]

He seemed about to argue, but then took a mouthful with nothing more than a grimace. I waited for him to finish it all and

---

1. A deficiency I have had rich opportunity to remedy in the intervening centuries. When the Vatican implemented entry-level ballistics training, I knew it was time to update my skill set—and not a moment too soon. The Arcane arms race made the Cold War look like a heated round of cribbage, and I've mined more silver slugs from Livia's backside than I care to count.

2. This was shamefully close to the truth. I had indeed considered leaving Jacques at an inn somewhere so I could make the rest of the journey in blessed solitude. I decided against it on the basis that I was fairly certain he would die. Please also see previous references to my crippling lack of funds.

3. The gunpowder was composed of several of the raw elements that fueled my alchemical treatments.

then passed him a water flask. His eyes glinted back at me as the horses clip-clopped over the stones and the wagon squeaked underneath him.

"Tell me more of yourself," he said suddenly.

"Myself? Surely you have heard enough about me from your father, young sir."

"My father said only that I must provide you escort," he replied. "He told me little beyond where to find you. In truth, he had never spoken your name before."

It stung to hear it said so bluntly. "He told you nothing of the Red Winter?"

"Only that he vanquished the Beast at the Bow and Brace, with the help of men in his employ. I had always assumed he meant the Normans sent by the king."

"Who do you—the *Ennevals*?" I laughed. "No, sir, they were not party to any 'vanquishing.' The one at the inn had lost his mind, and the other was fewmets by then. The Normans! Is *that* how the story is told in Gévaudan?"

Jacques was not laughing. "In Gévaudan," he replied quietly, "it is not a story. It hides among us, a sickness that has been growing day by day. It is too many orphans now fearing for their own children, wondering why the king's hunters were permitted to strip the baronies and leave nothing behind. It is neighbors committing murder over the price of bread, and animals devouring each other in the fields."

How interesting. Sarmodel's sudden attention was like bared steel.

"I am sorry, sir," I said, and meant it. But while I regretted my laughter, I knew what had so attracted my demonic Guest's interest. The woeful circumstances Jacques described were exactly the sort of discord I had feared. "I was surprised that your father did not say more about it, or me; that is all."

"Then tell me of *him*!" said Jacques, with a fire that I did not expect. "If you must slither out of my every inquiry about *you*, at least tell me how you knew my father."

The hollow under his jaw, below the earlobe, just on the line where his stubble gave way to soft skin. That was where he liked to be kissed. I would watch it all morning as we rode, seeing the muscles move beneath the skin as he talked or grinned or swallowed wine from his flask, thinking about the sudden gasp he would make as I placed my lips on it. . . .

"He was very different to you, sir. He sponsored me in the hunt. I do not know what else—"

"Tell me the truth! Tell me the truth about the Red Winter, as he never has. I deserve as much!" He was breathing too hard and color was rising in his face.

"Please, young sir," I said. "You must try not to exert yourself. And if I am cautious with my words, I have reason. Believe me when I say that the victims of the Red Winter are in many ways more fortunate than those who lived to remember it." The truth was the very last thing Jacques wanted, no matter what he thought. But was it fair to keep it from him? I took a deep breath and let it out slowly. "But you are right—Ocerne will be yours one day, and you should know what happened."

"I thank you." Jacques slumped back into his nest of bedding, exhausted anew. Only his eyes lived, red-rimmed and burning as he watched me.

"It began . . . it began twenty years ago. It was much the same then as now: reports of a wild animal taking people from the villages. The Baron d'Ocerne—your grandfather—posted a number of bounties for the creature. Like many others, I decided to lend my skills to the hunt, and went to Château d'Ocerne to assign myself . . ."

VIII

Château d'Ocerne
Gévaudan, France
1766

The parterre grounds of Château d'Ocerne were all but overrun with the hunters of France.

It was impossible to move without bumping into some hopeful nobleman or tripping over another's animals. I was enveloped in a soft crush of velvet greatcoats, curled horsehair wigs and dogs of every hunting breed, from formidable Norwegian elkhounds to piebald English setters. Everything was *expensive*. Waistcoats and britches were trimmed with embroidery and glinting with silver buttons. Every cuff and lapel foamed with lace. Even the dogs were brushed and clipped and wore burnished collars for their presentation to the baron.

Situated atop a forested rise in the Margeride Mountains, the château was a grand provincial estate, extravagantly appointed in rococo style. A legion of carved angels, lions and swans clung to every crevice of the portico, flanked by towering arched windows. From their lofty position, the Ocernes enjoyed a spectacular view across the valley: a bucolic patchwork of farms and villages laid out along the glistening ribbon of the river.

I'd been queuing for hours in the grand forecourt. I was one among hundreds of men who had flocked to Gévaudan in recent weeks—so many, in fact, that the Baron d'Ocerne had been forced to receive them in the courtyard rather than the parlor. We jostled among the hedges and fountains in a line that ran halfway back down the mountainside.

We were all there for the same reason: the Beast. A mysterious creature had been terrorizing the hills and pastures of the region for months, taking workers in the fields and travelers on the roads. Intriguingly, there had been numerous witnesses, but nobody could ever quite describe the creature beyond its enormous size and monstrous aspect. The whole continent was afire with the news, and when the king's call went out, it had attracted my attention immediately.

The Baron d'Ocerne watched over the proceedings from the shade of the portico in his (entirely unearned) military dress. Beside him were his wife and son—a stylish and rather handsome young libertine—along with a number of dignitaries and a royal delegation from Versailles. Everyone looked very tired beneath their curled wigs and pale cosmetics.

My attention was divided between three people.

The first was Bishop Fontaine of Mende—the real star of the proceedings—who fronted the king's delegation in a glittering clerical confection of red silk and cloth-of-gold. An ox of a man with a voice to match, Bishop Fontaine comfortably outranked everyone for a radius of several hundred miles. There was a distant, sleepy quality to his beatific smile, but behind the rosy jowls his eyes were keen and searching.

The second was a small man standing beside the bishop—Lord Bauterne, the Royal Lieutenant of the Hunt. He was dressed entirely in black: black leather, black wig, black furs, black gloves. He had even blacked his boot buckles and the metal parts of his weapons. Across his back was an impressive musket, taller than the man himself, and at his waist he wore two of the small blunderbuss pistols the French called "dragons." He had arrived with King Louis XV's personal endorsement for the bounty, and he was already something of a local celebrity.

And the third.

The third was the baron's son, Antoine Avenel d'Ocerne.

I would have placed him around twenty years of age. He wore a waistcoat of honey-colored velvet, trimmed with sable and gold thread, and black britches that were distractingly snug. Beneath the white curls of his wig, his blond hair was combed back and tied neatly at his nape with a black satin bow. He tipped his head very slightly when he caught me watching him, a sardonic gesture that somehow conveyed both amusement and profound boredom.

"*Professor Sebastian Grave, Thrice Laureate of the University of Modena, Engineer Emeritus to the King of Cyprus, come to assign himself before God to the hunt for the Beast,*" announced the herald.

Finally! said Sarmodel. *This had better be worth it. I hope we haven't come all this way for a minnow.*

I stepped up to a lectern that had been erected in front of the magnificent portico. On top of it was a weighty ledger decorated with the royal seal and the swan-and-staff heraldry of Ocerne. The document outlined a staggering bounty from King Louis XV himself—six hundred livres for the head of the terrible Beast of Gévaudan. Beneath the official proclamation were the signatures of those who had joined the hunt before me, including Lord Bauterne and the baron's son.

It will be more than worth it if we win that money, I said. *We haven't had a decent commission in months. And this Beast will make a decent meal, I am certain—it has attracted the attention of the Bishop of Mende. It's certainly no minnow.*

I reached for the quill to sign my name but found it had suddenly moved out of reach.

The bailiff leaned in close to my ear. "I believe you have made an error, Professor," he said, taking hold of my elbow with an usher's grip. Insultingly, he used the informal "*tu*" to refer to me, rather than the polite "*vous*."

"An error?"

I looked up from the ledger. It seemed I had failed to notice the change in mood under the portico. The official party, who had been quite disinterested as the other hunters signed the ledger, were now exchanging stern glances.

"The bounty is open only to His Majesty's subjects; Frenchmen of good and noble standing," said Bishop Fontaine, in a voice that was somehow quite serene but also came out of him like an organ blast. He did not address me directly but rather spoke *over* me to the crowd in the forecourt. "You will withdraw."

The holy man did not need to elaborate; my academic credentials could not hide the fact that I was a commoner. My humble origins aside, I suspected I was also a shade too brown to be considered a "Frenchman of good and noble standing."[1]

"Your Eminence, there are other men here without lands or titles," I objected, as the bailiff's hand tightened around my arm. "I have studied with the finest minds on the continent and beyond. It

---

1. Never mind that I had lived in France, at various times, for centuries before anyone present was born.

is my hope that the edicts of science may help us better understand and capture this Beast—"

"The Beast will be vanquished by the grace of the Church, not by the decadence of foreign academies," said Fontaine soothingly, as though calming a willful child. "I say again, you will withdraw."

"I see."

Fontaine inclined his head to the bailiff, who began to pull me away from the lectern.

What? Sebastian, get your name on that contract!

It's no use, Sarmodel. We'll just have to find another way to—

"Hold, gentlemen, please," said a new voice. "This man is in my employ. He will assign himself in my name."

Antoine Avenel d'Ocerne stepped down from the portico to shake my hand.

"Professor Grave, I am delighted to finally make your acquaintance," he said. The quick double squeeze of his gloved hand told me to play along. "I had not expected you to arrive until next week."

"The pleasure is mine, sir," I answered smoothly. "I made good time across the mountains from Aosta."

"Your Eminence, Professor Grave and I have been corresponding over the matter of the Beast. He is here to assist me in the hunt. I apologize for the confusion," said Antoine, with a collegial smile.

The official party watched stony-faced as the young lord ushered me back to the lectern. I picked up the pen and quickly signed my name beneath his signature with flowery, illegible script.

"Please, Professor, kneel for the blessing," said Antoine.

I dutifully knelt before the official party and presented my weapons. Bishop Fontaine did not hesitate for even a second; to those watching, he would have appeared gracious and unruffled. But behind the placid smile, he was attempting to slay us both with his eyes.

"The Lord Almighty watch and guide you, that you may acquit this righteous charge in His name," sang the Bishop of Mende, his voice still full of theatrical timbre after a hundred or more such displays, "and in the name of His Majesty Louis XV, by the Grace of God, King of France and of Navarre, and our patron in the hunt, the Baron d'Ocerne."

"My thanks, sir," I whispered to Antoine as I stood.

He replied with that same sardonic nod, his eyes dancing as we joined the baron's retinue under the portico. I did my best to disappear among the other dignitaries and hangers-on as the next candidate stepped up to the lectern. But I could not escape the gaze of the royal huntsman. The black-clad Lord Bauterne watched me from the other side of the portico, standing so still I could barely tell he was breathing.

Sarmodel, it looks like we've found our chief competition, I said nervously. *And I doubt the bishop is going to forget this. We should get away from here as soon as we can and start looking for this Beast. What do you think?*

What do I think? Let's see. In less than a minute on the job, you've fallen foul of the bishop, got involved with some fancy young twit and attracted the attention of a man with the biggest gun I've ever seen, he replied. *Even for you, this is* ***remarkable****. That's what I think.*

IX

Baron d'Ocerne feted us all that evening with a most immoderate banquet. Long tables were set out on the rear promenade with a view of the formal gardens and, beyond them, the wild, forested foothills of the Margeride Mountains.

Antoine was seated at the baron's table with his family, along with the bishop and Lord Bauterne. The places closest to them were reserved for the officials and local gentry, followed a little farther along by the hunters from noble stock, and so on all the way down to the various hired woodsmen, dog handlers, trappers and trackers who would be doing all the actual hunting, along with the hounds, the rats and me.

The food was excellent, of course. The bishop's presence ensured the tables were loaded with Gévaudan's bounty—hot loaves of bread, spits of venison and boar, honey-roasted geese, buttered artichokes, pastries sticky with black cherry jam—even while the rest of France recovered from riots over a widespread grain shortage.[1]

At my end of the table, the hounds received better service than the men. The hunters' charges were treated like favored children, and their pack leaders—distinguished with gilded collars—were served the leavings directly from their masters' plates, carried down to us by the château staff. The dogs seemed restless and agitated, in spite of their training. Many of them shivered strangely and strained against their leashes, putting their handlers to the test. One russet pointer in particular seemed quite unsettled; it hovered just outside the light of the lanterns, trembling and growling at its fellows.

Everyone was very thirsty after the ceremony and the baron's wine stores were seemingly bottomless. As the meal progressed, my companions traded tales of big-game hunts across the continent. I contributed a lascivious (and only partly fictionalized) account of my hunt for the Gorgon of Crete, which provoked laughter from the hunters and more skittishness from the dogs.

"The beasts are putting the handlers through their paces tonight. There are too many of them all together," said the man across from me, noticing my discomfort. He was the loudest voice at the table, a nine-fingered trapper from Gascony. "I know you. You're the Cypriot professor—the one with the baron's son."

"I am."

"Well, my sympathies to you, sir," he said, raising his cup in a mock salute. "You may be assured the young lord will get you nowhere near the Beast or the bounty. Though I've no doubt you'll see your share of whorehouses."

---

1. Now regarded as something of a dress rehearsal for the main event at the Bastille in 1790.

"And who do you believe will take the prize, sir? You and your lord, I suppose?" I asked.

"Yesterday I would have said so. But now—well." He drained his cup in a single, open-jawed swallow. "Now the prize is all but guaranteed to our new master of the hunt, Lord Bauterne. The man is a legend even down here in the provinces."

"Ha!" interrupted the man to his left, a Flemish dog handler with no teeth. "I think the Normans may have something to say about that."

"The Normans?" I asked.

"Lords Jean-Charles and Jean-Francois d'Enneval—father and son, and the previous masters of the hunt." He pointed to two large, blond men seated close to the baron's table. They were almost identical from a distance, with impressive mustaches waxed and curled in the grenadier style. "Most simply call them Enneval the Elder and Enneval the Younger. They have chased the Beast from Julianges to Velay these past few months—and marked it more than once."

"And yet it remains at large, which is why Lord Bauterne has been assigned to take over their charge," countered the Gascon.

"Well, let us see how the king's favorite fares facing a real killer in the wild, rather than chasing fat deer in His Majesty's hunting—"

"By the Lord!"

The hum of dinner conversation was suddenly shattered by the baying of dogs. I leaped to my feet, my Walloon blade in hand, and was nearly knocked over by two enormous hounds who came barreling out of the darkness, bound in a murderous tangle. They tore at each other ferociously, carrying their savage melee up onto our long table and through the remains of the baron's fine meal.

The banquet erupted into bedlam.

Chairs tumbled to the ground as the men around me sprang back from the bloody spectacle, crying out in shock. Handlers roared obscenities in all the dialects of France, struggling to restrain the other dogs, which had gone mad with fear. The air was suddenly rank with the stench of blood and shit.

It was over in seconds. The smaller dog—which I realized was the skittish russet pointer—howled as the larger, a darkly brindled female mastiff, bit deeply into its throat. With monstrous strength, she chewed through her victim's neck and then tore it out, sending a long rope of crimson over the white tablecloth.

I stood very still, watching the powerful hound on the table only a few feet away. Easily as tall as a man, she was imposingly muscular, with a thick neck and broad muzzle full of cruel teeth. Her coat was fawn mottled with black streaks, darkening around her face in a predator's mask. Her drooping ears and jowls glistened redly in the candlelight. Even amid the commotion, I could hear her growling with each exhalation, a terribly deep sound that promised more violence.

Sarmodel, if she comes for us, be ready.

Of course, my love.

"*Soeur!*" someone bellowed from the head of the table.

A small man pushed through the chaos. There was no mistaking the all-black uniform of the Lieutenant of the Hunt. Bauterne forced his way forward, scattering hounds and hunters alike with blows of his gloved hand. "Soeur! Heel!"

The huge hound cringed visibly at the sound of his voice and I suddenly noticed what the other hunters must have seen from the beginning. The animal wore a gilded collar around her bloody throat; she was the lieutenant's prized pack leader.

I slowly sheathed my sword.

"*Heel!*" The dog whined and lowered her head, all but crawling off the table to Bauterne's side. Already a diminutive man, he seemed a child beside the hulking animal, but she feared him like the flame. He seized her collar and dragged her away from the kill, ignoring her shrill cries.

A whine came from the mauled animal on the table, and Bauterne turned back toward it. "Soeur, my girl, what is this? What have you done?" he muttered. He drew his knife.

"For shame, sir!"

"Shame!"

Several of the hunters called their disapproval, like hecklers at a cockfight. Bauterne silenced them with a cold glance. There was the barest flurry of movement, as though he were flicking some mud from his glove, and then his black hunting knife was buried in the dying animal's ribs, piercing its heart. To my relief, he was very precise; I felt the poor creature's pain and fear drain away in an instant. Sarmodel claimed its anima with a pleasurable surge.

Bauterne wiped the knife on the hound's coat, and when he stepped away, he held another gilded chain collar, wet with blood.

"You dog-fucking bastard!"

Bauterne turned lightly to face his accuser.

Not one but two men approached him—the blond military men the Gascony trapper had called the Normans. The Ennevals were so equally proportioned and so uniformly weathered by sun and wind that it was difficult to tell who was the father and who the son. Even their grenadier mustaches were of identical styling and lush proportions. They advanced beside the banquet table with an identical gait, somewhere between a hunter's careful pace and a lord's strut.

Enneval the Elder rushed to the dog on the table, his large hands remarkably gentle as they cradled the animal's head.

His son stepped forward to meet Bauterne, his knife drawn. The lieutenant inclined his head, as though responding to a courtly greeting.

"Young Master Enneval. You have my apologies." Bauterne

proffered the dripping gilded collar to the Norman. "It seems my Soeur has taken issue with your pack leader for reasons I cannot explain, and with the most regrettable consequences."

The mastiff was growling again, her eyes on the young Norman as he approached Bauterne. "Consequences, yes," said the blond man, sheathing his knife. He stood nigh two feet taller than the lieutenant, and he plucked the bloody chain from Bauterne's hand as though taking a toy from a child. "Keep your bitch on her leash from now on, or someone will mistake her for the Beast and claim her hide. Those also are *consequences*."

"Such a man would be no friend to the people of Gévaudan. I assure you there is no better pack leader in France than my Soeur, and she will win us the Beast," replied Bauterne. "Surely, sir—surely you can see this was an accident. Again, I apologize." Bauterne seemed calm and his words remained exceedingly polite, but I was not fooled; he was as rattled as the rest of us. I also suspected he was a man unaccustomed to being questioned, especially in public.

The younger Norman stared down at him, tightening his fist around the chain.

"I well understand the blow of losing a favored hound, sir," Bauterne continued. "My Soeur is my own true companion on the hunt, and I am sure you felt the same about yours." He raised his hand for the enormous dog to approach him. She stood obediently by his side and he held her collar like the bridle of a horse. "You see? She heeds me in all things. This aggression is not in her nature."

"Which is it, then? She obeys you in all things, or she is so poorly trained she feeds on her own?"

"She must have been provoked, sir." Bauterne's conciliatory tone began to sharpen.

"Provoked?"

For just a moment, it seemed as though the altercation would indeed degenerate into violence between the two noblemen. I would have struggled to choose a victor in such a fight. Their physical differences aside, Enneval the Younger's sheer malice seemed quite evenly matched with Bauterne's blistering pride; both were being held in check quite poorly.

"Son, be quiet," interrupted Enneval the Elder. He did not raise his voice, but the other noblemen were immediately silent. The older man's mouth was bent in a deep frown beneath his blond mustache. His fingers stroked the ears of the russet pointer one last time before he let its head rest again on the table, amid the ruins of the baron's banquet. "There is no need to argue with Monsieur Bauterne. He is the king's emissary, and he will extend the king's courtesy, I am sure. He knows he has deprived us of our most valuable dog, who took years of care and training at my expense and must now be replaced. Just as we have been." Nobody was catcalling anymore; not even the drunkest of the guests dared interrupt. The man's eyes burned with bitterness and he suddenly seemed to show his age—there was no longer any mistaking him for his son. He looked to Bauterne and raised his gloved hand, shining with the blood of his most favored hound. Slowly, he stepped forward and wiped his thumb across Bauterne's cheeks, leaving two red streaks.

"First blood is yours, sir. I am certain you will compensate us accordingly, if we are now to hunt together, as you say," said Enneval the Elder, his voice taut.

Bauterne's eyes were wide with shock, his nostrils flared, but he did not bite back. Again, I was impressed with his composure.

"Of course, sir" was all he said.

Enneval the Younger was chastened by his father's words, but he was not quite finished. "My father and I will share our fire, our men and our hounds with you, Monsieur Bauterne, as the king commands. But a stupid cock in a wig is still a stupid cock, even with a royal decree. Do not presume to speak to me about 'provocation'—I know my own dogs."

Bauterne again tipped his head politely, color rising behind the bloody streaks on his face. The Ennevals had insulted and humiliated him quite acutely and very publicly, and he did not seem the type to forget such an affront. "I hope we may speak again when tempers have cooled. I will apologize now for a third time and I will remove myself, but such is the limit of my courtesy. Please, enjoy the rest of the evening and I will see you at the push tomorrow."

The Lieutenant of the Hunt left the Ennevals standing over the corpse of their best hound. I considered offering my condolences—I know well how hard it is to lose a beloved animal—but their quiet, furious grief seemed a private thing. The other hunters began to lead their dogs away from the banquet, which was certainly over now.

Antoine was suddenly at my side. He was flushed, and not only from the wine.

"Professor, my father is ready to burst into flames; I fear you have embarrassed him in front of the bishop."

"*Me?* Sir, I can assure you this had nothing to do with me!"

"And yet you are here at the center of the disturbance, again." He grimaced. "My God, the *smell* down here. What happened?"

"A very good question, sir."

I am no expert, but there was something amiss with the dogs—all of them. Do you sense anything? I asked Sarmodel.

Only that we seem to have attracted unwelcome attention again, he answered. *My love, it is time to leave.*

He directed my gaze to the baron's table, where Antoine's noble father and the Bishop of Mende were in stern conversation. Their eyes were on me and the bloody carcass on the table in front of me.

First blood, I echoed Enneval's words uneasily, taking one final cherry pastry.

X

The Western Alps
1785

"I do not recognize my father in the duplicitous libertine you remember, or believe my late grandfather was ever such a grasping lapdog, waiting on the Church's attention," said Jacques bluntly. "And the others—Bauterne, the Normans, Bishop Fontaine—these are not the men as my father described them to me."

It had been five days since my impromptu surgery on his shoulder, and he was recovering slowly. We were into the foothills of the Alps now, getting closer to the snow line with each step. Another week, perhaps a little longer, and we would be in Gévaudan.

And then . . .

I had told Jacques the story—the Mundane version—during his wakeful periods over the past few days. He had listened largely in silence.

"No?"

"No, sir," Jacques replied. "Lord Bauterne was a hero to the people of Gévaudan, and deeply troubled by their plight. My father has nothing but praise for the Bishop of Mende—Fontaine's scars are a sign of his selflessness and sacrifice, to hear him speak. And the Normans made the greatest sacrifice of all, giving their lives that others might live."

"Perhaps your father did not wish to speak ill of the dead."

"You do not seem to share his reservations," he said with a laugh.

"No indeed." In spite of myself, I was beginning to warm to the grim young Lord Ocerne. His illness had deflated his pompous pride to some extent and I was (if not exactly glad of his company) increasingly certain that I didn't want him to die. Jacques was still riding in the wagon, but his wound was healing with remarkable speed and he would soon be ready for horseback again.

It mattered little. To compound our problems, Aherin now seemed to be taking ill. The gelding was weak and haggard, and covered in sores and grazes from weeks of neglect at Jacques's hands. Each morning he was slower to move, and he was now without the strength to bear a rider. I walked alongside the wagon, doing my best to ignore our lackadaisical pace as we ascended into colder climes and the snowdrifts began to encroach on the road.

As our third night in the mountains approached, I knew the decision would have to be made. I had the great fortune to locate a campsite in the lee of an enormous fallen spruce. I unhitched the cart gently. It was shockingly quiet, sheltered by the tree's ancient trunk on one side and the snow-filled woods on the other. Jacques was sleeping, so I began to drag branches from the fallen tree across the remnants of a previous traveler's campfire. The fire I built was perhaps larger than necessary, but there was dry wood aplenty and I suspected that we would be thankful for the extra warmth tonight.

Jacques woke after a short while and climbed gingerly out of the cart, still very weak.

"Why have we stopped here?" he said irritably. "This is a miserable place to camp."

"Sir," I said quietly, "given our need, this is an absolute palace among campsites. It will be night soon and we can scarcely pass up the shelter. If you know somewhere else for us to go, I will await your lead."

Jacques seemed about to bite, but then bowed his head. "I apologize. You are right, of course. I admit that I am uneasy in these mountains and will be glad to leave them behind."

"Then I am doubly sorry, young sir," I sighed. "The time has come. I fear that Aherin can come no farther with us."

"Aherin?" Jacques seemed not to understand.

I nodded. "He is ailing, and grows worse by the day. Our journey through the mountains will be hard and it would be no kindness to take him with us. You must decide tonight if you will set him back on the path behind us, or . . . put him to rest here. I hold little hope that he will survive alone, but a sick horse will attract attention we cannot afford." Sarmodel had warned me several times of wolves following us, though none had yet been daring enough to approach. This would change the longer we were within their range.

"But he has come this far!" Jacques put a hand on the gelding's mane, stricken. "Have I truly treated you so poorly, my friend?" He looked very small in the shadow of the fallen tree. Then he turned to me. "No. You must be able to do something. If you are in truth a doctor, or a professor, or whatever gifts you claim to have.[1] Please. Aherin has been mine since I was a boy. My father gave him to me."

---

1. Do not be shocked by Jacques's sudden willingness to countenance a little occult assistance. When the chips are down, the God-fearing are always first in line to throw the baby on the altar.

"The road ahead will be trying enough, and whatever my 'gifts' may be, I cannot give him what he needs most: rest, sustenance and proper care," I said gently. "I am truly sorry, young sir."

"You refuse? You are here in service to my family, are you not?" he demanded. "Must I beg?"

Yes! Yes, Sebastian! ***Say it!***[2]

I ignored my Guest's goading. "You are technically correct, young sir, and if you *require* it, I will certainly do my best to take care of Aherin's needs alongside your own. In between times—and by your leave—I will also see to my own horse, and continue to set camp, hunt, cook and carry for us all. Perhaps I shall even find time for my own meals and private needs, or indulge in a few hours' rest. Shall we see who dies first, of the four of us?"

"Stop! I know—I know! You are right!" Jacques covered his face with his hands, shaking his head. "You are right, as always. And as always, I must apologize for my behavior. You shame me."

"It is no matter. I will take my gun and see if I can find us something to eat. Take some time to say farewell and do what must be done."

Jacques's hand fell slowly to his hunting knife; he was already practicing the stroke in his mind.

"Here." I took my sword from the cart and passed him the hilt. "This will be faster. The throat and the heart—and do it away from here. Hungry scavengers would be company most unwelcome."

---

2. Sarmodel takes an unhealthy—though entirely apt—delight in begging of any kind. This is partly because people who are begging are often willing to agree to anything, which opens the door to any number of unsavory Contractual possibilities. It's also a matter of taste; you might say that desperation is Sarmodel's favorite flavor of human misery.

He nodded. I left him standing by the fire, whispering close to Aherin's ear as he had on so many nights during his delirium.

The darkening woods were packed deep with old snow, and silent.

The soft crunch of my footfalls startled a fox. It dropped its meal and darted away, swift and pale as smoke in its winter coat. Otherwise the place was completely still; the creatures of the wildwood knew the dangers of the quiet twilight.

I spoke a Litany of the Hunt and waited.

The forest around me slowly sharpened into a stark shadowland of black and white. I could hear the friction of pine needles stirring above me and taste the steel-and-dust tang of imminent snow in the back of my throat. My movements became lighter and more liquid; among the hunters of the wilds, I was more the serpent than the wolf.

In my new perception, the snowy forest floor was a map of life and death. A wisp of down and a graveyard of tiny bones marked an owl's nest. Pale lichens consumed the deadfall with infinite patience. And every stone and hillock was contoured with tracks. I crouched low and followed them, passing my hands over the fresh snow to find those that still held traces of living heat.

Sebastian, stop. What is that?

Sarmodel directed my eyes to the remains of the fox's meal: a scrap of cold carrion flesh. I picked it up.

Man meat, he whispered.

What? Are you sure?

Sebastian, I have eaten more human flesh than leprosy.[3] *Trust me.*

---

3. I have no way to verify this. I suspect that my Guest was active in old Mesopotamia, however, which would put him in good company as far as man-eaters are concerned.

Very well. Shall we investigate?

I turned and followed the fox's back trail.

The creature's tracks took me in a lazy circle, first down to a frigid stream and then back up toward the road. A host of other tracks joined it along the way, left by rodent, wolf, weasel and badger; an informal guest list to a grisly banquet. The tracks braided together and converged back on a rocky overhang, where the roots of an aged cedar had split the stone of the mountainside.

Well now.

Two men sat there, side by frozen side. Without the grisly clue left by the fox, I might never have found them at all, so well concealed were they in their snowy nook. Their heads were half turned toward each other, as though I had caught them sharing some intimate secret.

The creatures of the forest had taken their due from the corpses; the men's faces were all but gone. But the lingering snows had kept them from decay and preserved much of their unfortunate resting place. I shooed away a nest of forest mice and gently brushed the snow from the bodies so I could see them in their entirety.

Killed by bandits? I suggested hopefully.

Certainly, replied Sarmodel. ***Hungry*** *bandits.*

The men's throats had been torn out; one had lost his jaw completely. Each wore a black apron of frozen blood, and I didn't have to look inside their shattered rib cages to know their hearts had been eaten. Their clothing told me they were travelers of ordinary means. They were young, and—most troubling of all—they were still in possession of their belts, boots and weapons.

I sat back on my haunches, thinking.

Their wounds suggested an attack by a powerful animal. But these men had not been killed and tucked away by an especially fastidious bear.

I closed my eyes. The forest around me was suddenly too close and too full of distractions. *Is it possible? Have we found the Beast so soon?*

My love, we are still days from Gévaudan. It is most unlikely—

I know! I know it's unlikely. But just think for a moment. Is it possible?

He twisted like an eel in my mind. *It is. But why would he come* ***here****? There are far better places to feed.*

Just so.

I laid my hand on the stock of my gun, suddenly wishing I hadn't left my silver blade behind.

"Who were you, gentlemen?" I murmured, leaning close to them. "And what were you doing up here?"

I was struck with something *familiar* about one of the men and it took me a few moments to work it out. Half of his scalp had been torn away and the remainder was peeling up like a matted military crest. The flow of his blood had darkened the snow around his shoulders like a crimson cape, and it was the Roman decurion I saw in his ravaged, eyeless profile.

"The gods of Rome have moved on," I murmured, imagining for a moment I could smell the smoking herbs of augury. I heard the loyal decurion's response once again.

Know that you are treating with a dark creature, he said in my memory, in the language of the ancient, beautiful empire. *It deceives you with every word. Be rid of it before it shows its true face.*

Again, I saw his hand, raised to point at something over my head.

Or *behind* me . . .

Behind me. Where a young man was shivering in his drug-induced stupor, already in the grip of a strange fever.

My thoughts turned in a troubling new direction.

I leaped to my feet.

Sarmodel, I need you! I turned and ran back for the camp, following my own tracks.

Yes! he answered. My blood surged as he *flexed* and came forward in my mind, filling me with new strength. My bones were shot with molten steel and my skin began to steam in the frigid air.

And Sarmodel . . . he was *close,* so close to the physical that I could taste his breath on my tongue. When he spoke again, I almost felt my lips moving.

Yes, I am here. Now ***run****.*

A scream pierced the snowstorm.

The sound was a jet of hot blood across the tapestry of my altered senses.

I flew through the snowdrifts, moving with Sarmodel's supernatural speed. To the animals of the forest, I must have seemed a black flurry in the night, like the shadow of a shrike. In my wake, I left eddies of vapor.

I came to rest in silence, poised in the shadows outside the camp. Through the trees ahead I could see the fire, dancing high on its fuel of fragrant spruce.

And beside it was the writhing silhouette of the kill.

Too late.

It was not a human voice I had heard screaming, but the final cry of Aherin. The gelding fought with the last of his strength against the death that had come for him. He had collapsed to the ground and his legs cycled weakly, kicking embers from the fire.

Hunched over him was a naked creature of monstrous aspect, covered in ropy muscle and tufts of pale, ragged fur.

In the flickering light, it might have been a man grown to huge proportions, with its long limbs and pink, newborn skin. The face, too, was manlike, bare about the eyes and nose with patchy fur that thickened like a beard along its jaw and down toward its throat. But there was nothing human about the bristly ruff and the sparse mane that ran down its back, or the clawed toes that gripped Aherin's hind leg.

There was an unnerving *pubescent* aspect to the creature, like a pup not quite come into its full coat. Grayish fur clumped densely across its shoulders and around the groin, but the muscular arms and legs were still ruddy and smooth. It was lean and wiry, but the broad skull and thick joints hinted at a strength as yet undeveloped.

It cradled the horse like a lover, with its jaws closed around the gelding's throat. One powerful arm tugged and worried at something I could not see.

With a moan, the monster threw back its head, tearing out the delicate channels of Aherin's blood and breath.

It raised its eyes and saw me—*knew* me.

I stepped into the light, steam pouring from my sleeves and billowing out of my collar.

The beast watched me, panting. Aherin, loyal to the last, struggled no more. Apart from the sound of the fire, the camp was utterly silent.

Be rid of it before it shows its true face.

Eyes as black and glistening as roe followed my hand as I raised the musket.

"That's enough, Jacques."

"Professor." The creature's voice was thick with red lust, but he still spoke with my young companion's Occitan accent. He sat back slowly and I could at last see what he had been doing. One arm slid wetly from within Aherin's belly, glistening red to the shoulder. The horse's innards spilled steaming onto the ground behind it. In his clawed hand, the monster brandished Aherin's enormous heart. "The throat and the heart, just as you said." He smiled at my revulsion and bit silently into the organ.

Sarmodel hissed in my ear, his ferocious strength ebbing slightly. *Sebastian, I can't do this forever. Kill him, now!*

How?! My gun and my hunting knife would be of little use against whatever Jacques had become. Worse, he was crouched right in front of my cart, where my silver blade and Arcane supplies were lying useless. *If I get any closer, it's my heart he'll be eating.*

Then think of something else. Quickly!

The creature spoke again, rolling his tongue around morsels of heart meat. "I wonder, Professor, what you are thinking. So often you say nothing, but your eyes are *eloquent*. What strange congress goes on inside that arrogant head?"

"I am wondering how long you think you can maintain yourself in this form, and what I should do with you afterward."

Jacques's laughter came from the monster's throat. "I would expect nothing less. Shall I tell you what is in *my* thoughts?" He stood, rising to his full height. He was well over seven feet tall, and every inch was taut with power; even with Sarmodel's help, I would be no match for him. The creature was aroused by the kill and reached down to wrap crimson claws around his protruding manhood. "In my thoughts, I hear a voice that tells me to *have* you as my father did. It tells me to spit you here like a hog before I kill you. Shall we see if my cock is to your liking, as his was? Would that please you?"

I knew he was trying to unnerve me, but I was speechless all the same. I edged away, stepping closer to the concealing shadows of the forest.

He knows about Antoine?

What does it matter, Sebastian? ***Kill him!***

The monster laughed again. "So, it is true! How did he like it?" He tore a mouthful from Aherin's heart as his other hand worked its pleasure. He was drunk on it all—the kill, the touch of his own flesh, my confusion and fear. "Was he the buck or the doe? I wonder. Will I taste him in your throat?"

"Be silent!" I took a few more faltering steps backward, feeling the snow-filled darkness close behind me. The monster's black eyes never left me.

"Come, Professor. Do you think to run from me, and so refuse my earnest advances?" He smiled with red, pointed teeth. "You will die before your second step, and I will be squatting over your bones by dawn."

I took another step, and another.

Sebastian, I am ***fading****!*

The creature swallowed the final scraps of the horse's heart and licked the blood from his fingers with a curling tongue. "Well? Have you no answer? No cunning words?" He laughed again. "Then come to me!"

Before his breath had cooled, the creature leaped.

A lot happened in the next second.

Without my augmented senses, I would surely have died, with the barest awareness of fangs at my throat and the warmth of my own blood on my skin. But my careful steps had placed the fire between us, and as fast as the monster was, Sarmodel was faster.

Now!

My hands moved with demonic speed as I cast the contents of my powder horn into the air. I spoke four Abject syllables and the creatures of the forest screamed as one.

With Arcane sight, you might have seen, for a sliver of that busy moment, the particles of gunpowder align into a quivering net of eldritch symbols and infinitely vanishing fractals above the flames—a net into which the monster plunged headlong.

With Mundane sight, you would have seen only the greenish explosion that followed.

The beast was thrown back against the trunk of the fallen spruce, howling as his ragged fur blazed. I followed him over the flames, quick as thought. With the last of Sarmodel's strength, I wrenched a burning log from the campfire and struck: twice on the skull and then—for spite—a third time in the creature's "earnest advances."

It was enough. The monster shuddered and gave a low, wheezing growl. His black roe eyes closed and he was still.

And suddenly I found myself standing ankle-deep in horse guts, struggling under the weight of a smoldering branch.

I collapsed to my knees, dropping the log.

Thank you, my love, I said as my sight began to fade.

My Guest retreated, his power spent. His voice was faint. *What's mine is yours. Now try not to die.*

The darkness came swiftly.

XII

Close behind the darkness, as ever, came the madness.

I retreated from the world, exhausted near to death, and the world retreated from me in turn. The blizzard's roar softened to silence. The blaze of the bonfire diminished, growing dim and distant. The frigid slurry of snow, mud and blood darkened to black around me.

And suddenly I was warm and dry, seated at a familiar table by a familiar hearth.

Here in the dim vault of my own mind I found, as I had so often in the past, a place of comfort.

I came back to myself gradually, slowly making sense of where I was—and *who* I was. A powerful magician? An esteemed professor? A famed hunter of monsters?

No. The man who was all of those things was in the real world, still convulsing in the bloody snow by the bonfire of spruce, prey to dreadful passions.

Here in this private sanctuary I was something else.

A child.

A serious child, with dark hair, olive skin and an aquiline nose. The young Cypriot boy I had once been.

I was seated at my mother's table, ready to eat. The table itself was rough and sturdy, made from the wood of a shipwreck; the pride of a fisherman's household. Around me was a hazy re-creation of my childhood home, conjured from my memories—a dirt floor strewn with wisps of grass, the faint smell of the ocean, the barest impression of a reed-bundle roof overhead. The fire cast a pool of ember-orange light that did not quite reach the edges of the room.

I could see nothing beyond it but darkness.

My chair was a white stone from the field by the seashore, just the right size for a child. It was cold against my bare skin. My arms were held down by my sides, bound with manacles that were in turn chained to a metal ring in the floor, no doubt salvaged from that same doomed ship. Each metal link was marked with the shape of Wanassa. Just as I remembered them.

Wanassa. The Lady. We do not say her name. I shrank from the word and the memory both.

Wanassa. She who bound me. Bound us. We do not say her name.

"Ssh. My boy, you must eat." From the darkness around me, a voice crooned; a low, rich voice but with a *burned* quality, as though the speaker were suffering a terrible thirst. Large hands emerged from the shadows, placing a wooden bowl on the table before me.

The meal was simple and unappetizing—a pulpy mash of grains and sour milk—but saliva pooled under my tongue; I was *hungry.*

The chains were short. The only way I could eat was by stooping forward and grubbing like a dog. I buried my face in the bowl, stopping only to turn my head and breathe.

"Good, good. Eat and grow strong." The hands came again from the darkness. The empty dish was removed and another took its place. Beans and salted fish. I moaned as I smelled it, using my jaw to tilt the bowl. My hunger was such that I wondered only for a moment why the food left a metallic tang in my throat.

"Sebastian."[1]

A new voice. A deep voice, full of command. I raised my eyes from the peasant's feast, my chin dripping.

A pair of golden eyes emerged from the darkness. Powerful footsteps made a slow circle around the table. A brilliant white light suddenly washed away the dim glow of the hearth, and a magnificent creature stepped carefully into the circle it made, shaking its mane.

Lion of Judah. Beautiful. Terrible.

He sat opposite me, looming somehow higher than the ceiling. His face was not entirely that of a man nor a beast. Jeweled wings with feathers like swords folded behind his back. In the white light, his claws and fangs shone with the luster of gold.

"So once again you have pushed your mortal flesh beyond its limits, and again you retreat within yourself. See yourself now as you truly are—a prisoner and a child you remain, trapped here these many ages," he said sadly. "Do you not tire of it? Will you spurn me still?"

I could not answer. My hunger was only growing stronger and I ran my tongue around my lips, desperate for the next bite.

---

1. He actually used one of my (much) older names. For the sake of simplicity, I've kept to my current English name throughout this account, but I've had dozens of names over the years, often variations on "Sebastian."

The lion sighed. "I feel your need. So long as you remain here, it will never end."

He raised his taloned right hand and pierced the palm with his teeth, releasing a cascade of hot blood. The liquid was thick and sang like crystal as it fell.

Where it struck the table, the bounty of empires sprang forth. Pomegranates and clusters of grapes burst from the red cascade. Candied figs and chestnuts, bright apples and plums swelled and tumbled against each other. The lion breathed over the feast, and unimaginable riches welled forth. Rubies and pearls rolled amid berries of the thicket. Amber and ivory were swept up in eddies of honey and spiced wine. Beads of molten gold pelted the floor.

It was too much to bear. I lunged forward, drawing my own blood as I strained against the shackles. But no matter how hard I pulled, the lion's gifts remained just beyond my reach. I began to sob, tears joining the line of drool that ran from my mouth.

"Such are the riches of the Kingdom," said the lion. "They are yours. Already they are yours." It licked its palm and the wound closed without trace. A final crimson drop rolled across the scarred wood and shattered in a tumble of dates and black garnets. "I have come to release you, Sebastian, and to give all of this to you. My very blood is yours for the asking, now and forever. Will you take it?"

I nodded frantically, close to delirium.

"Then you have but to tell me your name, and I will break the chain." The lion leaned forward and licked the tears from my cheeks. His breath was sweet and heady, like roses. "Come. I am strength. I am succor. The name your mother gave you. Tell it to me, and you will join me in the Father's Kingdom."

"My name?" My child's voice sounded very small next to his. "I . . ."

"MICHAEL! ENOUGH!" The words struck the lion like a blow. He recoiled, flexing his wings in menace, and the world flickered once again. The rich, burned voice seemed to come from everywhere at once. "This is not your place, Michael. He is *mine.*"

From the shadows, a shaggy creature swung up onto the table—a baboon, grotesque in its near humanity. Long-armed and lopsided, it drummed its hands on the wood with a screech. Its face was the lurid mask of the mandrill; crimson nose, bright blue ridged muzzle and gold beard. It grinned and showed its yellow fangs to the lion, and then it opened its mouth to belch, unfurling a forked black tongue.

I knew the creature. A terribly complicated word surfaced in my mind, seeming to mean a dozen things at once—*guest friend father teacher lover demon*—before it settled into a name.

Sarmodel.

With a cackle, the baboon set about scooping the lion's boons into its mouth, chewing noisily on succulent fruits and glittering gemstones alike.

The lion raised its lip in disgust at the mandrill. "And what do *you* offer, Lariel?[2] What has your abominable union given him but the promise of misery without end?"

The monkey continued to eat, smearing the feast across the tabletop. It regurgitated a vile slick at the lion's feet and then gorged itself anew, hooting with dark mirth. I watched in dismay as unimaginable bounty turned to ruin.

"Have you forgotten, Great Prince?" The mocking voice came from the darkness, but I knew it was him speaking—my Guest,

---

2. One of Sarmodel's oldest names, dating back as far as the time of the Fall. There are very few—a handful of the angels—who still remember it.

the baboon, Sarmodel, the one who was *always* here with me. "I am as much a prisoner here as he is."

"Then allow him to choose, and let me release you both."

The creature's laughter seemed to come from everywhere at once. "Such munificence! Release?" It turned and winked at me, food and bile dripping from its beard. "And I thought all the great deceivers were on *my* side of the Rift."

The lion huffed in exasperation and lowered its beautiful face to the level of the table. "If you will not treat with me, then I offer you—both of you—a warning." In the shadows, its wings flexed, glittering with blades. "Give up this pursuit. The Spirit you hunt has wronged me and stained the name of the Almighty. My mark of Justice is upon him and I will see it executed. Do not seek him out again; I will not countenance your interference a third time."

The mandrill leaned forward and kissed the lion's face with its foul lips. "My mark is also upon him, Grand General—I have staked my claim, a life for a life. And I knew him in Rome, *millennia* before your Almighty deigned to sully his loins with mortal issue. So, tell me: Who is interfering with whom?"

Michael shook his head sadly. "It will give me no pleasure to destroy you, Lariel, but know that if you step beneath the shadow of my sword, it will fall on your neck." He looked to me again. "And you, child of Cyprus. Yours is a trial I would not wish upon the Father of Lies himself. But as long as you refuse to redeem yourself, your torment will grow." His eyes softened in pity and he leaned over the baboon to tenderly lick my face again. "Sim Sala Bim," he whispered sadly.

He gave the baboon a final, weary glance and then, with a flicker of brilliant feathers, he was gone.

The white light faded and once more I sat in the glow of embers.

The baboon turned to face me and sat on its rump amid the fouled remains of the lion's feast. It watched me with implacable, intelligent eyes.

I lowered my face gratefully and continued to eat.

XIII

The dawn was bright and clear. The forest glittered with new snow, and the silvery chatter of snow finches joined the gentle clinking of chains in the morning air. A pot of lemon-mint tisane bubbled over the coals of the fire; I inhaled its fragrant steam as I stirred in a spoonful of honey.

Jacques was naked and chained to a tree behind me. My companion was slowly recovering from his eventful evening. He was still unconscious, but the convulsions had stopped and he was mostly human again.

My fine traveling clothes were black and stiff with dried blood. I had awoken from my delirium around midnight, weak and heaving, on my knees beside Aherin's torn remains. The blood that covered me and the foul taste on my tongue confirmed the true nature of my otherworldly banquet. But it was the feather clutched in my hand that dismayed me the most; a calling card from the Archangel himself.

Sim Sala Bim.

The words were a sudden fist around my heart. Sarmodel was distant, no doubt as debilitated as I was, and for those brief moments it seemed I was alone—*alone*—on the freezing mountainside. Worse, I was still hungry, in spite of my abominable repast.

I saw only horror behind me and more horror ahead; I had seldom felt more wretched. I wept there in the darkness. For misery, for despair, for the sheer futility of *still being there.*

I cast the feather into the campfire embers and turned to the slowly changing abomination that was Jacques. By dawn he was bound and secured, and the memory of Michael had lost its sting somewhat.

Sebastian, he is waking. If you're not going to kill him, you'd best prepare yourself.

I was indeed considering killing him very seriously. But the truth was that there were too many things I still didn't know—his condition hinted glaringly at some unfinished business of mine, and I would need his help to resolve it. There was also the matter of the six hundred livres I had been offered to complete the contract; I doubted the bounty would be forthcoming if I arrived with Jacques's corpse.

Sarmodel's warning was accompanied by weak coughing and a new bout of retching from Jacques.

Very well.

I checked my Wards carefully before pouring myself a generous measure of the infusion from the pot. My trapper's chain was sturdy enough, but I had encircled Jacques with lethal Admonitions in horse blood just to be safe. His monstrous flesh had sloughed away and dissolved in the meantime, and he now sat in a sticky puddle of mud and yellowish plasma.

Jacques only opened one eye (the other was swollen shut), but I was relieved to see that it was once again human.

"Professor?" he slurred. He flailed weakly in his chains, his eye blinking in confusion.

"Good morning, sir," I said. With my free hand, I raised my pistol, taking aim at his midsection. "Take a minute to collect yourself. Know that if you even twitch in my direction, I will be very pleased to end your legacy."

Jacques sat up slowly, his eye on the muzzle. He grimaced and cupped his hands over his manhood, which was no doubt quite tender. "You . . . you are insane, as I suspected. What reason do you—"

"Be silent." I cocked the gun in warning. "We are going to speak properly now, as two men who nearly killed each other last night."

"*Killed?* You are speaking madness, Professor." His face slowly changed as he took in the scorched wreckage of firewood and horseflesh scattered around him. He stared at my crimson face and my blood-soaked clothes. For a moment, he was almost endearing in his bewilderment. "By the Christ. What happened? What have you done?"

"Me? No, sir, this was all your doing. Do you not remember?"

"I . . . confess I do not, though my head is *aching*."

What do you think? I asked Sarmodel.

He seems sincere. And he's certainly afraid; I can smell it.

"Then tell me," I said aloud, "tell me what you *do* remember. Be truthful. I will know it if you lie."[1]

"Professor, *put down* your weapon! I will say nothing with a

---

1. A bluff on my part. One of the greatest limitations on a Contract of Truth is that it requires agreement on both sides, and I certainly wasn't about to step inside the Wards to shake his hand. Nor did I particularly want any deeper entanglements with Jacques d'Ocerne, the man-eating abomination.

pistol in my face." He shivered and gathered his legs close to his body. "And *must* I always be naked when you wish to speak?"

"You may have a blanket when I am satisfied." Nonetheless, I obliged his first request and lowered the muzzle of my gun. "Now *answer me*: What happened after I left you last night?"

His one-eyed glare was vicious. "Very well. I was—I was to kill Aherin." He looked down. "I remember that. At your behest, I was to kill my own horse. I had the blade. And I believe he knew. He was scared of me." He struggled weakly against the chains, trembling. "Professor, I don't *remember.* I spoke to him, to calm him. And then I awoke here."

"Why was he afraid of you, young sir?"

"I do not know."

"Shall I guess? Aherin was afraid because you have been feeding on him for at least the last week." I took a warming sip of tisane. "I found where you were cutting him on what was left of his neck. All those nights, whispering by his ear; I thought it was remorse driving you to his side, when instead—" I raised the gun as he tried to interrupt. "—*instead* it was a far different demon in charge. You were clever to hide your handiwork under the mane. But you must have known he would eventually weaken if you kept drinking his blood."

"*Drinking his blood?* I say again, Professor, this is madness! I—*believe me* when I say I would never do such a thing." But something troubled him; his words faltered. "How can you even suggest it?"

"Do you deny it? I am a madman holding a gun, so think carefully."

Jacques shivered again and his eye clouded. "Perhaps. Perhaps there have been dreams. A voice."

"A voice? What does it say?"

"It . . . he speaks of things I would never do, desires I have never had—not truly. Yet he knows me somehow. He speaks of hypocrisy and injustice, and it rouses the fury in me. And he speaks of *eating,* and I have awoken with a hunger such as I have never known. But I would *never.*" The young man grew quiet. "Aherin? I couldn't—I *mustn't.*"

"He" speaks of eating. No need to guess who "he" might be, I remarked, as Jacques seemed to lose himself in his fractured recollection. *It seems the Beast has been with us this whole time.*

What—this thirsty toddler? This hairless kit? Come, Sebastian, it makes no sense. This is a pitiable shadow of the Beast himself. You remember him as well as I do.

A shadow. Or a fragment, perhaps.

Indeed, replied Sarmodel. *My love, whatever the case—this one is dangerous. Be done with him now and let me feed. We could certainly use his strength.*

I do not disagree. But not just yet. He is still Antoine's son—and I need to know more.

"I am curious about this voice, sir, but let me inquire on a different matter," I said to Jacques. "Tell me again how you were shot."

And now he was silent.

"This is where it happened, is it not?" I pressed. "I wondered why you were so disinclined to camp here. Now I know, of course, that you have been here before."

"*Why?* Why must we revisit my every humiliation?" he snarled at me. "Yes, Professor, if you must have an answer. *Yes.* This is where I was betrayed. This is where my friends and brothers took my money, beat me and shot me with the weapons my family gave them. This is where they left me for dead with Aherin as my only companion. This is where I considered returning to my family in failure, stopped only by the knowledge that I may be the last chance they have, because my father is a stubborn pig who would save us with prayer and scripture!" He stopped, breathing hard. "Yes, Professor, you have deduced correctly: *this is the place.*"

He gave a nervous whimper as I again took aim at his crotch. "My loyalty to your father stays my hand this once, but if I hear another lie from you, the shot will fly. I found them, Jacques." I pulled a grayish, gnawed ear from my pocket and tossed it on the ground in front of him. "Your friends. I found them."

He recoiled from the ear, uncomprehending. "What is this?" Then his brow creased and he shook his head. "No. No! You are *wrong.* Gerard and Henri are halfway to Saint-Chély by now."

"They are where you left them after you killed them. It will be no trouble to bring them here if you so desire, sir; they are much lighter without their innards. I would warn you that they may be difficult to recognize, however." The severed ear began to shrink and blacken; my circle of Admonitions was quite unforgiving on foreign tissue. "Their hearts sustained you most of the way to Corvano, but your hunger has been growing, I believe—to Aherin's great cost. Do you deny it?"

His gaze was bitter, betraying a flash of the monster he had been. For several moments, he said nothing, and I feared he would indeed test my willingness to shoot him. But then his eye closed and he spoke again, barely above a whisper.

"I cannot."

"Go on."

He took a deep, difficult breath. "I returned from hunting to find my companions rifling my belongings. It was as I said: When I confronted them, they told me they were not returning to blighted Ocerne. They begged me to come with them, to start somewhere else with the money I had been given. I was so *angry* and the voice—*his* voice—was all I could hear." Jacques was barely audible. "And then nothing. It was as now. I awoke wounded, covered in blood—just over there, in fact." His sudden laughter was a mad, floating wheeze. "It was like surfacing from a dream. The others were gone. The voice was silent. Only Aherin remained."

"And was that the first time you awakened so? The truth—speak!"

"No. It has happened before."

"When?"

"The first time, perhaps a year ago." Now that he was resigned to it, the truth came quickly. "My father arranged a deer hunt for my birthday, with all the noble families of Gévaudan. My own grandfather, the Baron d'Apcher, killed a stag that was mine by rights—they were *my birthday honors*—and I was overcome by thoughts of vengeance. Not just vengeance; murder. I heard it—the voice—so clearly, telling me I could kill every man in the camp while they slept and they would never take anything of mine again. I did not listen—who would countenance such a thing?—but the next morning I woke naked and covered in filth in the middle of the forest. I thought it a prank, some elaborate jest for my birthday, and I managed to make it back to the camp before the others were awake. We learned on our way home that the local farms had been raided in the night, their livestock torn to pieces." He suddenly began to sob, a huge, ragged sound that was most of the way to screaming. It was horrific to hear in the snowy stillness. "I knew. I knew! I denied it, even to myself, but I knew I had done it."

"And it has happened again since? How many times?"

"I do not know. Ten? A dozen? The voice returns and it speaks of hunger and it must *eat*." Again, that terrible sob. "I do not remember—please believe me!"

"I do, sir."

A man who becomes a monster in the night, and is only satisfied by the kill,[2] I reiterated. *What did we leave behind in Gévaudan? Is this my fault, Sarmodel?*

Almost certainly. How many loose ends must come back to eat us before you start listening to me? Come now, time to pull the trigger.

"Kill me, then," said Jacques suddenly. He was clearer than he had been since we met. "If I am half a monster already, if this is how it will be, I cannot bear it. But you must first promise me you will continue on to Ocerne. At least take the news to my family, even if I am lost."

"Lost? I will not concede defeat so easily, and nor should you, young sir." I holstered the pistol. "And no, I am not going to kill you."

*What?! Are you **joking**?!*

His red, bleary eye narrowed. "Why not?"

"Because I believe you and Gévaudan can both be saved."

"Must you frustrate me even in this?" He shook his head. "How can I return to the château—to Eloise—knowing what I will become?"

"Leave that to me, young sir." I lifted the pot of tea from the fire and splashed it across the bloody marks in the snow. My Admonitions dissolved along with them. "Now, let us get you out of those chains, and we will set some new rules for the remainder of our journey. And have no fear—I am also half a monster, and I have a great deal of unfinished business with your Beast."

---

2. Yes, I see you there, hurling your peanuts and bawling, "He's a werewolf, you idiot!" Please be aware that the contemporary "werewolf" with which you are familiar was quite unheard-of up to this point—and then suddenly they were everywhere. Perhaps you are beginning to understand why this is such a landmark case.

PART TWO

The Beast and the Maiden

XIV

Château d'Ocerne
Gévaudan, France
1766

If I had any doubts about the Beast of Gévaudan, they were dispelled on the first day of the hunt.

The day Lord Bauterne led us in the push.

The new master of the hunt called us to gather at noon on the green slopes outside the château, forming a line on the border where the fields met the mountain forests. There was no talk of the humiliating events of the previous night's banquet, at least not within earshot of the Lieutenant of the Hunt and the stony-faced Normans.

"*Form up! Hold your marks!*" came the command, passed from man to man along the line. Hunters spread out with their hounds, each party a spear's length apart from the next. It was a surprisingly orderly process given how many hounds, horses, dialects and hangovers were in play; these men had all been drinking the baron's wine until well into the small hours.

Antoine was among the worst afflicted. I suspected he had ended up at the brothel in Saint-Julien-by-the-Stream. There was something very endearing about the young lord, cranky and disheveled with wisps of blond hair hanging in his face.

"Sir," I ventured in the tense silence before the hunt, "forgive me, but I must wonder why I am here."

"For the push, Professor, which is about to start. For all the good it will do us."

I understood these "pushes" were a weekly affair, led by the master of the hunt—this would be Lord Bauterne's debut. Each Sunday after Mass, the villagers of Gévaudan would gather at assigned rally points in the wilderness with pots and batons, creating a great wall of noise and malodor with which to drive the Beast from hiding. The hunters waited in a line on the far side of the forest, snaring every startled piglet and badger with the poor luck to be passing through.

"My thanks, young sir, but that's not what I meant. I don't wish to seem ungrateful, but I must ask—why did you intervene on my behalf yesterday, at the ceremony?"

"Do you object to being in my employ?"

"Not at all. But—if we may dispense with the ruse for a moment—you roused the displeasure of both your father and the Bishop of Mende for the sake of a stranger. A *foreign* stranger."

"Ah. That. Perhaps I simply felt it was unfair to deny you a place in the hunt, after making the journey to help us." He squeezed his eyes shut, placing a hand to his tender head. "I might have reconsidered had I known you were so fond of talk."

I laughed and handed him my brandy flask. "Here, this will help—not more than a mouthful, mind."

Antoine's eyes snapped open and he accepted the flask with shaking hands. He took a long swallow and then another, his eyes watering.

Sarmodel shared Antoine's skepticism. *What sort of Beast do you imagine will be flushed from hiding by a line of screaming meat-bags banging on pots?*

Who knows, my love? I answered. *But hopefully we may at least set eyes on it.*

I took the flask back from Antoine as a hunting horn sounded across the forested hilltops. A distant clamor rolled through the trees, the sound of shrilling voices and clattering saucepans. The push had begun.

The fastest animals came first. Hares and a few small deer burst from the bracken with their hind legs kicking high behind them. The hunters let most pass by. Then came the big game. A furious boar emerged not far from us, attracting a staggering thunderclap of musket fire. Somewhere to the north, voices chorused "*Cérvi!*" as an impressive stag fled across the hillside, chased by a keen pack of hounds.

And then came the wolves. Surprisingly large and utterly terrified, there were perhaps a dozen of them in the pack, driven before the throng of villagers. They bolted from the cover of the undergrowth not far from our mark, breaking through the line of hunters in seconds.

"Men! To me!" Bauterne was suddenly there, barely more than a shadow among the trees in his black hunting leathers on his black horse. "For God! For the king!" The hunters turned as one and we followed him in the chase.

I will admit it was tremendous fun to ride with the army of hunters, swooping after our quarry through the creeks and gullies of Gévaudan. Antoine's mood improved almost immediately and his mad laughter was audible above the fray. In the end, the senior Enneval took down two of the poor animals with his musket, Bauterne another, Soeur yet another, and the largest fell to the nine-fingered trapper from Gascony. It was bloody and exhilarating and, perhaps most importantly, it made everyone feel as though they were *doing something.*

Afterward, we reserved the stag—a noble creature with twelve points—to be presented to the Baron d'Ocerne as patron. The hunters who had made kills bloodied their faces and claimed the finest cuts for themselves, and then hunters and villagers alike celebrated over a feast of wild game.[1] We gathered, greasy-lipped, to watch as Bauterne cut the wolves open and examined their stomach contents for human remains. He was genuinely downcast when the search proved fruitless, and he left the carcasses for the dogs to fight over.

I was disappointed too, of course.

I'm sorry. Perhaps this was a mistake after all, I conceded.

An abysmal waste of time, but we managed to feed, at least, said Sarmodel. He was preening after consuming the anima of the wolves, rich with the energetic bounty of their predatory lives. In my mind they left an aftertaste of black pepper and butter caramel.

A very different sort of hunt began a few hours later, as the villagers returned home to horror.

The Beast had not been idle while we played the great huntsmen in front of the common folk.

The first body was just outside Saint-Julien-by-the-Stream, a stone's throw from the château. A young shepherd was found broken over a hitching post, his head on a nearby rooftop, crushed like a pumpkin.

Next was the toothless Flemish dog handler, raked to ribbons behind the church and then left to be devoured by his own hounds.

---

1. If you are thinking that this practice would quickly strip the region of its wildlife, you are absolutely correct. Anything that was not eaten or killed for sport quickly learned to avoid the forested foothills in favor of less accessible climes, at least on Sundays.

The animals had to be put down, so wild had they become with fear and bloodlust.

And the last I saw with my own eyes.

Many of the Gévaudanais had come to the push in wagons, stuffing the drays with hay to help make the bumpy ride more bearable. For two young lovers, one such soft bower had seemed the perfect place for a secret tryst. They had decided to hang back while the other villagers were distracted, beating pans in the forest.

"Professor," said Antoine. His words failed as we joined the wailing onlookers surrounding the wagon.

They were around sixteen years old, I would say. The boy had been torn in two; everything below his ribs was gone. The girl was at least intact, but her wounds were almost too savage to look at. Their hearts had been taken and the wagon was filled with their blood. Perhaps worst of all, their hands were still entwined in the crimson-spattered hay between them.

But it was not the gore or the tragedy of their deaths that drew my attention.

Sebastian—there! said Sarmodel.

I see it!

There were enormous bloody tracks leading away from the cart and back along the road. They were similar to wolf prints, but there were five long toes on each paw.

I spurred my horse after them at a trot, eager to follow the tracks before the other hunters arrived. The footprints went a short distance, until they disappeared into the forest again—just over the hill from the place where the hunters and villagers had been carrying out their push.

I dismounted quickly, my heart quickening at the sight of a telltale shimmer in a particularly deep paw print.

"Professor? What is it?" called Antoine, stepping down from his horse behind me.

"A trail, sir!" I answered, my voice cracking in excitement.

Do you see this? Do you see it?! I said to Sarmodel. I knelt in the mud, using my gloved fingers to scoop clear, yellowish slime from the paw print.

Plasma!

I was holding the unmistakable by-product of a supernatural transformation. It dripped off my glove, evaporating rapidly into fumes.

No wonder the Beast has been so elusive. He's not hiding; he's changing form, I said. *Sarmodel, he must be* **big***—I haven't seen this much since that lamia in Corinth in the twelfth century!*

Sarmodel whooped in my mind.

Spirit made flesh! Sebastian, I take it back—this has been a magnificent day! he crowed.

We were definitely not chasing a minnow.[2]

---

2. Plasma is the transition phase between anima and biological tissue—think of it like spiritual stem cells. It disintegrates rapidly in the Mundane world, so finding it in noticeable quantities usually means something powerful has been constructing/deconstructing living flesh, for whatever reason, very recently. Note that this is a significant undertaking for any Spirit; your garden-variety Arcane nuisance doesn't just go around shifting phase or shaping flesh.

I assumed we would return to Château d'Ocerne after the push, but Antoine took us in the opposite direction. We even avoided Saint-Julien-by-the-Stream and its alehouses, where the day's events were no doubt already being recounted and embellished.

We did not speak much, but not, I think, because Antoine had nothing to say. He seemed consumed by his thoughts and there were moments he seemed on the verge of posing some important question, but then reconsidered.

The beautiful stone paving of Château d'Ocerne's high road gave way to pebbles and then, eventually, to mud. As the sun grew low, Antoine took us off the path completely, deeper into the forested foothills. He crested a stony hillock and stopped, surveying the villages we were leaving behind, with their lazy columns of chimney smoke and fields of fat sheep. In the distance, the château was still visible, watching over the lowlands from its forested perch. Antoine finally began to talk, unbidden.

"In the beginning, it was the farms. Some sheep were found

killed in the fields, and a few pigs in the stalls," he said quietly. "It was nothing unusual to lose some animals in spring, when wolves and foxes are feeding their young. But then there were rumors from the Upper Allier. A woman claimed she had been attacked by a beast—an animal such as she had never seen—in the pasturelands. Without her oxen to protect her, she said, the creature would surely have killed her. A wild tale."

"You did not believe her."

"Of course not. None of us did," said Antoine. "But the following month, there was a week when the fog did not lift—five blind-nights when even the owls did not fly. And when we finally saw the sun again, they began to find people. The d'Ilvé boy and his friends at the crossroads. Travelers near the Bow and Brace. The charcoal burner and his wife on the gully road—not an hour from Château d'Ocerne. We could ignore it no longer. Captain Duhamel and his soldiers emptied the villages of able-bodied men, beating the bracken from Fournois to Langogne with a force of thousands. They saw the Beast many times—and injured it many times, to hear it told. But still the attacks continued. We have lost nearly a hundred good people in little over two years. All killed by this one Beast, most savagely. All brutalized—mutilated."

"Mutilated?"

Antoine's eyes were bright; I suspected he had refilled his wine flask more than once during the day. "Yes. As you saw today, the Beast does not stop at killing. They were savaged. Gutted. He ate their faces. He took their hearts. And some of them had been . . . indecently dealt with, do you understand?"

"I believe so."

Sarmodel was listening as intently as I was. This was a story familiar to us, from many centuries of hunting monsters. I ran quick calculations in my mind.

At least one victim a week, on average, I commented, *and as many as five in a single day, as we have seen this afternoon.*

Sebastian, it's something big! His excitement was palpable, like a tiny trembling sun in my mind. *And it's almost certainly getting stronger.*

"Then came the stories," Antoine continued. "The Beast is the size of a barn with eyes like cartwheels afire. It can be in three places at once. It has been shot, poisoned and stabbed, and still rises to kill again. It speaks and laughs like a man. Did you know the Normans even claim they saw the monster emerging from the wildwood in a pair of britches? Little wonder the king has sent Bauterne to replace them." He laughed. "And now the Bishop of Mende has arrived and we are to believe the Beast is the Devil himself, come as punishment for our transgressions."

Oh, the Devil![1] *Naturally!* snorted Sarmodel.

I sat beside Antoine on my horse, watching the shadows of the clouds chase each other across the hilltops.

"And what do you believe, sir?" I asked him.

"You have seen what we face now, Professor. It humbled us today. It *mocked* us, killing in the stoops and byways while we toasted each other around the firepit. It is not the first time. What do I believe? I believe the Beast has grown bolder; it is no longer satisfied with lambs and piglets. And it has grown smarter as well, I am sure of it. But more than that, there is something *wrong* in Gévaudan. Fear has become a sort of sickness; the villages are filled with

---

1. I want to make this absolutely clear: the Spirit you know as Lucifer, Satan or the Devil hasn't been seen for several thousand years, thanks to the Almighty and the Host. It is safe to assume he has been consumed. While we are on the subject—the idea of Hell is both impractical and improbable. Please tell everyone you know.

suspicion and the animals have become wild. You saw what happened at the banquet last night, and that dog handler was eaten by his own hounds today—these things were unthinkable only a few months ago. I fear it is only getting worse." He didn't look at me but his mouth twitched into a wry smile. "I apologize. You must think me a lunatic."

"I put more stock in 'stories' than you might believe and certainly I do not think you a lunatic. But I must question your wisdom in joining the hunt alone," I said. "Your father has given you no men or hounds, and you have not been invited to join the royal hunting party. If I may be blunt, it appears you are not being groomed for success."

"Most astute, Professor!" Antoine laughed again. I would learn that it was his most common reaction; that easy, open laughter. He sobered quickly. "My father does not trust me, I fear. He expects me to play swashbuckler in the shadow of the château and return in time for dinner. He is giddy under the attention of the king and the Bishop of Mende and gives little thought to the greater questions."

"And what are those?"

We turned our horses down the eastward trail, our shadows leaping along the path ahead of us as the sun fell.

"What is the Beast, really? Why has it come to Gévaudan? *Where* did it come from?" Antoine said, shaking his head. "It seems to me we must answer these questions before we can hope to kill it, but the bishop and the king are not interested in a solution that is not a gun or a dog. So we need to have the courage to find the answers ourselves. *Sapere aude.*"

"'Dare to know,'" I said. "A scholar's maxim, though hardly a Christian one. I approve."

"Wise words for wise men. Christian or otherwise," he replied. "You asked me this morning why I intervened on your behalf at the assignment ceremony. The truth is I don't believe this Beast is a wild animal to be captured by conventional means. There is something more happening in Gévaudan—and I want to ***know***. It is my hope that a scholar's approach may succeed where the hounds and the hunters have failed."

"A scholar's approach? ***That's*** why you defied and embarrassed the Bishop of Mende and your own father?"

"Perhaps I also thought it would be fun."

"*Fun?* Forgive me, but I feel you are either mocking me or giving me half the truth."

He laughed again. "Perhaps I am. But truth begets truth, does it not, Sebastian Grave of Larnaca, slayer of the Gorgon of Crete?" Antoine said, again with that sardonic grin. "If I may say so, you are also a most unusual scholar."

"How so?" I smiled despite myself; the young man's humor was infectious.

"You are a long way from any university, for one. You are also very well armed. A couple of pistols and a sword—a *very* beautiful sword—are interesting accessories for a man of learning, no?"

"And why not? Perhaps I intend to defeat the Beast in a duel." I played along, more than a little intrigued by the dashing young Lord Ocerne.

"It would be the only approach we have not yet tried. Why not, indeed?" he replied. "And if I may say so, you are terribly clumsy."

"Clumsy?"

"I believe you spilled every drop of wine you were given last night," he said.

That surprised me. I do not consume alcohol, for a number of reasons. But I have become adept at pretending to drink in company, for the sake of either politeness or subterfuge. During the banquet, I had indeed poured my wine out under the table whenever nobody was watching—or so I believed. The young lord had clearly been watching me very closely.

I had no response, so I followed Antoine's laughter into the darkening woods.

He is quite unusual, I remarked to Sarmodel. *Not at all what I expected from the baron's son.*

"Now, Professor, one more very important question before we set camp," Antoine called back to me. "Can you cook? I am getting hungry."

Perhaps not so unusual after all.

XVI

The Eastern Alps
1785

"My father spoke those words?" Jacques interrupted. "*My father* questioned the wisdom of Bishop Fontaine?"

It was the dead of night; we both kept very strange hours of late. Three days had passed since Jacques's transformation and my fears about sleeping in the mud had become a depressing reality. Jacques was a lit powder keg and I was keeping him as far away from people as possible.

I was changing the dressing on his shoulder; the wound was healing very slowly, but it was thankfully clean and no longer oozing pus.

"Certainly, sir. It was clear to your father, as it was clear to me, that the Beast was not a rabid boar, or a rogue pack of wolves, or any of the other fantasies concocted by the bishop. Why does that surprise you?"

"It is surprising to me that he was ever such a skeptic. Now, you would think the Bishop of Mende speaks with God's own tongue, the way my father follows his every word."

"Well, I suppose," I said, talking quickly to blunt the prick of betrayal, "I suppose all men learn to find truth where it best suits them." I finished the dressing, tugging the bandage perhaps harder than I needed to.

Jacques nodded. "But you believed the Beast was one of us? One of the Gévaudanais?" Jacques asked.

"I did. Among other things, I am a hunter of monsters. The most dangerous—and the most successful—are not monstrous at all.[1] They dissemble. They watch. They hide their true natures until they are ready to strike." I gave Jacques a pointed look. "Do they not, sir?"

He exhaled through clenched teeth. "Must they all then endure your wit?"

"Only the ones who owe me money," I replied. I was rewarded with a momentary, self-conscious smile from Jacques across the flames.

I took it as something of a duty to jostle these moments of levity from the boy when I could. He had been through something unimaginable, and I have found that a little black humor can help to minimize the scars of the psyche.

"Speaking of money," he said. "I don't suppose you found my father's allowance with . . . with Gerard and Henri?"

My hands slowed briefly in their work. "Do you believe I would keep it from you if I had?"

"No, I suppose not," he said. And then his dark frown returned. "Am I damned, Professor? Is this a punishment for my own wickedness?"

"Ha!" I did not catch the laugh in time. "I apologize, sir, but

1. Livia: QED.

what do you imagine God has to gain from punishing a nineteen-year-old boy—"

"I am a man already married," he grated.

"Very well—what do you imagine God has to gain from punishing a nineteen-year-old *man already married* with a curse that causes him to become a man-eating monster?"

"Again, you must mock me," he answered wearily. "Professor, who are you really? I feel that I cannot believe a word you have told me. Are you really a Cypriot scholar? A witch? A monster?"

I paused in my ministrations. "Have a care, young sir. If you are concerned about damnation, this is a dangerous line of inquiry." I held out a jar of willow tincture I had made for his pain. "Please, drink this."

"Not until you answer me."

"Very well. A Cypriot scholar? Yes. A witch? Perhaps. A monster? On occasion. Now—drink, if you please."

"What kind of monster?"

I guffawed. "*What kind?* The kind that must eat to survive. Much like yourself."

"And yet you are also a killer of monsters?"

"When required."

"But you will not kill me?"

My humor began to fade. "No, sir. Not even if you ask me to."

"Because of my father?"

"Sir—"

"Because of my father? Tell me."

Because I am afraid this is my fault.

"My God, you stubborn, insufferable—yes! Because of your father. Now drink, before I force it on you."

Jacques took the tincture from my hand. "Does he know? Does my father know what you are? Is that why you parted on bad terms?"

I turned and fussed over my medical instruments, so that he would not see my face. "So many questions! You have had quite the change in temperament, young sir. Three days ago, you would sooner have spat in my face than wished me good morning," I said. "And now I cannot get you to stop talking."

"Oh, very well!" He took a sip of the tincture. The concoction was utterly primitive compared to my paregoric (which my companion had already guzzled), and it would have tasted absolutely dreadful. Jacques nearly inverted his face with his expression of distaste. "By the Lord, Professor—this is the worst one yet! Could we not sweeten the draft with honey, or perhaps some wine?"

"Is that how the young lord receives his medicine in Ocerne?" I smiled at him sidelong. "From a favored nurse—called Lorette, perhaps?"

This time I had chosen my jest poorly. Jacques blanched and his mouth tightened unbecomingly. When he spoke again, his voice was very quiet. "Are even my thoughts not my own? How do you know that name?"

"Forgive me, please. I did not mean it as an insult. It was something you said during your fever, that is all," I answered.

"Truly I have not been the master of my own actions," said Jacques. He looked utterly mortified. "Please, speak no more of this. Lorette is a childhood friend and I would not bring her into this abominable mess."

"Of course not, sir. You have been confused and unwell, and I should not make fun—again, I apologize."

I think we may confirm that the young lord has a mistress, I said to Sarmodel.

Indeed—another "childhood friend," he replied. *Did he eat this one? Perhaps we will find out.*

Jacques was placated, though his pallor had been replaced

with a glowing blush. "It does not matter, and I take no offense. Please—are you sure you can rid me of this sickness? I cannot bear the thought of it happening again."

"I am, sir. As I said, I have an acquaintance in Gévaudan who I am confident can help you. Then, if that fails," I said, brandishing my surgeon's knife, "and *only* then, I will kill you, as you have requested."

"Then I suppose I must trust you. Please, go on. You were telling me of the hunt. Your suspicions bore fruit, did they not?"

I secured the fresh bandages with a pin and helped Jacques to dress. "They did. But not in the way I expected."

"Oh? Did the Beast outsmart even you, Professor Grave?"

Jacques smiled sardonically and suddenly I could not look at him anymore. His similarity to Antoine in that moment was more than I could bear.

"Yes, he did," I answered finally. "At every turn."

ADDENDUM:

On the Imprisonment of Jehanne d'Arc

Rouen, France
1431

*Six years since the events of the turnip field, Jehanne is in a terrible pickle. With the help of the voices in her head, Jehanne the peasant has become Jehanne d'Arc, "*la Pucelle,*" breaker of the siege of Orleans. The precocious teen has taken to the Hundred Years' War like a professional, outsmarting the generals, out-churching the Church and predicting the most unlikely victories at a distance of several hundred miles. As the war simmers away and she performs more and more improbable miracles, she attracts attention from all sorts—including my master and the old one, the one you know as Sarmodel.*

But they are a long way away on a job in Halicarnassus, and events are moving quickly. Captured by enemies, surrounded by the Almighty's clergy and on trial for heresy, the Maiden is quickly being carried beyond their reach.

Who to send into the vipers' nest? Who can be trusted to infiltrate the homoerotic circus of the tribunal and get close to the most famous virgin[1] *on the continent?*

Who can be coerced with the threat of torture, long-distance, per the conditions of her Contract, signed under similar duress?

Who indeed.

There were no footsteps. One moment the prison corridor was empty, and the next she was there, a wimpled silhouette peering through the grille in the door.

"My lady?" the nun called softly, her accent strange.

Inside the cell, the prisoner stirred, lifting her head from the table. The chamber was barely two paces across, the floor strewn with hay. Its occupant was filthy, dressed in men's clothes that hung loose on her thin body.

"My lady Jehanne?" the newcomer called again.

"I am here, Sister." The prisoner stood unsteadily. Her voice carried the weary defiance of one who has been mistreated often and long.

"So I see. Please, stay where you are." The nun opened the cell door and stepped inside. The hem of her gray habit was flocked with grass seeds. She carried a basket, covered with sackcloth, which she set on the table. From within she produced food—good food—and a bundle of blankets. Last, she set down a flask of wine and two cups, along with a thick red candle. The candle she erected carefully, using her fingertips to straighten the dark fiber of the wick.

1. Is nobody except me a little embarrassed that she is quite literally named for the fact that she never popped her cork? The tribunal made a case of her enduring cherry for *weeks*, with her standing right there.

The prisoner's eyes widened and she stepped back, raising her hands. "You are not Sister Elise."

"No." The strange nun unfastened her wimple, revealing a long coppery braid. "Please, sit down and eat." Her face was a perfect oval, regal and sensuous. A pair of silver earrings glittered by the soft curve of her jaw. Even disguised in her nun's habit in the gray morning light, the woman was breathtaking.[2]

There was only one chair in the cell, so the stranger seated herself on her upturned basket, motioning for Jehanne to join her. The prisoner stepped back against the stone wall, her arms crossed. "I will not. Did Beauvais send you to kill me?"

The woman laughed. "The bishop? No, my lady, he'll do that himself. Somewhere everyone can watch." She tore apart a loaf of bread with strong hands. It was still warm and steaming inside. She smeared it with soft cheese and placed it on a plate for the young woman, sighing as she inhaled the aroma. "Please eat something. You're going to need your strength. And I wouldn't kill you with food, believe me."

It took only a few moments. The smell of the food was more than Jehanne could stand. She sat at the rough table and *ate.*

"So, you're *la Pucelle.* The *Maiden.* Truly?" mused the red-haired woman. "I suppose the guards have taken care of that by now."

Jehanne narrowed her eyes at the stranger, but then simply shrugged. "They have tried. But their molestations have been

---

2. I am what I am.

unsuccessful. Why do you suppose I wear a soldier's trews?"[3] The prisoner spoke between mouthfuls, wiping her chin. "Now tell me. Who are you?"

"My name is Livia. I'm here to help you."

"I've had many such offers of help, none of them without cost," replied Jehanne, with a shrewd smile. "You've been sent by someone who wants something. If not the Bishop of Beauvais, then who? Gilles de Rais,[4] my devoted lieutenant?" She grimaced in distaste. Then she paused as though listening, her eyes downcast, dark and strange. "No. It's a different man. An old man. He has two faces. One is fair and the other is—what does that mean? Two faces?"

Livia laid one hand gently on the corner of the table; the other fell nonchalantly to her side, finding a hidden pocket in the skirts of the habit. "Tell me, my lady—how do you know that?"

"I listen, and I am told the truth," replied Jehanne simply.

"Told by whom?"

"The Lord has sent his saints to me, the wise Catherine and fearless Margaret, guided by the Messenger himself. You know this. It is known across the land." Her voice grew stronger. "It is known across the sea to the lords of England, who keep me here because they fear the truth: that the Lord Almighty is on our side."

"Tell me about this messenger. What is his name?"

---

3. Effective, but not the smartest choice long-term. In preserving her storied virtue, Jehanne inadvertently ticked a different box under the "Punishable by Death" category: cross-dressing.

4. Remember this name; he's important.

"Are you not a Christian? He is the Messenger, the herald of the Lord, whose name is Michael."

"The Archangel." Livia's beautiful face was impassive. "I see. And he brings you these visions?"

Jehanne chewed for a few moments in silence, returning the strange woman's gaze.

"Is this why you've come? To test me?" She laughed. "I have seen distant battles and augured their victors, time and again. I have lifted the siege of Orleans with nothing but my banner, and raised our country from its knees with triumph after triumph. And still every lord must have his proof. I wonder what miracle will satisfy yours." She sobered quickly. "Well, you have wasted your time, though I thank you for the food. I will be tested by Beauvais's heretics again tomorrow, and for many days to come. You may see for yourself how the charges against me are answered."

"Oh, meatbag," Livia sighed. She leaned forward and made a curious gesture above the red candle. The wick kindled with a steady flame that began to burn deep crimson as it consumed the wax. "Please. You think yourself extraordinary, but you are witless cattle like all the others."

"Devilry!" Jehanne drew back from the light. "Lord protect me!"

Livia spoke a few words not heard in the world for centuries. The red flame intensified with the sound of sizzling fat, blazing halfway to the ceiling. Jehanne was suddenly silent, her eyes black and deep. Her shadow, no longer that of a young woman, grew huge, a menacing darkness on the wall behind her.

The succubus stood slowly, her stance wide and her teeth showing. In the red light, her horns and talons were clear to see, and beneath the habit her tail was flicking. When she spoke again, it was in Latin, the first human language she had known.

"Your name please, my lord."

Jehanne's whole body heaved, and she clutched at the edge of the table. Her throat clenched with spasms and she belched, her tongue extended grotesquely.

"Your *name.*" Livia removed her hand from the hidden pocket, producing a small glass globe of silver fluid.

Jehanne's convulsions stopped suddenly. Her voice grew deep and sonorous. "You presume much, half-breed." She leaned forward and drew in a long breath over the red flame. Behind her, the Maiden's shadow resolved into a bestial silhouette; a monstrous wolf, perhaps. "And you know you burn the blood of creatures offered *in my name* a thousand years ago.[5] You do not need to hear it from my mouth."

"I will have it nonetheless," she replied. She raised a talon to one of her earrings, engraved with fine symbols which answered the red glow with a faint blue luminescence of their own. "You understand."

"A pet! How far have the Daughters of Ishtar[6] fallen, that

---

5. The votive candle was made in Rome at the Temple of Mars Gradivus, just after the Feriae Marti. A sheep, a bull and a pig were sacrificed in the name of Mars, and their blood mixed with sacred beeswax from the Shrine of Mellona. Sebastian must have paid an absolute fortune for it.

6. According to the oldest accounts, succubi were created by Ishtar, the Mesopotamian deity of love, sex, war, death and new life. Frustrated that even the sharpest meatbags were unable to comprehend the beauty in her paradoxes, she made us, her daughters, to teach them. I can neither confirm nor deny this—I was born in Rome and I never got to meet Ishtar before the Almighty gobbled her up in the 600s.

you allow yourselves to be Shackled?" Jehanne showed her teeth in a frightening smile. "Very well, bitch. Call me Avstamet. Call me Barron. Call me Ares and Mars, as did the empires of old. My True name[7] I will keep, lest it melt the brain inside your beautiful skull. Will that suffice?" She inclined her head, regarding Livia with an appraiser's eye. "Do not fear me. I pity you, half-breed. When last I walked in flesh, your kind were our favored children, masters of our temples and bearers of our word. In my House, you would have gorged yourself on mortal stock."

"I know, my lord," replied Livia wistfully. Her eyes were on the candle, now half consumed by the eldritch flame. "And now that I have your name, I am charged to offer you an exchange."

"Already the carcass is on the table!" Jehanne's laughter was rich and too deep. "How are we to carve it, your master and I? You offer freedom for the Maiden, no doubt. What does he want in return?" She leaned back, folding thin arms across her chest. "In which direction would he have me take this holy war?"

"My master has an interest in seeing the war *ended*. He would rather it happened without the Almighty acquiring your essence."

"Ha! An accomplished magician who is also a man of peace?" said the creature that was Jehanne. "I think the world has not changed quite so much."

---

7. Yes, they got this right in the movies. Knowing an entity's True name does indeed give you the upper hand in negotiations. And yes, in case you are wondering, Sebastian knows mine and included it in every line of my Contract, like the tiny tyrant he is.

"He simply fights a different war, my lord. The One God is not a threat to be ignored—or provoked," Livia replied. "My master asks that you consider the consequences of impersonating an Archangel of the Covenant as you make your decision. Your ruse is clever, but Michael is no warmonger. Do you think nobody else has guessed your true nature?"

The Maiden clucked her tongue. "Hurry up, half-breed. What are your terms?"

"I will take this gullible *phlam*[8] away with me today. It will be dangerous but you will convince her to come. My master rides to meet us, and he will free you from her flesh—on the condition that you remove yourself from the field. Indefinitely."

"Oh *certainly.* Would he like her maidenhead in the bargain?" Jehanne's mouth began to seep red. The girl's body, already weak, was starting to deteriorate. "And should I agree, what do I get in return?"

"You survive. How much longer do you think this meat can sustain you?"

Jehanne laughed again. "But she is a most worthy vessel! The land is awash with blood spilled in her name. This war is *glorious,* with its religious fire and ingenious exploding powder! And it serves me well. Every execution, every revenge slaying and holy victory—dedicated to the Maiden. Every battlefield prayer and dying curse, made *in her name*—and through her, to me. She has laid out a feast for me, and I have not yet had my

8. Generally speaking, *phlam* is mortal stock, designated for consumption. It's most often used in reference to virgins, who have always been in high demand, though tastes have changed in the last few centuries. A literal approximation would be "veal."

fill. Soon I will have regained my strength completely—and men will know the glory of the Empire once again."

"'Soon' may still be too late if you are trapped in a burning corpse,[9] my lord," replied the succubus.

"Ha! Jehanne will die a crone before they can agree to burn her. So far, they have produced naught but their own rhetoric, and they are easily ensnared in it."

The girl's hulking, lupine shadow began to stretch along the walls.

Livia took a step back toward the cell door. "You have slept long, my lord. I fear you underestimate the reach of the Almighty and the agents of his Covenant." The crimson flame was a bare inch above the table now, surrounded by a puddle of boiling red wax. The food around it had begun to shrink and blacken. "Do you think Michael sits idle while you paint his name in blood across the continent? Even now he guides the clergy in their scheming. He *will* see your deluded heretic committed to the flame, and ensure that her anima—along with yours—is dedicated to the Almighty."

"I see." Jehanne was silent in thought, her black eyes unblinking. "Tell your master." The Maiden smiled again and her terrible shadow lunged, pinning the succubus to the wall with a dozen dark, questing limbs. "Tell him I must decline his terms. End the war? I am not fooled by your ruse, succubus—

---

9. A Spirit cannot just abandon a mortal vessel when it's not fun anymore. Possession is a lifelong commitment, much worse than marriage, and a Spirit will share the fate of its meatbag host unless lifted out by Arcane means or fire, or transferred to another willing host. Or—worse—it will end up trapped for centuries in the tissue of a corpse. I often wonder how much otherworldly talent is off the market because it's stuck in a pelvis or a finger bone in a museum somewhere.

he will attempt to devour me as soon as I have left the flesh. And he would be welcome to try." Livia sucked a sharp breath through her fangs, helpless as the quicksilver globe was squeezed from her hand and tumbled harmlessly into the straw. "Ah, yes. You are *ripe,* half-breed. How much mortal meat has perished in the heat of that black quim?"[10]

"My lord—"

"Be *silent,* bitch. You sought my answer and you shall have it." Blood welled in Jehanne's dark eyes as the shadow grew to fill the cell. "I do not fear this faceless Almighty, who allows his flock to feed upon him like a flea-ridden dog. He has taken my Empire, but Rome can fall again. I am *most* interested in this master of yours, however. Who is this man I see in your mind, with the nectar of a hundred lifetimes sweetening inside him? And who is the one *behind* him . . . so very *old.*" Jehanne's tears made crimson scribbles down her face. "Tell him to come. If he would bargain with me, tell him to come. He will need no votive candle, no Arcane ordinance. He will show himself and we will deal."

"Your word," Livia hissed, straining against the creature's grip. Its touch was agony, so hot that it felt *cold,* and Livia knew she was likely to die if it continued. The red flame sputtered and Jehanne nodded.

"On my own True name and by the blood of this vessel, I swear it." The creature worked its mouth and spat a spray of bright blood into Livia's face. "Make no more demands of me, bitch."

---

10. One of the questions I am forbidden to answer to anyone except my master, under the clauses of my Contract. Suffice it to say I've enjoyed more hot meals than you have.

The succubus licked the droplets from her lips. “Done and done!” she hissed.

Jehanne nodded. She coughed, and then coughed again. The thing within her was fading.

“Tell him to hurry, half-breed.” The candle was all but spent, sputtering angrily as it consumed its last. The shadows melted away and Livia slid to the floor. “I would hate to see the Maiden perish before we have a chance to meet.”

XVII

Margeride Mountains, France
1766

The Beast went to ground in the days after the push, and Antoine took us ever farther from the main hunt and the château. Lord Bauterne had all but commanded us to patrol the river lands, but my young companion took us instead east toward the mountains.

I was directing him, of course. While I was technically in his service, Antoine was among the worst woodsmen I had ever met, unable to follow a trail and seemingly devoid of instincts. He was, fortunately, very suggestible and easily influenced by flattery.

So it was that we found ourselves alone a week after the push, in the foothills where I suspected the Beast had its bolt-hole. We set camp late; the light was almost gone by the time we secured the horses. I found us a sheltered campsite, between a stony overhang and an ivy-choked stand of alders.

I use the word "we" very loosely. As usual, Antoine was reasonably drunk by the time the sun had set, and I handled the lion's share of the work while he sang to the horses, gathered firewood and urinated on a cluster of puffballs. His attempts to light the fire were as misguided as they were unsuccessful.

"This wood—it's wet," he announced finally, striking his flint for the umpteenth time over a pile of green alder twigs.

"Allow me, sir," I said. He sat back against a tree and watched as I built a cheery campfire. Light snoring alerted me to the fact that I would also be taking first watch.

Antoine slept like the dead, so I took the opportunity to make some preparations. I took a few lumps of coke I had acquired and marked them with a series of alchemical symbols in pyric chalk before arranging them in the fire.[1] Next, I took out my jeweler's tool kit, positioning my little ceramic crucible atop the coke "forge." Inside it I placed a handful of beautifully engraved silverware.

While the metal was melting, I busied myself cleaning out my shot mold and sharpening my tools. The mold was necessarily small, yielding only a half dozen pellets per cast. Sarmodel brightened my vision and offered a few instructions, directing my positioning of Arcane engravings inside the mold. It was fine, repetitive work which he found tedious, but I took an artisan's pleasure in the details.

"Did you steal those?"

I started, jabbing my thumb painfully with the point of my burin. So consumed was I in my work that I hadn't noticed that the young lord had awoken. I glanced at the crucible, where a couple of filigreed spoon handles were slowly sinking into the melt.

"I did, sir," I answered lightly; there was no point in denying

---

1. A handy trick I learned from an Arcane artificer, this elemental succession causes carbon to "accumulate" heat energy, allowing the fuel to burn at temperatures normally only found inside a forge.

it. I sucked the blood from my thumb and added a careful scoop of mercury salts to the mix. "Are you hungry?"

Antoine took a small ham and a loaf of bread into his lap, carving thick wedges off each and chewing as he watched me work. He said nothing, but I could feel his curious gaze following my movements.

"I am casting my shot, sir, if that is what you are wondering," I ventured, without looking up.

"Yes, I deduced as much." He drained the lees of his wine flask. "Though I must ask why you require such precious ammunition."[2]

"An old technique I learned hunting lions with the Shah of Persia. Silver ammunition holds its form better and flies truer than lead," I lied. "The great hunters of Araby use nothing else."

"I see," he said.

I aligned the hinge and closed the dies. There was barely a line to mark the join. "You may wish to look away, sir," I said. Then I gripped the neck of the crucible with sturdy tongs and carefully poured a stream of liquid silver into the funnel. There was no concealing the jet of cerulean flames that erupted from the hole, like the tail of a meteorite, as the cooling silver took on the Arcane compulsion of my sigils.

"By the Christ!" Antoine started and almost fell backward where he sat. "What was that?"

---

2. Please forsake all of your fast-food pop-fantasy ideas about silver bullets and werewolves. Silver is useful because it's a lightweight and (reasonably) affordable metal with the stability to hold and withstand Arcane compulsion—a lead musket ball marked with Violations would disintegrate into oxides almost immediately. Silver can instead carry the Arcane charge for an extended period, without succumbing to it. Platinum is even better than silver; titanium is better still; and today's tungsten carbide is the absolute pinnacle—it also makes an exceptional sushi knife.

"A secret of the smith's craft," I improvised with an enigmatic smile. I quenched the mold in a small tub of water. Antoine whooped as the steam mushroomed out. "A reminder that the forge is a wonder as much as a tool."

I opened the mold and gently tapped the spheres free of the core, like silver berries shaken from the branch. Each was nearly three-quarters of an inch in diameter; even one would humble this Beast, whatever it turned out to be.

"A wonder indeed! May I try?" Far from fearing the crucible and its volatile contents, Antoine was putting on his leather riding gloves, ready to try his hand.

Absolutely not, said Sarmodel.

But Antoine's eyes were shining with enthusiasm and he was already reaching for the tongs. After a moment's consideration, I passed them to him. "Of course. Let me show you first. . . ."

There was a disdainful rippling in my mind, which I have come to interpret as my Guest rolling his eyes.

After the second batch, Antoine no longer needed my help. He took inordinate glee in provoking the explosive reaction and only laughed when he managed to singe his hair.

I took the time to buff and examine each pellet, trimming away excess from the mold. It was too dark for Antoine to see exactly what I was doing, so I also took the opportunity to ensure the Arcane sigils were clear and properly joined. We developed an easy rhythm and I was for a precious hour or so utterly absorbed in the pleasure of just making something together with him—good work in excellent company.

Our work was interrupted by the sound of swiftly approaching horses and the excited baying of dogs.

"Who is there?" I called, standing up. I had not anticipated company this far from the main hunt.

The dogs arrived first, surrounding our secluded campsite in a snapping, barking circle. Leading them was an enormous brindled mastiff of unwelcome and familiar aspect: Soeur, the Lieutenant of the Hunt's most favored. She stood facing me at the edge of the firelight, growling in menace.

"Monsieur Bauterne!" called Antoine with easy, accustomed authority. "Call off your hounds, sir!"

Out in the darkness beyond the dogs, the hoofbeats slowed and grew much closer.

"Young Lord Ocerne." Bauterne came into the light, mounted on his black gelding. He looked very small indeed sitting astride the powerful animal. "Have no fear, sir; they will do nothing without my word." Behind him followed the Ennevals, also mounted, their faces creased in identical scowls of disapproval beneath their thick grenadier mustaches.

"The baron's pup?" snarled Jean-Francois. It seemed the younger Enneval had not improved his rapport with the Lieutenant of the Hunt since their very public disagreement at the banquet. "*I told you* it was a false trail. Your 'instinct' has led us to a cookfire, Lieutenant."

Bauterne said nothing. He did not even look at the glowering huntsman; the Norman might not have spoken at all. I wondered again who might win in a fight between the two—the huge, embittered Enneval or the cunning, prideful Bauterne? It was difficult to say who I would rather see humbled in such an exchange; rarely has my dislike for two men been so evenly mixed.

Antoine filled the silence. "Messieurs Enneval—senior and junior both. A pleasure to see you again, good sirs." His tone was light and genial. "There is room by the fire. Would you care to join us?"

Be ready, I sent to Sarmodel. If Bauterne was trying to intimidate us, he was succeeding. While I doubted he would openly attack us,

I did not trust his control over his hounds, many of which seemed almost crazed in their excitement. I noted with unease that several were also shivering strangely, like the poor pointer at the banquet.

Of course. My Guest's presence alighted delicately on my centers of consciousness, like the fingertips of a harpist poised to play.

"Regretfully, we must decline, sir," said Bauterne. "We are returning to our lodgings at the Bow and Brace and we have ground to cover tonight. As do you, if you are to attend Mass tomorrow and take part in the push." Bauterne still had not recalled his dogs, and his manner was icy. "I believe you are supposed to be in Langogne with the other hunters, are you not?"

"We will unfortunately not be able to join the push this week, sir. The professor and I are following a promising trail and I do not wish it to go cold," replied Antoine, raising his voice over the chorus of excited hounds. "Your *dogs,* sir. Please—call them off!"

"A trail—here?" Bauterne scoffed. "Within reach of the hunting lodge, where we have slept every night this week, with no sign of the Beast? I believe the *professor* may have misled you, young sir." He motioned in my direction but barely glanced at me.

"I do not believe we have met, sir," I interjected with a smile. "I am Professor Sebastian—"

"I do not require an introduction," he interrupted. Just like the bailiff at the assignment ceremony, he issued a grave insult by referring to me with the informal "*tu.*" His inflection rose toward mockery. "The Cypriot. I remember you from the château. The publican at the Bow and Brace has mentioned you also."

"Oh?"

The Bow and Brace was a beautifully appointed—and very expensive—hunting lodge along the mountainous eastern road. I had stayed there on my first night in Gévaudan, enjoying my last taste of civilization before what I expected to be weeks of camping in the wilds. The lieutenant and the Normans had made it their base of operations for the hunt. It was also where I had "acquired" the silverware that was now bubbling away in my jeweler's crucible.

"Yes. I must wonder now, as I did then, why an Ottoman man of letters would involve himself in the hunt for the Beast, here in Gévaudan." He looked at me steadily. It was not really a question, but the Lieutenant of the Hunt waited for my response.

"I simply seek, with humility, to bring the methods of science and physics to bear upon a thorny problem," I answered smoothly. I could feel Sarmodel counting dogs in the periphery of my vision. "A problem that has resisted resolution by other means."

"Then my misgivings are not without basis. I have met men like you before," he replied. Behind my smiling lips, my teeth were clenched painfully. Though entirely typical of men of his station, Bauterne's arrogance was particularly galling to me; I decided that I disliked him most of all. "Your 'science' will get you and those around you killed. I take it you are responsible for the strange lights we followed here?"

Clumsy, my love, admonished Sarmodel gently. He was right; I had allowed the tranquil spring woodlands and my charming young companion to dull my sense of caution.

"I confess that I am, sir," I replied. "I have been casting my shot and I fear that my methods are lively."

Bauterne was silent for a moment. Then he leaned forward in the saddle. "Indeed? Show me. I would see these 'lively' methods for myself."

"It takes some time, sir," I answered. "I do not wish to delay you on your way."

"Then perhaps I might see what you are making with such a conspicuous display."

I opened my mouth to offer another obfuscation, but Antoine was faster.

"Of course, sir," said the young Lord Ocerne. He rummaged in the dark near my tools and retrieved a handful of musket balls, which he poured into the lieutenant's gloved palm. "We have plenty more, if you are in need," offered Antoine.

There was only the dull sheen of lead in the huntsman's hand; Antoine had given him the shot from his own pouch.

Bauterne examined the small pellets in the firelight, his face blank. "It is unremarkable."

"For the love of God, man!" interrupted the younger Enneval. His anger was directed not at me, but at Bauterne. "The Beast is not here! Come!" He wheeled his horse around, whistling for his hounds.

Bauterne barked a short command. Suddenly Soeur was there at his side. She made no threat beyond a low growl, but the Norman's hounds shrank from her, scrabbling back to join their packmates.

Enneval the Younger pulled up short, swearing.

"Father!" he snapped. "Come! Will you sit there like a clubbed lamb?"

"Get back here, you fool," his father answered. His voice was surprisingly soft. "Before you embarrass us any further."

But Bauterne appeared to have changed his mind. He waved a black-gloved hand. "No, no, we should indeed be on our way. I apologize for the intrusion, young sir."

"It was no intrusion, Lieutenant. But I will thank you at our next meeting to remember that Professor Grave is here at my invitation and speak to him with the respect he is owed."

Bauterne looked down at Antoine for a long moment before returning the musket balls to him, dropping them one by one into his hand. "You are not baron, sir. Not yet. Do not forget upon whose invitation *I* am here." But when he spoke to me, he retained the polite formal register. “Have a care with your ‘methods,’ Professor Grave. Next time you may attract the attention of less amicable visitors.” He turned his horse around and then stopped, looking back over his shoulder. “And you would do better to place your faith in the Lord God Almighty than in the false edifice of your science—I know which will claim the Beast in the end.”

I did not trust myself to respond, so I simply returned his nod. Bauterne gave a warbling, birdlike whistle and the hounds mercifully melted away into the dark woods. The last to disappear was the formidable Soeur, her gilded collar glinting as she left the circle of firelight. The Normans did not even acknowledge us as they followed Bauterne into the night.

I am not confident that the hunters were entirely out of earshot when Antoine began to laugh.

“Gévaudan’s greatest hope!” he said, shaking his blond head. “Have you ever seen a bigger bunch of co—”

XVIII

The French Alps
1785

"Professor, I fear we need to move faster," said Jacques, interrupting me mid-story.

I was digging the wagon out of a shallow snowdrift on the road while my horse waited patiently. We were close—so close—to leaving the icy forests of the Alps behind, but winter was chasing us hard and this was the third time we had been forced to stop and deal with the snow.

Five days since his monstrous transformation, Jacques was still too weak to be of much help, though his injuries were healing well under my care. His swollen eye had opened again and he could now walk around without clutching his tender manhood. He was not yet strong enough to ride, which was a happy coincidence now that we had only one horse. He was more than content to remain in the wagon most of the time, reclining in his nest of blankets and sipping on willow-bark elixir.

"I am digging as fast as I can, sir."

"I know. I know." His voice cracked. "But we need to keep moving. I can hear him again, do you understand?"

"Him?" I put down my spade slowly. "This 'voice' you spoke of?"

"Yes."

"Since when?"

"These past few days. I didn't want to believe it would return so soon." His mouth was a red crack, the only color in his face. "I am sorry; he speaks only of hunger and sometimes it is all I can hear. I want . . . he wants you very badly and I don't have the strength to withstand him should he return in earnest. If there is help to be found in Gévaudan, we must get there very soon."

Well, sadly it seems the time has come to nip the young man's wick, said Sarmodel. *It's unfortunate, but his anima will not go to waste. The hunting knife will be fastest—it's in the left saddlebag.*

I'm not going to slit his throat in the mountains like a bandit. There is still time, surely.

Sebastian, you know we won't survive if he transforms again! Why take the risk?

Because I suspect whatever has happened to Jacques is my fault. I must try to fix it, for Antoine's sake at least.

Shit on that, Sebastian, and shit on you! You are risking our lives in the hope of earning another tumble in the sheets with some French meatbag who has likely forgotten all about you—and who will likely be dead in ten years.

Come, Sarmodel. He is forty, not eighty.

You know what I mean! And may I remind you what happens if ***you*** *die out here? Even if by some chance the young lord does not kill and devour us, we are in a terrible state—every minute brings us closer to* *death by exposure or starvation*, he snapped. *And where does that leave me? Trapped in your frozen corpse, that's where!*[1]

You are being very dramatic.

"Professor? Have you nothing to say?"

"Apologies, sir—I am thinking." We were still days from Gévaudan. Even if I got us moving again and pushed my horse to her limits, it was time Jacques very likely did not have.

"I believe I have a solution, but it's going to be very unpleasant."

"More unpleasant than your vile tinctures?"

"Very likely yes, but still better than shooting you like a dog on the side of the road." I retrieved my musket from the wagon. "It looks like we are making camp here for the night. Do your best to set a fire and try to stay warm. Now, pass me my shot, please. You say you are hungry; I hope you mean it."

---

1. In case you are wondering—yes, my body is indeed susceptible to starvation, exposure and injury like anyone else's. While Sarmodel's presence prolongs my life and makes me somewhat more resilient than the average person, I can (theoretically) still be killed, my heart being the most obvious point of weakness.

ADDENDUM:

On the Fate of the Maid of Orleans

Rouen, France
1431

Whatever has become of Jehanne?

She's smart and courageous, if a little dowdy and in need of delousing. And she's always been a chatty little thing—surely she can talk her way out of her latest predicament.

The "Archangel" on her shoulder has helped her outfox the Almighty's company men for weeks now. The tribunal is a shocking mess, with priests questioning their vows and even the executioner unwilling to commit.

Is it possible that, with her pure heart and natural pluck, Jehanne has exposed the steaming pile at the heart of the Church and forced them to release her? Do we dare hope that the Bishop of Beauvais has been chased out of Rouen? Does Holy Jehanne the Maiden now lead the charge to push back against the invaders who cooked up this travesty of an inquisition?

I'm just teasing—of course not.

They stitched her up and burned her, cherry and all.

The crowds were leaving, trickling away across the flagstones into streets and alleyways. Rouen's taphouses would soon be full to bursting, abuzz with the telling and retelling of the spectacle in the Place du Vieux Marché.

The wooden tribunal seat was empty beneath its red ecclesiastical heraldry; in the morning, it would be dismantled. Only a few clergy remained in the fading light. Many were kneeling in prayer across the square, their eyes red-rimmed from smoke and weeping, wondering what they had done.

The pyre was all but spent. Three times, the Bishop of Beauvais had ordered it built and set ablaze. Three times, Jehanne d'Arc had burned, until there was nothing left but ash. And still the bishop seemed unsatisfied. He had retired early in disgust and posted guards on the smoking remains, lest the devoted come picking for relics of the Maid of Orleans. The ashes would be cast into the River Seine, and with them the last traces of France's famous heretic would be flushed from the town.

A solitary man walked slowly against the flow of the throng. Swarthy and dark-haired, he surveyed the square with intelligent eyes, running a careful gaze over the pyre and the men guarding it. Beneath his dusty cape and hat, he was unusually dressed in a long, embroidered tunic and loose trousers, with only rough sandals on his feet. He bowed his head as he stepped into the open.

A nun knelt by the edge of the public viewing area, weeping gently into her hands. She was pale and haggard, like so many of the Church retinue, and she glanced continually at the pyre, as though waiting for some miracle from the ashes. The newcomer approached her and removed his hat. He did not cross himself like the other faithful.

"Might I pray with you, Sister?"

The nun nodded dejectedly and the man knelt beside her.

"What are you *wearing*?" she hissed between sobs. "I thought we were trying not to attract attention."

"I didn't have time to change," he replied through his teeth.

"Well they just burned a woman—three times—for wearing the wrong thing." Livia looked at him sidelong. Sebastian was gray and unappetizing, as exhausted as she was. Above him, the many eyes of the old one burned only faintly in their rippling constellation of ether. The Spirit's gaze seemed to come from a great distance, as though he were looking down on them from a height; even indoors his presence loomed vastly overhead. "You're late, meatbag, And you *stink*. Where have you been?"

"Halicarnassus. I came as fast as I could." They bowed their heads as a solemn group of monks shuffled past. "You look terrible."

Livia grimaced. She knew it was true. "I am hungry, nothing more."

"Livia. Show me."

She made an impatient sound and twitched back the sleeve of her habit. A band of withered skin marred her wrist, covered with oozing sores. "Lord Avstamet's touch was unkind."

"So, it is truly him?"

Livia nodded and hooked a finger inside her wimple, revealing more blighted flesh around her throat. "Call him Barron. Call him Ares. Call him Mars."

I knew it! exulted the old one. *I would recognize his handiwork from the far side of the Rift. Tell me, half-breed—where has the Warfather been hiding these last centuries? As far as the world knows, he perished with the other Olympians.*

"He did not say, my lord," she said, "but he was sleeping for a long time. I would guess it was one of his relics, surviving somewhere."

"I am inclined to agree. I'm sorry, Livia. I did fear that unmasking him might make him . . . disagreeable."

She lowered her hand and looked at him in distaste. "Your pity is unbecoming, as always, meatbag. I did as you bade me." The marks on her skin pained her, but worse—so much worse—was the burning cold Avstamet had left within her. Like an icicle slowly growing in her chest, the ancient Spirit's black touch abided. She returned to her display of devout weeping, a fast disguise for the real tears rising in her eyes. "He agreed to treat with you, not that it matters now. And you've missed the Maiden, body and soul. The Almighty snapped up her anima before her undergarments were properly alight."

The master and the old one swore together. "I suppose that was to be expected."

Half-breed, what of the Spirit?

"That's a more interesting story," she said with a dark smile. "I think he may have regretted his pride as his earthly vessel burned up around him. He was running out of meat to hide in and then, suddenly, he was just . . . gone."

"What? How?"

"Nobody knows!" Livia laughed wickedly. "The bishop keeps setting the poor Maiden on fire in the hope that she'll give up her demon. But there's nothing left of her now, and there's still no sign of our elusive Avstamet."

"Livia. *Where did he go?*"

"Calm yourself—both of you," said the succubus. "He's right here, sleeping."

She discreetly pointed to one of the guards standing by the

embers. "That one. He took something from the pile when they were raking her up the first time. A bone, I think."

Sebastian narrowed his eyes. "I see . . . a devotee to the Maiden's cause? Or a vulture looking to sell some holy remains? And right under the nose of the bishop and his tribunal." He rubbed his chin thoughtfully. "What sort of man risks his life for a dead woman's bones?"

And does he know he has a demon in his pocket? the old one ventured.

"We will need to find out." The master looked at Livia seriously. "Has Michael shown himself?"

"No, but he's here, playing the bishop like a lute. He walks my dreams." She shuddered. "Be grateful that you do not sleep, meatbag." Whenever she closed her eyes, Livia saw the general and his Host encircling Rouen like storm clouds, driving the mortal cattle with their flaming blades and throbbing song.

"It seems the Archangel was angry enough to make an example of the Maiden. He will be doubly displeased that her demon has eluded him," said Sebastian. "I'll handle it from here, Livia. We'll need to be careful."

"Careful?" The corners of her wimple began to smoke as the succubus swore in her native tongue. "I have *been* careful! 'Careful' got us a pile of ash instead of a virgin! Give me a minute alone with that guard and he'll give me every bone in his body—but we need to move *quickly.* Do you think we are the only ones watching?"

"You may be right." The master's eyes were distant for a moment and he seemed to come to some internal agreement, no doubt with the old one. "Very well, Livia, we'll do it your way. Tonight, you are going to pay a visit to the guardhouse.

And then—once you've collected what I need—you may satisfy yourself however you please until dawn."

Livia closed her eyes and laughed gently. She ran her hands down the front of her habit. "Oh, meatbag. *Yes.* You can trust me."

Sebastian looked at her for a long moment. "Trust you like I trusted you in Rome? Do I need to remind you of what happened when you *broke* that trust?"

"No, meatbag. I am reminded every day. A thousand-odd years of servitude tends to stick in the mind."

"For both of us," he muttered as they stood together. "I'm going to find a room nearby and see if anyone else comes poking through the Maiden's remains. If you see Michael—or any of the Host—come back to me immediately."

XIX

Margeride Mountains
1766

The Beast killed with shocking frequency.

As the spring ripened into summer, Antoine and I chased it from corpse to dismembered corpse across Gévaudan. It covered impossible distances, often striking several villages in a day. It was both everywhere at once and nowhere. Most concerning of all, its tracks—when we could find them at all—seemed to be getting bigger and deeper.

Sarmodel's disapproval grew like the weight of a (very bad-tempered) stone in my mind with each new body and each cold trail. He finally voiced his displeasure one afternoon as we pushed for the third time into the trackless woods north of Château d'Apcher, high up in the mountains.

Sebastian, what are we doing up here again? How many times must we cover the same territory?

I am trying to narrow down the Beast's home range—

Well do it faster! You have been here for weeks, with nothing to show for it but saddle sores.

I know! I know.

And have you considered in your ramblings that I might be hungry? Does it ever cross your mind that—

"Professor, I think I know this place!" said Antoine suddenly, as we forded the shallow stream in search of somewhere to camp. "Yes! I used to come here as a boy. Come, follow me."

It took us some time (Antoine's memory was not quite as accurate as he claimed) but we eventually found the place he sought; a rocky ledge overlooking a fast-flowing branch of the stream. Antoine's eyes brightened as he spied several dark shapes gliding beneath the surface.

I set about securing and caring for the horses. The day had been very demanding on the poor animals, and I took my time settling them in for the night. I took special care to check their hooves. The mountains were notorious for what the hunters called "trail teeth"—small, sharp flakes of slate that were easily wedged inside the hoof and had crippled many a horse in Gévaudan.

Antoine was filling our water flasks in the stream, singing as usual.

"I am sorry to say that dinner will be very spare tonight, sir," I called over my shoulder, rummaging through our bags. "We did no real hunting today, and it has been some time since we restocked our victuals."

"Have no fear, Professor," he called back to me. "Tonight, I will provide for us."

I turned to find him standing on the bank in nothing but his drawers and undershirt.

"Are you planning to bathe, sir?" I asked. "Brace yourself. The stream is pure snowmelt."

He wriggled out of his shirt and then his drawers, leaving me quite distracted and unable to speak.

Oh Sebastian. Oh, yes. Sarmodel kindled obscenely. His lust overlaid mine with unspeakable passions; Antoine was suddenly a morsel I wanted between my teeth as much as between my legs.

"I told you, did I not, that I used to come here as a boy?" Antoine said. He took a long drink from his wine flask and set his shoulders, like a man going into battle. "There was a game we used to play, the village boys and I, which may serve us well now." He knotted the legs of his drawers and stepped into the icy stream. "Though there is some unpleasantness to begin . . ." He waded out until he was knee-deep, gasping and wincing. With a grin, he lowered his knotted underwear into the current between his knees, letting it balloon out behind him like a fishing net. ". . . the rewards will be more than worth it."

"I see that you are outstandingly drunk tonight, sir."

Antoine simply winked and began to sing to the water. It was a tune I had not heard from him before, in which a baker hawked his wares to local women, with various double entendres around his "hot loaf, rising firm." "Have you ever seen a fish serenaded?" he asked me after the first verse.

I could not help but laugh. "No, sir, I have not. I do not believe, in fact, that I have ever met a man willing to invite a fish into his smallclothes, with song or otherwise."

"Silence, unbeliever! I have lured more than fish into these drawers, and they have never failed me."

He continued his ribald song with another verse about his "bulging bag, full of goodness." The fat trout in the stream ignored him completely, busy with their own crepuscular foraging. I returned to the fireside, prepared for a very lean evening.

It cannot have been more than a few minutes later that Antoine gave a whoop of excitement. I turned to see him hoisting his drawers from the water, with a long, dark fish thrashing inside one of the legs.

"I told you!" he exclaimed. "I told you it would work!"

But his prey was not so easily captured. His elation turned quickly to dismay as the fish began to struggle in earnest. He grasped at the linen, trying to trap the slippery creature, but somehow ended up chasing it hand-over-hand up to the opening. It leaped into the air, silver flanks flashing in the dying light.

"Whoreson!"

Antoine managed a last valiant attempt to catch his prey, succeeding for a few seconds in grasping the fish with his hands. Then, with a final flick of its powerful tail, the trout slapped Antoine once on each cheek—*one-two!*—like a woman affronted, and slipped free. With a startled cry, Antoine staggered back and toppled into the frigid stream.

He was laughing even as he resurfaced, naked and empty-handed.

I would struggle to push the image from my mind, both in the coming days and in the years that followed. I remember Antoine climbing drunkenly to his feet in the stream, his wet, naked skin shining like the fish that had just bested him. I remember the faint blue veins visible just below his collarbone, and the thickness of his body hair as it descended toward his manhood. I remember his blond hair stuck to his face and his maple-colored beard shedding drops of water like rain. I remember all of it, still.

"My lord? Are you hurt, sir?" I asked, somewhere between helpless laughter and helpless arousal.

"I am not," he said, his teeth chattering. "But you have witnessed the loss of my dignity and my drawers to a trout—I think you may safely dispense with your 'my lord's and 'sir's." He gave me another smile. "Find me a dry blanket and promise never to mention this again, and you may call me Antoine, as my friends do."

Do not misunderstand.

For all of his surprises, Antoine was in many ways entirely consistent with a young French nobleman of the time. He was a keen reader, a self-proclaimed polyglot and a critical thinker.[1] He could play the harpsichord. He had learned the fine arts of the hunt: the gun, the knife, the kill and how to care for his horse and gear.

The more practical arts—most notably setting a fire—had clearly been left to others. Each night he knelt, tongue-in-teeth, smacking his flints over whatever tottering pile of twigs he had constructed. And each night, I offered cheerful advice (which was just as cheerfully ignored) until I could stand it no longer and did it myself. He watched me closely with suspicious, narrowed eyes, sipping on his wine flask, hoping to re-create my technique the next time. And the following night, invariably, the ritual would play out again.

I soon learned not to underestimate him, however. Though he couldn't track a herd of oxen through a snowdrift, he was a far better marksman than me, and was responsible for a large proportion of the game we killed. This was doubly impressive given that he was usually drunk by lunchtime.

I also probed gently into his unmarried status—a nobleman who was still a bachelor at nineteen was certainly enough to raise eyebrows.

"I am betrothed to the Lady Ninette Voltours d'Apcher," he replied evenly. He said the name very precisely, as though it were something he had committed to memory. "We are to be married in the spring, when she comes of age."

"Congratulations—a fortuitous alliance for both your families, Antoine."

1. All of which made him, much like me, an insufferable know-it-all.

Antoine made a wry face. "'Fortuitous' is perhaps not the word. Lady Ninette is the fourth of the Baron d'Apcher's daughters to whom I have been betrothed. The first died of consumption before we had a chance to meet. The second—her twin sister—did not survive a fall during a riding lesson. And Annalise, the third, succumbed two years ago to a fever caused by the scratch of a cat, to hear it told."

"Perhaps condolences instead, then? My God, Antoine—*three* dead brides? That's some atrocious bad fortune. Let us hope at least that you may welcome your latest betrothed to a land free of the Beast come springtime."

"Indeed! May she survive so long," he said dryly, raising his flask.

Oh, I like him, said Sarmodel. *And what is this cat sickness? Can we get some?*[2]

It sounds like superstition to me. And no, we can't.

Antoine was looking at me sidelong. He indicated the gold fede ring (a useful sham) on my left hand. "And what of your wife? You speak little of her."

"My beloved Livia awaits me back in Padania," I replied easily. "Though we have not been blessed with children,[3] she busies herself with the affairs of the household."

"There is always hope," he said. "How long have you been married?"

"A long time," I answered. "A very, very long time."

---

2. Infectious diseases are popular, if unpredictable, subjects of demonic experimentation. Leprosy, bubonic plague and Spanish flu have all earned their creators (Oribet, Veles and Caligern, respectively) endless torrents of anima and bragging rights to match.

3. Can you imagine? If memory serves, Livia was in fact in Africa somewhere at the time, sourcing diamonds for me.

ADDENDUM:

On the Fate of Jehanne's Remains

Rouen, France
1431

What a night. Try to imagine it if you can.

Jehanne the Maiden's live execution has made the local meatbags extremely hot and bothered.[1] *The smell of burning human flesh has turned on some strangely colored lights deep inside their heads. They are all at once excited, disgusted, intrigued, awed, ashamed and terribly hungry, and Rouen is absolutely awash in their juices.*

In short, they are ready to mate.

I am also hungry. See me there among the crowds, just another nun chafing off her nipples in a woolen dress. I'm following the bone thief—a single guardsman among the many—toward the barracks. He is almost panting in excitement and he holds one hand over the front of his doublet. Within is a pouch containing a fragment of the Maid of Orleans, and within **that** *is a vast, wounded, sleeping presence that smolders and murmurs.*

1. Not nearly as hot or as bothered as the Maiden herself, though.

But the thing I want you to see most of all is something I missed altogether.

There's another man watching, too. He's not looking at the bone thief; his golden eyes are following me, and not for the usual reasons.

He should be easy to see in the crowd. His hair and beard are completely white, and he's making no particular effort to hide.

But I'm weak and injured, and it's been a very long time between meals.

And with all the pheromones in the air, I'll admit I am a little distracted.

She was at first no more than a flicker by the door. Like the last traces of a dream, impressions of her hovered in the predawn darkness. She was but the suggestion of a long-fingered hand on the frame, and the contrary curves of candlelight along her back and hips.

And then she stepped into the room, shedding the shadows like a gown. Naked but for the jewels in her ears, Livia stretched and shook back her auburn hair.

Her evening's feeding had restored her. She was full and flushed with health, her skin unblemished. Her blood hummed through her limbs like liquid crystal, and she felt as though she might strike sparks from her fingertips. It had taken time and perseverance, but the terrible chill inside her was also gone, melted away in the heat of her repast.

She stepped over the corpse on the floor—no doubt the room's original occupant—and turned her attention to the man on the bed.

Though his eyes were closed, the master was not sleeping—not really—and he was still fully dressed. She approached with a sinuous strut. Ahead of her she pushed a wake of heady scent, filling the bedroom with the aromas of hay, night jasmine, spun flax and sex.

Sebastian was not immune. In his trance, he murmured and stirred.

"Ssh, my darling," she whispered. "I have returned." She crawled onto the bed, her body flowing over his. Gooseflesh rose on her arms and she drew in a long breath. His anima was *rich* with the centuries of his life, and being this close to him was very near to ecstasy. She guided his hands across her too-warm skin and he sighed. "Yes, love, take your pleasure. I want you to."

He was swelling hard against her thigh, with only the linen of his trousers between them. Her hands worked at his clothes as he raised his mouth dreamily to her breast. The scent in the room grew overpowering as she teased him, lowering her face close to his.

"Kiss me, Sebastian. Please," she murmured in his ear.

Their lips met and the man's eyes slowly opened. "Hmm . . . ?"

"Hush—"

"Livia!"

He thrust her away with a strength that was not his, bellowing in dark speech.

The succubus was lifted bodily and thrown back, striking the wall.

She screamed and clutched at her throat as the Shackles in her ears blazed with blue fire, illuminating an immaterial collar suspended around her neck. Composed of the sigils of her punishing Contract, it had no true substance and barely flickered as she clawed at it. The agony was blinding, searing beyond her flesh to the anima within.

Sebastian rose from the bed, his clothes in disarray, and stood over her. Livia writhed as her glamers burned away, exposing her horns, talons and tail. He muttered another impossible word, and the fire was extinguished.

The succubus knelt panting on the wooden floor.

"One day, meatbag," she said, with a fanged smile, "one day you won't be able to help yourself."[2]

"*One day* I'm going to eat your heart," he replied. He muttered below hearing and Livia's earrings pulsed darkly, sending a weighty throb through the Contract around her neck. "That's another twenty years!"

"Come, Dominus, I was only—"

"Fifty!" The earrings pulsed again, growing noticeably heavier.

"You—*Fifty years?!* Are you serious?"[3]

"Question me again and we will make it a round century! Livia, tell me—*please*—that this ill-conceived attempt is not an indication of failure. Do you have what I sent you to retrieve? Speak!"

Livia lowered her face. "I was tardy."

---

2. If Sebastian were ever to (finally) succumb to my charms, he would effectively be giving me permission to kill him, which voids a number of fundamental clauses in my Contract. While I doubt my usual methods would actually dispatch him (he's quite the banquet), I'd be free for the first time in hundreds of years.

3. Excessive! Of course I expect to pay the piper when I breach my terms, but this was unnecessary—I was at this point already Contracted well into the 1980s. When Sebastian drafted my Contract back in Rome (about which I will not say more here), it was with specifically this kind of brazen exploitation in mind.

"Tardy?" The air around the master was suddenly charged with danger, like a tree before the lightning strikes.

"I do not have it, meatbag," she said bitterly, closing her eyes. "Scathe me as you will, and be done."

The master was robbed of his reply by a snarl of fury from the old one. His myriad eyes, hanging in the ether above the master, were incandescent with fury. The air around them became a black, infinite spiral, bristling with fangs.

Useless half-breed! *Scathe you? In my time you would have been peeled like an orange and fed to the flame! If the Olympian has escaped me, I will—*

"Sarmodel—*Sarmodel,* enough!" The master collected himself with an effort. "I *knew* I should never have listened to you, Livia!"

With some effort, she began to cry. "I . . . have no excuse. I followed the thief to the barracks as you commanded. But . . . it took some time to find him again."

Sebastian's eyes narrowed. "How many?"

"What do you—"

"Livia. How many soldiers perished on your loins tonight?"

Livia hung her head. "Four."

"Four?"

She swore miserably. "Six, damn you!"[4]

"You dallied with *six men* before you thought to carry out your charge? No wonder, Livia," he snarled, jabbing a finger at her, *"no wonder* you were 'tardy'! And no wonder you are looking so beautifully refreshed."

"Truly?" She dared the faintest smile through her weeping. It was a thin compliment, but at least he had noticed. She

4. Nine.

allowed her fingertips to alight tantalizingly atop her trembling bosom.

"Stop that," he snapped. "Now, tell me what happened."

"Oh, but you are *dull*!" she sobbed, letting her hand fall. "Very well! After . . . after the other men, I found the thief. He was easy meat." The memory was near and sweet. She could still feel the guardsman's warmth flooding into her, a silver torrent of anima that wreathed her nerves in pleasure as it carried his life away. He was there yet, with all the others, his anima utterly devoted to her, beating in her flesh like a second pulse. "He liked my teats, so I let him suckle awhile at first. He was quite drunk, though, so I had to use my mou—"

"Not that part," the master grated. "Tell me what happened *to the relic."*

"Oh." From somewhere in the shadows, she produced a leather pouch, heavy with coins. Her face downcast, she held it up to him. "I don't know. This was all I found on him."

"Money—payment, no doubt. Let's see what a heretic's bone fetches." He hefted the pouch and tugged at the drawstring. *"Gold?!* By the Almighty! Did you open this?"

"Of course."

Sebastian made a quick count. "So you prowled the streets of Rouen all night with some *fifty florins* in your pocket?"

"Are you . . . pleased?" She looked up hopefully, wiping her eyes.

"I suppose it is better than nothing.[5] And it may be a clue in itself," mused the master. "This kind of money must have been arranged beforehand. Your guardsman was no opportunist.

5. The ingrate! Fifty florins in the 1430s was more money than most would see in a lifetime.

Someone very, very wealthy made him an offer in advance, an offer he could scarcely refuse—and he collected in a hurry. But who?"

Gold leaves a trail we can follow, said the old one. *I have . . . an associate who can assist, but she is greedy. We will need fresh bait—a female—and one of those coins.*

Livia looked up at the swimming ethereal presence, her eyes wide. "*Clauneck?* Are you so desperate?"[6]

We would have no need if you were able, just once, to manage a simple task, succubus! Even a dog can fetch a bone!

"Clauneck. Why do I know that name?" asked the master warily.

She is a Spirit with an . . . affinity for gold. The world has never again seen splendor like the riches she drew to the Court of Solomon.

"Until he discovered where the gold was coming from, and by then it was too late,"[7] added Livia. "Clauneck built the mint at the Temple of Juno Moneta in Rome, which I'm sure you remember, Dominus. She claimed she was also a consort of Midas. Think carefully before you draw up your Wards for this one, meatbag. Better to keep that gold and find somewhere quiet to pass the time for a few hundred years." Livia gently massaged the muscles of her neck, where the weight of the Contract had settled like a millstone. She winced as she brushed her throbbing earlobes.

---

6. I might have taken a little more care if I'd known the old one would get Clauneck involved, but you know what they say about hindsight.

7. Have you ever wondered why the fabled King of Israel had a harem of thousands and only three children?

Afraid of some competition, succubus? mocked the old one. *Do not fear, Sebastian. I can handle Clauneck.*

Livia laughed. "No, you cannot. She will get what she wants, one way or another." She stood up unsteadily. "Now, may I be dismissed?"

No, succubus. You have work to do. We will need something to bargain with. Clauneck will not sign for anything less than a vessel.

"Possession?" The master seemed far from certain. "Is Mars . . . Barron . . . Avstamet—whatever he's calling himself now—truly worth it after all this time, Sarmodel?"

Oh yes, my love. He will be power and pleasure like you have never known. We will be drunk on his anima for a thousand years. His tendrils caressed the master's shoulders. *And the world will be free of the Warfather, of course. This interminable war will find its conclusion quickly enough without his interference.*

"That is reason enough. I suppose. Very well, then—go, Livia."

She restored her glamers with a gentle shiver. Her tail, talons and fangs vanished. Lovely once more, she inclined her head to her master and pulled the shadows around herself like a blanket. "This city is crawling with *phlam.* I will return soon."

Mind me, half-breed, called the old one as she left. *Do not tarry this time, or it will be your flesh waiting for Clauneck in the Circle.*

I noticed it first as a kind of persistent distraction.

Antoine would tie a brace of rabbits and I'd spend the morning—the entire morning—playing the scene over in my mind, watching his hands move through the knots, the long, slender muscles in his forearms bunching and kneading as he worked. Neither of us bothered to shave while we were living in the wild, and I studied the way his hair changed from pale, burnished gold on top of his head to the honey-colored curls of his beard and nape. I wondered why he snored for about ten minutes at the same time every night. I pondered the fact that he put on his breeches starting with the right leg, but then when it came to his boots, always started with the left.

The story of the trout became a game, a tale we would tell with greater and greater embellishment at inns and firesides. We played pranks on each other (often trout-inspired) and I would devote my long nights to devising new ways to surprise him with a salted water flask or bedroll full of stones. He in turn would rouge my cheeks with crushed berries while I was deep in meditation and introduce me as Madame de Pompadour to anyone we met, to my great puzzlement. Antoine's impulsiveness was infectious and his carnal appetites unpredictable, to the point that we became known as *les belettes*—"the weasels"—for our many late-night raids on the local "henhouses."

It sounds strange, given how many people were dying, but that summer was a dream. There was danger and hardship but there was also a sense of possibility I hadn't felt for centuries. Antoine was young and full to bursting with every pleasure he could find, and once again, somehow, so was I.

It wasn't until one frosty morning in autumn—right before what would become known as the Red Winter—that Sarmodel drew my attention to the obvious.

I can't **wait** *for the fornicating to start,* he said, interrupting my daydreaming. Antoine and I were riding through thick bracken and drifts of fallen leaves, on our way down to Saint-Julien-by-the-Stream. I had been remembering my young companion, naked and knee-deep in the stream, whooping in surprise as the silver trout leaped from his grasp. *You're quite the jackrabbit when you're in love.*

The what—and the **what***? With whom?*

Come, Sebastian. This one is a good match for you, he said. *What's wrong?*

Nothing is wrong and you are mistaken.

His sigh carried the threat of a waking furnace.

Very well. I am scared it's a disaster waiting to happen, I confessed, chewing my lip. *This is absolutely ridiculous. I'm here—we are here—on serious business.*

Would it be the first time you paused to sample the local fare?

This is different! Antoine is technically my employer, and he has no interest in me, or any other man. No. I shook my head. *Leave it be, Sarmodel. This is not a distraction I can afford in the middle of a hunt, not right under the nose of the Holy See.*

Sarmodel only laughed. *Isn't it delicious? And I wouldn't be so sure about the young Lord Ocerne. He's a long way from the château and he certainly doesn't object to your company.*

I narrowed my eyes. *You want him.*

He laughed again. *Of course I want him. Because* **you** *want him. Though I think we both know it goes a little deeper than that.* He settled in my mind, coils upon coils. *Don't misunderstand; he'll die one day, like they all do, and I hope we're there when it happens.*[1] *But not right now.* **Now** *he's young, and mortal flesh is so exquisitely designed for pleasure—why not enjoy each other?*[2] *I can think of a dozen ways he might be compromised out here in the wildwood. Let me show you—*

I do **not** *need your help with this, Sarmodel.*

If you ignore the quat, it will only grow larger—much better to give it a squeeze and enjoy the mess. I don't understand why you won't follow your instincts. Just take him! Get it over with so we can focus on the task at—

Leave me be!

Very well! But if you won't take my advice, could you at least take your eyes off his rump long enough to get me something decent to eat? It has been weeks and I am **starving.**

It has not been **weeks***—*

---

1. Cathexis, or emotional connection, is what allows the exchange of anima from one entity to another, such that even inanimate objects (e.g., money) can become repositories of spiritual energy. This is why Sarmodel derives such exquisite pleasure from consuming those with whom I share a strong personal connection. He does not understand why this would upset me.

2. I have come to regard with great suspicion anything Sarmodel says beginning with "Why not . . . ?"

"Are you well, Sebastian?" Antoine's voice startled me. "What are you scowling at?"

"I am just thinking," I replied, "that we need to move faster if we are to reach the market before everything is gone. My heart is set on pork and mushrooms tonight, and I will be satisfied with nothing less."

"Then you shall have it. You are riding with the baron's son," he said with his easy smile. He hefted a bag of black walnuts from a tree we'd had the luck to find that morning. "I think the market will provide most generously."

Nonetheless, we hastened our horses through the foothills toward Saint-Julien.

The charming hamlet was situated in the shadow of Château d'Ocerne, at the foot of the long road up the mountain. It had become a hub for the visiting hunters, and its monthly market was usually stripped to the boards by midday.

Antoine was correct, naturally. Everyone of any consequence recognized Antoine Avenel d'Ocerne. Sold-out provisioners suddenly found stock for him to buy. Antoine knew their names and which villages they came from, and he inquired after their families. He hulled the walnuts one by one and handed them out in place of payment, assuring each shopkeeper that his account would be settled by the château. In return, we received wedges of cheese, coveted *petit salé* salted pork, round loaves of bread and small, sweet pumpkins. And Antoine, of course, refilled his wine flask.

I was very uncomfortable with the entire exchange. The food was most welcome and I would certainly not have been able to afford it otherwise. But it felt like an abuse to take it on little more than good faith. There was something naïve and presumptuous about Antoine's behavior that bothered me. While it was impossible to dislike the baron's handsome, laughing son, I detected a tone of resentment beneath many of the greetings we received.

Some did not bother even to conceal their disdain. Antoine was all but ignored when he approached the Normans. They offered little beyond the barest requirements of courtesy. The genteel, black-clad Bauterne was there too, showing off a trio of fresh wolf carcasses to his legion of admirers. He simply inclined his head to us, shadowed by the hulking Soeur. The Lieutenant of the Hunt reserved an especially patronizing smile for me.

We were also being watched.

Sebastian, mark that one. She sees me.

A young woman with white-blond hair stared at us from the open window of a small cottage. She was unkempt and ragged, even in comparison to the other villagers, with homespun clothing and no evidence of face powders or rouge. On the sill in front of her was a collection of half-filled bottles and jars, and the eaves were hung with drying herbs and fresh pelts.

Truly? Then she may be able to help us.

I excused myself and slipped away from Antoine's side. I approached the herbalist slowly, smiling.

"Good day, Mademoiselle," I ventured. "Might I see what you have for sale?" She had barely reached womanhood, her face still plump with youth and spotted with pimples. But this one would be overlooked in Saint-Julien's matrimonial lottery. She was the village *sage-femme* and would spend her life tending her neighbors' ailments, bringing their babies into the world,[3] and enduring their scorn and suspicion.

I knew immediately that Sarmodel was right—the young woman had a strong touch of the Arcane, and she could see him.

3. Or making sure they never came into the world at all.

I was most surprised to see a potent hagstone[4] hanging on a cord around her neck. It was almost certainly a gift from a powerful patron Spirit; she was being groomed for greater things, it seemed. She was also clearly frightened, and her gaze roved high over my head.

"Who are you?" she demanded, shrinking away from the sill. She clasped a hand over the hagstone and I felt her power—untrained but not inconsequential—gathering protectively. "To whom are you bound, foul thing? I did not call you!"[5]

"He is mine, never fear," I replied, with forced laughter. "My name is Sebastian Grave, and I have come to join the hunt for the Beast, like the other men here. My Guest will not harm you." I extended my hand, the Sigil of Amity[6] shining in golden fire on my palm. "Perhaps we could speak somewhere privately?"

She shook her head fiercely. "No! I will not treat with you. You—God help me, you have *eaten* men, hundreds of them. I see it!"

And if we meant you harm, phlam, *you would already be among*

---

4. A stone with a natural hole through it, worn by the water of a sacred waterfall, stream or fountain. Hagstones bestow Arcane sight and can provide a measure of control over minor Spirits, even for the uninitiated. They are traditionally given as favors by powerful Spirits in exchange for devotion, and they take a very long time to form. I hadn't seen a genuine one for centuries by the time the 1700s came around.

5. Do not ever speak to a Spirit of any consequence this way. There are a raft of protocols to be observed, and good etiquette can make the difference between sharing a meal and becoming one.

6. Not a Contract so much as an MOU, the Compact of Amity is a common gesture of good faith between Arcane practitioners, establishing peaceful relations for as long as both parties agree. Breaking the Compact is considered the very worst manners, and word gets around quickly.

them, said Sarmodel. The girl flinched as though from a thunderclap.

"Leave me, I said! You were not invited!"

I did not see where the dog came from. Between one moment and the next, it was there inside the hut, with her hand resting on its head.

"Please, be calm," I said. In my Arcane sight, the animal was a violet serpent as thick as my leg, rearing under her palm. Blind as a worm and fanged like a lamprey, the creature doubtless had a head full of venom.

Sarmodel laughed heartily. *A Spirit of the wash!*[7] *Do you have a ratcatcher back there as well, O supreme enchantress?*

"He is my boon companion,[8] demon. He will protect me with his life."

He will kill you in your sleep and mount your corpse, hedge-witch. Sarmodel laughed again. *By the Rift, where are your Wards? We could turn him against you in a second!*

"There is no need for threats," I said. "I seek only information on the Beast—and I will be happy to share information in kind."

"The Beast! No! I hate him—*we* hate him. He brings only discord. I am forbidden to speak of him."

"Forbidden? By whom?"

Tell us what you know, meat, or this will end badly for you.

"I will tell you no more!" The girl tugged at the hagstone and

7. A common name for the nenekt, a type of primal Spirit found most often near streams and marshes, and familiar to many a local wise woman.

8. The creature under her hand was, like many domestic Spirits, a caster of glamers. I had no doubt about what sort of "companionship" he provided to the lonely young herbalist of Saint-Julien after dark.

shook her head again. The serpent tensed, ready to strike. In the Mundane world, her ragged mutt was growling. "Now *go*!"

"Please, we must know—"

"Mademoiselle Cecile? Is something amiss?" A grim, middle-aged man shouldered past me, placing himself in front of the open window. He was clearly wealthier than the majority of the townsfolk, with a long sapphire-blue waistcoat and embroidered ivory britches. His hair and his eyes were both a pale, silvery gray like freshly honed steel. There was something forceful and muscular about his stance; though he walked with a cane, he looked more than capable of cracking skulls with it. He seemed vaguely familiar, though I could not place him among the hundreds of Gévaudanais I had met in my time on the hunt.

"No, Monsieur Chastel. Just another of these hunters come to vex me," replied the herbalist.

Chastel.

I recognized the man now. Jean Chastel was the publican of the Bow and Brace, the sumptuous hunting lodge near the eastern border. Formerly an infantry officer, he retained the bearing of a much younger man. We had met during my brief stay at the lodge, when I had first arrived in Gévaudan.

He looked me over. "Hunter? Hardly. He rides with the Baron d'Ocerne's son. You should leave, *Professor*. And take the young lord with you. I believe he has finished licking the cream from Saint-Julien for this month."

I gave a slight bow and retreated from the herbalist's window, extinguishing the mark on my palm. "I did not mean to disturb you, Mademoiselle Cecile. I will not trouble you or your companion further."

They conversed quietly, watching me as I left.

XXI

I found Antoine by the gallows. There were two ragged old corpses hanging there in the autumnal air, too dry for even the scavengers to show much interest, though one optimistic corax[1] perched patiently on the beam.

My young companion was talking with Monsieur Comtois, whose incomparable cheeses were wrapped in cloth and stowed in my saddlebag. Antoine was eating one of the golden, buttery apples from the late season, a sheen of sweet juice on his lips. The two men were discussing the changing of the year and, of course, the Beast.

---

1. A diligent scavenger, usually found where the corpses are plentiful and the anima of low quality. In the Mundane world they appear as you would expect: crows, rats and other vermin.

You should have taken the nenekt, Sarmodel insisted. *The thing is feral.*[2]

I think Cecile might have objected to that, and we can't really afford to make any more enemies here, I replied, *especially anyone with her sort of talent. She may also be useful to us—she clearly knows something about the Beast, and we don't have a lot of leads right now.*

He snorted but did not press me further.

"Sebastian!" called Antoine. "Come! I was just telling our good cheesemaker how we shall be the only two men who return from the hunt fatter than when we left."

"Not if you are in charge of meals, I fear," I replied.

I made genial conversation but I was impatient to leave. Our encounter with Cecile and steely Jean Chastel had soured the day for me. The presence of so many other hunters also made me uneasy; I disliked especially the watchful eyes of the Ennevals and Bauterne.

"Sebastian?" Antoine peered at me, his brow creased. "Are you well?"

Sarmodel!

I feel it. His presence sharpened like an icicle.

A vertiginous pressure rose around us. For a moment, everything yawed sickeningly along the axes of matter and energy. The market was saturated with impossible Arcane hues and the air was tinged with the stink of burning metal. The sensation built and then broke like a wave, receding to nothing.

I feared to think what it had washed up in the world.

---

2. A Spirit summoned without Wards or Contract is considered feral. While it's unfair to generalize, and every life is precious etc., a feral Spirit is almost always up to no good and should be put down as soon as possible.

*It's **him**. The Beast—he is here!* Sarmodel was a nest of sucking, snuffling mouths in my mind. ***Oh, but he's big! I smell him!***

I looked around desperately, drawing my silver Walloon blade. Antoine and Monsieur Comtois recoiled in confusion at my sudden ardor; they had felt nothing, of course.

"Sebastian! What—"

I silenced him with a shake of my head. The bucolic bustle of the marketplace was suddenly filled with peril.

Sarmodel Projected in front of me, taking on his child form.

"That way, quickly!" he urged, pointing to a gated laneway on the far side of the fountain. It was little more than the space between two houses, barely wide enough for a horse to pass.

In there? Are you sure?

"You felt it, Sebastian! Something just shifted phase![3] We may not get another chance like this!" He faltered for a moment. "By the Rift, he's *enormous*."

I walked slowly toward the wooden gate.

Quickly then, I need you, I said to the Projection.

I waited for him to come forward, but Sarmodel's anima was sluggish and barely warmed my fingertips.

"I'm not strong enough," he snapped. The child scowled at me. "You never listen! I told you I was hungry!"

I swore and curled my fingers nervously around the handle of my pistol. He was right; absorbed in my sylvan daydreaming about

---

3. When a Spirit shifts phase (either by assuming control of a host or by manifesting directly) it requires two things. The first is energy in the form of anima. The second is an induced aberration in the laws of the Mundane world—a rupture of sorts—to allow the crossing. Generally speaking, the more powerful the Spirit is, the more anima will be required, and the more noticeable the aberration will be.

Antoine over the last week, I had indeed neglected to take proper care of my Guest.

And now it was too late.

"Sebastian?" I barely heard Antoine's voice.

The gate was open slightly.

Time to see what we've got.

I pushed it with the tip of my sword.

There was a quiet sound, a gentle sound, coming from the shadowed laneway. At first, I saw a touching tableau: a big, cloaked man comforting a red-shirted little boy in his lap, his arms cradling the child protectively.

But the shadows resolved into horror. The child's vest was dyed with his own blood. The whimpering cries were his last breaths as the man nuzzled at his torn throat, one hand kneading savagely inside the poor boy's rib cage.

And the killer was of course no man.

Covered not in a cloak but dark, ragged fur, the thing in the laneway rose towering onto its hind legs, dripping gore and fresh plasma onto the stones. It raised the child's heart to its mouth and crushed it like a grape between its fangs.

Sarmodel and I were both silent in shock.

It wasn't dread of the monstrous Beast or the sickening act it had committed (though these were terrible enough) which so disconcerted me.

I met my Guest's wide eyes and knew I had the right of it.

It's him!

It was not his physical body I recognized; that was just the keyhole through which glimpses of his true form were visible, looming mightily just outside the Mundane world.

Similar recognition flashed in the monster's eyes; three hundred years had not dulled his memory.[4] The Beast knew me—knew both of us—and his gaze was even and unafraid.

And now, as then, he spoke to us.

"*TU! QUOMODO?*"

They were words I might have said myself—*YOU! HOW?*

Momentarily stunned by his sudden appearance, I could not respond.

"*Yes!* I see you, Avstamet!" crowed Sarmodel-child. "*MARS VIGILA!*"

"By the Lord!" Antoine's voice was distant; I had all but forgotten he was there. "The Beast! ***The Beast!*** Save yourselves!"

Silence bloomed across the village like a shock wave.

Then all was screaming—hunters screaming for their dogs, parents screaming for their children, children screaming for their lives.

"Sebastian—the Yoke!" barked Sarmodel-child.

I started the Tartaric syllables, but the Beast leaped before I could finish the opening pronouncement. Only the tight confines of the laneway saved me from disembowelment. The creature snagged the swinging gate as it lunged, slamming me to the ground in a cascade of splintered wood.

The screaming intensified as the Beast emerged into the open, a nightmare suddenly made flesh in sleepy Saint-Julien-by-the-Stream.

They could not remember exactly what it looked like, the survivors of that fatal market day, when later they tried to describe the killer. Like the other witnesses before them, they would recall the dark fur, the pointed ears and the muzzle full of fangs. ***Like a wolf, but as big as an ox,*** they would say.

4. Please refer to Livia's supplement for the outcome of our previous encounter.

But the whipping, tufted tail and matted mane did not belong to anything they could name. And the human proportions, the intelligent eyes, the *face*—these were beyond comprehension. They could not bear to look at it in the daylight, and their recollection would shy away from it for fear of madness. They had only one word that might capture it.

"Beast."

I knew better.

I recognized the animal that speaks with a man's voice, the father of orphans. I saw the impetuous, violent Spirit that Greece and Rome had pacified with worship and nourished with the blood of legions. The god they called War and Glory, Ares and Mars. I recognized the devil on the shoulder of poor Jehanne d'Arc, and the voice that seduced Gilles de Rais into depravity.

The ancient Spirit Avstamet, walking the Earth again—somehow—after all this time.

He tensed on the flagstones, a single point of stillness in the churning, shrieking press of people, like a bowstring drawing taut.

And then the Red Winter truly began.

PART THREE

The Massacre at Saint-Julien

XXII

Prior to the Red Winter, Saint-Julien-by-the-Stream had a reputation for both excellent hams and a particularly piquant form of soft cheese. From the moment the Beast revealed himself to me in that laneway, it would be known for only one thing: the massacre.

If not for the narrow lane and its quaint gated entrance, I would certainly have been among the first victims. Instead, I lay winded on the ground beneath a spall of shattered wood.

It took me a few seconds to collect myself. In that small space of time, the marketplace had become a carnival of crimson.

"*Get up, you useless meat!*" Sarmodel-child bellowed, railing painfully in my mind. "Did you see?! Avstamet! By the Rift! He will *not* escape me this time!"

I shook the splinters from my blade. The boards and banners of Saint-Julien's market were suddenly drenched in spatter. Everything dripped.

The Beast moved with impossible power.

Some people were frozen in a rapture of terror at the monster come to life in the afternoon sun. He tore them apart where they stood.

Others fled before him like mice, but they were all too slow; far too slow. A green-suited mummer was raked to the bone as he tried to run. Madame Pradels tumbled among the last of her golden apples, fountaining blood from the stump of her neck. The stablehand was pulled aloft by the hair like a turnip, his body opened onto the flagstones as the Beast tugged out his innards.

And with each kill, the Spirit claimed another heart and another draft of coveted human anima to fuel his eldritch flesh.

By the Almighty.

If there had been any doubt about what we faced, it disappeared in those few nightmarish seconds. I leveled the point of my sword at the monster and once again began the Crippling Yoke.

The Beast snarled as Arcane polyhedrons began to proliferate around him. His terrible eyes found me again in the throng.

But now a second tumult rose to rival the screaming: the baying of hounds. Just as the Beast drove the villagers before him, so he drew the hunters of France behind.

"*Soeur! Allez!*" Bauterne's voice was unmistakable as he swept past me on his horse. His hounds splashed through the blood toward the Beast, led by the formidable Soeur. The Ennevals were not far behind, their own pack of sturdy northern dogs keen on the trail.

The Beast roared and cast the stablehand's corpse into the oncoming pack. With a powerful leap, he fled along the street.

Shit! My Arcane focus slipped away as he moved out of range, and the Yoke failed a second time.

"Follow me!" the elder Enneval bellowed over his shoulder. "We will catch it at the bridge! Do not let it reach the woods!" Perhaps a score of Gévaudan's hunters were storming the small town with their army of hounds. They called back to him and half of them wheeled around to follow him, driving their packs east along the riverbank.

Idiots! I fumed inwardly. *Where are they going? Do they believe they are going to herd him into a treadle snare?*

"Be silent and *get moving*!" Sarmodel's child Projection shrilled at me. "Why are we still—Wait!"

He drew my focus to the fountain, now swirling red. A young girl panted on the ground beside it, struggling to sit upright. The monster's parting attack had thrown her from her feet and inflicted a mortal wound. Her lifeblood streamed over her pinafore from a horrific gash across her throat.

"Avstamet has not claimed her!" Sarmodel hissed. "Quickly! We will use her strength!"

His Projection flickered eagerly toward the girl, clutching at the first traces of escaping anima.

But two people ran over to kneel by the victim. I recognized Père Arnaud, the priest from the château, in his black cassock.

And with him was Mademoiselle Cecile the herbalist.

"Hurry, Father!" she cried, taking the girl in her arms. "Before the end!" Her eyes were not on the priest, however, but fixed firmly on Sarmodel. She scooped water from the fountain and began to wash the victim's face.

"No!" snarled the demon child, opening a mouth suddenly full of fangs. "You little *bitch*!"

Père Arnaud sobbed such that he could barely enunciate his prayers, but already the crown-like manifestation of the Almighty was forming about the dying girl's head. The holy man was performing extreme unction. He applied sweet oil to her hands and forehead, speaking softly in Latin.

"Ssh, Therese, go now," crooned the young witch, stroking the girl's face. "The Lord will take you."

The priest pressed a sliver of bread into the victim's mouth. I caught a few words of viaticum before her anima welled up. It shone and trembled briefly before it was gently embraced by the glowing corona.

Sarmodel whirled on me, his boy's face grown bestial.

"I *need* that *phlam*! Stop them—"

Sarmodel, she's already gone! I interrupted, closing my eyes against the light of her final Communion. *And I cannot do anything with you shouting at me!*

"Sebastian! Here!" Antoine's voice broke through the wailing.

He was leading our horses through the market. The animals were all but mad with fear, surrounded by blood and screaming and the ripe smell of dogs.

There was no time for subtlety. I whistled a snatch of melody that ascended above hearing. The horses stilled immediately.

I ignored Antoine's raised eyebrows as we both mounted. "Come! You heard them—the bridge!"

Cecile the herbalist glared and raised her chin defiantly as we passed.

Draw up your Wards, witch, Sarmodel hissed at her. He withdrew his Projection, settling back into my mind. *Get your "boon companion" to help. When I am done with the Beast, I am coming back for both of you.*

The Ennevals and the other hunters pushed their packs hard.

The cobblestones of Saint-Julien were overrun with a tide of dogs, funneled by the narrow laneways down to the poplar-shaded promenade overlooking the river. They poured out onto the open ground, spurred on by their masters and drawn by the Beast's bloody trail.

They caught him at the bridge, for all the good it did them. Hounds surrounded the monster like rats, but it barely slowed.

We emerged onto the road behind them at a gallop.

"Hold!" the elder Norman was bellowing. "Hold, you bastard, *do not—*"

A gunshot cracked through the barking chaos. Dogs screamed and dropped away like swatted bugs. Cries of shock and anger rose over the general cacophony; it was utter folly to attempt to shoot the Beast at this distance, particularly when it was surrounded by hounds. There could only be one man responsible.

Bauterne knelt on the near bank. He was right in front of the *lavoir,* where a group of villagers had just abandoned their laundry, and he was surrounded by tubs of fresh suds. His long, black musket smoked and I could hear him shouting as he reloaded. But he was not replying to Enneval; I doubt he even heard the man.

"*You are my strength! Into your hands I commend my spirit; you have redeemed me!*"

Bauterne's Litany was not going unanswered. His musket was positively singing with Divine radiance. In my Arcane sight, jeweled wings unfolded over his head like a banner.

Michael is here?!

The Archangel was doing more than announcing his presence. He was warning us off, and I was keenly aware of the many ways he might eliminate his chief competition in the chaos.

Somehow, Sarmodel's agitation escalated; his presence was like a steel wasp trying to grind its way out of my skull. *Of course Michael is here! He must have known what we were really chasing. Did you think the Almighty would miss another tilt at such a prize?*

Well, he has a gun, Sarmodel. That Litany is going to put holes in both of us if he turns it in our direction.

You know he can't commit harm under the Covenant,[1] he snapped. *But he can find plenty of other ways to get underfoot.*

The black musket thundered again.

"What is he doing?" demanded Antoine, horrified. "Bauterne—he's hitting the hounds!"

"The Lieutenant of the Hunt did not earn his colors without making some sacrifices," I shouted back, equally shocked; Bauterne's ruthlessness was on full display. "Come! Onto the bridge!"

We pushed forward, driving our horses onto the span with the other hunters.

"Take care, Antoine!" I called as we moved along the arch of the bridge. The drop on either side was significant and the water below was shallow, rolling over a pavement of smooth stones. A fall would be unforgiving, if not fatal.

Bauterne fired again; the hornet buzz of flying shot was very close to us. More dogs fell, but the Beast roared its own fury this time; the Archangel's blessing was yielding results.

A heavy runnel of blood snaked down the Beast's hind leg.

The monster stumbled.

It was enough. The dogs swarmed over him like a second pelt.

Now, Sebastian! interjected Sarmodel. *Get closer and finish the Yoke! Kill every mutt on this bridge if you have to.*

Of course, my love! Watch as I ensnare an Olympian with the Crippling Yoke, on horseback, in the middle of a bridge covered in

1. The Covenant that all of the angels have signed forbids (among many, many other things) physical violence, willful harm and/or deliberate killing of mortals without provocation. I would note that "provocation" has been very broadly interpreted over the centuries, hence my cautious approach.

dogs, with the Archangel shooting a musket over my shoulder, I snapped back. *Shall I stand on my head and fart the Pater Noster as well?*[2]

His only reply was a snarl of frustration. He Projected ahead of me in the form of a monstrous mandrill, a demon baboon skipping over the sea of hounds. He capered across their backs, calling to the Beast in sulfurous Tartaric.

"Welcome to the flesh, Avstamet! We are here for your heart! Come, come!"

He bared his yellow fangs and hooted with murderous mirth.

The Beast stopped.

At the far end of the bridge, only a few steps from the forest and freedom, he rose from the fray and turned his unbearable gaze back on the hunt. I knew it had all been a ruse.

Smiling cruelly, the Beast scattered the hounds with an easy swipe. He plucked the dogs from his hide, biting the heads off the most tenacious. Only the indomitable Soeur, the single hound who came anywhere near matching him in size, remained steady. She hunkered down, snarling on the flagstones as her terrified packmates churned around her.

The Beast set his feet and howled. A horrific cry vibrated beyond sound into Arcane frequencies.

And he received an answer.

A hundred wild voices rose in the eternal hymn of the hunt.

---

2. The Crippling Yoke is the "nuclear option" among the many disciplinary measures in the magician's tool kit—most practitioners would be driven to invoke it perhaps once or twice in a lifetime. It is also exceedingly difficult to execute. Sarmodel naturally advocates its use for almost everything, which has earned me a reputation as something of a sadist—albeit a very competent one—in the Arcane community.

The men on the bridge faltered. Their eyes followed the sound to the deep, autumnal forest behind the Beast.

Wolves.

From the thickets and the hollows they emerged in their dozens, shivering and drooling. Driven to madness by the cry of the ancient Spirit who wore their likeness, the animals trembled and whined, drawn to his side by the promise of blood.

We were perhaps halfway across the bridge, in the midst of the throng of hunters. And all around us, their dozens of hounds began to shiver.

"Back—Antoine!" I shouted. "Get everyone off the bridge! Back! Now!" But none were listening to me.

I held my beautiful sword, my Walloon silver, out to one side, softly intoning the succession of Violations carved into the fuller. It began to keen. In my Arcane sight, it was a tongue of blue flame.

"*Yes!!* Masterfully done, Avstamet! Come, War! Come, Discord!" shrieked the baboon. It perched on the corpse of a mastiff. "Join in the sublime sacrament![3] Eat and be eaten!"

The Beast had brought his own pack to the hunt, and the men on the bridge were almost close enough to taste.

The trap was sprung.

---

3. The consumption of human flesh—or more specifically the heart, which is the richest repository of anima.

XXIII

We were overwhelmed in seconds. The wolves poured out of the forest and across the bridge. They left a twitching red wake. The hunters sounded their horns and realized too late that many of their own hounds were answering the Beast's call instead. The Gascon trapper was torn apart by his dogs in front of me, his nine fingers gripping the gold collar of his favorite as the animal chewed through his face.

Again and again my blade flashed. My silver was designed to bring down even eldritch flesh, and it dispatched Gévaudan's wolves, as fierce as they were, with frightening ease. As always, I had to take care to guard my own safety without attracting undue attention. The Violations in the metal were not visible to the Mundane world; their effects[1] most certainly were.

The hunters on the bank behind me were sorely beset. Horses

1. If I recall correctly, this configuration deconstructed matter at the molecular level, producing an effect not dissimilar to a bandsaw.

screamed as they were dragged to the ground by hounds and wolves alike. The carnage was indiscriminate, and above it all, the howling Beast presided.

He advanced through the massacre, soaking up fresh anima from the corpses on the bridge. Where he found a human body, he twisted out its heart and devoured it. Always his eyes were on the capering baboon, now screaming obscenities over the bedlam.

Sarmodel, come back! I called, panicked. My Guest's Projection was immaterial, but he was still vulnerable to Arcane injury.

The mandrill ignored me, devoting all his attention to committing the ultimate affront to the proud, ancient Spirit. As the anima of wolves, dogs and horses rose up around us, the baboon Projection snatched it from the air, sucking it into himself like breath. It was only the leavings from Avstamet's table, but it was enough of an insult to draw his anger.

The Beast lunged toward the mandrill, but the bodiless Projection flickered away. He reappeared on Soeur's brindled back, raising his inflamed pink rump to the monster.

Soeur, one of the few hounds who had not succumbed to savagery, saw her opportunity and leaped for the Beast's flank. It barely deflected her, and she pressed her advantage with a vicious bite to his forelimb. Again, the baboon flickered away to safety.

Now! The Yoke, you cretin! Sarmodel boomed in my mind. *While he is busy!*

Oh, very well! It was perhaps the best chance I would get. The Projection had drawn the Beast within range and Soeur had indeed provided a valuable distraction.

I raised my sword, using its straight line to focus the Crippling Yoke through the chaos.

But no sooner had I opened my mouth than Antoine cried out in distress.

"No! *Back!*"

A huge timber wolf leaped at him. Antoine dodged awkwardly in the saddle and—bizarrely—began to laugh, as though he were rollicking with one of the château dogs.

"Whoreson!" He made a swing with his sword, but the animal was already too close. The momentum of the attack carried Antoine off his horse and they were both—man and wolf—dragged scrabbling over the side of the bridge.

"Antoine!"

There was no decision to be made. I went after him.

It took only moments to beat my way back along the bridge. My horse was on the verge of bolting, but I barely registered the carnage happening all around me; my eyes were on the riverbed far below, searching for Antoine.

I reached the poplars on the promenade and dismounted in haste, scrambling down the steep bank.

Down on the riverbed, the chaos of the melee above was muted and distant. The twin arches of the bridge cast a long shadow and I was suddenly very cold. A few animals limped out of the trickling flow. The rest were corpses.

The timber wolf lay in a wide puddle. The wretched animal had broken Antoine's fall, and its blood was slowly clouding the water.

"Antoine!" I called out. "Where are you?"

To my relief, he was crawling toward the shelter of the bridge. He flailed through the stony shallows, tangled in his own clothing. His movements were ungainly and lopsided; I suspected he had been injured in the fall.

"Sebastian!" he gasped. "Here!" He drew in another sharp lungful of air and made a strange hooting sound. In his shock, Antoine was still laughing like a lunatic.

"Cretin!" Sarmodel-child appeared, fists clenched, not far from me. "What are you *doing* down here?"

Following my instincts—on your advice! I snapped back, pointing at the wounded young nobleman.

For a rare moment, his confusion rendered him speechless. He looked at Antoine, and then back to me.

"You're going to fuck him *now*?!"

I was robbed of my response by a tremendous splash and a primeval roar. I recoiled, falling back among the pebbles of the riverbed.

The Beast had descended.

The monster landed in the water near Antoine and the flow turned red around him. He was covered in a slick of blood; it dripped from his jaw, his shaggy shoulders and the tip of his lurid, erect member. The Beast was afire with the darkest passions; Arcane heat rippled off him in waves. His too-human eyes found the young nobleman struggling in the shallows. He smiled with crimson teeth.

"Antoine, *get up*!" I yelled, panicked. I struggled to my feet, babbling incantations.

The monster shrugged off my blinding Extirpation and kicked aside the corpse of a horse. One step closer, then another.

There was no other choice.

"*Parley!*" I yelled in Latin. "Avstamet, attend!"

XXIV

What? Sarmodel-child stared at me.

"Parley!" I said again.

The Beast heard me. He bared his teeth.

"I call you Ares. I call you Mars. I call you Avstamet," I continued. "By your own name and the blood of Jehanne d'Arc, you have agreed to treat with me. Attend!"

It was a long shot—circumstances had certainly changed in three centuries, and I had very little with which to bargain.

But Antoine. I could not watch him die.

I breathed hard, my eyes wide as I waited for the Beast's response. He was most displeased at being interrupted in his feast, but he had made an agreement with Livia all those years ago and the Contract held.

A burning white ideogram flickered to life on my palm.[1] The

1. This symbol is known colloquially as "the Table." It denotes a ceasefire for negotiations.

Beast's half-human paw was similarly marked; he was bound to reply.

"*Vin hanc carnem?*" The monster's voice was more than sound. I felt it inside my chest. He wrapped a clawed hand around Antoine's ankle and lifted him from the riverbed. In his terror, the young lord did not make a sound—he had, for now, stopped laughing. He hung, limp and trembling, from the Beast's grip. Avstamet's Latin was crisp and imperious, and he asked his question again.

"*This* meat, Magician?" He looked at Antoine in bewilderment. "You invoke your Contracted right—for *this*?"

"No! No! He does not!" interrupted Sarmodel-child. "He misspoke! What he meant to say was—"

The Beast made an Abject sound that could not rightly be called speech. In my mind it was all at once a Roman spear, a striking viper and a black meteor. It shot invisibly through the air toward my Guest's obnoxious Projection.

"Sarmodel!"

The demon child's chest burst like a ruptured melon. He howled, his anima pouring from the wound in streams. The injured Projection winked out of existence and he fled back into my mind, gibbering.

"Do you wish to treat?" demanded the Beast.

"I do!" I shouted, sounding far more certain than I felt. "I claim this man. What are your terms?"

The Beast looked at me, richly amused. "You are shrewd, Magician, but you are no different to these other mortals—a gnat, aspiring to the eagle's nest." He spat blood onto the pebbles at my feet; he was now close enough for me to smell the miasma of brimstone and plasma that surrounded him. "You seek to devour me? You might strive as well to drink the ocean. Your life is mine already—as is yours, nettlesome Spirit. But I will honor my word, given to you so many years ago." He regarded me for a moment and then spoke again. "My terms are simple. In exchange for this single, unremarkable sack of meat, my price is Truth."

"Done," I said, without hesitation.

His bestial tongue flicked from his mouth, his eyes narrowed. He certainly suspected a trick. "Such human folly. I agree. Done, then."

Avstamet cast Antoine aside, skimming him like a stone over the shallow rapids.

That's your bargain? You're saving the lordling? Have you lost your senses?! Perhaps we might save our own lives first? Sarmodel whimpered. The Beast had dealt him a fierce blow. He dragged on my life force as his anima hemorrhaged away. ***Please tell me this is one of your clever ploys!***

I did not respond.

The Beast advanced on me. He lumbered over the riverbed, dragging the hind leg that had taken the Archangel's bullet. His engorged, bloodied phallus thrust with every step. I raised the silver blade between us; the melee would be on again as soon as his terms were answered.

"Now—tell me True," said the Beast. "Who are you? ***What are you,*** to pursue me so over three hundred years?" He looked *into* me with a mixture of fascination, disbelief, revulsion and naked hunger.[2] "The world has seen countless changes in my absence. This Almighty which grows like a cancer has become something I would

2. This is an expression I have endured countless times over my lifetime. Undying flesh is something of a Holy Grail for Spirits—their greatest limitation on the Mundane plane is the lifespan of their host. My unique condition and my many centuries of life make me a great white whale to other Spiritual predators, including the Host of the Almighty.

never have imagined. But *you*—you remain a singular abomination. I have never seen your like—mortal flesh that does not die! A miracle even we, the Olympians, could not achieve. And yet here you stand."

"Are these your terms then?" I insisted, praying that Antoine was taking the opportunity to get as far away as possible.

His face split in a red grin. "You are impertinent, Magician, and your heart will taste the sweeter for it. I will ask again—*what are you?* A Spirit mistaken in transition? A magician's bargain gone awry? A chimera of the soul? What Abject dealing gave rise to such a delicious freak?" He inhaled deeply, drawing in my scent. "My terms are Truth, and you will meet them. Tell me how it was done. I will know the secret to your long, long life—your undying flesh—before I take it."

He was a scant few paces away now. I had glimpsed Avstamet once before in that long-ago encounter, but still I was almost physically stunned by his presence. The Spirit's gestalt was complex beyond imagining. This close to him, I could feel the living circuitry he had built and built and built over millennia of bloodshed committed in his name. In my Arcane senses, he stood out from the Mundane world like a fountain of magma; an exposed vein of gold; a lightning strike.

This, then, was a true Olympian, who had been called a god by the empires of old.

Sarmodel was correct. We would be drunk off his essence for centuries.

"Speak! Answer me now or forfeit! What are you?"

I managed to hold the Beast's immortal gaze. The compulsion to kneel, to abase myself before him, was almost overwhelming, like the weight of the sea.

I was possibly about to speak my final words, and they were pitiful.

"I do not know."

A familiar Arcane rush marked the fulfillment of the Contract.

"Impossible!" There was confusion and something like pity on the Beast's face. "Your undying flesh—tell me how it was done. You are bound to speak the Truth, or I will split your mortal darling from crotch to crown!"

But Avstamet had received his Truth. The Sigil of the Table faded from my palm and I dared a devious smile.

The Beast was close enough now. With my free hand, I reached down to my belt.

Oh my.

A terrible blunder.

A hot wave of nausea accompanied the realization that my quicksilver ampoules were tucked away safely—and uselessly—in my saddlebag, next to my brandy and silver shot. In my concern for Antoine, I had descended to the riverbed with only my sword and two empty pistols.

"Oh my"?! Sarmodel shrilled in my mind. *"OH MY"?! If we die, Sebastian, I want you to know—are you listening to me?—**I want you to know** it's your fault!*

"You truly do not know?" The Beast looked at me in wonder. "A miserable Truth, and a worthless bargain. Tell me why—"

"*For the Lord!*"

We had both forgotten the Lieutenant of the Hunt. The man had moved into position atop the bridge, his musket throbbing with the Archangel's Litany. The Beast flinched with a snarl as gunfire cracked the air again. Divinely infused shot from Bauterne's musket punched into the riverbed at his feet, kicking up a spray of shattered pebbles. The Beast leaped back, retreating beneath the northern arch of the bridge.

"Soeur! Now!"

Bloody and half mad with fury, the giant mastiff seemed to come from nowhere. She leaped from the shadows, catching the Beast by the throat. He was thrown off balance, and their savage dance began in earnest.

Sebastian, Sarmodel hissed, *if you are going to do something, do it now!* He was doing his best not to falter, but my Guest was in agony. I could feel an echo of his pain, as though I had scalded the inside of my skull.

Very well.

Soeur's tenacity would buy me little time, and my resources were limited. The beleaguered Beast moved farther out of reach beneath the bridge. I looked with some regret at my immaculate silver Walloon sword. The curved basket handle was still exquisitely polished—without even a dent—and the blade beneath the blood was mirror bright. It would cost me a fortune to replace.

With a sigh of frustration, I reversed my grip and cast the sword like a spear, directly at the Beast's terrible head. The Violations blazed into life and the blade streaked through the air like a ribbon of lightning.

But the Beast was moving too quickly. The sword arced a little too high overhead and lodged, singing, in the masonry above him.

*Oh, **excellent**,* said Sarmodel. *Quickly, throw your breeches as well, that we may be completely defenseless!*

Ignoring him with some difficulty, I began to speak. Not the Crippling Yoke (I was quite certain I no longer had the strength to finish it), but a rank bastardization of the Violations engraved into the sword. I spoke louder and louder, deliberately breaking every rule of pronunciation and Arcane grammar. The blade's crystal song began to oscillate, jarring and warbling unpleasantly.

Overhead, a thin crack snaked across the stonework, spreading from the trembling blade. I mangled the last syllable wretchedly and my beautiful weapon disintegrated with a silent, actinic flash and a cascade of white powder.

The underside of the stone arch was suddenly crazed with blue-white light—the dangerous Arcane spatter of Violations undone.

Then, with a sound like high thunder, the stone burst.

The entire northern arch of the bridge collapsed. Even the Beast was not fast enough to escape a thousand tons of falling rock.

The monster was buried instantly. Wolves, dogs, men and horses rained down atop the rubble.

Then silence.

XXV

Eastern Tournel, France
1785

Jacques forced another dripping chunk of deer heart into his mouth, gagging.

He knelt over the animal's carcass where it had fallen among the pine needles, its head blasted almost clean away by my musket. In the chill of the autumnal forest, he belched steam like a dragon, screwing up his face against the urge to vomit.

"Quickly now, sir—don't stop." I knelt beside him, my hunting knife still wet with the deer's blood.

"I need. Just a moment," he gasped, glancing back through the trees to where the horse and wagon waited, perhaps a hundred yards away. Over the past week—had it only been a week?—this had become our habit; I would make a kill and then bring him to it, to do what must be done. Thankfully, the road cut through deep forest and I seldom had to go far to find him a beating heart.

"Very well, but only a moment. I have told you; it must be alive or it will do you no good."

"The thing is still moving, Professor—I assure you it is still alive."

I looked appraisingly at the heart in his hands; as he said, it was still twitching weakly, and there were glimmers of golden anima swimming within it. I turned away quickly; Sarmodel's obscene appetite was bringing me very close to devouring it myself. "Excellent. *Eat.* If you do not, I will have no choice but to chain you again, as we discussed."

And what about **me***?* Sarmodel asked. *Are we going to give every drop of anima to the young lord while we starve? I'm hungry, Sebastian, and I know that means you're hungry too.*

I am. But Jacques comes first, I'm afraid.

I watched hungrily, making sure Jacques finished the heart, down to the last arterial scrap. He swallowed, heaving, and then bolted down water from his flask.

"Well done, sir," I said. "The voice?"

"Quiet again. For now."

"I am pleased." I handed him a rag. "Clean your face and your vest before we head back—you are a horror."

Jacques complied and then threw the rag back at me. "Professor, how much longer until we reach Gévaudan? I cannot take much more of this."

"We will be there very soon, sir," I said. "Now please, try to calm yourself. Breathe deeply and slowly, as we have practiced. You must avoid becoming agitated."

"And you are certain I can be cured?"

"I am."

Sebastian, is it wise to lie to the young lord?

I think he has enough to worry about. Let him believe it for now.

Or—let me finish—you could ***kill him and be done****.*

“Come, sir,” I said to Jacques. “I apologize that we must keep moving, but neither of us will survive long should the snows catch us. Do you need a moment to rest?”

“No . . . no. It gets easier each time.” Jacques shook his head, defeated, and I assisted him back through the trees to the wagon.

We were—finally—out of the Alps, and the memory of Aherin’s brutal demise was no longer so fresh. Winter was following us out of the mountains, however, and we woke each morning to a bitter white frost; it was set to be a very cold return to Ocerne.

“Will you continue your story, Professor?” Jacques asked as we resumed our journey. “Though it is an ungodly tale, I cannot bear the silence.”

“It was an ungodly business, I’m afraid—as you well know, sir,” I told him.

Jacques was quiet for a moment, his eyes thoughtful as the wagon wheels creaked beneath him. “I don’t understand. My father—how could he keep all this from us?”

“I cannot answer for him. We parted on bad terms, as I’m sure you have deduced. But he has his reasons,” I said. “Just as the other survivors do.”

“It is strange to hear you speak so of the Gévaudanais. Père Arnaud and the others—these are people I have known since I was a child. It is as though they lived other lives, to have seen these things and never once spoken of them to me.” He shook his head. “How is it possible? The good père held mass at the château only weeks ago. Comtois the cheesemaker’s wagon is still first to the market every month. And Mademoiselle Cecile still makes her tisanes and poultices, of course.”

Oh ***her***, said Sarmodel, with sudden bile. *I was sure she’d be warming the bowels of her familiar by now.*

“Truly?” I said. “And how fares the *sage-femme* of Saint-Julien?”

"Cecile? Well, she is still our midwife—she was there at my birth, and I have no doubt she will be there for my firstborn as well."

Jacques looked as though he would go on, but then stopped talking abruptly, his lips pressed firmly together. My suspicion was roused immediately.

"I should very much like to pay the midwife a visit—I believe she can help us." Apart from Antoine or perhaps the Bishop of Mende, Cecile the *sage-femme* was the only person in Gévaudan with any knowledge of the Beast's true nature. She might be very helpful with a number of questions I had, if I could get her to speak to me. "We will pass through Saint-Julien on the way to the château. Perhaps Mademoiselle Cecile will be more amenable to guests this time—unless you object, sir?"

Jacques looked as though he did indeed want to object, but he simply nodded.

"Very well. Now—where was I?"

"You destroyed the bridge—which took us years to rebuild, incidentally—and crushed the Beast with one of your unholy tricks. But that is not how it died."

"No, of course not," I said. "That happened later, at the Bow and Brace, as you know."

"So tell me, then—how did you allow the Beast to escape from beneath a thousand tons of stone?" I noted with unease that, in spite of his revulsion, he absently licked his lips, picking up the last traces of blood from his beard.

"Very well, sir. Take another measure of your tonic and I will continue—I fear you will need it."

XXVI

Saint-Julien-by-the-Stream
1766

The chaos subsided for a few precious seconds after the explosion.

The massacre on the bridge ceased abruptly. With half of the span collapsed, the hunters scrambled to get off the remaining structure to the surer footing of the riverbank. At the same time, the wolves and the hounds began to flee, the Beast's hold on them broken as he was buried under the collapsing bridge.

I was left alone and panting on the riverbed, surveying my handiwork.

You are the very worst kind of clever, grated Sarmodel. *But he is still alive in there. What now?*

We finish. Somehow.

I approached the mountain of rubble. My silver sword had quite literally just gone up in smoke, and conventional weapons would be useless.

But I had again forgotten about the Lieutenant of the Hunt.

"Remove yourself, Professor Grave!" barked Bauterne. He moved against the stampede, running nimbly along what remained of the bridge. He knelt at the shattered edge, reloading his musket with a practiced hand. "This kill is mine!"

I squinted up at him. The Archangel's radiance almost completely obscured the man; I could barely stand to look at him in the Arcane spectrum. Beneath the flashing blades of Michael's wings, I caught ephemeral glimpses of the Lion's bright mane and golden talons. The Archangel was descending to claim his prize.

Sebastian—don't let him, Sarmodel whimpered.

"Soeur! Hold!" called Bauterne.

I was astounded to see the huge hound crouching in the shallows, growling at the rubble.

I was shocked to see the state of her. She had somehow managed to leap clear before the bridge fell, but her savage engagement with the Beast had left its mark. Her flanks were red and ragged where he had clawed at her, and one side of her face had been torn away, flapping loosely against her neck. Though she was not looking in my direction, I was not foolhardy enough to believe she had forgotten me; a step toward the Beast would be a fatal mistake.

I considered a dash for my Arcane supplies, up on the bank in my saddlebag, but Bauterne would have made the kill before I reached my horse. I even thought about some last-ditch Tartaric Words—witnesses be damned—and quickly concluded that the attempt would kill me in my current condition.

So all I could do was swear impotently as the lieutenant knelt and took aim with his singing musket, waiting for the Beast to reappear. It seemed I was to be granted the pleasure of watching the Almighty steal the food from my plate.

"No more, you bastard!" A new voice tore through the stillness.

A huge figure rose over Bauterne, followed by a mighty splash.

The Lieutenant of the Hunt swore, nearly falling from his perch on the edge of the bridge as he was suddenly drenched in a deluge of dirty suds. Above him stood Enneval the Younger, holding a now-empty laundry tub from the *lavoir* in the circle of his arms.

"You *dare*?!" Bauterne gave a crazed, almost hysterical shriek. He tugged frantically at the lock of his musket, knowing as he must that the powder was irretrievably soaked. There was something disconcerting about seeing the urbane, courtly huntsman so incensed.

The rubble heaved, and heaved again. Soeur barked sharply.

He is coming! sobbed Sarmodel.

I drew my hunting knife, hoping valiantly to give the Beast something more than indigestion to remember me by.

"No! *No!*" Bauterne screamed again, desperately trying to reload his weapon. The Archangel was all but flogging him from the ether.

With a roar, the Beast burst free. Chunks of masonry tumbled into the shallows as he shrugged and kicked his way out of the rubble. Bloodied and covered in dust, he was incandescent with rage. Bone crunched as he swatted Soeur to the ground. She did not stand up again.

But Avstamet was also diminished. It had cost him much to preserve his mortal vessel beneath the tons of stone. The monstrous, wolflike form was shedding its fur, and clear yellow plasma was beginning to drip from his flesh; pink, human skin showed beneath it. Avstamet was losing his grip on the material plane.

He paused only a moment there, trembling on the riverbed. His eyes marked us all with a vengeful glare—me, Sarmodel, the Archangel, Bauterne, Enneval and Antoine.

Antoine.

He was still there, lying in the shallows where the Beast had cast him aside. The monster dragged himself over to the helpless young nobleman.

"This one," the Beast said to me, his Latin derisive. "*This* is yours, as we agreed, is it not? Shall I show you what you have won with your bargain?"

The baron's son was paralyzed where he lay. His eyes were wide as he was brought face-to-face with Gévaudan's Beast for the second time. He raised a hand in terror as the monster loomed above him.

The Beast looked not at his victim, but directly at me as he closed his jaws, slick with blood and plasma, around Antoine's hand. The young man screamed as the monster's teeth sank slowly into his flesh.

But Avstamet had made his bargain; this sack of meat was not his to kill. With a bitter glare, he released Antoine's hand and kicked him away.

"There are your spoils. We shall see, in time, if you still wish to call this a victory," he said in Latin. "Draw up your Wards, Magician—and you, old Spirit; make a fortress of your impossible soul. It is mine already."

And then, snarling, the Beast fled. Up the wreckage of the bridge he bounded, and then along the road away from Saint-Julien as his bestial form began to deteriorate in earnest. He followed the wolves into the forest, leaving a trail of vital fluids.

I closed my eyes in profound relief.

Still alive in there, my love? I probed gently.

Barely, Sarmodel answered weakly. *Sebastian, we are hanging in the breeze. Get us out of here.*

He was right—the Beast was not the only danger we faced.

As though to emphasize the point, a scream of fury rose from the bridge.

"*Shit-eating Norman!*"[1] raged Bauterne. He threw his musket to the flagstones and stood up in a liquid, twisting movement, drawing the dragons from his belt. "I had him! ***I had him!***"

He faced Enneval the Younger with the pistols raised directly at his chest. I distinctly heard the twin clicks as the hammers dropped, a point-blank shot that should have blown apart the Norman's rib cage.

But Bauterne was dripping wet from black wig to black boots. The dragons did not even smoke as their sodden charges failed. Enneval glowered at him and dropped the wooden laundry tub at his feet.

"You shot my dogs, pig," said the Norman, spit flying from his mustache. Without another word, he turned his back on the fuming lieutenant and returned to his father's side on the riverbank.

Bauterne stood there trembling dangerously. The Archangel's blessing rippled off him in sheets, dissolving into nothing as the Lion departed. We had all been stymied, it seemed.

I took the opportunity to disappear.

Antoine had crawled far under the remaining arch of the bridge.

I spied him on a pebbly embankment. He sat in the shadows, shaking against the stone abutment, his eyes wide. His clothes were wet from the shallows and he held his wounded hand strangely, as though cradling a child. I feared the Beast's bite was the least of his injuries; his arm was almost certainly broken.

"Sebastian, I lost the pork," he said as I approached. We were

---

1. What he actually said was "Norman shit-sausage," though from his tone it was clear that he considered "Norman" the more offensive part of the phrase.

both breathing hard. "I saw it fall out of my saddlebag, but it's gone now."

"Never fear. I will find it, my friend. I promised you *petit salé* and mushrooms, did I not?" I replied. I knelt beside him. My heart was sprinting in my chest from my confrontation with the Beast, and my hands trembled. "I could make a braise if you like, and we could share one of Monsieur Comtois's fine cheeses afterward. What do you say? Here, let me look at your arm."

Antoine's eyes were glassy and his pupils wide. He stared at me as I examined his shoulder with my fingertips, following my face as though he had never seen me before.

"Shall we look for the horses?" he asked me, struggling weakly to rise. "You could whistle for them again. Will you teach that to me?"

"Later, later, my friend." I held him down gently. "Later, Antoine. Rest here for a moment. Can you move your fingers?"

This close to him, I could smell the fear and excitement of the chase still rising from his skin, and the sweetness of apples on his breath. I tried to ignore the low instincts[2] that thrilled at his closeness, at the feeling of the warm flesh beneath his wet clothes. At how he needed me.

He's fine. He's going to be fine.

The arm was not broken, thankfully. But Antoine's hard landing had dislocated his shoulder, and perhaps cracked a few ribs.

"Antoine, may I see your hand?" I asked.

"Yes, of course," he said courteously, as though I had asked to borrow his handkerchief. I gently took him by the wrist and he extended his arm. "Please, have a care. I cannot seem to—*whoreson!*"

With a single, rolling movement—and before he could protest—I

---

2. Unfortunately all mine, as much as I'd like to blame Sarmodel.

leaned in and rotated Antoine's shoulder outward. It snapped back into place with a dull pop. He looked at me, mouth open. His eyes shone with a naked mix of pain, gratitude and childlike betrayal.

"Is that better?" I asked softly.

He blinked, slowly flexing his fingers. Then he nodded and heaved in a long breath. "I think I would like you to take first watch tonight. I will cook if you like, but in truth I am not hungry."

"I will manage, Antoine."

I still had one hand on his shoulder and the other wrapped around his wrist; I could feel his chest rising with each breath and his wounded anima aching like liquid fire under my fingertips. He was still staring at me with his wide, black eyes.

"I saw you," he said. "I saw what you did. How did you—"

"You are confused, Antoine," I interrupted, feeling suddenly sick. "I don't know what you saw, but you are safe now."

"Sebastian . . . who are you?"

I don't know!

"No." I shook my head. "No, Antoine. Do not ask me. Not you."

"It's only . . . I'm . . . I am glad of you," he said finally.

I would say I could not help it, but I've lived enough lifetimes to know that's just a sweet lie we wrap around unpalatable acts. Temptation always offers a choice. He looked at me in silence, this young, wounded man, in need of my help and so completely at my mercy.

I raised my hand to his face, and to my shame, I kissed him.

XXVII

Antoine gave no reaction to the kiss. He simply blinked slowly at me with his wide, wide eyes.

Seconds later, shock carried him into unconsciousness. I quickly cleaned his bitten hand in the clear shallows and made a sling for his arm. Carefully, I wrapped him in blankets and tied him to the saddle; the last thing he needed was another fall.

Then I took the opportunity to get us away from the bedlam of Saint-Julien, as quickly as I could. I was shaken, for many reasons, and I needed somewhere quiet to be.

The Beast's trail had proved impossible to follow, so intermingled was it with the blood of wolves and dogs. Most of the hunters had already given up the pursuit, and instead devoted their time to recovering what was left of their packs and their wits.

I took us away into the trees.

I had no real destination. The mountains seemed to be pulling the autumnal forest up around them like a blanket, and I was grateful just to disappear into its golden gloaming.

Sarmodel was silent. His agitation was like a warren of ants in my head. His anima no longer dragged on mine, but he was in bad shape.

Sarmodel, this may not be the best time, I said gently, *but I think we're in trouble. The Beast is* ***Avstamet****. An Olympian.*

I was there, Sebastian.

Have we perhaps overcommitted on this one?

Overcommitted? We have struck an unimaginable fortune! he hissed. His voice was whisper-thin. *Must you always lose your nerve at first blood?*

First blood? Sarmodel, you can't be serious. We very nearly died! It's not just the Warfather we're up against—Michael is staking his claim as well! I'm going to need quite a few more silver bullets to contend with an Olympian ***and*** *an Archangel.*

Yes indeed. Perhaps next time you might even bring them to the fight, he snapped. His anima spasmed weakly.

I'm sorry, I said. *You're in pain. We can discuss it later.*

No, no—you are right, he conceded, uncharacteristically thoughtful. *And the fault is not yours alone. I misjudged our quarry. The signs were there that the Beast was something extraordinary, but I dismissed them. An Olympian, in the world again after so long. It barely seems possible.*

He remembers us, I remarked. *That's flattering, I suppose.*

To my relief, he managed to laugh. *Perhaps. But he is not Avstamet as I remember him. The Mars we knew—the Father of Rome—would not have stooped to this slaughter in the streets, not with his own hands. And why has he taken the form of the Beast?*

He is the Spirit of War, Sarmodel, and what is war if not slaughter in the streets, decorated with a banner? Rome was built on it, I said. I had attended the Holy City's soaring temples to Mars Quirinus, the Protector of the Populace. His shining greaves and sacred *ancilia* had defended the citizenry for centuries, at the price of constant warfare in the provinces. *Rome dressed him in the trappings of civilization—the city's faithful watchdog—but he was always the wolf underneath the uniform. Perhaps the Beast was there all along. I cannot believe I'm saying this, but I wish Livia were here. She knew the Olympians better than either of us.*

Sarmodel's swearing was murderous crimson in my mind. *Oh, indeed! Do not forget where her "assistance" got us last time. The half-breed would have greased her loins with half the barony before she thought to inquire after the Beast.*

I do not doubt it.

Sarmodel's assessment made me uneasy. Avstamet had changed; that much was obvious. He was cruel in a way he had not been in the past. Jehanne d'Arc would have been horrified to see her "Archangel" now; a general does not soil his hands with the blood of civilians. But mad? I could not believe it. The monster who terrorized the folk of Gévaudan was no desperate, crazed animal, whatever form he might wear. While the eight baronies, the king and the Church emptied their coffers to hunt him down, he danced around them all with impunity. There was some greater game we were not seeing.

Antoine came back to himself as we climbed higher into the foothills.

"Sebastian, I'm sorry, but I must rest," he said. "I am nigh frozen to death, and I cannot stop my eyes from closing."

"Of course, my friend."

I had barely looked at my young companion since leaving Saint-Julien. The kiss seemed unreal, a moment in a dream that I had left beneath the bridge. I dared to hope Antoine would not remember it, and yet I could not shake it from my mind.

In truth, I was disgusted with myself. I'd let Sarmodel's

suggestions get the better of me, and pushed myself on Antoine in his state of shock.

I found us a campsite out of the way, in the shelter of a leaning maple. Its fallen leaves made a soft nest for Antoine's bedroll. He was soon asleep next to a snapping fire of pine branches.

I cooked but did not eat. I took extra time to soothe our horses and see to their care; the poor animals had earned it after the day's events. I cleaned and oiled our tack, and took stock of the supplies we had purchased at Saint-Julien's ill-fated market. Most had survived, but there were things we had lost in the chase. I made careful count.

Pointless busywork, all of it.

I could not summon the stillness to meditate, so when there were no more distractions to be found, I sat beneath an opening in the forest canopy and searched for comfort in the eternal, sparkling firmament.

Vain Cassiopeia still followed her endless circle around the pole star, chained to her throne. Aquarius and Pegasus would, as ever, fall from view with the last autumn leaves. Ominously, Orion the Hunter and his hounds were beginning their winter ascent, fast on the heels of the great monster Cetus.

"You do not sleep." Antoine's quiet words startled me.

He came to sit beside me. He was still wrapped in a blanket, with his injured arm held close to his chest in the sling. In his other hand, he held a flask of wine.

"I thought it prudent to stand watch tonight," I replied. I did not meet his eyes.

"That isn't what I meant. You do not sleep—ever—do you? Not like other men do." He sipped the wine and I could feel him watching me in the silence. "How is that possible? You do not sleep, or drink, or pray. There are so many things about you . . ."

His words trailed away and I closed my eyes. I knew what was to come.

"I saw you," he said finally. "Today, with the Beast. You *spoke* to it. And what you did—that was not science, or secrets of the smith's craft, or whatever clever flummery you would claim."

"No."

"Then what in the Lord's name—"

"Antoine, I think it might be better for us to part company," I interrupted, all but choking on the words. "I should have left you in Père Arnaud's care. You are injured, and the path will grow only more dangerous from here. Whatever you believe you saw—and your very worst suspicions are true—will be called for again, and always with consequences.[1] You will not be spared them."

He was silent for a long moment, his eyes relentless.

"Why do I feel that you know the Beast of Gévaudan better than any of us, Sebastian Grave? What did he say to you? You did not join this hunt for the bounty, did you?" he demanded.

"Antoine, these questions will do you no good. You will not like the answers." I turned to look at him. "Please. Rest now, and I will take you back to the château tomorrow."

"I am not a child, Sebastian. And I will not return to the château while the Beast continues to slaughter our people—in open daylight, no less. My father puts his faith in the bishop and the Normans—and that cock, Bauterne—but they will not protect us from the creature we saw today. They cannot. I know that for certain now."

---

1. I was referring to real-world consequences like thumbscrews and the guillotine, not mystical blowback from "ye olde laws of magick." I am not a big believer in karma, though on revisiting these notes, I may reassess that stance.

"And you believe me a more promising prospect? An interloper from a foreign land?"

"Why not? You asked me why I intervened on your behalf, all those months ago, and this is the truth of it. I could tell, even then, that you were something we have never seen, and you have proven me right. The way you think, the way you see things that others miss. You are our best hope, surely you see that."

I shook my head. "I am nobody's savior, Antoine. You are correct: I am here for my own reasons. I have known the creature you call the Beast for a very, very long time. You wish to know what he said to me? He asked me what I am. And I had no answer, Antoine, not for him and not for you. All of this—the hunt, the manners, the genial professor from Cyprus—is a sham. I am not your best hope; I will kill the Beast and take his power for my own, using any means, and then I will leave," I told him.

And then I will move on, as ever, and find the next Contract, the next patron, and the next and the next . . .

"And the people of Gévaudan will still owe you their lives," he replied.

"Ha! The people of Gévaudan will call me ungodly and degenerate—and worse—and they will be right. Do you believe your father or the bishop would countenance my presence if they had seen what you saw today? The Church would burn me alongside the Beast."

"Why should that concern me? What has the *Church* done for us here in Ocerne?" Antoine demanded angrily. "The Bishop of Mende squats like a toad over the château, while his cat's-paws get their hooks into Ocerne's revenues and ledgers. His family in Mende have had their eyes on our lands for decades, and he has not come all this way in person just to oversee a wolf hunt. I see what is happening, even if my father does not. Your ways may be . . . irregular, and your reasons are your own to keep, but I know you are a decent man. I would sell you the barony for a tin livre before I trusted Bishop Fontaine to deliver us."

"No, Antoine. You cannot in honesty call me a decent man after what happened today, my friend." I turned back to the stars, unable to hold his gaze. "I'm sorry, Antoine, for . . . for what I did. To you. I took advantage of you when you needed me. I am ashamed."

He studied me in silence again, and I felt I would catch fire if he continued to stare at me. "No, Sebastian. I don't want that," he said finally. "Your sorrow, or your shame. And I don't want to leave."

"You—Antoine, you are impossible! Have you no fear?"

"Of you?" he said. His fingertips cupped my chin, and he gently turned my face back toward him. "Yes. From the first."

The second kiss was his, as the first had been mine.

He pressed his lips to mine with simple, candid affection. I felt his stubble against my skin and tasted the wine in his mouth. He was sure and tender, as though I were the one in need of reassurance.

It lasted only a moment. We looked at each other, our faces almost touching, the mist of our breath mingling between us. I started to pull away, feeling how near I was stepping to disaster.

"Antoine, I am . . ."

I am not who you think I am, I wanted to say. *I am a witch. I am a monster, a murderer. I am an abomination older than the House of Avenel, older than France.*

He silenced me with another kiss, more forceful this time. "I don't care," he murmured against my lips. He pulled me closer. "Don't you see? You are a wonder. More—you are a miracle, when we need one most. I know you have secrets. Just do not send me away. Stay with me." I felt his smile as he kissed me again. "Dare to know."

I forgot the stars above me and the centuries behind. I forgot the Beast and the hunt and the Host of the Archangel, all of them somewhere, somewhere. But not here, not now.

We left our clothes on the forest floor and filled the shelter under the maple tree with our warmth. He pressed his hands and his face against my skin in wonder, making me gasp with the hot shock of his tongue on my throat. He shivered as I took him in my hand, and he twisted his fingers in my hair.

There was no more talk that night. Antoine was afire with hunger and delight. The day's events—the nearness of death, perhaps—made us reckless and daring, and Antoine devoured every pleasure I could offer him. Between times we slept, wrapped in each other beneath the blankets. We kissed and made love and slumbered, and awoke to begin again.

And all the while Sarmodel coiled around us, drinking our desire like wine and sighing with a hundred mouths.

XXVIII

Saint-Julien-by-the-Stream
1785

"Sir, wake up," I called over my shoulder, bringing my horse to a halt. I pointed to a forested rise in the distance, where Château d'Ocerne shone like a crown of ivory and glass in the morning sun. Below it on the valley floor, a cluster of rooftops dozed under a blanket of chimney smoke. "Look, sir. Château d'Ocerne—and Saint-Julien. We have arrived."

Jacques sat up briefly in the wagon behind me and gave a half-hearted smile.

"You seem less than excited, sir," I remarked.

I could not blame him; I wasn't thrilled to be back in Gévaudan either.

At least Jacques was in reasonably good health again, all things considered. With a steady diet of living hearts, we had kept the monster within him at bay, but it was certainly not a permanent solution.

"I am sorry, Professor," Jacques said. "You have brought me

this far and I am grateful. But I cannot be a danger to my family—are you certain this acquaintance of yours can help me?"

"I am. She is an associate of Mademoiselle Cecile, and I can care for you in the meantime. You must only promise to tell me if that voice in your head grows too insistent. It is not much farther—we are almost there."

Abandoned fields and blackened ruins were bleak markers on the road to Saint-Julien. The ragged homesteads of the farmers—those who remained—spoke of profound poverty. Many were burning their own fences for warmth. Jacques told me that most of the farms had been torched during the Red Winter and then purchased for a handful of crumbs by the wealthy mercantile families of Mende, most notably the Fontaines.

"The bishop's family shares his ambition, though not his vow of poverty," Jacques said darkly.

It was fitting that the first Gévaudanais we met were in a funeral procession. As we neared the crossroads to Saint-Julien, we came across a small group of mourners. Beyond them was a huddle of brick buildings and animal pens; a weather-beaten shingle identified it as Saint-Julien's piggery. Pallbearers emerged from the homestead bearing a cloth-bound figure on a pallet. The first corpse was followed shortly by a second and then a third, much smaller than the others.

I bowed my head respectfully as we passed them, close enough to overhear a whispered conversation.

". . . barely a handful of sows left," said one man to his neighbor. "They ate him, and the wife and the boy, and then they ate *each other . . .*"

Didn't I tell you it would be awful here? said Sarmodel. *Didn't I tell you?*

I didn't respond. We took the southern road toward Saint-Julien.

Little wonder there was talk of treasonous discontent in France.

Twenty years had passed since last I was in Saint-Julien-by-the-Stream. They were years I had spent nursing my injuries—both visible and invisible. Years I had spent trying to forget the Red Winter.

And years of utter misery for the people of Ocerne, it seemed.

Saint-Julien had deteriorated noticeably. It looked smaller to me. There was less movement—less life in general. The people had a terrible sameness to them; a likeness born of hollow eyes and thin cheeks. They were strangely colorless, in spite of their cosmetics and various crude vanities. Their clothing was dun and their skin gray. More than anything, they looked hungry.

Their lot had improved little since the days of the Red Winter, though their circumstances were still far better than those of their countrymen in the farmlands.

We arrived by the southern road, passing by the church and its little cemetery. There were a number of fresh graves and a few pits waiting to be filled—no doubt by the pig farmer and his family, following close behind us. I could hear the bite-and-scrape of the gravedigger's shovel, performing its grim duty somewhere out of sight. A man's ghost stalked the street ahead of us in his waistcoat, his immaterial musket raised—undoubtedly one of the many hunters who had died here. I decided not to disturb him.

Jacques raised the hood of his cloak when we arrived, concealing his face from the townsfolk.

"Far better that I am not seen," he said in response to my

questioning glance. "There is little goodwill for Gévaudan's noble families of late. I would rather avoid trouble."

"As you will, sir. You have nothing to fear, in any case; you would scarcely be recognized in your current condition."

"A small blessing."

"Now, you said we might visit Mademoiselle Cecile, did you not? Where might I find her?"

Jacques stiffened. "Professor, what exactly do you hope to gain from visiting our *sage-femme*?"

"Information. She may be able to help me find a cure for you, in fact."

Jacques wanted to protest, I could tell, but there was no reasonable objection he could make. "Very well. That way, toward the river."

We passed through the busy village square. My gaze alighted on the places I had so recently described to my young companion. The stalls. The charming fountain. The gallows, now adorned with a neat quartet of hanging bodies and a well-fed little community of coraxes. The gated laneway where the Beast had made his first kill of that horrific market day. And behind it all, the high road leading up the forested mountain to beautiful Château d'Ocerne.

A group of people were gathered by a stand of books, sniggering at some sort of pamphlet. As we approached, a scuffle erupted among two of the men, encouraged by catcalls from the rest. To my horror, the smaller man threw his opponent to the ground and began stomping on his face, his eyes wild and saliva flying from his mouth. Far from intervening, the others gathered around, laughing and applauding; I realized they were all quite drunk.

In the melee, one of the pamphlets landed on the ground by the wagon; Jacques passed it up to me wordlessly. It was rough in texture and cheaply produced, but it made its point eloquently. It was a pornographic political cartoon, depicting the queen, Marie

Antoinette, in her private chambers. Her much-lampooned hair towered ridiculously overhead, while she exposed her vulva and invited a procession of courtiers to "pledge their allegiance."

"Come, Professor," said Jacques. "I do not wish to loiter here."

"No indeed." I discarded the lurid cartoon, disturbed in a way I could not quite define. "Let us conclude our business and be gone."

It did not take us long to find the midwife's house.

Cecile the *sage-femme* had significantly improved her circumstances, if not her station. Her home was a little clay-brick cottage on the edge of town, with its back to the river. She was still far from the homes of the other villagers, however, tucked in between a bulrush thicket and an old barn, where visitors could come and go with discretion. I counted more than a few potent reagents among the flowers of her sweet front garden—monkshood, yarrow, poppy and pennyroyal.

Really, Sebastian? asked my Guest. *The hedge-witch? Let us hope her temper has improved since the last time.*

If it has not, we have lost nothing. And if it has, she may be able to save us a lot of time.

As you like, he shrugged.

I dismounted and tied my horse to a post by the door. Jacques climbed out of the cart, rising to his feet with some effort.

I raised my hand to knock on the door, but it opened—seemingly of its own accord—before I had the chance.

"Mademoiselle?"

A pleasant smell of chamomile, licorice and warm bread drifted from the small parlor inside the door. I entered hesitantly, noting the exquisitely Warded metal mirror hanging on the wall opposite; it appeared that Cecile had upgraded her practice significantly since our last meeting.

I followed the gentle clink of crockery to the kitchen.

She had her back to us. Her long blond hair swayed as she arranged a tea set on a tray. Her stays and pinafore were a deep, burned yellow, likely dyed with madder root. Warm light filled the room from the open window and glittering motes floated through the air. A jar of honey on the sill glowed such that it seemed to be nothing less than liquid sunshine. From the ceiling hung bunches of drying herbs and wildflowers. A russet fox dozed on the floor, soaking up the sunbeam next to a very plump white rat. Through the window I glimpsed the herbalist's private garden, filled with nodding flowers and the lazy humming of bees. I found myself smiling, my eyes half closed, as I inhaled the smell of the bread, a fresh baton rolled in poppy and thyme. Jacques gave a gentle sigh beside me.

"I had a feeling," said Cecile, her voice so rich it was almost a melody, "that I should expect important guests." She remained facing away from us, her hands occupied in their dance of counting pastries and turning cups.

Oh a "feeling" indeed, scoffed Sarmodel. *Are we to believe you didn't have every roach and pigeon in town reporting back to you?*

Cecile ignored him. "Come, you must be hungry." Her white-blond hair rippling in the light, she began to slice the bread. "You have traveled such a long way."

"We . . . have indeed . . ." My smile grew as I saw the steam rising from the loaf. In the light, it was golden and soft and *golden.*

Sebastian? What is the matter with—

"Sweet," murmured Jacques beside me. "Honey sweet. Apple sweet. Golden sweet."

"Yes truly, young sir," Cecile said (sang). "I have honey rolls and apple tart. Follow me outside; my daughter has set the table under the willow. She has been looking forward to seeing you again." Still she did not turn around.

I really *was* hungry, and so very tired after our long journey, just as Cecile had said.

"Yes—Wait, no!" I snapped, shaking my head. "Stop that!" I screwed up my face and quickly bit the tender pad of my thumb, using the pain as an anchor for my senses. The soft world inside the witch's kitchen began to sharpen back into focus.

*What? A **trap**!* Sarmodel was shrill in his outrage (which I suspect was somewhat confected). *You dare, witch?! Sebastian! Attack!*

Now that I was awake to it, Cecile's enchantment was plain to see. The warm light, the inviting scents and even the clinking of her tea set—each was a thread in the golden cable she was looping around us. As it fell away, the kitchen resumed its natural aspect. It was still warm and comfortable, but no longer suffused with her dreaming compulsion; still charming, but no longer *charmed.*

Cecile froze momentarily as she felt me slip free. The red fox was suddenly on its feet, fixing me with a calm stare. Its eyes were completely white. Behind its benign Mundane façade, a hook-nosed, wrinkled creature[1] regarded me with suspicion.

Then the hedge-witch turned to face me, the tray in her hands. "Forgive me, Professor," she said simply. Her voice was no longer musical, but it was pleasant enough. "You can understand some caution on my part after our last encounter, yes?"

I found I could not reply immediately.

Even without Arcane help, Cecile was unexpectedly lovely. The ragged, pimply young woman I remembered had blossomed into something of a beauty. The lack of artifice which had made

---

1. A Contracted canult, a very professional and exceedingly useful choice of familiar.

her seem unkempt as a girl now bestowed her with a natural grace. It was clear she cared nothing for the bouffant coiffures and lily-white faces to which the other village women so aspired. She let her hair fall in a wild cascade of sea-foam around her face and down her back. Her skin was tanned from her days outdoors, with freckles sprinkled across her cheeks and the soft ridges of her collarbone. With clear gray eyes and a careful smile on her lips, she was far from the grubby, hysterical creature who had so vexed me twenty years ago.

And there, positioned perfectly in the cleft of her bosom, was the hagstone. It throbbed like a second heart.

I realized I was staring, at risk of falling under a very different sort of spell.

"No indeed!" I blustered. "Well, yes. Perhaps."

"Then please, follow me," she said. She turned to leave through the back doorway, into the garden. "And it may be better not to wake the young lord, if we are to discuss business. Don't you agree?"

Jacques was leaning dreamily back against the wall, his eyes following the glowing motes that drifted through the sunbeam. He was smiling, his eyes half closed, more peaceful than I had seen him in our short time together.

"Sir, would you care to join us for tea?" I asked gently.

"Yes please, Professor," he said immediately. "May I also have something sweet?"

Cecile gave a shrug and a half smile.

"Very well," I conceded. "But if he comes to any harm, there will be consequences."

Cecile laughed. It was a joyous, raucous sound, heedless of propriety and with a sharp edge of mockery. "I shan't blacken his eye or club him in the cullions, if that's what you mean." She shook her head and led us outside, still laughing.

XXIX

The *sage-femme*'s garden was larger than I expected, a perfect circle surrounded by a low stone wall. The garden beds, positively foaming over with flowers, encircled a clover lawn. Its centerpiece was a wide, circular pool, ringed with flagstones and marigolds but otherwise unadorned. At the far end of the garden, a gate led out to a narrow path through the bulrushes, and beyond them no doubt to the river. A black goat—entirely Mundane as far as I could tell—was secured to a peg in the ground, happily grazing.

Sarmodel flinched as though he had been stung. *By the Rift, look at these Wards! What merry devils is she raising in here?*

I blinked my way through the Arcane spectrum. *Almighty God.*

Cecile's garden was an immaculately configured Circle. We were essentially stepping into her workroom—a frame for her to set her Wards upon.

And set them she had. I counted no less than three Majestic Vaults, along with a dizzying succession of Prevaricating Clauses. There were others, hidden deeper, which I suspected were a Sudden

Jaw and perhaps a Flower of Hands. Cecile was not taking any chances with her Arcane guests, it seemed.[2]

*Do not touch **anything**,* I warned Sarmodel.

An old willow cast its shade by the eastern edge of the lawn. Beneath its canopy, a young woman smoothed a green cloth over a three-legged round table. The twisted trunk of the willow was set with so many melted candles that it seemed partly made of wax itself. By night, this is where Cecile would ply her trade as fortune teller, soothsayer and matchmaker.

"Come, Lorette," said Cecile. "We have important guests, as I expected."

Lorette!

Suddenly much about Jacques's strange behavior was explained.

So, this is she . . . "darling" Lorette.

"Do you need the cards, Mama?" called the girl over her shoulder. Lorette seemed about the same age as Jacques and she was blond like Cecile, though it was a warmer, caramel hue. Her skin, like the hedge-witch's, was brushed golden by the sun. Her dress was simple and fit her poorly, but it was far from shabby. The pinafore was a dusty shade of pink, crisscrossed around the hem with grass stains.

"No, my sweet. These gentlemen are not here for a reading."

Lorette turned to greet us and stopped dead. She looked suddenly as though she were standing in a fire.

"I'd like you to keep company with young Lord Ocerne for a time—you are well enough acquainted," Cecile went on. "I fear the

---

2. I had a similar framing arrangement inlaid in steel in the floor of my basement back in Corvano, though without the entire Arsenal of Tartarus hanging over it.

professor is going to scold me." There was light ridicule in her tone. Sarmodel began to simmer in the back of my mind.

"But—Mama!" Lorette's face flushed red and her hands twisted in her skirts. She looked first at me, and then at the dazed Jacques. Then she adjusted her cloth cap and lowered her eyes to curtsy, though not without a glint of defiance. "Of course. My lord Ocerne, it has been too long since we saw you in the village," she said, with painful formality.

Cecile placed the tray on the table and handed Jacques a sticky roll glazed with honey. "Something sweet, as promised. Now go."

"Thank you," said Jacques, like a child practicing his manners. "It is nice to see you, Lorette." The herbalist's daughter stiffened as he took her by the hand.

"Come, my lord," said the witch's daughter. "There's work enough for us both."

I approached the table cautiously, still not quite ready to accept Cecile's hospitality—certainly not here at her oracle's tripod, standing within her ferociously Warded Circle. Lorette and Jacques crossed the lawn, hand in hand, as Cecile poured the tea.

"Oh, come—sit down," she said, sweeping her long hair back behind her shoulders. "I apologize for the charm; I am necessarily careful about visitors. Do you think I'd kill you in my own home—and with *him* sitting on your shoulders? Here." She held out her right hand, the Sigil of Amity glowing golden on her palm.

*Oh—**now** a truce!* said Sarmodel. *Twenty years too late, I think!*

Cecile looked up at him and then back to me, her hand still extended. "Please, Professor. I am not the witless craven I once was. We have things to discuss, and I didn't make all this food for myself."

"No. I suppose you didn't." Slowly, I reached forward and

clasped her hand. The golden fire pulsed between her skin and mine, writing the sigil on my palm.

We sat down. Cecile covered a slice of bread with pale butter and handed it to me. I devoured it in seconds.

Tell me, what happened to your "boon companion," hedge-witch? asked Sarmodel, with lavish scorn.

Cecile laughed her magnificent, crowing laugh. "He did in fact try to kill me in my sleep, as you predicted. Whether he would have mounted my corpse . . . well." She shrugged and laughed again.

I could feel Sarmodel's surprise; if he had expected hostility, he was to be disappointed. Cecile was changed indeed. *Well. A near miss, then, and a lesson learned. I am almost glad.*

"One of many lessons I've learned since you were last in Gévaudan." She made a circular motion that encompassed her charming cottage and walled garden, along with their formidable Arcane defenses. "I no longer consort with unbound Spirits. Or the pastor, for that matter."

"Good principles. They have served you well," I remarked. For all of her tenuous social status, Cecile was certainly living comfortably—far more so than most of her neighbors.

"Saint-Julien has been kind to me," she replied. "And there are still those with wealth and power who value the humble services of a *sage-femme.* Along with her discretion."

"I am pleased for you—and impressed." Cecile had attracted patronage both otherworldly and Mundane, which was no small accomplishment in this era of religious rule.

We were interrupted by a snatch of song, floating across from where Lorette and Jacques were kneeling by a bed of mullein. The girl had lost some of her shyness and was singing gently, showing Jacques how to pick the delicate rosettes of leaves. He followed Lorette's movements like her shadow and she touched his hand fondly. Even without her obvious discomfort, that single gesture revealed everything about how "well-acquainted" Jacques and Lorette really were. Beside them, the fox watched with its white eyes, the fat rat perched on its head.

Darling Lorette. The witch's daughter.

I might indeed have believed that Lorette was Cecile's daughter. There was some passing resemblance to the blond herbalist of Saint-Julien.

But Cecile was, among many other things, a midwife. I suspected that at least one child she had brought into the world had not gone home with its mother.

"Lorette is a lovely girl," I remarked, "and a keen student, it seems. You must be proud of her. Will she follow after you?"

"I hope so. She has natural talent as a midwife. She's stopped death at the doorway of many a laboring woman," replied Cecile. "And she has been . . . a great gift to me."

"One among many," I remarked, pointing to the hagstone, throbbing on its cord around her neck.

Cecile's eyes were deep with thought. She wrapped a hand around the stone. "That's why you're here, isn't it? Your business with Lady Dayane—that's what this is all about."

Dayane.

My eyes were drawn to the pool in the center of the garden.

I had been avoiding the thought of her. Of all the unfinished business in Gévaudan, my dealings with Dayane troubled me most. It seemed almost like a dream now.

In many ways it had *been* a dream.

Petrichor. The curious flick of a doe's ear. White hands, white breasts, a soft white abdomen with no navel. Footsteps on the surface of the pond, and the emerald fronds of mare's tail beneath, waving, waving . . .

"Will you treat with her again on my behalf?"

Cecile's eyes narrowed. "Professor, I can guess why you are here—the young lord fair reeks of sickness. But I will not treat with my lady for you. Not this time."

"Then I have no choice but to go uninvited. I can find the way by myself."

"I would ask you to reconsider," she replied, with forced patience. "Professor, you think you know best, but hear me when I say there are things happening in Gévaudan that you cannot possibly understand."

"Then tell me, please! What is happening here? I have seldom seen such a state of misery—the Beast is certainly not responsible for all of it."

She heaved a deep breath, looking at the golden sigil on her palm. "I'm not sure how much the young lord has told you, but there's an easy word for it: 'trouble.' So many different sorts, it's hard to tell where one ill gives way to the next."

"Go on." I almost swilled my entire cup of tea. It was a blend of chamomile, rose and licorice, with a touch of honey, and it was absolutely delicious.

"I believe the Red Winter has returned to claim Gévaudan properly. Now, as then, my neighbors are being slaughtered at night, in the forests and byways. I am hunted in my dreams by the wolf with the hands of a man. The beasts of the field and the fold become wilder and more savage with every generation—many have become ungovernable, or worse. It is like a sickness that has begun to spread. I believe it's *bleeding out* into the villagers, do you understand? There is an anger I have never seen before—neighbors suddenly turned into enemies, and violence in so many homes."

I began to interrupt, but she raised a hand. "There's more. The lord of Château d'Ocerne—well, I think you'll find him a changed man. Your young charge did well to hide his face here in Saint-Julien. His father has few friends here now."

"Antoine? But *why*?" It was not a surprise to hear that Antoine had changed; Jacques's account of his father had confirmed as much. But it unsettled me to think the charming young man I had known—and yes, loved—was now so poorly regarded.

"In part, because the people are hungry. They feed the cow and must watch their children starve as the cream goes to the nobles and the meat to the Church. But it's not just about the price of bread anymore—villagers are being murdered and the baron is doing nothing to stop it. The people . . ." Cecile stopped, glancing at Lorette and Jacques.

"Oh dear," I said. I have witnessed the life cycle of oppressive regimes countless times; every one starts and finishes with talk of "the people." "Go on, please."

She leaned forward and spoke in softer tones. "The people are getting desperate, and their rage is aimed squarely at the nobility. There are gatherings in cellars and barns at night, where the young and the loud talk about things like 'freedom' and 'equality.'" Cecile took another sweet roll from the table, her eyes distant. "It worries me, more than a little. Lorette has been swept up in it—they see in her a leader, and a pretty face to rally hot-blooded young men to their cause. The young lord among them."

"And here is the scandal, at last!" I said. I almost laughed; there was something deliciously absurd about the prospect. "Jacques Avenel d'Ocerne sneaks out at night to join the local malcontents in airing their grievances against his father."

"Not openly, not yet. He attends in secret, as many do, with the sense to keep his face covered. I have kept my distance from the whole tinderbox. Secret nighttime meetings seldom bode well for women like me—I'm sure you would agree."

"'Trouble' is the word. You had the right of it." It seemed Jacques's difficult relationship with his father had very deep roots. It would be a great embarrassment to Antoine to have his heir sympathizing with the peasants who furnished their lifestyle.

Cecile poured more tea for me. "Professor, there are no coincidences. You say the Beast is not the cause of Gévaudan's troubles, but I see his hand everywhere. The Red Winter was the beginning of it all." She looked again at her daughter. "I don't need the cards to tell me where this is all headed."

War, said Sarmodel. *Naturally.*

"All the more reason for me to take Jacques to Lady Dayane—she may be the only one who can help us. What aren't you telling me?"

Cecile seemed troubled—scared, even—as she wrapped her hand once again around the hagstone. "I can say no more."

"Cannot or will not? Please, you know how important it is," I insisted.

Her brow creased, showing a flash of the embittered young woman she had once been. "Important for whom? Professor, I am not a fool. You and your *companion* did not come to save Gévaudan during the Red Winter. You came here to take the Beast's power for yourselves. Why should I trust you any more than him?"

Because we are not—yet—the ones devouring your neighbors, witch, said Sarmodel. *And what are* ***you*** *doing, you and your lady? What masterful strategy against the Beast have you concocted in consultation with your patron?*

Cecile bit her lip, and I was surprised to see tears in her eyes. "It is time for you to be on your way, I think."

"Cecile, *why*? Why won't you help me?"

Her tears brimmed over, and she wiped them angrily from

her face. "Because I cannot! There, you have the truth! My lady no longer answers when I call."

"Is she . . . ?"

"No, she is not gone. I feel her still, here." She held up the hagstone. "But she cannot or will not speak to me, not these past several years. Please, Professor, there are things you don't know. Do not seek her out again, I beg you. Do not take the young lord to her. My lady has not been the same since the Red Winter."

"What do you mean? Why?"

"Because you betrayed her, Professor. And I don't know how, but I fear that is the root of it all—the young lord's illness, the madness, the misery, all of it. The bargain you struck has been *broken*, and now we are all paying the price."

ADDENDUM:

On Summoning Clauneck

Rouen, France
1431

How would you choose the perfect bait for an avaricious, duplicitous grub like Clauneck? She's attracted to anima that is fairly basic, easily excited by shiny things and without much willpower. Think carefully.

It's a trick question, of course; that's essentially all of you.

Picture me, then, theoretically spoiled for choice as I hunt in the benighted alleyways of Rouen. But it's not as easy as I'd hoped. The nun's habit has been a lightning rod for almost every cock in town,[1] *but Clauneck prefers females, which is a slightly more difficult brief in the 1400s. Women are seldom outside on their own unless they're prostitutes, and tonight all of* **them** *are busy.*[2]

So you can imagine my delight when I see, in the light of a baker's window, the face of the perfect young woman. She's blond and pretty under her chaperon, with round cheeks and a sweet button nose. Her

---

1. I was as surprised as you are.

2. I try not to prey on prostitutes in any case. Call it professional courtesy.

eyes are faraway and there's a sleepy smile on her face as she kneads the dough in the hour before dawn.

Is she thinking of the husband she's left at home, warming the bedbugs? Will she return to him at noon with a fresh, knotted loaf in her apron? Or is she still unplucked? Is she betrothed to a handsome young miller somewhere, who aches to wipe the flour from her cheek with his hand? Is her mind full of plans for her wedding and the sticky mysteries of the first night?

Is there any point in speculating?

The Circle was perfect. Each ideogram was sharply drawn in white wax onto the floorboards, and the Abject geometry between them was as crisp as the facets in a jewel. Livia could not begrudge the master his due; his Arcane practice was impeccable.

The room at the inn had been stripped of its lean comforts. The bed was tipped on its end to make space, and the corpse of the former occupant lay discarded in a corner. With the shutters closed and the presence of the old one hanging like tar fumes, the room seemed especially, oppressively dark.

In the center of the ring stood the girl. She was flushed and staring. She did not protest as the beautiful red-haired woman slowly began to undress her.

"You are exquisite, Anna," whispered Livia, close to her ear. "You are beauty itself. And now we are alone." The naked succubus kissed the girl's throat and unbuttoned the back of her dress. "I can scarcely believe I have you to myself. Can you imagine how I want you?"

Anna's hands and face were still dusted with flour. Her hood and apron lay on the floor of the bakery, back where the magnificent stranger had come in suddenly from the night and begun her seduction. The baker, furious at the oven full of burned bread, would find the garments later and begin to fear for his young assistant.

Barely able to speak, the girl shook her head. Her eyes were distant, not blind so much as saturated with Livia's presence. "Tell me—oh, please."

Livia's whispers floated from her lips like moths. The succubus let the girl's dress and chemise fall to the ground, and kissed her again. "Anna, I must have you." Her breath was hot against Anna's white neck as she caressed her breasts. "Do you want me to?"

"Yes," she breathed, her eyes half closed.

In the shadows, Sebastian was pleased, though he was trying not to show it. He had thankfully changed his clothes; the corpse in the corner was now wearing his Eastern garb.

Watch yourself, half-breed. She is not for you, warned the old one.

"Indeed. Livia, do not get carried away," added the master.

The succubus gave them a cool glance. She kissed Anna one final time. "I have a gift for you, my dearest. A fancy for our bower, before we make it our own."

"Oh, but you are *lovely,*" sighed the girl. She had begun to slide one hand into the hollow between her legs, unthinking. "I feel I have known you such a long time."

Livia stepped carefully outside the Circle. Her glamers rippled like water as they crossed the barrier. "We were in love when the world was young, Anna." She laughed enchantingly, but she looked only at her master. "And we will be in love when the last sun sets."

"Yes." Anna's eyes were shining. "Always and always."

Sebastian began to mutter, his words inaudible. He cast something into the Circle: a coin that flickered merrily as it spun, in spite of the dim light. It clinked loudly as it hit the wooden floor.

"Take it, my love," purred Livia, safely outside the Circle. "It is yours."

"Oh, Lord! Is it gold?!" Anna stooped to collect the coin. The metal was bright, as though freshly minted, but the surface had been gouged with a circle of strange letters. Livia could not see it—did not want to see it—but she knew it was identical to the Circle of sigils on the floor. A Contract. "I can't—this cannot be for me!"

"But it is, Anna," replied the succubus from the shadows. The master's low words were cycling faster now. The Circle kindled, gathering Arcane power like static. "I am buying you, my precious poppet," she said, with another playful laugh. "That little piece of gold, for all of you. Does that sound fair?"

"You are teasing me!" Anna laughed as well, her eyes never leaving the coin in her palm. "You could have me for half a denier, or nothing at all, if you like. Come, where have you gone? Will you . . . oh it is *gold* . . . *beautiful* . . . will you kiss me again?"

"All of you for the price of a gold coin? Truly?" Livia insisted gently. "I will not take you unwilling, my darling."

"Yes, oh yes," breathed Anna, enraptured. "Anything. It shines."

"Done, then," sighed Livia, folding her arms.

Done! crowed the old one.

"And done!" came a terrible third voice, speaking from Anna's mouth. The girl clapped her hands over her face and began to scream.

In Livia's Arcane sight, something crawled into the world, wriggling up inside the girl like a rat into a carcass. Anna's anima blazed in silent agony as it was pulled from her living flesh and devoured by the creeping thing. It lasted only a few moments.

Then the naked girl was silent. She trembled in the center of the Circle, hunched over and breathing heavily.

Clauneck! called the old one. *Attend!*

The girl straightened slowly to look at them. Livia grimaced, and even the master seemed shaken.

Anna's lovely face was changed. In the center of her forehead, like a brand, was embedded the gold coin. From its rim, a slow line of blood lengthened toward the tip of her sweet button nose. Her eyes glittered with shining motes, like flecks of precious metal.

Her mouth fell open. "Gold," she said. "I see it, master!" Her lips did not move when she spoke; the voice bubbled up from her throat like an echo in a well. Her sparkling eyes flicked back and forth, searching and searching. They found Livia and stopped.

Anna gasped low in her chest.

"*Bitch*,"[3] came the underwater voice.

"*Salve*, Clauneck. You are revolting, as ever," replied Livia, in Latin.

"Clauneck, you are bound by the Contract I have written," said the master. "It is graven into your very flesh.[4] Heed me."

---

3. What she actually said was "*c'fauch*," which is a portmanteau of the Tartaric terms for "tool" (*c'fant*) and "slave" (*auch*). You may see it politely translated elsewhere as "pet," but there's a bit more color to it than that.

4. Witness Sebastian's unhealthy penchant for Shackling his pets. Once a Contract has been accepted, a physical iteration is not strictly necessary. Such objects are known as Shackles, and they usually signify an insulting lack of trust (entirely warranted in Clauneck's case).

The master produced another florin and held it up. "This gold was used to purchase something very important. You will help me follow it to its source."

"I can. I will." She snatched the coin from the air as he flicked it into the Circle. She raised it to her open lips with a sound between a sigh and a hiss.

"Gold!" The coin disappeared into her mouth and she closed her eyes in rapture. "Ah me . . . Riches . . ."

The master waited.

"Well?"

Anna's naked abdomen bulged and rippled strangely, but she did not make a sound.

The minutes marched on.

What is taking so long? demanded the old one.

"Clauneck, you will carry out your charge," said the master. "Whence comes the gold?"

Perhaps the Singing Thread will inspire a response?

The naked girl opened her eyes again. They were now utterly dark, like orbs of black glass, and they swarmed with shining golden flecks. "I see it! I smell it! There, master—he is this way!" She turned to the south, pointing.

Finally! exclaimed the old one.

"Who is he?" asked Sebastian.

The demon worked her tongue. The voice within her belched words. "Soldier . . . baron . . . marshal . . . madman . . . He builds a kingdom, but it will not be his."

*What is **that** supposed to mean? Clauneck, speak clearly—and get control of that meat before you embarrass yourself,* snapped the old one. *Sebastian, next time you are moved to complain about my presence, just remember how much worse it could be.*

"Perhaps you might do the same, as the one who does

most of the complaining," replied the master. "Now, for God's sake—tell me his *name,* Clauneck!"

"Yes, master. They call him troubadour and murderer and monster. He gives them gold for their warm hearts and they call him Gilles, the Baron de Rais."

"Gilles de Rais," mused the master outside the Circle. "I have heard of him, I think."

"He was Jehanne d'Arc's lieutenant," offered Livia. "She was none too fond of him from what I gathered."

"And yet he was willing to pay a fortune for a fragment of her corpse," he said.

"Those two things may not be unrelated."

"He has *gold,*" said Clauneck in her drowned voice, her black eyes still staring to the south. "His line is seeded with coin! I taste it. It has left a trail. Yes, I can take you, master."

"Excellent, Clauneck! Sarmodel, this one will be useful!"

Livia did not join them in celebration. Her eyes were on the naked girl, who stood nosing the air like a hound. "Sebastian. If you value your long, long life, drive her out now. There must be another way. Clauneck does not enter a Contract she cannot twist to her own ends. And she will spoil the meat. Do you trust that she knows how to operate that body on her own?"[5]

The creature in the Circle looked over at the sound of her name, but said nothing.

You will be silent, half-breed, or I will make good on that Scath-

5. Most Spirits have very little idea what goes on under the hood when they take over a mortal vehicle. Usually they will leave enough of the host's anima intact to manage the drudgery of breathing, digestion, etc., unsupervised, or they risk some fairly distressing biological consequences.

ing, hissed the old one. *Clauneck is coming with us. Just clean this up and disappear!*

"I agree. You've done quite enough tonight, Livia," snapped the master. "Now get out—and *put some clothes on.*"

"You . . . you're leaving me here?" Livia demanded incredulously. "With Michael and the Host perched in the rafters? Are you joking?"

"I don't have anywhere to send you, Livia, as you well know."[6]

"But where—"

"I don't care where you go, just stay away from us. I will summon you next time I need somebody pleasured to death."

"But—"

"I have spoken, Livia! I do not want to hear you or see you—or find you in my damned bed. Go!"

Livia's eyes flashed but she said nothing more, wary of the smoldering presence of the old one. Shaking, she gave a deep curtsy.

"If so you command, Dominus," she replied. What was she supposed to do now? Shackled without a charge was no way to live.

"I do! And *do not* question me again," said Sebastian. He turned to the demon in its new coat of flesh. "Come, Clauneck. We leave at once, while the trail is fresh."

The thing in the Circle did not reply. She cast about with her black, glittering gaze. A flour-dusted hand pointed to the

---

6. I wouldn't like to guess how many homes the master lost to fire/mob in the 1400s, and it wasn't always my fault. I think this one might have been, however.

master's belt, where the bag of florins was fastened with a silver clip. "Gold," came the bubbling voice. "If you please, master."

Do not test us, Clauneck, said the old one. *Come!*

"Gold!" A fresh trickle of blood oozed from the rim of the coin in Clauneck's forehead. Her black, glimmering eyes did not leave the master's purse. "Ere we begin the chase! I will have it!"

The master swore. "Does nobody know how to follow instructions? Clauneck—"

"GOLD!"

Livia laughed, shaking her head. She picked up the corpse in the corner and heaved it over her shoulder.

"She's all yours, meatbag. Farewell—and remember, I warned you."

XXX

Saint-Julien-by-the-Stream
1785

We left Mademoiselle Cecile's home before the afternoon grew too late.

The hedge-witch and her daughter walked us to the door, under the watchful eyes of the red fox. Jacques was beginning to recover from Cecile's enchantment.

Cecile handed me the remainder of the fresh-baked loaf, wrapped in cloth, along with a package of useful herbs—willow bark and poppy in white pouches; deadly foxgloves and monkshood in black.

"My thanks, Mademoiselle Cecile—and to you too, Lorette. Your hospitality has been a balm after a very trying journey."

"A pleasure, sirs," said Lorette, her tone so gracious it was almost certainly affected. "And please pass on my regards to your wife, Lord Ocerne." She gave a deep curtsy and then, inexplicably, her smile crumbled and she began to cry. She pushed past her mother and disappeared once more into the garden, sobbing.

Jacques, still somewhat dazed, looked after her and sighed.

"I—I apologize," I stammered. "I did not mean—"

"No, Professor," said Cecile, raising a hand. She looked weary. "The apologies are mine to make, and not only to you. Sometimes I forget that Lorette does not often spend time . . . in company."

"Ah," I said, suddenly understanding. What Cecile really meant was "in company with young men." Lorette's obvious affection for Jacques was only half of the picture—just like her mother, Lorette would not be considered a suitable wife for any of the local bachelors. She was already past the age at which most of her peers were courting and planning for marriage. That she was also destined to deliver their babies was bitter recompense.

"Please, reconsider," said Cecile. She clasped my hands in hers and the Sigil of Amity faded; our business was concluded. She looked fearful as we said farewell. "I wish I could tell you more, but I cannot."

"I will set this to rights, Cecile, I promise you."

Sarmodel offered his own fond farewell as we stepped outside.

Watch yourself, witch.

Before I lost my nerve, I put us on the high road to Château d'Ocerne. The time for delays was over, and I suddenly found myself with a great deal of business to manage. My impending reunion with Antoine had become the least of my concerns.

"What did you speak of, you and Mademoiselle Cecile?" asked Jacques suddenly, sitting high in the wagon. The road was steep and I walked alongside him to ease the burden on my poor draft horse. "I can scarcely remember—did I fall asleep?"

"You swooned, not long after your first sweet roll. An aftereffect of your medicine, I'm afraid," I improvised. "Lorette took care of you. The 'childhood friend' of whom you spoke?"

"Yes," he said, a little too quickly. "Growing up, I was friends with a number of the village children, Lorette included."

"Really? And how long have you been in love?"

Jacques swore and closed his eyes. "Oh, but I would slap that pander's grin from your face."

"Surely I am not the first to notice, young sir. The girl looked as though she were about to fly apart the whole time we were there," I said gently. "You have betrayed your own feelings before—do not forget whose name you spoke during your fever in the mountains. Close to death, it was not your wife you called for, but the herbalist's daughter. And it is Lorette's likeness on that cameo in your pocket, is it not?"

"Very well." Jacques looked miserable in every way. "As children, Lorette and I were close, and had I been one of the village boys, she would surely have been my sweetheart. As the baron's son, I was always bound to marry my Eloise, but . . ."

"But?"

"But, Professor, I allowed my affection for Lorette to grow beyond respectable bounds, for much too long. It does not matter now—I am married, and it is time to set such selfish folly aside. I have made plain to Lorette that we will remain friends, but no more," he said, sighing. "I am not proud of myself. You must think me a villain."

I adopted my most conciliatory tone. "Sir, I will offer no judgment on your romantic affairs—adultery is the very least of your misdeeds, as we both know. But might I suggest any future liaisons take place away from Lorette's . . . political associates."

Jacques swore again. It suited him. "Cecile told you. Must you know everything?"

"I try to. It helps prevent unpleasant surprises." I looked at him pointedly. "Rubbing elbows with rabble-rousers and agitators, for the sake of a pretty girl? I thought you a smarter man than that."

"I am not a complete fool, Professor. Do you believe I went for

Lorette's sake alone?" Jacques's cheeks were burning now, and it was not with fever. "No. You have seen the ruinous state of Gévaudan. You have seen the way the common people starve, while the noble families fete each other with banquets. We believe—I believe there must be another way."

"Another way? Noble families indeed! You speak as though you were not one of them."

"Professor, you may sneer—you are doing it right now, in fact—but Gévaudan has been broken since the Red Winter, and there are those who would see it rebuilt for the good of the many. Lorette is one, yes, but there are others. I went to hear them."

"Of course—you went to hear them, at clandestine meetings, late at night. Meetings at which I am certain your father received a ferocious roasting from the pulpit," I said.

Jacques showed a flicker of the monster within—a slitting of the eyes, and a peeling of the lips. "My father received nothing he does not deserve!" It lasted only a second, and then he was once again remorseful. "I . . . I went only a handful of times. It was always in secret, and always in disguise. Lorette made sure that nobody knew who I was."

"Yes, yes. And afterward I'm sure the two of you spent some time in private discussing the emancipation of the Third Estate." I gave him a sly smile. "And the emancipation of your underclothes."

"You are vulgar as ever," he snapped, though I could tell his heart wasn't in it. I wondered just how far down this dangerous path he had strayed.

"Does Antoine know?"

"About Lorette?" His mouth twisted. "Yes, since we were children. He forbade me to see her even then. As for the meetings and the rest . . ." He gave a defiant shrug that I'm sure drove his father mad. "I suppose he must. We have certainly argued about his treatment of the working people in Ocerne, though he will see none of it. He is stubborn."

"In that regard, you are certainly your father's son. Your family disputes must be spectacular."

"It matters little in any case. I have made it clear to Lorette that I can no longer join her in the village and that whatever we have had was only a child's fancy kept alive too long. There was never a future for us—a baron's son and a midwife's daughter—but I lacked the courage to end it until I was married." He looked as though he wanted to be sick. "I wanted to give her the cameo as a keepsake, that she might know how much I care for her, even if we could not be together. She refused it. Quite forcefully."

"You tried to buy her off."

"I did not! I swear it! It was meant as a parting gift, nothing more."

"Then you have much to learn about love, young sir."

Jacques gave a small shudder. "This I certainly know. Now tell me, who is Lady Dayane? You mentioned her once before. And please—no tricks, no lies."

I raised my eyebrows. Jacques had obviously been more aware in the parlor than I thought. "As you wish. She is an acquaintance I made during the Red Winter, and I believe she can help you. I will introduce you, soon."

He seemed less than satisfied with my answer. "This is more of your weaseling, I can tell. I know every noble family in the eight baronies, and none of them bear that name. And still—*still* you have not told me what happened at the Bow and Brace."

"In good time, sir. There are things you need to know before the truth about that final night. And still other things you should know about before we reach the château today—including the truth of Lady Dayane, yes. I am not the only one with obligations unfulfilled in Gévaudan, you see. Your father, also, has debts to pay. . . ."

Margeride Mountains
1766

The weeks that followed the massacre at Saint-Julien were intoxicating. Exhilarating. Scandalous. Magnificent.

Antoine and I disappeared into the wilds of Gévaudan, utterly consumed in each other. As a lover, he was as shameless and fearless as he was in all things. We spent our days following tracks through the mountains, taking every opportunity to indulge our carnal desires. We met fewer and fewer hunters as the days grew colder and shorter, so we took ridiculous risks, cavorting naked in the northern cascades, or bucking in sudden, violent heat against the trunk of an ancient cedar.

I would be crouched, perfectly still in the bracken, sighting a hare with Antoine's musket. Then suddenly I would feel him behind me, his beard brushing my ear and his hands reaching around to unbutton my breeches.

"Do you think you can make the kill, Sebastian?" he would whisper, with a playful bite at my earlobe. "Do you want to know what I'll do to you, if you can? There were other games we used to play, the village boys and me." His hands wormed inside my clothes, searching and stroking. "Let me tell you . . ."

I didn't *always* miss.

Antoine delighted me, I think, most of all because he surprised me.

"I've figured it out!" he said suddenly one evening, bolting upright where he sat. We were camped in the mountains once again, not far from where the Beast had taken a traveler on the eastern road.

I smiled wryly, looking up from my notes.[1] "I am apprehensive. What have you figured out?"

"The fire—that's how you've been doing it!"

"Doing what?"

His mind was clearly racing. "I *knew* there was a reason you always managed it when I couldn't. It's magic, isn't it?"

Sarmodel's derisive laughter made it difficult to keep a straight face.

"Antoine, are you suggesting that I've been using the dark arts to light our campfire?"

"Well, have you?"

Yes—confess, Sebastian!

I had the seed of an idea, so I decided to play along. "Most astute, Antoine. I have indeed. Tomorrow night, I will show you—it's a simple enough trick, if you are willing."

"Whoreson!" He glared at me, pointing an accusatory finger at our cheery campfire. "I knew it! And yes—I am willing, by the Christ. Tomorrow night!"

The following evening, we sat by the unlit fire. Antoine's face

1. I was indeed still devoting some of my time to the hunt, in spite of all the fornicating.

was pinched in concentration as he focused on mentally reciting the "cantrip" I had taught him that morning.

"Good, Antoine," I said encouragingly. "I can feel it working."

"How much longer, Sebastian? These ridiculous words are going to fly out of my head," he said. I smiled to myself.

"Try it now, just like we practiced." I shuffled back slightly.

With a grave expression, Antoine pointed at the pile of logs and took a deep breath.

"*Sim Sala Bim!*" he boomed.

With a thunderous roar, the logs burst into flames. A ball of fire ballooned up into the treetops, provoking hysterics from the horses and loud swearing from me. I scrambled to calm the animals, casting a panicked gaze skyward to make sure we hadn't set the forest ablaze.

"By the Almighty, Antoine—did I tell you to *shout*?"

Antoine sat in wide-eyed shock, his finger still outstretched. Then he began to laugh.

"An inferno!" he whooped, as the fire settled to more domestic proportions. "I knew I could manage it! Tomorrow I will do it again—and *better.*"

I considered telling him the truth—that I had written those nonsense words[2] in pyric chalk on the wood while I was gathering it, and that anyone with the power of speech could have triggered them. Then I observed his sparkling eyes and fierce grin, and knew I'd tied my own noose.

"Very well, but in more civilized tones, mark me," I said. I felt

---

2. Yes, they are meaningless, in spite of what you may have heard—they are firmly in the "abracadabra" school of Mundane twaddle. And no, I can't really teach someone magic words if they're not gifted with some Arcane capacity.

a little better about it when I sat down beside him and he rewarded me with a kiss.

Sarmodel had been remarkably quiet through the whole "lesson," but he spoke up now.

Be careful, Sebastian, he said lightly. *Best not to play with your food.*

No harm done, I replied. But I didn't teach Antoine any more "magic" after that night. My Guest was wagging his finger in my face for good reason.

I was telling Antoine things. Arcane things. Dangerous things. Things that would give the young baronet a robust case against me for any number of capital offenses, if he were so inclined. Either way, I was initiating him into a world for which he was certainly not prepared. But he was curious and unafraid—always unafraid—and it made me ever bolder. So I shared perhaps too much with him: my secrets, my body and even my heart.

Not *all* my secrets, of course. For all the wonders I could show Antoine, there were things whose horrors could never be disguised as "ancient arts" or "folk remedies." I was host to a demon. I had eaten people, body and soul, at his behest. Together, we were a life-drinking aberration of the natural order, centuries old. These were the realities I could not deny or justify or laugh away as small-minded superstition. And so I kept them to myself; let Antoine be dazzled by my fire-lighting cantrips and musical horse charms.

And what of the Beast?

The hunt went on, never fear. The attacks had stopped briefly after that day at Saint-Julien, and many hoped that the Beast had in fact perished. I knew better. Now that I understood what we faced, I spent time making preparations for his return.

By the time we received word of new victims—travelers on the eastern road—Sarmodel had taught me a dangerous new Word which he promised me would leave a mark even on the ancient Spirit of War. He would not tell me what it meant or permit me to say it aloud, but it made the world flicker alarmingly when I recited it in my mind. I also envenomed my hunting knife with a potent poison made from powdered Bombay thorn apple and the gland of an amphisbaena.[3] It was a tense and risky procedure I hoped never to repeat. But Avstamet would come for us, now that he knew who we were, and I wanted to be ready.

And come he did, though not in the way I imagined.

I realized something was wrong as the moon grew full, perhaps three weeks from the massacre at Saint-Julien. Antoine's dislocated shoulder and cracked ribs had healed in days, with a little Arcane help, but the Beast's bite on his hand was concerning me greatly.

In objective terms, the monster had barely nipped him; the Beast's mighty jaws could easily have dismembered my young lord. But Avstamet had bargained away his claim on Antoine's life. The creature's bite was a parting insult, nothing more—or so I had believed. It left a semicircle of deep punctures on his hand, from the tip of his little finger across the heel of his palm and all the way to the tip of his thumb. This same neat line was mirrored on the back of his hand, where it had miraculously missed the vital nerves and ligaments of his wrist.

But in spite of my best efforts, the wounds would not close. They no longer bled after the first day, and Antoine said they caused him no pain, but his flesh would not heal where the Beast's teeth had pierced it. And Antoine grew sicker by the day, in turns possessed of a feverish energy and debilitated by exhaustion.

---

3. Two-headed snakes found in the deserts of Mesopotamia. Their venom is almost universally fatal, but it's particularly effective on mortal tissue infused with Spiritual enrichment, i.e., victims of possession.

What is it? I asked Sarmodel. I was changing Antoine's bandages and discreetly inhaled the scent from the cloth—completely clean, even with the open wounds beneath. *Can you find anything?*

Nothing, he answered. *If there* is *something there, it's working outside my range.*[4] *Keep an eye on your young hobbyhorse—we'll know soon enough, I think.*

That evening, after a fiery, bruising round of lovemaking, Antoine rose from our nest of blankets to relieve himself.

The night was cold; winter had begun its march. I lay smiling, breathing white clouds up at the moon, enjoying the warmth Antoine had left.

I sat up suddenly. There was movement in the darkness, strong and violent.

Sarmodel.

Of course. My Guest brightened my vision and I stood up slowly. I wished, not for the last time, that I still had my Walloon silver.

"Antoine?" I could still see nothing with my augmented vision. The black-and-white shadowland outside the firelight was utterly still.

I heard a low voice and felt my heart quicken. Antoine was talking to himself.

In itself, this was no great anomaly; Antoine often talked or sang to himself when he was busy with a task. But this was different. He sounded angry, or terribly confused, or both.

"Antoine? Who are you talking to?" I was naked and very cold,

---

4. Much like a spectrometer, my Guest has a certain "range" over which his senses operate. While Sarmodel is a reliable enough bloodhound in the Mundane, Abject and Arcane realms, there remain entire spectra of supernatural realities that are as imperceptible to him as they are to me.

but fetching my clothes would mean turning my back on the low, bestial muttering coming from the darkness.

"To the Gorgon of Crete!" he called back suddenly. His voice was too high and too distant; how had he moved so far away in those few short moments? He laughed at his own jest, and then he made a strange choking sound.

Oh, Antoine.

I spoke a Litany of the Hunt and slipped, snakelike, into the forest.

I smelled blood immediately and turned after it. It was grim confirmation to feel the residual warmth of Antoine's footsteps beneath me as I followed the scent.

He was there, as I feared, where the trail ended.

"Antoine, please, come back to the fire," I said softly, suddenly wishing that I could dispel my augmented senses; that the darkness would hide even a little of what I saw.

Antoine was surrounded by a miasma of vital traces: the twin plumes of his breath misting from his nostrils; the lingering scents of sweat, hormones and sex; his urine on the trunk of an alder. And vapor from the fresh blood that ran down his torso, shining black in the moonlight.

Antoine had found a pine marten, no doubt busy with its own nocturnal hunt. The poor creature had ended its life bludgeoned against a rock, with my lover's fist around its neck. And now he held its sleek body close to his face like a child with a cherished toy, his teeth working into the animal's soft innards.

"Please," I said again, not sure what I would do if he refused.

He looked up at me suddenly, discarding the bloody corpse on the forest floor. "Sebastian, aren't you cold?" Antoine's teeth were long and pointed; a predator's weapons. He absently sucked his fingers clean, one by one. He seemed oblivious to the blood that dripped from his beard and down his chest.

"I am. Why don't you come back to bed with me?"

Antoine followed me back to the fire, picking gingerly over the forest floor with his bare feet. He made no objection as I washed his face and body clean of blood, even allowing me to inspect his teeth when I was finished. The elongated fangs were already reverting, dissolving into plasma. His eyes were very bright but somehow empty; I wondered how much of this he would remember in the morning.

Then suddenly he staggered into the brush, heaving. He disgorged his grim repast in a crimson stream and then cried out for water.

Afterward we sat by the fire, wrapped in blankets. I watched him watching the flames. He breathed deeply and seemed to come back to himself gradually.

"What was she like?" he asked suddenly, meeting my eyes over the fire.

"Who?"

"The Gorgon of Crete." There was a shadow of a smile on his lips. The tight fist of fear in my gut began to loosen its grip.

"She was . . ." I let out a heavy breath. "More than anything, she was terribly sad. In the end, death was a mercy for her."

But Antoine was already asleep where he sat.

Sebastian, watch him tonight, said Sarmodel. *Or think about killing him now. There's no telling—*

Yes, I know! I know, Sarmodel! I snapped. *I saw what happened.*

My love, I am only being careful. This is a curse, or something similar. Avstamet has done something to the boy. It will certainly get worse.

This is my fault. I showed the Beast my weakness and he stuck his teeth into it. Of course he did.

All true, he said. *Now be smart. What are you going to do?*

I will find help, I answered, looking at Antoine's wounded hand, glistening in the firelight. *And I believe I know where to start looking.*

ADDENDUM:

On the Search for Gilles de Rais

Orleans, France
1437

Jehanne's legacy has grown like a boil.

As the master and his foul new companion chase the trail of Gilles de Rais's gold across the continent, they can scarcely hitch their mounts without hearing another account of the Maiden's exploits.

But the woman's relic and the potent Spirit it contains have so far eluded them. Clauneck has naturally found a loophole in her Contract, which requires her only to "follow the trail" of the gold. So, she has dutifully sniffed out every merchant prince and high-end pander who did business with the master's florins, much to his frustration.[1] *Gilles de Rais, the man who used the money to buy the Maiden's relic, is very*

1. I would like to point out that if I ever performed this badly, I would be Scathed down to the gristle. I will also note that while Clauneck was permitted to eat up the master's gold like popcorn, I am still, after more than fifteen hundred years, scarcely trusted with my own weekly expenses allowance.

busy with the war and his own personal affairs, and never seems to spend long in one place. He remains, somehow, always a step ahead.

The Hundred Years' War is very inconvenient. Every battle and siege they must avoid only adds to their journey. The master grows impatient and the old one is absolutely fuming; years have now passed. It should not be this difficult. Is Clauneck stupid? Has she misunderstood her charge? Is she just dragging her heels because she's an ancient, joyless maggot who doesn't need the work?[2]

And what of me? What has the master's discarded (but not emancipated, never fear) succubus been up to this whole time? I won't spoil the surprise, but I will tell you that I've been having even less fun than the master with his new pet.

See them with me now, two grim travelers, approaching the outskirts of Orleans. There is almost nothing left of the master's fortune, but this time—surely **this time**—*Clauneck is on the right track.*

But hark! A mighty crowd is gathered there outside the town walls. The people of Orleans have come together in their thousands, along with their animals, vermin and children, not to mention a storm of mosquitoes and an absolute orgy of fleas.

But what are they here for? To what end this brazen enticement to the Black Death? Is it a battle? A natural disaster?

No. They're here for entertainment! An enormous stage has been constructed by the river, purpose-built for a theater show—and what a show it is.

Hundreds of little meatbags prance across the boards, reenacting the siege of Orleans and Jehanne the Maiden's miraculous victory. There's a naval battle, a skirmish on a bridge, the breaching of the walls and a real live woman ***in public with no hat on****; the common folk in the crowd are dangerously overstimulated.*

2. No, no and yes, respectively.

Every night, the silken costumes are burned together with all their finery, and new ones are made for the following day. Every night, a fortune in golden beads and silver buttons is melted down, turning into a strange white slag that crumbles into nothing. And every night, Gilles de Rais weeps over the bonfire, calling devotions to Jehanne as he consigns his riches to the flames. The Loire River has become a milky soup of makeup, soot and shit.

Do the spectators ever wonder, as they clap and hoot like monkeys, who is paying for it all? Do they question what sort of man would throw the wealth of nations, not to mention years of his life, into a spectacle about a dead virgin?

Surely such a man must be utterly, catastrophically mad.

The wooden tower tilted and swung open on concealed hinges. A dozen straw dummies dressed in blue and red Orleans heraldry spilled onto the stage, bursting concealed bladders full of pigs' blood. Smoke poured from grates in the floor. Sunlight flashed from gilt-edged swords as soldiers fenced along the ramparts. From either side, organs joined with ranks of harps and viols in a booming crescendo as bugles called across the theatrical battlefield.

Thousands had gathered on the hillside to watch the performance. The play, *The Mystery of the Siege of Orleans,* had grown in reputation, and its miraculous subject remained a source of pride for the city. So magnificent in scale that it could not be performed within Orleans itself, the spectacular took place outside, against the fitting backdrop of the walls.

At the back of the audience, hidden in a stand of poplars, two people watched the mystery play with unusual interest. The man was olive-skinned and dark-haired, with an aquiline nose and distant, intelligent eyes. While the crowd cheered and cried out in awe at the spectacle, he remained unmoved.

Beside him, his companion stood motionless, pale and red-lipped. She was almost completely swallowed up in a capacious woolen dress, with her chaperon hood pulled low over her face. A terrible smell soured the air around her, redolent of sickness, unwashed flesh and scorched metal.

At a glance, she might have passed for an old woman. But there were signs that something terrible ailed her. Her face and hands were thin, but there was a strange, lumpy fullness to the body inside her clothing. Her skin sagged loosely, like an oversized costume. Hair which had perhaps once been blond now hung like damp straw. She studied the performers like one transfixed, rubbing her fingers and thumbs together.

The man turned to her.

"Clauneck," he said. "Attend."

The woman blinked several times, but said nothing.

"Well?" he demanded.

She pulled her gaze unwillingly from the performance and found his face. Slowly she shrugged, the dress bulging oddly. She raised a hand and lifted the edge of her hood.

The coin in her forehead was bright. She touched the golden surface, where the symbols of her Contract were engraved. Her mouth fell open and a thick voice spoke from somewhere inside her.

"Gold, if you please, master."

The man seemed faraway for a moment, as though lost in his own thoughts. Then he retrieved a coin from his belt pouch and pressed it into the woman's hand. "A warning, Clauneck. This is your last chance. You have led me to every fop and princeling who so much as glanced at these coins, and we have still not found Gilles de Rais. If you fail me this time, you will submit to the Crippling Yoke. Again."

She nodded with lethargic calm and closed her fingers around the coin. The man snatched his hand back.

"Oh me, oh aye," burbled the demon, closing her eyes. "*Gold.* Oh, riches." The coin was heavy, a precious florin. Enraptured, she raised it to her unmoving lips. "Gold, with a man's face. A king's face! They speak his name, from the sea to the summits! Ah, me." The coin disappeared into her mouth and she shivered.

Onstage, the figure of Jehanne d'Arc rode out of the smoke on horseback, her banner held aloft. Her gilded bascinet helm answered the sun with its radiance, but the Maid of Orleans was in distress. Gravely wounded, she delivered her lines of verse with desperate passion, in a final attempt to rally the French troops in the name of the Lord.

At the back of the crowd, Clauneck's eyes opened again. They were black and deep, and filled with swarms of glittering sparks. Her lips were wet and so flushed they were almost purple. From her mouth emerged a forked white tongue that flicked through the air, scenting the breeze.

"There! That one," came the drowned voice from her throat. She pointed to the foot of the stage.

A strange figure danced there. He wore a white silk robe—an angel's costume—and he conducted the orchestra with a gilded ceremonial rapier. His thick beard was dyed royal blue with woad and his face was painted with a stern lion's visage. His attention shifted again and again from the scene onstage to the furiously bobbing bows of the musicians.

The master squinted. "That's him? That's Gilles de Rais?"

Clauneck trembled. Her eyes were wide, drinking in the silks and gemstones anew. "Oh, me . . . gold . . . it runs from him. Like water, like blood . . ."

"No doubt," the master replied. "And somewhere in his collection, it seems he has what is left of the Maid of Orleans and her demon, purchased with the fortune which is now lining your gullet."

"Hmm." Her hands came to rest on the lopsided swell of her abdomen.

He started and turned from her as the final fanfare shattered the afternoon. There was joyous outcry in the audience. The Maiden strode to the front of the stage, delivering a dramatic plea to the Lord and his angels, her hair whipping in the wind. Regal and righteous, even in her wounded condition, she was the promise of France made flesh.

"Rise, Jehanne! Rise, France! To glory, to glory in God's name!" chanted the chorus.

The conductor cheered hysterically, his voice rising momentarily above the clamor.

"Yes! My lady! Onward, Jehanne!"

The master looked bitterly at his demonic companion. "Clauneck, I will proceed alone from here. You have stretched your Contract to its limit. Six years is a long time to hold your leash, and you have—finally—done as I asked. Prepare to depart this flesh, which you have treated so very poorly. I hope you have enjoyed yourself."

Clauneck's eyes swiveled back to him. "Gold. Fifty pieces, marked with a king's face. So we agreed. So it is written." She pointed to the coin in her forehead and then to the money pouch on his belt. "So it is graven in my flesh, by your hand. Fifty pieces of gold."

"I have *given* you—"

"Nine and forty. The price was fifty."

"Surely—"

"Gold."

"But I—"

"Gold."

"Oh, shut your mouth, damn you!" he snapped. He took the last coin from the purse and threw it at her feet. "Gold, *gold*! Take it then—may you choke on it."

Cannons fired from the city walls and an army in silken regalia stormed onto the stage behind the figure of Jehanne. The heroine called them forward with her tattered banner, exhorting the crowd to join her in victory.

"To glory, to glory in God's name!"

Clauneck gave a gurgling sigh and reached down to retrieve the coin, her fingers flexing with too many joints.

But the demon was not to receive her price.

"There they are! *Take them, now!"*

There were suddenly men all around them, their cloaks cast off to reveal the lamb-and-cross heraldry of the Rouen Guard.

"Who—?!"

The master was seized in a moment. The men pinned him to the ground.

But he was not so easily disarmed. He uttered a single unearthly syllable and one of his captors screamed as his eyes ruptured from their sockets. The others quickly stuffed the master's mouth with rags, and he subsided, glaring.

Clauneck was a different matter. Belching and writhing inside her dress, she struggled with inhuman strength as four of the soldiers attempted to hold her. One fell to the ground twitching, his face clawed down to the skull. The others she cast off with a rippling shrug, her whole body convulsing to dislodge them. Her hands stretched out in desperation for the fallen coin.

"GOLD!"

"Demon!" One of the men, presumably their leader, lunged at her, brandishing a large, elaborately ornamented silver cross.[3] Though he wasn't old, his hair and beard were almost completely white, and his eyes were a fierce, tawny gold. "Down! *Down* in the name of the Almighty God!"

Clauneck recoiled from the holy artifact. The white-haired man held it close to her face, driving the demon to her knees.

"Hold them!"

The soldiers, emboldened, bound her wrists and ankles with intricately wrought chains. The master was likewise restrained on the ground, and the white-haired man stood astride him, regarding him with his strange, golden eyes.

"And so I have, at last, found you. How disappointing to finally see you up close, witch. You are quite unremarkable now that I see your face." He leaned low, tapping the master's chin with the cross. "I am Captain Renard of the Rouen Guard, and you are now a ward of the Almighty. I will unstop your mouth now, for I have questions—and you will answer. But do not attempt to foul the air with your sorcery again. I have

---

3. A cross does not in itself present any threat to Spirits or half-breeds (but please feel free to try your luck). This particular specimen was inlaid with a martyr's bone and engraved with Samadhic ideograms—a true idol of the Almighty, which is now exceptionally rare, even on eBay. If you're really attached to your little mortal bag of meat, then invest in some real protection, like a handgun.

bound you, not only with chains of iron, but also with the divine bonds of the Lord's will."

The man plucked the wool from the master's mouth. He continued to hold the cross over him, wielding it more like a club than a talisman. Where its shadow fell, Sebastian's skin darkened with bruises.

"Divine bonds? Do you think I've never seen the Choking Braid,[4] you cretin?" the master snapped, holding up the strangely twisted links of his chains. "This is some fine Arcane craftsmanship—just like that idol you hold. If I am a witch, then so, Captain, are you."

The white-haired man struck the master's face with the cross, bursting his bottom lip like a grape. "You are disgraceful in word as well as in deed. My hands, like my eyes, are devoted to the Almighty. These instruments of Divine justice were created with His guidance." He leaned in closer, his lips almost touching the rough hair on Sebastian's face. "I *see* you, unwilling as you are. And I see the one behind you, with his claws in your soul."

"Truly?" Sebastian squinted in suspicion. "See *how,* exactly?"

"The Archangel has opened my eyes. You cannot deceive me."

"Michael!" Sebastian swore. "It seems I'm not the only one with claws in his soul. Tell me, Captain—how long has the Archangel been whispering in your ear?"

---

4. An ancient charm invented by one of the Egyptians (probably Horus) that permits speech, but no Arcane utterance or activity. Included in the first cycle of every major Grimoire since the Pharaohs, it's quite literally the oldest trick in the book.

"Do not dare speak the Messenger's name, witch, lest he blind you where you lie." Renard struck his face again and the master cried out. "I have been charged with recovering the relic you stole from Jehanne the heretic's pyre. Give it to me now and you may yet be redeemed. Resist me, and you will share her fate."

"The relic?" The master grimaced. One side of his face was now turning livid purple, where the shadow of the cross fell. "You think *I* have it?"

"So says the Archangel," answered the captain, with utter certainty. "So it must be."

"I will not deny that I am seeking it. But if I had it already, do you really think I would be wandering the continent with Clauneck for company?" demanded the master.

The captain's golden eyes were distant and deep for a moment, and he shook his head grimly. "So. I am denied again, and the search must continue." He straightened and turned to his men. "But we will yet draw the lode from the dross. Bring him back to the abbey, and his vile bloodhound too. Keep them apart, mind. I will interrogate them separately."

Sebastian closed his eyes in resignation. "Torture, is it?" He spoke to the empty air above the captain's head. "Are you there, Michael? This is most unworthy of an angel of the Almighty."

Captain Renard smiled, dangerously handsome as he menaced the master once again with the painful aura of the silver cross. "For the fallen, mortification of the flesh is the only true path to redemption. You will tell me everything you know, and the heretic's relic will yet be mine. I hope you will be more forthcoming than your abominable strumpet."

Sebastian gave a small moan of trepidation.

"Strumpet?"

"The half-breed you left behind in Rouen. She escaped me eventually—maimed herself like a wolf caught in a snare. But I could not have found you without her."

Renard reached into a satchel at his waist.

From within he produced a severed hand, still attached to several inches of wrist. Slender and feminine, it was pink with health and somehow still moving, as though freshly shorn from the owner's forearm. It was, oddly, quite beautiful, like a piece of a statue. It was marred only by the melted, scarred stump, and the wicked talons that extended from the fingertips as it flexed.

The captain held the thing close to his mouth. "Where lies the one who holds your leash, succubus?" he asked.

Like a compass finding north, the index finger pointed squarely at the master's chest.

Sebastian swore.

"Livia."

"Bitch," agreed Clauneck miserably.

XXXII

Saint-Julien-by-the-Stream
1766

I found Mademoiselle Cecile in the fields behind Saint-Julien.

It was the day after Antoine's disturbing transformation, of which he remembered nothing. We returned to Saint-Julien in the morning and I sent him to get more wine, salt and thread—enough to keep him busy for an hour or so. I took the opportunity to seek out the young *sage-femme* in the commons behind the village. It was not difficult; in my Arcane sight, her hagstone pendant winked across the field like a star.

The young herbalist was also swearing like a soldier. She knelt in a patch of cotoneaster, harvesting the berries with a curved knife. A cloud of tiny biting marsh flies surrounded her, and her bare arms were covered in red welts.

"Get off me, you little pricks!" she hissed, slapping at her shoulder. They covered her back and her dirty blond hair like pepper.

"Next time, use lavender and some geranium, if you can find them," I said, approaching on my horse. "Either press them for oils or rub them straight on the skin—you'll have no more trouble with bugs."

"You again!" she said, scrambling to her feet. Her pinafore and apron were stiff with dried blood; Cecile had doubtless been very busy since the massacre in the marketplace. "I told you to leave me be!"

And I told you I was coming back for you, witch, said Sarmodel. *Where is your boon companion? I am going to juice him like an orange and I would like you to watch.*

She raised the pruning knife with one hand and clasped the hagstone with the other. It throbbed formidably in her fist. "Leave me be—now—or I will burst your heart."

"Young lady, please calm yourself—and watch your tone. Père Arnaud is not here to rescue you this time. And I would remind you once again that I am not your enemy." I leaned forward on my saddle horn. "Rather, I have come seeking your help."

"My help?" She slowly tucked the knife into her sash, but did not release the hagstone. "Every house in the village needs my help right now. I have nothing left for you—either of you."

Oh please, we are not here for pile cream, said Sarmodel. *We don't need you—we need whoever gave you that stone.*

"My lady?" Cecile's suspicion was plain. "You have no business with her."

"Mademoiselle, I need help from a powerful Spirit, and yours is the only one here. The baron's son has fallen victim to some strange affliction and it is the Beast's doing. This 'lady'—can she help him?"

"I have no doubt she *can*. Whether she *will* . . . I would not presume to say."

"Please, it is important."

"Important? Is the baron's son more important than the dozens of others who are waiting for me?" she asked. "Is he more important than the man whose legs were crushed when the bridge collapsed, or the girl whose face was nigh bitten off by a crazed hound?"

"He is. To me," I said, despising myself for the blush I could feel rising in my face.

Just tell us where to find her, said Sarmodel, *and then go back to your bugs.*

Cecile's stubborn jaw trembled and her eyes were suddenly bright with tears. "By God, I hate you. All of you. Why have you come here? Why can't we just live our lives as we were, without Spirits and demons and the fucking Beast?"

I was about to give her a fitting response, but she looked so utterly miserable.

Sarmodel, let us try a different approach, I said privately.

I was just thinking the same thing. We can dump the body on the road somewhere—they'll think the Beast got her.

Not exactly what I meant. Let me handle this for a moment, please.

"Cecile. I—I apologize. I understand how you feel, better than you know. I was exactly like you once—"

You were never anything like this puling slattern.

"—and I know how unfair it is. You asked for none of this and it asks *everything* of you. I can help you; *we* can help you. Do this one thing for me and I promise I will do everything in my power to rid you of the Beast for good."

Cecile shook her head but did not speak. She knelt and returned to her work, her face turned away from me.

"Mademoiselle?"

"You don't know what he is. You think you do, but you don't." I realized she was crying as she worked, pulling the stems and nicking away the berries with a practiced hand. "My lady has forbidden me to speak of him—she does not wish me to attract his eye—but he sees me already. I see him in my dreams; he hunts me through the village, a wolf the size of a barn with the hands of a man. He speaks in Latin, and he opens his mouth as wide as the sky, and when I look inside, I see hundreds of people, each devouring the one in front like sausage links—the farmers and the villagers all the way up to the bishop and the king, who eats all the rest, and of course the wolf, who holds them all in his mouth. And then he eats me." She stopped and looked up at me. "I will tell you the way and petition my lady on your behalf, as you have requested, and she may treat with you as she sees fit. But make no mistake, Professor—he is going to eat you and your arse-talking imp as well."

"You have my thanks, Cecile. You may well have saved the young lord's life."

We followed Cecile's directions to the foot of the mountains, where an alpine stream cascaded into the river. On her instructions, we were to follow the stream to its source.

Arse-talking imp? Sarmodel was still fuming. *There are some occultists, Sebastian, who would not countenance such an insult to their Arcane associates.*

Just let it go. Cecile has given us what we want, and there is certainly something powerful in these mountains.

Perhaps, he replied, *but if you are wrong, I want you to promise me something.*

Oh?

You will kill the young lord. Today.

I did not make any promises, but his point was clear.

Antoine and I left our horses tied by the stream. There was fresh water and plenty for them to eat, should we fail to return before dark.

I told my young lover only what was essential. He was weak and unwell, and I thought it best not to trouble him any more than necessary. As far as he knew, the Beast's bite had succumbed to an infection and I was taking him to someone who could help. He seemed more dejected than concerned—he still remembered nothing of his bloody deeds the night before.

It was difficult going for Antoine, but I could spare little attention to helping him. There were signs along the way, things I would have missed without Cecile's guidance. A rowan, split by a lightning strike. Red verbena flowering there at the threshold of winter. A standing stone with the shadow of a face on its pitted surface. A circle of gray toadstools, undisturbed in a glade. Each was a marker on a very specific trail.

I took a deep breath and began to sing.

It was a low, wordless song,[1] taught to me centuries ago by creatures without human mouths. I hummed and whistled through the melody where I could not make the sounds with my voice alone.

And the world around us answered. Like the chimes in a great instrument, each stone and tree resonated with its own vibration. The mountain stream was a thrumming bass tone, lifting and leading the rest. We were in the right place. We followed the stream up and around the mountain.

Antoine began to wander as the song took effect. He crouched to examine a clump of snowbells, his eyes wide.

"Sebastian, these are beautiful," he croaked.

"Yes, they are. Come, we still have a way to go."

He gently plucked one of the flowers before I helped him to his feet.

---

1. Yes, it has a name, and no, I'm not going to say what it is. Forgive me if I am overcautious in this age of the internet.

"Antoine, can you hear that song?"

"What song?" he answered absently, humming the refrain. He twirled the little white flower between his fingers. I smiled and took his hand.

We walked hand in hand like children, ever deeper into the forest.

The woods changed as the Fey melody filled the world around us, like water soaking slowly into sand. Wild Spirits became apparent. Antoine marveled at a nenekt rolling in the rapids. I drew him quietly away before it noticed him. A red-winged orneger bored for anima-rich sap in the trunk of a fir tree, uncaring as we stepped close enough to touch it. Eyes watched us from the shadows and the treetops.

There were tears on my face as we followed the stream still farther, past the shallow run where Antoine had been so humiliated by the trout. A swarm of tiny flying Spirits danced on the surface, leaving V-shaped trails on the water.

I remembered the world like this, when there was worship in wild places and people did not shackle their gods to mortal concerns and mortal civilization. A traveler through the wilds might slip into the Fey realm and find himself speaking to a sentient tree, or treading on the scaled back of an ancient serpent.

Do not get lost, Sebastian, said Sarmodel. His voice was so close that I glanced at Antoine to see if he had heard. I felt strong hands on my shoulders, guiding me step after step beside the stream. I have no doubt that, without him, Antoine and I would both have lost ourselves up there in the Fey dreaming.

We came at last to a place where the treetops seemed to swallow the sun, and a green gloaming lit the way to an eldritch place. We had arrived.

The pool was wide, perhaps ten steps across, shadowed beneath a stone rib of the mountain. It was, of course, a circle. The edges were overhung with bracken and flowering grasses, nodding at their own reflections. Beneath the surface, a forest of mare's tail glowed gemstone green in the sunlight, waving in some deeper current.

On the far side, a mossy black overhang delivered a constant trickle of meltwater. It fell in a single, clear stream onto a flat tongue of granite that rose just above the water's edge. I recognized it immediately as the place where Mademoiselle Cecile's hagstone had formed over centuries. Beyond the ripples of the cascade, the water of the pool was very still, disturbed not even by the wind.

None of it should be here. This flower-strewn clearing with its emerald pool, here in the mountains with winter beginning to bite—it was impossible.

A sacred pool. There could be no doubt.

Antoine collapsed to his knees by the water, his face shining with awe. "I never knew such a place existed," he said. "And *here* in the mountains, so close. Can we rest here, Sebastian? I . . . I do not think I can go farther."

I didn't answer him. I could feel the pool's custodian Spirit hovering just beyond my senses. The presence was primal, yes, but not threatening. It was unmistakably feminine.

I knelt by the water, my head bowed. From my pack I took out a wooden bowl, which I floated on the surface. I had bought it from a local man who assured me it was made from the pines of the forest around us. The Spirit stirred; we had her attention.

Oh, she is very, very old, said Sarmodel. I could feel his awakened appetite. *Under other circumstances . . .*

Do not **dare** *challenge her, Sarmodel. That is not how we work, remember?*

Calm yourself, my love. It was just an observation, he said. *But have a care. I cannot help you once the deal is made.*

I know. Now, please, do not scare her away.

I began to sing again; a different song this time. The words were a poem in Ancient Greek, an ode to a wild mountain stream. I sang of her leaping cascades and life-giving waters, her grassy banks and her unknown depths. Into the floating bowl I placed a handful of barley and four silver pellets from my shot pouch, followed by a measure of wine and a twisted sprig of mistletoe. I sang the last stanza of the devotion and placed my final offering in the bowl: a handkerchief in which I had collected a quantity of Antoine's semen.[2]

Seemingly of its own accord, the bowl floated away from me, out into the center of the mirrorlike pool. There it burst suddenly into white flames and disappeared beneath the surface.

And there she rose.

---

2. Oh, come now. It's a little late for squeamishness.

XXXIII

From the green depths she emerged slowly, her sleek head rising from the surface without even a ripple. The water of the pond slipped away from her skin like a sleeve, as the laws of the Mundane world found no purchase on her eldritch flesh.

Antoine and I could only watch in rapture as she ascended, rising until she stood on the surface of the pool. The air filled with the green smell of crushed grass and petrichor.

She was white, so very white, like a young woman molded from living ivory. Her hair was as black as the granite of her shrine and flashed green like the depths of the pond when it caught the light. It hung long down her back, twined thickly with strands of water chestnut.

Sarmodel, she's a naiad. My God, I had believed them all gone.

He said nothing; I think even my Guest was a little stunned.

"My lady, I have come," I said. I can't say how, but I knew without doubt that *she* had been waiting for *me*. We had not impelled her into physical form—she had always been here and simply chosen to reveal herself. I could not help but return her smile as she stepped across the surface of the pool toward us.

Even now I can barely explain. There was something at once compelling and unnerving about her. The water nymph was one of Pan's cohort and she bore his likeness. Tiny, bud-like horns protruded from her forehead, covered in velvet. Her ears were long and furred with soft black down, like a doe's. Her abdomen had no navel, and her long white hands were without fingernails. She wore no clothing, but she was not ***naked***, just as a fish or a deer is not naked. Nor was it the sight of her bare flesh that so ensnared me. She had a primeval, unsettling beauty, far removed from the swooning sensibilities of the time. She was dragonflies where I expected butterflies; eelgrass where I was accustomed to lilies.

"You *found* me," she said. The eyes that regarded me were pellucid brown and fringed with long black lashes. Her smile was innocence itself. "I have watched you, many times, Magician. The chase! The trout in the stream—*one-two*—ah! You would have my favor as victors of this hunt, certainly." She clapped her hands and laughed, and the surface of the pool shivered with the sound. "My handmaiden told me you would come, and I have so wanted you to find me. And now you have *come*!"

"I was not certain you would answer. It has been many years since I made such a call," I said. "We have come seeking your aid, my lady."

She shook her head playfully. "But there will be time for everything! Come, let us first spend a moment in company. Would you like to hear me sing? We can weave rainbows from the water together. Or perhaps a race?" she offered, her eyes sparkling.

"No, my lady. I regret to say our need is great." I indicated Antoine, who seemed nigh delirious.

"So it is, always." The naiad seemed disappointed, but she

acquiesced. "And who is this young petitioner you bring to me, whose seed you have offered in my sanctuary?" she asked, her long ears flicking with curiosity.

"He is Antoine Avenel, the son of the Baron d'Ocerne."

"Ah. Then you know me already, son of Ocerne!" she said with delight. "My waters have nurtured the great houses of Gévaudan for generations."

"But who are you? Where did you come from?" murmured Antoine.

"I have always been here, my young lord," she said. "I am Dayane, the Water from the Mountain. I have tended these woods since the first men arrived with their stones and furs. I nourish root and river, the shepherd and the wolf. All who call are answered." She looked up at Sarmodel and bowed low, her hair dipping below the surface of the pool. "Even you, old one. Your challenge would not have gone unmet. It has been a long time since I was so honored."

Sarmodel gave a low growl, a sound of naked hunger. ***The honor is mine. You are pure nectar, Dayane, and I would drink you to the lees.***

"Ha! There were those who called themselves gods who claimed as much. They chased me through these mountains for three days and nights, until the final sun rose on the Lupercalia. None could outpace the stream." Her smile as she straightened was full of wild pride. Small yellow flowers opened in her hair, forming a victor's crown. "Would you hear the story?"

"It pains me, but I must decline, my lady. It is one such god who has caused our current troubles, in fact," I said. "Please, Dayane. We have little time, and the young lord's illness grows worse by the hour."

She grew suddenly very sad, and the pond seemed to lose its glowing depth. "Is there truly nothing else you would speak of? Do you not wish to hear a poem, or a song? You *must*! Kings once came to hear me sing—kings and queens and great sorcerers."

"I am afraid we cannot, Dayane," I answered gently.

She nodded, her eyes downcast. For a moment she was silent, her doe's ears flattened in consternation. Fingers of frost began to creep over the surface of the pool.

"I know him, the one you speak of," she said softly. "We all know him, the wild Spirits and I. He is the Warfather. Ares. Mars. Avstamet."

"Yes, Dayane," I answered. "Avstamet. Your priestess[1] Cecile would not speak of him." I glanced at Antoine. He was watching us with confusion written plainly on his face.

Your gift is wasted on her, my lovely, said Sarmodel. *The favor of a demigoddess for a village witch? A hagstone for a midwife?*

The naiad's voice held a trace of defiance. "She is strong and worthy, and with my boon, she will grow to greatness in my image. It was I who forbade her to speak of the Warfather. I do not wish for her to draw his eye."

"Can you help us, then? Do you know where he is?"

Dayane looked at me askance. "No. I know only that he wears the flesh of a mortal and moves among you, as you have no doubt discovered."

"But why take the form of this Beast? What does he hope to achieve with this massacre of the people?"

Dayane shook her head. "You do not understand. You remember only the golden greaves of the general, the Olympian, Mars the

---

1. The word I used was Ancient Greek: "*hiereia*," which translates as "priestess" or "diviner." There is a lot more to the role than either of these words really communicates, but you might say that Cecile was a sort of living "outpost" for Dayane in the Mundane world.

Father of Rome. You forget that the Spirit of War was already old when Greece and Rome sent their armies across the sea. Avstamet was born when the first man decided to kill his neighbor to take what was his, rather than share the world with him. He is the hunger for conquest within every man, that you have tamed with comfort and law and the promise of a warm hearth. He has always been the Beast, just as you have."

"And you will not help us against him?"

She shook her head and the surface of the pond seized violently, becoming a jagged flower of ice beneath her feet. "He is diminished, but he remains the Warfather. He violated and devoured untold numbers of my sisters in the groves of Arcadia. I do not wish to join them now that he has returned."

Cowardice, said Sarmodel. *I am disappointed, Dayane.*

"Patience, rather," she countered. "With patience, the stream will cleave even the mountain."

"Then what of Antoine?" I asked, motioning to my ailing lover. He held out his wounded hand. "Will you not help him?"

Dayane's limpid eyes were full of compassion. "Yes . . . yes, perhaps this I can do." The ice slowly dissolved into the pool, leaving it once again still and shimmering within. "You are very unwell, young one. This is Avstamet's doing, is it not?"

"The Beast. His teeth. His blood," replied Antoine. Clearly he was more aware of what was happening than I realized.

"I fear a curse," I added. "The wound will not heal, and Antoine is *changing.*"

The naiad inclined her head. "A curse, perhaps. An invasion, certainly. A poison of the soul. Avstamet has left a part of himself in your anima, my young one. It strives to conquer you; I can see it."

"A part of himself? What do you mean?" I asked.

"His very essence is in the wound—the plasma of his disintegrating form, thanks to the fearsome blow you dealt him. It was an act of desperation but also a lesson. He wishes to make an example of your young lover."

"An example? Of what?"

"You still do not understand. The Warfather has become a fountainhead of discord, a hunger that seeps into every living thing. You have already seen its first fruits."

"The hounds," I murmured.

"Just so. The beasts you have tamed over generations are forgetting themselves and returning to savagery. So it will be with the young lord's people, in time. As he feeds, Avstamet's influence flourishes, spreading into the world like a contagion. He will stoke and encourage the lowest instincts in man, and strip away the mask of civilization." She pointed to Antoine. "And now this. You ask why? He has done this to spite you, Magician. He has kept his word and spared the young man's life, but now he will show you the beast you have risked your life to save. His very flesh will be a mirror to his darkest appetites."

"Can he be cured?" I insisted.

"Yes," said the nymph, her eyes clear. "What is Mundane flesh but earth and water? I do not know if it can be destroyed, but I can take the thorn from him. But you know there will be a price, Magician."

"I do. But I cannot answer for him."

She turned to Antoine, stroking his face. "Poor young one. Your throat burns, and you hunger so. The one you call the Beast has left a terrible barb in your flesh. I can take it from you, if you will it."

Antoine trembled under her touch. "Please," he whispered.

"Of course." Dayane smiled. "There was a time when your people honored me with gifts and service and songs. I would have answered you with charity, and asked nothing more than a kiss from a handsome young man. But you and your people have forgotten me, young Lord Ocerne. Your love of the Almighty has eclipsed all others, and so my favor will come at great cost. Do you understand?"

He only nodded.

Dayane did not take her eyes from Antoine, but she spoke to me. "This is not for your ears, Magician—or yours, old one." She bent low, speaking close to Antoine's ear. He gave no reaction to her words other than a slight widening of his eyes.

I knew it was unfair. Antoine was so weak, so ill and so deeply adrift in the Fey realm he would have agreed to anything.

"That is my price and my requirement," said Dayane, straightening. "Be warned; though the bargain is a costly one, the price for breaking it will be far worse. Do you accept?"

"Is there no other way?" he asked mildly, as though he were simply curious.

"None, my young one," she said sadly. "Avstamet has planted a hunger in you that will never be satisfied. If I do not remove it, you will devour your rivals to the last—such is the nature of war."

There was never any question. Antoine accepted the naiad's bargain, with a shrug and a nod.

"Done."

I let out a great sigh of relief; I did not realize I had been holding my breath. Dayane laughed in delight and danced away from us, standing once again in the center of the pool.

"You are so easily pleased! Come, then," she said. The words were more than an invitation; they were a compulsion. I let her Fey magic settle over me like strands of spider silk. "Your love is a spark of the Divine in the Mundane world. Let us share it."

"Are we to sing, after all?" I asked, as the pond filled with mossy green radiance.

A fine spray leaped from the surface of the water as she laughed again.

"No, Magician," she said. I looked down and saw my own hands unbuttoning my waistcoat and then my breeches. "This is a rite of the flesh, and in flesh it will be performed."

Antoine rose to his feet. He was already naked, his manhood hard and ready. His wide eyes were shining with lust. Without a thought, he walked out onto the surface of the water, into Dayane's waiting embrace.

She wrapped her arms and her legs around him, guiding him inside her. As their lips met, Dayane's pool began to ripple again—a steady double beat. The rhythm of Antoine's heart.

She would accept nothing less than complete surrender, and I gave it willingly. I shed my clothes and joined them there in Dayane's sacred pool. Antoine and I were lost in a joyous, wordless world where she was all at once there with us, twined around us like the ropes of mare's tail, and flowing through us like bright liquor in our veins.

When we woke the next morning, clean, clothed and refreshed by our horses at the foot of the mountain, I heard the distant sound of Dayane's laughter. The wounds on Antoine's hand were healed completely, leaving only faint scars under the skin, like twisted cords.

XXXIV

Saint-Julien-by-the-Stream
1785

Jacques was quiet for a few minutes after the tale was done. Our pace up the high road was slow, and we were only halfway between Saint-Julien and the château gates.

When previously I had recounted the story of my time with his father, I had omitted many of the more intimate details, for the sake of good taste if nothing else. But in this instance, there was really no way of obfuscating the facts, and I felt it was time that he should know.

"My father broke his word," Jacques said finally. "That's what you think, isn't it?"

"It is—Cecile as much as said so. I believe your father betrayed his bargain with Lady Dayane, and Gévaudan's woes—along with your condition—are the result."

"A bargain he made under your guidance," he accused, and then he seemed to catch on his own thoughts. "I have seen those scars on his hand, though he is almost never without gloves. Is this why he has never spoken of the Red Winter to me? Because he made this demon's pact?"

"In part, no doubt."

Jacques's thoughts were sprinting now. "By the Lord. This is your remedy for my illness, isn't it? You mean for me to make another deal with this Dayane."

"If she is the cause, then I can think of no other way to cure you, Jacques."

"But?"

"But, as you have correctly deduced, your father betrayed her. Dayane may be unwilling to treat with us a second time. Or she may still be waiting to claim her payment."

"And what payment is that? Can we procure it?"

I let out a long breath. "That is the question, isn't it? This is one of the many things I will need to ask your father," I replied, with what I hoped was a reassuring smile.

I had expected that Cecile might be able to simplify my task or offer some guidance, but Dayane's disappearance only complicated matters further. Why would the nymph abandon Cecile, her mortal advocate, now that danger had come again to Gévaudan? Was she afraid? Was it some sort of reprisal for Antoine's betrayal?

What do you make of it? I asked, daring to hope that my Guest had intuited something I could not.

I hate to agree with the hedge-witch, but she has the right of it: trouble.

Very helpful. Thank you.

Sebastian, this is ***your*** *unfinished business. What do you expect me to say?*

Nothing! Nothing. I am frustrated, that's all.

I was also becoming increasingly distracted by our impending arrival at Château d'Ocerne. I had not seen Antoine for twenty years. His invitation to return had the air of a summons and I was not altogether sure what sort of welcome I should expect. Had he finally forgiven me, or was it a reckoning he sought? I hoped for the former, given he had offered me the bounty anew.

"Professor, I must speak to you about my father," blurted Jacques, as though reading my thoughts.

I gave a small moan of trepidation. "More? Sir, I apologize if my account is not to your liking, but I am doing my best, and it is not always an easy tale to tell."

"No, no. This apology is mine to make. I . . . I have not been truthful with you in one final thing."

"By the Christ," I muttered. "What now? Your falsehoods have nearly killed us both already, sir."

"I know, and I can only hope you will forgive me one last time." Jacques took a deep breath. "I am sorry, Professor, but my father did not send for you. He does not know you are coming, in fact."

What?

"What?"

I stopped the horse in the middle of the road, earning some colorful rebukes from fellow travelers.

"Whatever do you mean, sir?" I asked, as calmly as I could.

"We had begun to despair! The Beast was claiming a new victim every night! My father refused to seek help from the other barons, or to speak to the villagers about the attacks; not even a word of reassurance. And you must understand—he *would not tell us what happened* during the Red Winter!"

"'Us'? 'We'? We who?" I felt the beginnings of some strong emotional upset. My heart was thundering, my face became very hot and my stomach seemed to be filling with simmering vinegar.

"Eloise and I," he said. Then his brow creased. "Now that I

think on it, I believe she knew. She knew something was . . . wrong with me. Perhaps that is why she refused to wait any longer."

"And what did you do, your wife and you? Speak!"

"I knew a trick to get into my father's study. We sought a way to reach the others at first—the Normans and Bauterne, the heroes who vanquished . . . the ones I knew had hunted the Beast in the past. But Papa had kept nothing, only the original contract." Jacques swallowed; he seemed afraid to continue. "And then I found your letters."

"You—*you* read my letters? My *personal* letters?" I closed my eyes in chagrin. I remembered the state I had been in when I sent those letters to Antoine.

"We had no other avenues to pursue! What were we to do?" he countered, growing angry now. "Do you believe I *wanted* to read the sickening prose of my father's foul—"

I seized Jacques by the front of his waistcoat. "Have a care what next comes out of your mouth, boy," I said very quietly, biting the end of each word. "This is not an apology like any I have ever heard. If you wish to resume your journey home in my wagon, you will explain yourself properly."

I would like to point out, offered Sarmodel, *that I wanted you to kill him* ***weeks*** *ago.*

I did not trust myself to respond. I released the young lord and stepped back from the wagon.

Jacques collected himself, simply breathing in and out for a few seconds. "I *am* sorry. Please. You have come this far. Please, Professor. We need you!"

"Do you expect me to believe that—My God, the *money.* I take it this means the new bounty is also a lie?" I could barely get the words out.

"It is. Please, Professor. Papa cannot turn you away now that you are here."

"Oh, but he can, sir!" I snapped, clutching my head in my hands. "And what fantasy did you concoct to explain your absence?"

"I . . . I quarreled with my parents the day I left. I told them only that I was leaving Gévaudan to find help."

Back in the mountains, I think it was. I said, "Kill him now," right after he transformed into a—

*Be **silent**, Sarmodel!*

I stared at Jacques, trembling. "You are asking me, young sir, to arrive unannounced and unexpected to your father's house after decades of estrangement, and there to throw myself upon his mercy."

Jacques looked ashamed, but no less earnest. "I am. I will not let anything happen to you, I swear it."

"Oh!" I raised my hands heavenward. "Such reassurance from the young lord who can barely wipe his own backside! Do you understand, you little *idiot,* that your father could have me committed to trial for heresy? Or clapped in irons and drowned in the sea—your own words, I believe. The things I told him—the things I have told *you*—my God!"

"One night, Professor. Stay just one night, and see." Jacques's hollow eyes implored me.

We remained thus, staring at each other, for a painful few moments.

Then I stepped in close to him. It was gratifying to see him flinch, but I had decided against a physical confrontation. I elbowed Jacques aside and opened my trunk, situated beside him in the wagon. With a sound somewhere between a sigh and a grunt, I took my courtly wig out of its case and placed it on my head, adjusting the cloth cap and powder-gray curls over my hair as best I could. Then I fastened my sword and pistols to my belt; best to be prepared for whatever awaited.

"One night," I said, thrusting a finger in Jacques's face. I whistled the horse into motion again. "And I expect my expenses to be paid in full before dinner."

It was a strange feeling, returning to the courtyard of Château d'Ocerne after twenty years. Even bereft of its crowds and pageantry, the parterre courtyard with its gurgling fountains had an imposing grandeur.

There were differences. It had been springtime when I first assigned myself to the hunt before the Bishop of Mende; it was close to winter now and the gardens were shedding the last of their autumn foliage. The outbuildings were as I remembered them, though in better condition. And everywhere were people occupied with the business of running the château, carrying wood or flour or baskets of linens. It seemed the Ocerne estate had not suffered the same dilapidation as the rest of the barony—on the contrary, Antoine as lord had added conspicuous luxuries and embellishments. I did not see this as a good sign.

The château's state of high alert was also much in evidence. Guards watched us as we approached the gatehouse, and the walls were bristling with armed men. We were stopped within moments of stepping inside.

"Do you have business at Château d'Ocerne?" asked a young guardsman.

"We do indeed." Jacques stood with some effort, removing his hood. "Notify my mother that I have returned."

The ensuing commotion was quite exhausting.

A short while later, I found myself in the opulent marble-floored parlor of the château, sharing a very uncomfortable silence with Jacques. At his request, the guards had cleared the room of staff and attendants, and closed the doors behind them.

Sebastian, I am hungry, complained Sarmodel.

I know, my love. As am I.

In truth, I was ready to jump out of my skin. My eyes flicked back and forth between Jacques and the grand doors, expecting Antoine to enter at any moment.

"Jacques—*Jacques*!" The doors swung open and a tall woman entered the parlor. She was flanked by the elderly château butler and the housekeeper, who were both hurrying to keep up with her. I felt an uncomfortable heat creeping up beneath my collar. She could only be the Lady of Château d'Ocerne, Jacques's mother. Antoine's wife.

"My God, where have you *been*?" Lady Ocerne crossed the floor with rapid strides, lifting the skirts of her ivory gown. She enfolded her son in an embrace that looked almost painful in its intensity.

I could barely look at her face. I remembered her only from a distant glimpse twenty years prior, and she had been but a girl, newly arrived to meet her betrothed. And now this was her house, and I an uninvited and very likely unwelcome guest.

Now in her thirties, Lady Ninette Avenel d'Ocerne was taller than her children and, I deduced, impeccably fashionable. Her cream-colored gown was decorated with cerise ribbons and white lace, with a sumptuous stomacher of embroidered gold peonies and blister pearls. Her face was powdered to milky whiteness, and her dark brown hair was piled up on her head in elaborate curls.

"I went to get help, Mother," answered Jacques, when she released him.

"Without leave from your father? Or from me?" she countered. "We needed you here, Jacques. Your *wife* needed you here."

"Where is Eloise?" he asked.

"She does not know you are here; I decided to let her rest. She has barely slept these past few weeks, with the worry of your disappearance and the killings in the villages. She has requested more than once to return to her family in Saint-Chély. I suggest you go to her as soon as you have bathed and dressed properly. And where are Gerard and Henri? Their father is near mad with worry. I have had to give him time away from his duties in the kitchen."

Oh dear, I said to Sarmodel. *I had forgotten about them.*

Indeed.

"Mother, I'm sorry." Jacques's eyes brimmed over again. "They will not . . . they will not return. There was an accident in the mountains, and . . ."

Lady Ocerne was silent in shock, her eyes wide. "No, Jacques. Oh no." The housekeeper behind her gasped and covered her mouth with her hands.

Jacques's mother took a step back from him and slapped him sharply across the cheek. He did not resist or even react. Her own tears cut through the powder on her face and she looked at him in despair.

"Oh, my son. Now, perhaps you will begin to learn that you are not a child anymore. My God—your father." She shook her head. "I cannot tell him."

"I will tell him myself," said Jacques, with some bitterness. "We have *many* things to talk about. Where is he?"

"He is not here, Jacques," replied his mother. "When you absconded, he traveled the length and breadth of the barony seeking word of you. And when he found none, he went himself to find aid against this Beast."

He's not here?

"Aid? From whom?"

He's not here!

I was relieved beyond words. Though it was only postponing the inevitable, it would at least give me time to prepare myself before I saw Antoine again. Or at least to have a bath.

"I do not know, and *you* have no right to ask," Lady Ocerne said. "Were our troubles not great enough? Did you think to prove yourself by abandoning your home—your *family*?"

"Mother, I went to find help and I have returned *with help*." He gestured to me. "This is Professor Sebastian Grave. He helped defeat the Beast during the Red Winter."

Lady Ocerne closed her eyes in a moment of private mortification; she had clearly failed to notice me in her agitated state, and this was a scene most unbecoming for the lady of the house.

"I apologize, Professor Grave. This is quite unforgivable. You are not meeting us at our best."

"My lady, please do not trouble yourself," I replied with a bow. "I remember well the terror of the Red Winter. It is an extraordinary household that can keep decorum during such a scourge."

She looked at me steadily. "The Red Winter. You must have been a young man indeed. Did you know my husband?"

"I did, my lady."

"Mother, please," interrupted Jacques. "Professor Grave has saved my life more than once. He has earned our hospitality at the least."

Lady Ocerne seemed to gather herself. "Certainly, he has. Marguerite, please prepare a room and a bath for our guest," she said to the housekeeper, who curtsied and left immediately. "Professor, you must join us for dinner. Please allow me to make amends for this most discourteous reception."

"I would be honored," I said, though there was nothing I desired less than to spend the evening exchanging witticisms with the bewigged nobility of Gévaudan.

"Of course. I have much to do before dinner, beginning with deciding how to tell my cook that his sons are dead," said Lady Ocerne. Then she turned to Jacques once more, pointing a shaking finger at his face. "Go and see your wife."

Lady Ocerne took her leave, along with the housekeeper Marguerite. We were left with the butler, who introduced himself as Dimitri.

"I will have your belongings brought up to your chamber, Professor Grave," he said. "Your horse is being cared for and should be ready by tomorrow, should you require it."

"My thanks," I said. Then I gave Jacques a meaningful look.

"There is one more thing, Dimitri," said my young companion. "The professor has incurred expenses on my behalf, not least of all in caring for me after I was injured."

The elderly butler scratched nervously under his wig. "My lord, I recall a great sum was disbursed for you, only last month. Yes indeed, you came to me with Gerard and Henri—"

"Yes indeed." Jacques spoke through his teeth. "And the money was lost in the mountains, along with them."

"My lord, you *lost* three hundred livres?"

"It was closer to two hundred and fifty[1] by then, but yes."

"If it is of any assistance, gentlemen," I interrupted, offering the butler a rolled sheet of paper, "I have run an account."

1. Two hundred and fifty-seven, to be precise.

XXXV

She wasn't beautiful, but her face was pleasant and her smile easy. I hated her. She was polite and gracious and intelligent, and I hated her even more.

Sebastian, what is wrong with you? Sarmodel asked. He can't *exactly* read my thoughts, but he knows when I'm feeling strongly about something, or someone. *I feel like you're about to burst into flames.*

It's nothing, I grated. *You wouldn't understand.*

You're always so sure of that. I might be able to help.

I ate something to keep my hands busy. *I doubt that.*

I could feel Sarmodel strumming my senses with unusual attention. *Ah,* he said. *It's the wife. The Baroness d'Ocerne. She got something you wanted.*

Yes, Sarmodel. She got something I wanted very much, and without even trying.

Was that so hard to admit?

You do not have a heart, I replied harshly. Outwardly I was talking light philosophy with Eloise; Jacques's young wife was surprisingly inoffensive, and quite well-read. I feigned a spell of coughing to disguise the tears in my eyes—of hurt, humiliation or rage, I couldn't have said. *But if you did, you would understand that there is nothing harder to admit in the world.*

Sarmodel was silent for the rest of the meal but I could feel him turning in my mind.

I was treated as an honored guest. The table was set with an extravagant porcelain dinner service, decorated with a wolf-hunt scene in exquisitely detailed relief. Everywhere was the sparkle of silver, from the engraved cutlery to the scallop-and-swan candelabra. Lady Ocerne must have emptied her stores for us. We ate watercress and pheasant soup; roasted duck and quails in pots of sage butter; wine-glazed pork; potatoes crushed with garlic and leeks; mushrooms as large as plates, dripping in mustard cream; soft bread, cheeses and tart plum pastries.

It was all so much dust in my mouth. I acquitted myself well in the face of Lady Ocerne's munificence, accepting with courtesy all that was offered and complimenting both the cook and the lady herself. She was distracted—concerned for Antoine, and confused by the behavior of her son, though she hid both very well.

I loathed her poise and her easy rapport with the castle staff. I even found something despicable in Jacques and Eloise's cow-eyed devotion to each other.[1]

I retired to the guest quarters early, pleading weariness.

It had been a mistake coming back to Gévaudan after all. How

1. Something of a rarity among married couples in the nobility, who usually made a career of despising each other as soon as the vows were done. It was also interesting to see Jacques so enamored of his wife, given what I knew of his past with Lorette.

could I have believed that Antoine would send for me after all this time? Jacques was not redeemed by his apology. If I had been more alert, I would have seen that there was something amiss with the whole proposition, from the very beginning.

Yes, more alert, and less blinded by the desire to return to something that was no longer there.

The fire had been lit in my chamber. A pair of elaborate high-backed chairs basked invitingly before it and I sat with gratitude, watching the flames. I resolved to depart in the morning, before Antoine's return. I would leave it to his family to tell him as much or as little as they wished of my visit.

The edges of my vision flickered as Sarmodel Projected into the chair opposite me. He was watching me in his favored human guise, my child self. His sharp nose and dark, serious eyes were too grim for a boy's face.

I am sorry, I sent to him. *About what I said. About not having a heart. It wasn't fair.*

I was surprised by my own reaction. Jealousy of any kind is quite out of character for me, and I had always known Antoine would marry. Perhaps it was the final dashing of my lovelorn fantasy—that Antoine had in fact been desperately yearning for me all this time, miserable in an arranged marriage to a witless *madame*—which had so poisoned my mood.

Sarmodel reached over and placed a spectral hand on my arm. *I have eaten hearts, Sebastian,* he said, not unkindly, *and they are as any other meat. The only one that matters to me is yours, and I have shared it with you for lifetimes. These Mundanes are not worthy of it.*

Even Antoine? I smiled ruefully.

Even him. The boy I had been smiled back at me.

I suppose I won't need that quicksilver after all. I used my foot to give a little shove to my trunk, loaded with my arsenal of the high occult. *I've been a fool from the beginning. What a ridiculous waste of time.*

You're really going to leave? He raised a dark eyebrow. *With all of this trouble unresolved?*

Unresolved? We nearly died the last time we tried to "resolve" this particular trouble, I said.

You do not believe the risk is worth it? What about Antoine? He seemed genuinely perplexed.

Antoine doesn't want my help, Sarmodel! He never did. Whatever is going on here can run its course without me. I drew a sigh that somehow turned into a sob. I covered my face with my hands and wept.

Sebastian. I felt Sarmodel's hand on my shoulder. *You have lived thousands of years. Do you truly have more tears for this one man? You cried so many for him.* I felt him flowing, flickering around me. *This one Mundane, mortal man . . .*

Sarmodel, stop.

. . . this one, dying, imperfect creature . . .

I turned to see him Projected again, now on the great wooden bed. My breath caught and I could only stare, utterly ensnared.

. . . this one product of mortal tissue, so easily re-created . . .

He was Antoine as I had known him, naked and beautiful. His blond beard was dusted with snowflakes and his skin was like polished wood in the firelight. Sarmodel extended a hand to me. It bore the bite I remembered so clearly, the punctures welling with bright jewels of blood. A fallen maple leaf was stuck to his thigh, from that first night we spent as lovers. He saw the longing in my eyes and broke my heart with Antoine's smile.

I know everything you loved about him, Sebastian. I loved him with you. The voice in my mind was Antoine's. *Come. Take comfort with me.*

I moved to the bedside, powerfully drawn to him—drawn to

both of them: the man I remembered and the demon I had always known. I knelt and he touched my face, leaving streaks of blood across my cheek. He stroked my ear as Antoine once had, and his lips as he leaned forward were firm and eager on my mouth.

"Antoine . . ."

Yes, my love. He smelled of the wilderness—pine, leather and horses. Smoke. Sweat, sex and blood. I tasted brandy in his mouth; the publican's best from the Bow and Brace. And underneath it all was the tang of Tartarus, a trace of hot sulfur and burning metal. *I can give him to you. And you can give him to me.*

I felt him reaching tenderly into the parts of my mind I guarded the closest. He pulled at the memories I held so painfully, teasing them gently away from me as he guided my hands to his body. He was hard and willing in my grip, and his skin was burning. His kiss grew more intense and his hands tugged at my clothes as I responded to his touch.[2]

The temptation was overwhelming. It would be easy to give it all to Sarmodel, to just . . . let him. The betrayal would lose its sting. The memories of Antoine would lose their color and he would be just another face among the multitude in my mind. Soon, I would have trouble remembering his name. Sarmodel would grow stronger on the charge of my anguish and I would never have to feel it again. One day, the memory of Antoine would be gone altogether and I would be none the wiser.

---

2. I have been asked whether Sarmodel is physically *there* on occasions like this, or whether he's just playing shadow puppets in my mind. The short answer is, fortunately, the latter. It takes significant anima for a Spirit to create matter of any kind, let alone a functioning, sensate human body; he wouldn't waste it turning tricks for me. If Sarmodel and I do ever "touch," be assured that it is an entirely simulated experience, albeit an immersive one.

But . . .

But . . .

I couldn't.

"Sarmodel, stop," I said, gently pushing his hands away. "This isn't—"

Ssh. Let me take it from you, and tomorrow you may look at all of this with a clear head.

"I don't want to. Not this time."

Antoine's eyes regarded me gravely and I thought my Guest was about to insist. But then he leaned forward and kissed me again, softly.

Then speak no more of leaving. You know we still have much to do here, and your business with Baron Avenel d'Ocerne is the least of it.

I pulled away from him sharply.

"I see! Yes—yes, indeed! Let us not forget the fragment of the Olympian *you* have come so far to claim. Best not to let your mortal bag of meat complicate things!"

Sebastian, please. ***We*** *have been hunting Avstamet for over three centuries. This may be our last chance. Even if you won't kill him, the young lord is likely to die one way or another—let us be here when it happens.* Antoine's hand caressed my throat. *And are you not eager for your own restitution? For all the humiliations of the past?*

"And then what?" I asked. "Then what? The next Contract, the next Beast? The next great hunt? The next Antoine? Let us consume all of them, for there will always be another and then another, will there not?" I stood and turned my back on him, my hands shaking. "Please change! This is a cruel trick, Sarmodel! Change now, or go away." I could no longer bear to look at his perfect re-creation of Antoine. "Must you always have your way?"

He was silent for a few long seconds and I thought that he

had mercifully decided to dispel his Projection. But then his voice thrummed in my mind again, and it was no longer Antoine's.

I am cruel, Sebastian, he said, *but not to you. Never to you.*

I turned around slowly, feeling the Arcane ripples of his transformation. On the bed he lay, with his arm outstretched, his form shifting from one heartbeat to the next. From moment to moment he was Helen, Narcissus, Dayane, deadly Belqis, Ayesha, Alexander and innocent Percifal, each of them breathed into life from my memories. Even Livia appeared, smiling wickedly around her fangs, and Johan Weiss, and Hannah the Brewster; lovely, shunned and doomed. Sarmodel was an ever-changing idol of desire, cracking my resolve with every object of my lust over thousands of years. All except one; Antoine's face did not appear again among the many.

Come. No tricks. Now he was Wanassa the Lady, unimaginable in her splendor, and unthinkable in her depravity. *What are we if not lovers?*

I was lost with my first step, and we took each other hungrily.

The blissful morning of meditation I had anticipated was not to be.

Frantic knocking on my door drew me back to the world from my trance.

"Professor Grave!" The man's voice was unfamiliar.

It was perhaps an hour after dawn, and my chamber was filled with peaceful, rosy light, quite at odds with the insistent banging. I became aware of a more distant disturbance as well; there was shouting and movement out in the courtyard.

I answered the door to find a breathless young attendant.

"Professor Grave, you are needed immediately in the chapel."

"The chapel?"

Well, this is unexpected, said Sarmodel wearily.[3] *An invitation to the House of the Almighty.*

"Yes, sir. Lady Ocerne is waiting for you."

I put on a silk banyan robe in midnight blue, picked up my valise and followed him back through the château's sumptuous corridors to the courtyard.

Sebastian—blood. Sarmodel drew my attention to a number of small stains on the ground leading into the chapel.

I see it.

Guards had been posted outside the chapel doors, and they let me pass with a nod. The attendant was not so permitted.

The chapel was very well appointed, particularly given its diminutive size. Elaborate plasterwork and stained glass gave it a slightly overstuffed opulence.[4]

Lady Ocerne was standing in front of the altar, facing one of the left-hand pews. She was frowning, her eyes dissecting a figure who slumped there, sobbing. The lady was freshly risen from her chamber, wearing a rose-colored redingote to cover her nightclothes. One of her maids had wrapped an embroidered violet scarf into a turban around her head, so she was at least passably attired for public viewing. In one hand she held a decorative silver pitcher, which I surmised was full of altar wine. The other hand she rested

---

3. We were both quite tired after our evening of debauchery. That sort of recreation requires a decent amount of energy—both Mundane and Arcane—from both of us, which is one of the reasons we do it so rarely.

4. This still grates on me. Putting aside the flagrant corruption and/or money which could have been spent on feeding the poor etc., the Church's many crimes against good taste during the Baroque remain difficult to forgive.

on her hip, in a posture that spoke much of her impatience. Her sleeve was smeared with blood.

"My lady?" I ventured, stepping inside. My voice echoed sanctimoniously.

She greeted me more with exasperation than relief. "You have arrived, sir," she said, and then turned to the figure sitting in the pew. "He has arrived! Will you speak now?"

I hurried to the front of the chapel, my footsteps very loud on the marble floor. The person on the pew turned in her seat, revealing her tear-streaked face to me.

"Mademoiselle Lorette?"

The girl was clutching a fine glass goblet full of wine with shaking hands. She looked very out of place in her ill-fitting, grass-stained pinafore.

"Come, girl. You are a friend of my son's, and for that I will excuse this intrusion. But now you will speak, or I will have you removed. And flogged in the square," warned Lady Ocerne.

"Professor! I . . . I . . ." Lorette seemed to be in shock. Her hands shook to the point of spilling the wine.

"Calm down, ssh," I said, kneeling beside her. Her hands and the front of her skirts were covered in blood, still fresh. "Come, drink up."

Lorette drained the goblet in a matter of seconds and Lady Ocerne wordlessly refilled it.

Lady Ocerne noticed my shock; a French noblewoman did not serve others, especially not with her own hands. "Forgive me if I do not trust the discretion of the staff. I wish my husband to know as little of this as possible," she said. "It is not *appropriate* for Lorette to be here, as she knows," she added coldly.

"Of course." It was hardly surprising. Lord Ocerne would

scarcely approve of his son's former sweetheart visiting the château in the early hours.

Lady Ocerne was regarding me with suspicion. "Professor, the young lady arrived not half an hour ago, in this state. She asked for you specifically and would not speak—or leave—until I sent for you. Perhaps, before you spend another night in my house, you will tell me *why,* along with who you really are."

"In good time, my lady."

"In good time, then." None of the suspicion left her eyes.

I returned my attention to the trembling girl. Lorette's expression was grim and haunted; she was barely keeping her composure. "Can you tell me what has happened, Lorette?"

She drew a deep breath. I feared for a moment that she might faint. "Professor," she said. "I was going down to bathe and I found her."

A hot, heavy weight began to grow in my gut. "Found who?"

"Mama," she said. "She was on the path." Lorette suddenly began to sob in great, gulping breaths that racked her entire frame.

"Mademoiselle Cecile?" asked Lady Ocerne.

"I went down to the river to find her and she was—she was—" Her voice suddenly rose to a wail. "Oh Mama! By the Christ, he killed her! He killed her in the night and he ate her heart!"

PART FOUR

A Number of Betrayals

ADDENDUM:

On Captain Renard

Abbey of Sainte-Anne
Loire Valley, France
1437

Goodness gracious. Here we are, back in a cell.

Distracted by his pursuit of Barron/Avstamet, the master has not noticed that he is himself being pursued, and now he's a prisoner, with a private room in the cellar of a local convent. I can picture it well—I left my hand there, turning purple in a vise.

Unlike Jehanne d'Arc, Sebastian Grave the witch will not receive the dubious benefit of a tribunal hearing. Archangel Michael's cat's-paw, the handsome, white-haired Captain Renard, visits him personally to extract information. The captain is an Arcane artificer of some talent, and his creativity takes flight in the abbey's smithy. He arrives at the cell every few days with all manner of hooks and hammers and burrs, or occasionally a glowing brand if he's feeling puckish. He always leaves frustrated and furious, his uniform generously spattered from his day's work.[1]

1. My experience of Captain Renard leads me to believe that not all the spatter was on the outside.

The questions are always the same. Some are clearly coming directly from the whiskered lips of the Archangel, but others betray more human preoccupations. Where is the relic? Who has the relic? What is the master's True name? Has he lain with another man? What was it like?

The master's spirit is strong, but so is the Choking Braid the captain has forged into his chains. Without access to his Arcane talents and no way to feed the old one, Sebastian is just meat on the rack—meat wrapped around information that the Archangel wants.

The captain is very happy to do the unwrapping.

Captain Renard's golden eyes were, as always, the first thing Sebastian saw when he returned to consciousness.

The righteous captain had climbed onto the rack atop his captive, his face very close and feverishly intent. He roused his unconscious prisoner by worming the pommel of his knife between the man's ribs until the pain brought him back to waking, screaming life.

"I see you, Sebastian Grave," he whispered, when the master's cries subsided. The captain was close enough for the prisoner to taste his breath. "In that first moment when you open your eyes, between sleeping and waking, I *see you*. Without artifice, without vice; innocent as Adam. You are naked to me, do you understand?"

"I am naked to anyone who wanders past the doorway!" croaked the master. His body was thin and filthy, and covered in the marks of his abuse. He had seen nothing but the inside of the abbey's cellar for months. The small stone room, lit only by a slant of sunlight from the ceiling grate, had become all he knew. Every few days, they would bring in an apple-wood table and it became the rack upon which he was tortured. "And I was not 'sleeping.' Perhaps the next time I lose my senses, you might cover me with a blanket for the sake of decency."

"Do you truly feel no different?" the captain asked in earnest. "Lighter, perhaps?"

"The only thing I *feel* is you poking me—both places."

The master screamed again as the pommel pushed deeper, burrowing slowly into the tender flesh.

"And your venom returns, as ever," sighed the captain. "Next time I shall use the sharp end."

He climbed down to the floor and returned the knife to its sheath. He picked up a flask of water and positioned it for the prisoner to drink, which the man did greedily. "Sometimes I despair that I will ever bring you to the Father's light. Every day, I hope that the change will take root; that you will awaken with your pure soul drained of its corruption. And every day, you fall anew." He smiled sadly. "The demon within you is an anchor you will not relinquish."

The captain turned to a bench beneath the window. On it were arranged several of his dearest, cruelest tools, made with his own hands. "All of my ingenuity, inspired by the Archangel himself. To what end?" He ran his fingertips lightly across them.

"Oh, chin up, Captain," said Sebastian, his voice stronger after the water. "Soon I'll be dead, and you may diddle my remains with as many toys as you like." He shifted on the rack, wincing. "Come. What shall we discuss today?"

Renard looked over his shoulder at Sebastian. "You are trying to anger me. And you will not die without embracing the Lord, I promise you." He moved to the head of the table, where the Arcane chains secured the prisoner and stifled any eldritch utterance. The captain checked the intricate links as he spoke, thumbing them like a rosary. "No, there will be no questions today. I have decided on a different course. If the mortification of your flesh will not bring you into the light, then I will turn to the power of the Holy Spirit to free you. Perhaps then you will tell me what I need to know."

"The power of the Holy Spirit—an *exorcism*?"

The captain nodded grimly.

Weakly, Sebastian began to laugh. "You can't be serious. Do you believe you'd be the first to try?"

"I have enlisted a champion of the Almighty," said Renard implacably. "Your soul will be burned free of its demon."

"As far as I can tell, they are one and the same," said Sebastian. "Who exactly have you got coming down here to help? The abbess?"

"Your mockery ill becomes you, witch," replied the captain. "No. The bishop himself rides in secret to meet me at Montargis. I leave today to provide him escort."

"The Bishop of Beauvais? Of course. No doubt he is still smarting after losing the Maiden's relic the first time." Sebastian lay back and closed his eyes. "Captain, listen to me. I have a different proposition, if you would hear it."

The captain huffed, on the edge of a rebuke. Sebastian's eyes were closed in exhaustion, but he could hear the man breathing, as though enduring some private struggle.

"Unless . . . unless you offer the information I seek, pray hold your tongue!"

"I offer freedom, for both of us," answered the master wearily. He opened his eyes again and looked directly at the captain. "Are you not tired of the Archangel's charge on your head? Set me free. It will take only a few words to unlock my bonds.[2] Forget this maddening, thankless service. And *come with me.* You can, you know."

The captain sucked in a sharp breath. It was a sound of mingled shame, fear and shock, as though the master had caught him undressing.

"Yes, I know you have thought about it. You are wasted here, Captain. Do you not wonder about the voices you hear and the things you see with those strange eyes of yours? The miraculous devices you create with your hands? The shapes in your head? I can help you understand where it all comes from. I can help you understand *who you are.*"

Captain Renard did not speak. He was breathing heavily, his eyes downcast. His hands opened and closed uselessly.

"Come, Captain. Michael sees your gifts—and *uses* them—but he does not trust you with your own power." Sebastian smiled. "He is denying you your birthright. I can teach you. And Livia—I'm sure you haven't forgotten her. She has her own secrets to teach. The world is so much more than prayer and duty."

"Stop!"

The captain stepped up beside the rack again, his face transformed with passion. He reached out toward the master; he might have been preparing either to embrace the prisoner or to strangle him.

"Yes. Let me go," whispered Sebastian. "Say the words. Please. Come with me."

Renard trembled there for a long moment.

---

2. The Choking Braid can only be unlocked with a spoken phrase, chosen by the artificer. The diabolical beauty of the charm is that, even if the prisoner knows the words, the Braid itself prevents him from speaking them.

And then his hands fell to his sides. He wiped perspiration from his face and shook his head slowly as his ardor subsided.

"So, this is temptation," he said. "The Archangel warned me, but I did not understand." Tears ran down his face as he looked once again at the man on the rack. "No, witch. Here you will remain, until I return with the bishop. He will test you with a light such as you have never imagined."

"It doesn't matter, Captain," said Sebastian, defeated. "I can't count how many times I've had some zealot take a wedge to my immortal soul. I've tried it myself—with the assistance of a manifest demiurge, no less. It will not work."

"Then you had best pray the bishop can succeed where the others have failed," said Renard. "If you will not be redeemed, Sebastian Grave, then you will burn. I will find the relic for the Archangel, on my own."

The captain left without another word.

The master's bravado fell away. He shouted desperately to the empty cell, his face gray. "Michael! Are you there? If you want the Olympian, you will show yourself!" His lips were tight across his teeth. "This mortal cruelty is beneath you. *Show yourself* if you would treat with me!"

But the Archangel, if he was present, did not respond.

Perhaps an hour passed, and the prisoner heard footsteps on the stairs.

A nun entered the room.

"Livia?" Sebastian said hopefully, raising his head. "By the Rift, I thought you were never—"

But no. Though the gray woolen habit was the same, this was a true woman of God. She was old, with a wary, squinting aspect, and she wore a large pectoral cross on a chain around her neck. She carried a bucket of soapy water and a bundle of clothes.

"Abbess Agace," said the master, disappointed. "I do apologize for my condition. The good captain cares little for my dignity of late."

"I've lived over fifty years of this war; your shame does not interest me. But Captain Renard has left instructions for you to be respectable and in good health when the bishop arrives," she replied.

"It seems lowly work for the woman in charge," the master said.

"It is," replied the abbess dryly. "But I need my table back." She took a soapy rag from the bucket and began to wash the prisoner, scrubbing him roughly, as she might a horse.

"Ah! Please, Sister, have a care!" Sebastian winced as the cloth dragged over his wounds.

The nun seemed about to chastise him, and then she softened. "Beg pardon." She inclined her head and assumed a gentler manner, dabbing cautiously at Sebastian's torn skin and tender bruises. Abbess Agace shook her head. "One would think the captain had seen enough bloodshed out there on the battlefield. I will see to your wounds in a moment, when you are clean."

"I don't suppose you might unchain me?"

She snorted. "Certainly. Why don't I go right ahead and stab myself with yon shears as well?"

The master laughed in spite of himself. "I had to ask."

The nun's mouth pursed briefly, and then she resumed her work. "You are not like the temptress, or that gold-crazed abomination locked up beneath the chapel. The captain scourged them just as deeply as you, and they screamed and wept and raged. You are different. Unbowed. Civilized. Charming." She rinsed the cloth in the bucket. "But I know you are a demon, just as they are demons. So save your clever words, if you please. You will need them when the bishop arrives."

"And when will that be?"

She shrugged, wiping carefully at a shredded flap of skin under his arm. "Several days. You will have time to rest and eat some proper food. Bread and barley soup. Eggs, if you keep your manners. You will need to be strong for the rite."

"Yes indeed," he murmured.

Abbess Agace worked quickly. When she was done, she straightened slowly and pressed her fingertips to the small of her back, groaning. From inside her habit, she produced a little bottle of pale golden liquid and took a swig.

The prisoner came alive at the sight of it.

"Sister! Sister, please," Sebastian said. His eyes were wide, following the bottle, which glowed amber in the light. "What is that?"

The abbess belched brandy fumes. "It is my elixir, for my pains."

"Might—might I have a measure?"

The old nun puckered her mouth. "You presume much for a man on the rack."

"Please, Sister. If it is a tonic, then *please*—share a mouthful with me." He implored her with his eyes, rattling his chains pitifully. "If you would claim any mercy at all—my pain is also great, and there is every chance that I will not survive the bishop's purging."

With a sigh, the abbess uncorked the bottle again. "Very

well. With God's grace it will put you to sleep and I will be able to dress you in peace."

She placed one hand under his head and carefully held the bottle to his lips. Before she could stop him, the prisoner took the neck between his teeth and bolted down a mighty draft.

"Well—*well now*!" Abbess Agace snatched back the bottle and let his head fall with a crack. She brought her hand back around in a sharp slap. "Ingrate! It is down to the lees—and what now?! What is left for me, when my pains return?"

"I don't know," said the prisoner. His eyes were closed, his face transfigured in rapture. His breathing was suddenly very loud. "I don't know . . . what will happen . . ."

The abbess stared at him, first in fury, then in confusion, and then finally—when she realized what was happening—in terror.

XXXVI

Saint-Julien-by-the-Stream
1785

I departed the château immediately, leaving Lorette in Lady Ocerne's care—the girl did not need to return to the site of her mother's murder. I paused only to secure my horse at the midwife's stoop.

I found Cecile on the path outside her back gate.

Outside her back gate, and outside the Circle of her formidable Arcane Wards. Cecile had been defenseless when her assailant had struck.

The *sage-femme*'s laundry tub and its load of linens lay discarded in the reeds, miraculously upright and undisturbed. Her killer had opened the front of her body like just another layer of clothing beneath her stays and chemise. The bulrushes and the stones of her garden wall had been sprayed with her blood. And, just as Lorette had said, he had eaten her heart; there would be no lingering specter for me to question.

As I feared, there were five-toed prints in the mud leading back down into the river.

I swore.

It appears the young lord got hungry overnight, said Sarmodel.

Or there's another heart-eating monstrosity in Gévaudan.

Come. Do you think that's likely?

You're right. I should have locked him up, back at the château.

Locked him up? You should have killed him weeks ago!

But I didn't, Sarmodel! I didn't. I decided to come back, because I know I can fix this.

You're off to a cracking start, I must say.

I knelt by Cecile's corpse, careful not to disturb the puddle of blood that had lengthened from her body down toward the river. Cecile's gray eyes were open, but they showed only the reflection of the sky. I lifted her blood-matted hair away from her face, searching for the cord around her neck.

Nothing.

Frustrated, I returned to the witch's walled garden, where we had shared tea only the day before. It was tranquil and filled with the sleepy drone of bees about their business. The circular pool was a deep green mirror. Cecile's Wards overhead were in the late stages of collapse; by now it was only the residual charge in her Circle keeping them alive.

But then there, under the indigo crests of the irises, I detected the familiar beat of primeval power.

Cecile's russet fox sat in the shade of the waving stalks, watching me with its white eyes. The familiar was leaking blood and plasma from two deep gashes along its back, and to my great relief, it held the hagstone between its teeth. Its Arcane form, the wrinkled canult, was weeping, and not only from the pain of its injuries, I think.

I walked slowly toward the witch's familiar and knelt on the clover. "You served bravely, little one," I said. "Your mistress would be proud."

Limping, the fox came forward and dropped the talisman into my palm. Then it rested its head in my hands for a moment, panting. With a sigh, it discorporated into glowing vapor, its duty done.

Don't you dare, I said, feeling Sarmodel's Arcane jaws opening. He subsided with a grunt and the familiar's essence left the world unimpeded.

There was no time to waste.

I moved to the edge of the still pool in the center of the garden. Even in the clear morning light, its kinship with Dayane's shadowy, sacred pool was unmistakable. I knelt in the clover and held the hagstone up between my thumb and forefinger. The hole in the center, worn over centuries by the stream of Dayane's sacred waterfall, seemed to wink with passing shadows.

Sebastian! What are you doing?

"I need to make things right with Dayane—and to do that, I need to know what she was promised twenty years ago." With a deep breath, I held the stone to my eye, looking directly through the center. "Cecile used this to commune with her, and her heart was not the only place she kept her secrets."

No! You have no idea what might be in there!

I allowed my vision to shift through the Arcane spectrum and beyond, telescoping through the tiny circular aperture. The stone pulsed, and then pulsed again.

Then it grew suddenly immense, a planetary void looming around everything, an endless loop that bounded not only my vision, but the world entire.

With a nauseating lurch, Sarmodel and I were pulled inside.

I still knelt by the pool in Cecile's garden, but now I was also somewhere else.

At the edges of my vision were flickers of another place—the beautiful emerald pond that should not exist in the winter mountains. If I looked into the pool, I could see the reflection of the wildwood and hear the cascade trickling eternally onto the black granite slab. Beneath the surface of the water, the mare's tail swayed.

It was a green, dreaming place, an Astral simulacrum halfway between Cecile's garden and the naiad's shrine. It was both places at once, and not truly either. Here Cecile would have communicated with her patron over the years of their relationship, receiving instruction on her Arcane journey.

Dozing beside me in the clover was not Antoine this time, but rather a frightful thing; a filthy, ragged baboon with a garishly painted face. It roused itself to wakefulness with a shriek, showing its fangs.

"Sebastian, get us out of here! This is not safe!" The voice came from all around me, but I knew it was the mandrill speaking. The animal whirled around, hissing in threat.

"I need to know," I said, my voice echoing with a thick, underwater quality. "Courage, Sarmodel."

Dayane was not here; Cecile had been correct about that much. Whatever connection the naiad had to this place was gone.

But Cecile herself . . . something of her lingered here in her garden, in this eternal, impossible glade. Nothing as useful as her ghost, but there was still an echo of her, an enduring imprint she had left over many years, like the impression of her body in her bedclothes.

"Help me, please," I murmured. I sensed more than saw a figure walking among the flower beds. I felt her kneeling there among the salvias, digging at the soil, and—*over there*—heard the slosh of water carried in a bucket from the river. All around me, Cecile still labored in her garden.

"Yes, Cecile. I am here. Show me. *Show me.*"

At first there was nothing. Whatever shadow of the herbalist remained here seemed unwilling to communicate with me.

And then I saw her.

She was Cecile as I had first met her—a ragged, pimply young woman, her face serious and her gray eyes full of scorn. She knelt by the pool opposite me, and in her arms was a sleeping baby wrapped in a fur blanket. She crooned and tutted as the child began to wake, and snatches of some soft lullaby reached me across the water.

The baboon hissed and leaped onto my shoulders. He dug painfully into my flesh with his hands and feet, snarling close to my ear.

"We are exposed here, Sebastian![1] *Get us out!*"

"Just a moment longer! I *know* she has something to tell us!"

I reached up to squeeze his arm in comfort and he gave a threatening hoot deep in his chest.

"You owe a debt, my lord," Cecile said suddenly, to someone I could not see. Her face was drawn in distress and the baby was beginning to cry. "Will you bc truc?"

"Please! What do you mean, Cecile? What was the debt?" I asked.

But she did not answer—or could not. Tenderly, she set the baby down on the ground. With gentle care, she rolled back its skin, like peeling the soft husk from an ear of corn. From within the shed skin, she lifted a new child—a boy child, a little older than the first—and wrapped him in the fur again.

---

1. Just as Sarmodel is open to Arcane assault when he Projects, I am vulnerable when I send my consciousness outside the Mundane world. In their own realm, Spirits have me very much at a disadvantage.

Then he, too, began to whimper, and Cecile set him down. Her fingers delved beneath his skin once more and she lifted out another child, older again. Cecile continued her tearful protest and repeated the ritual once more, bathing the babe in the pool and wrapping him in the fur blanket.

A fierce gust barreled through the garden. The surface of the pool rippled ominously and the otherworldly glade filled with streaming white illumination, like the radiance of a star.

"No!" howled Sarmodel, clutching at my neck with his baboon's claws. "*No! Sebastian!*"

With a shower of celestial light, the Archangel descended. He landed on the far side of the pool, his bladed wings folding behind him. Their flashing green jewels and golden plumes seemed to draw the color and substance from the naiad's glade, as though the Lion were a lantern and everything else simply a play of shadows.

"Sebastian Grave," he said. "I offer you one last chance. Cry off. You will find only sorrow in this chase."

The baboon rose on his hind legs on my shoulders, and I could well imagine the obscenities he was performing for the Archangel's benefit. Cecile paid no heed to any of us, absorbed with her task.

"I cannot, Michael, and I would not," I answered him. "I have given my word and my heart and I will see this finished. Leave me be!" Cecile pulled another child aloft now; this one was a boy already half grown.

The Lion's half-human face betrayed neither surprise nor anger. "I am not your enemy, Sebastian—nor yours, Lariel[2]—but

2. Again, this is Sarmodel's most mysterious alias. He refuses to tell me anything about it, other than the fact that it's his oldest name—I would know nothing of it if not for Michael and his ilk.

I am bound by a greater Covenant. The midwife of Saint-Julien is one death that might have been averted had you heeded my first warning. There will be more if you persist."

The baboon shrieked and Sarmodel's voice came from above. "Such compassion for the hedge-witch! Tell me, Great Prince—had our young monster not claimed her heart, would Cecile have taken her place at the Almighty's side?"

Cecile was now pulling forth another child from within the body of his predecessor. With each bloodless birth, the child grew older, with strong limbs and pale skin. And with each child, Cecile herself aged a little more, becoming less the ragged girl and more the woman I had met in the garden, her hair a tumble of sea-foam and her bosom dusted with freckles from the sun.

Michael shook his head. "You know she would not, Lariel. The faithless do not Commune. In her foolishness and her desire for power, she was ever devoted to her lady," replied the Archangel. He looked at the sobbing echo of Cecile, distraught in its task. "And look at this shadow she has cast—a thing of misery, broken with the guilt of her life of murder and degeneracy."

"Too late! She will not listen!" babbled Cecile. "Why did you break faith?"

Michael showed his teeth in a grimace. "If you are seeking a message here, Sebastian Grave, it is right before you. Say Grace."

"Then why are *you* here, Michael?" demanded the baboon. "The witch is beyond your help."

"I came not for her sake but for yours, Lariel," said the Lion, with some annoyance. "If you cannot be grateful, at least be silent." Then he spoke to me. "Sebastian, I have returned to claim what remains of the Spirit Avstamet in the name of the Almighty. I would spare you the pain of a confrontation. I say one final time: Cry off, or you will know terrible remorse."

The Lion's brilliance grew brighter, and brighter still. With it grew an unwelcome, subtle heat that I felt not on my skin but somehow within my flesh, like radiation.

"Sebastian!" hooted Sarmodel. "We can't stay here!"

Cecile sloughed away the skin of the final child and lifted from its husk not a boy but a monstrous wolf, a hulking thing that bore her to the ground with its weight. The creature had not paws but clawed hands on the ends of its long legs, and it pinned Cecile where she lay. Its eyes were full of cold intelligence.

"*Vin hanc carnem?*" it said to me with a leer. "This meat? What are you, Magician?"

"Sebastian! *Out—now!*" The baboon bent down and sank his yellow fangs into my shoulder. In that same moment, the wolf closed it jaws around Cecile's throat.

Cecile and I screamed together, and then there was only darkness.

XXXVII

It was approaching noon when I came to my senses, still kneeling there by Cecile's pool.

A feather-light, fragile thing crumbled between my fingers. I lowered my hand and saw the hagstone, now hollow and translucent white like an empty chrysalis. It collapsed into pale ash[1] and then dispersed on the wind. Its rich Arcane energy erupted into the air like the blood from a punctured vein.

Aha!

Sarmodel's essence flew wide and fast, a smothering net ensnaring the hagstone's anima. He drank it to the last.

And then I felt the welcome surge of fresh anima effervescing through my every tissue. The long journey, the exhaustion of

1. Known as holy ash, this fine white powder is the transition phase between inorganic matter and Arcane energy. It is commonly left behind as a residue when a Spirit claims the anima within an object, through dedication or similar ritual. As previously mentioned, the biological equivalent is plasma.

caring for Jacques, the restless night in Château d'Ocerne—they were all rinsed away in the roaring tide of vitality. My skin tightened deliciously over flesh now full and firm. The hagstone's anima had a cool, earthy purity, like drinking directly from the naiad's cascade.[2]

Ah, my love, said Sarmodel. *That's better, isn't it?*

I smiled, closing my eyes in bliss. *It is indeed. We haven't fed properly for quite some time.*

The garden was peaceful again. In the Mundane world, nothing had changed, but somehow everything was different, too. Without Cecile's influence and care, the little enchanted bower she had created would slowly decay. I was witnessing the final poise of the bloom before it withers; the soft edge of the full moon before it wanes.

I hope that was worth the risk, Sebastian! You realize the Archangel could have discorporated us in there—or worse? my Guest said. *And naturally the witch would vex us with her twaddle, even from beyond the grave. If she had something to say, why not just leave a note?*

"She had good reason to be cautious with what she knew." I rubbed my eyes. "Sarmodel, we need to find Jacques. If he was out killing last night, there's no telling where he's ended up."

Why?

"Because Cecile showed us eighteen children, Sarmodel, each older than the last. One for each year of his life. And the last—the nineteenth—was the Beast."

And?

"It's *him,* Sarmodel. The price Dayane asked for saving Antoine

2. As unspecialized repositories of anima, artifacts like hagstones are readily consumed by even the most rudimentary of Spirits, which is one of the reasons they're so rare nowadays.

was Jacques. His firstborn." I stood up, every movement charged with new energy. "You heard Cecile. She said we were all paying the price for Antoine's betrayal. All of this—Jacques's curse, the violence in Gévaudan—is her vengeance come to pass. I can think of no other remedy. We must take him to her."

It was with renewed vigor, along with no small amount of foreboding, that I mounted my horse and prepared to head back toward the château. There was no telling where Jacques might be, or whether he would have returned to himself.

But my search was short-lived.

Jacques d'Ocerne was waiting for me by the fountain in Saint-Julien-by-the-Stream. He was mounted on his new horse, a rose-gray gelding from the château stables, and he wore a wide tricorne hat, pulled low over his face.

Jacques was a brighter, steadier man this morning and I was almost glad to see him. Freshly bathed and clean shaven, he was dressed in a sky-blue waistcoat and riding jacket, trimmed with fine gold embroidery. Under the tricorne, his blond hair was tied at his nape with a black ribbon and he wore smart black riding gloves and boots—very respectable indeed. It was already a busy morning in the plaza, and he was painfully conspicuous.

"Good morning, Professor. You are looking well."

"As are you, sir."

One would almost suspect he'd eaten a nutritious midwife in the night.

"Forgive me for following you—I heard what happened from my mother," he answered. He swallowed hard, his eyes haunted. "I could not come to Mademoiselle Cecile's home, I am sorry. Is she truly . . . ?"

"Dead. Yes, I am afraid so, sir."

"Lord help us." Jacques swallowed again and passed his tongue across his lips. It was not his fear that he was holding in check. "Was it . . . was it my doing?"

"Sir, there is no point in—"

"Professor, do not lie to me," he interrupted. "It happened again, didn't it? Last night, with Eloise, I almost . . . I had such terrible dreams, and the voice was talking and talking about Cecile, giving voice to such dreadful impulses." He took a deep breath. "Then I awoke this morning in the orchard, with no memory of how I got there and only blessed silence in my head—*silence*—when there had been no respite from the damned voice for days. Please, I have already killed my dearest friends and I can scarcely bear the remorse—I say again, do not lie to me."

"Then yes, sir. It is safe to assume you killed her," I answered simply.

"My God. Professor, this stops now. I am afraid to think what I may do to my wife, or to my family. I will come with you, to Lady Dayane, or to Lord Lucifer himself—wherever you think I must go to be rid of this curse."

I swore inwardly and gave Jacques a reassuring smile. "I will certainly help you, sir, but I fear you may not understand the full extent—"

Sarmodel twinged in the back of my mind.

What is it? I asked.

Be prepared was all he said.

"Professor? Are you well?" asked Jacques.

There was sudden outcry as a large group of people on horseback entered the square from the west, crossing directly in front of us. Jacques and I were corralled against the fountain as the crowd drew back to allow them passage.

The foremost were military men, more than a dozen well-armed soldiers wearing the yellow sun of Mende. Behind them came a coterie of attendants in red and white ecclesiastical garb.

Church retinue, I remarked, my sense of trepidation growing. I felt supremely exposed; mounted on our horses, Jacques and I stuck out from the rest of the crowd like trees in a field.

My worst fears were confirmed when a herald stopped in the center of the square and sounded a silver trumpet.

"His Excellency, the Most Reverend Bishop of Mende!" he announced.

After a suitable pause, a stocky charger followed him into view, bearing an equally stocky rider. Jacques swore murderously beside me.

Bishop Fontaine of Mende was in poor health. He had seemed plump and pampered during the Red Winter; now his oxlike frame had a lumpy, sagging aspect and he looked terribly haggard. One side of his face was livid pink and scarred with an old burn; his eye on that side was nearly completely closed. Both he and his mighty white horse were conspicuously well dressed in impoverished Saint-Julien. His bishop's cassock with its exquisite embroidery was probably worth more than the village he rode through. Fontaine held his hand high to display his gold-and-amethyst ecclesiastical signet, and he wore his bejeweled golden pectoral cross—dead giveaways that this was a carefully planned entrance.[3]

"Take heart, children of God. I have come to return the Lord's light to Gévaudan, in this dark time." The bishop's voice had lost

3. No, a clergyman would not normally trot about in his nicest frock with all his jewels on, even when on official business. But it seemed that not even the challenges of riding a horse in a thousandweight of silk and gold were enough to deter the Bishop of Mende from a little theater.

none of its theatrical timbre in twenty years, and he still wore his placid, sleepy smile. I despised him, certainly, but you must understand that there was also something *beautiful* about him, in spite of how much he had deteriorated physically. The gold, the exquisitely decorated vestments, even his enormous horse—they all combined to make him something more than just a man, something almost otherworldly. The effect was quite breathtaking.

A susurrus of low muttering rolled across the crowd as he rode through. There were those who genuflected, but others who shook their heads, and others still who made their displeasure clear with audible profanity. Far from encouraging the people of Saint-Julien, the bishop's divine splendor verged on an insult.

Nor did the people rejoice for the man who came behind him.

I suddenly found myself open-mouthed and unable to breathe.

I felt the overpowering need to hide, but there was nowhere to go. I do not know if I could have moved in any case; all I could do was stare at him.

Antoine.

XXXVIII

I knew he would be older, but it still surprised me to see he had *aged.* Twenty years had passed, yes, and it showed in his thinner face and the deeper set of his eyes. His blond hair was lighter, more than half turned gray, and it was neatly tied back above his collar. He was also clean-shaven now, as befitted a nobleman of France, and his green riding attire spoke of both sophistication and wealth.[1] He was still handsome, but it was a weary handsomeness, underscored by the bitter line of his mouth.

Antoine was not introduced by the herald; I believe the Baron d'Ocerne knew what kind of reception he could expect from the villagers. He barely raised his eyes from the ground as his horse followed the bishop's retinue through the square.

A small group of Mende's soldiers brought up the rear of the

---

1. I suspect that the fashionable Lady Ninette d'Ocerne had a hand in dressing her husband.

procession and I began to breathe again. By grace and good fortune, neither the bishop nor Antoine had noticed me.

But I had forgotten, of course, Jacques's strong predisposition toward ruining my life.

"Father!" he bellowed across the square. "What lunacy is this?"

Antoine turned immediately, his expression fierce. I was helpless to do anything but wait as his eyes found us above the crowd.

And then he saw me.

A feeling of warmth ballooned in my chest as he smiled, the shock on his face replaced instantly by the delight of recognition. I raised one hand from the reins in a tentative wave.

But no, I was quite mistaken. Antoine was not smiling; his mouth was drawn up in a grimace of dismay.

"Guardsmen!" he called. "Soldiers of Mende! To me!"

Jacques and I were surrounded in moments. Bishop Fontaine's soldiers had us backed against the fountain, their muskets all aimed at me. Behind them, a hundred pairs of shiny peasant eyes were suddenly all fixed on us.

"This man—this man is a witch and he has bedeviled my son!" said Antoine, holding his place in the line of military men. Beside him, the Bishop of Mende stared at me with wide eyes, his charger fidgeting beneath him. "Jacques, *get away* from him!"

"I will not!" Jacques retorted. "And do not hide behind your accusations. You bring the Bishop of Mende back to Gévaudan? Have we not seen ruin enough? Is he here to buy out the little land that remains to us?"

"Be silent, Jacques!" shouted Antoine. "Monseigneur! This is—"

"I know him, sir," said the bishop in his resonant baritone. His round eyes narrowed. "Yes, Professor, I remember you. I see you are unwholesomely preserved—unchanged to my sight after these many years. I should have ended your life at the Bow and Brace, after your foul deeds, but Baron d'Ocerne persuaded me to let you live. I see now that was a mistake."

I heard him only distantly; I cared nothing what I looked like to the bishop. It was Antoine's eyes I wanted to see. His stone-gray eyes as I remembered them, half closed in laughter or pleasure.

Look, Antoine! I wanted to call to him from the center of the menacing circle of soldiers. *Do you remember? Isn't this just like the time we were surprised by the king's hunters in the woods? When I was casting my silver shot and you burned your hair, and the hounds came to surround us?*

But Antoine would not even look at me; this time he was on the side of the hounds and the hunters.

"We have come to find the source of Gévaudan's troubles, and we have met with swift success, it seems," the bishop went on. "Be alert, men. This man is not only a witch but an abomination; I have seen his depravity with my own eyes." He leveled a thick finger at me. "You will submit to me now and come with us to Château d'Ocerne. We will have the truth of your crimes from you, by the grace of God."

"Monseigneur, please—he will give us nothing but devilry! He can bewitch with a song, and raise a fire with nothing more than a word!" protested Antoine. "Please! He must be dealt with here and—"

"I have come at your request, Lord Ocerne," interrupted the bishop, at volume. He kept his eyes locked on my face. "I will seek the truth wherever it hides, and no matter what snares the Foul One sets around it. Service to the Lord Almighty demands courage; little wonder that Gévaudan finds itself so beset, when its lords shrink from the first test of faith. No! The witch will come with us to Château d'Ocerne, now."

I managed to find my voice again. "In fact, I have a chamber there already, Monseigneur. And your accusations are without basis. I have come once again to render aid to Gévaudan, and waited only for the return of—"

"Be silent! You will not speak unless commanded!" barked Fontaine, outraged. He turned to Jacques. "Young lord—you have suffered the devil to sleep beneath your roof?" he demanded.

"Professor Grave has already saved my life more than once, Monseigneur. Believe me, he is no enemy to Ocerne or its people. Even now he is on the trail of the Beast."

"Jacques, he *lies*!" cried Antoine. "Do not listen to him! Please, my son, get away from him!"

"*Lies?* Shall we speak of lies, then, Father?"

I kept my silence, weighing up the situation in my mind as Jacques and Antoine engaged in a very public and most unedifying family argument.

There was a part of me that wanted to go with my captors, on the thin hope that they might allow me the opportunity to plead my case.

And yes, if I am honest, it was mostly because it would mean being close to Antoine again, that I might have a chance to speak to him. A chance to explain.

Do you . . . do you think he might forgive me? I asked Sarmodel.

For what, Sebastian? One day you must stop seeking forgiveness for solving people's problems, he said. *And it is time to stop making decisions from your breeches! We have things to do.*

So we do.

I placated my Guest, but I was still so unsure. I *knew* I could convince Antoine to help us, if only I could speak to him alone.

But the decision was about to be made for me.

Sebastian! He is here! hissed Sarmodel.

There was no need to ask who he meant.

The Archangel's radiance shimmered suddenly into being overhead and the warm, heady scent of roses momentarily filled the air. The Grand General's glittering wings flexed wide, firming his claim and marking his chosen.

But it was not the Bishop of Mende who bore the Archangel's flame in his heart.

It was Antoine.

My own heart shrank within me.

Sarmodel—how?

How could he?

Antoine—laughing, mad, drunken Antoine, who had "dared to know"—had bowed so deeply in service of the Church that the Archangel had found a perch on his back. I remembered suddenly Jacques's many idle comments about "prayer and scripture" and the stern, pious father who had raised him. And I remembered the warning Michael had given me that very morning: *I would spare you the pain of a confrontation. Cry off, or you will know terrible remorse.*

Antoine had been lost to me all along.

My plans for a reconciliation were revealed in that moment as hollow fantasies—Antoine was no longer the man I knew. And now the Archangel had claimed him.

I hate you, Michael, I sent, clenching my teeth against the shame and rage that battled within me. *I know you can hear me. You are crueler and lower and more deceitful than any demon and I hate you.*

Hear, hear! added Sarmodel.

"Gentlemen! Please!" I said aloud, interrupting a choice invective from Jacques. "I submit—I submit! I will come to the château and we will get to the truth, if so you wish."

Jacques gaped at me. "Professor, you cannot be serious. You know they are not interested in the truth."

"It is a little late for misgivings now, sir," I replied sharply. "I am here at your behest, to honor the contract I signed so many years ago, which you hold unfulfilled. Or have you forgotten?"

Jacques's grimace of shame was most gratifying to behold. "I have not."

"Then prepare to leave, sir. I will assume your horse is fit to ride, for once," I said, with a meaningful glance at his mount.

"He . . . he is, sir." The young lord's eyes widened and he gathered the reins more tightly in his hands.

"I am glad you have seen sense, vile thing that you are," said the bishop, his peaceful smile returning. "Now it is time to see you tested in faith and in intention."

"Monseigneur, I implore you, do not allow him to speak another word!" admonished Antoine. "Do not trust this show of compliance—he will kill us all before we are halfway to the château! Deal with him here if you must, or—or kill him and be done."

Kill him and be done?

I stared at Antoine, truly unable to speak. He still refused to meet my gaze, and I dared to hope that he looked ashamed. Had he really just called for my death?

Ready? I asked Sarmodel.

Oh yes, he chuckled. *Remember those triphthongs.*

I took a deep breath, not only drawing air into my lungs but also gathering together all of the prodigious energy we had so recently absorbed from the hagstone.

I released it all with a Word.

I do not know what they heard. For a moment they all wore the same face—Antoine, the soldiers, the bishop and the colorless villagers were united in sick terror as the Tartaric syllables smacked into them like a line of breakers.

I had modified the Word only slightly since that day at the

crossroads. With some simple adjustments for magnitude (and with Sarmodel bearing down hard), the Tartaric compulsions that had so neatly unhorsed Jacques now ricocheted among the soldiers of Mende, spinning off and replicating countless times in the crowded square of Saint-Julien. The hagstone's energy, accumulated over millennia in Dayane's sacred pool, was almost completely expended in the space of a second.

I could not have orchestrated a better outcome.

Closest to the epicenter were the soldiers who surrounded us. They cried out in alarm as their muskets popped apart and clattered to the ground, smoking. Then the air was suddenly full of wheeling arms and red-hot shrapnel as their bridles and tack shot their fastenings and fell away like shed skin. Horseshoes spun across the cobblestones and saddles began to slide. The golden chain of the bishop's pectoral cross began to glow and flew apart in a spray of red-hot links. Both he and Antoine joined the soldiers in cursing as their stirrups, too, dropped away and their gear fell apart around them.

But the real chaos started when their clothing began to unravel.

I was almost tempted to stay and watch. The laughter of the common folk was a joyous counterpart to the shouts of dismay from the soldiers of Mende. It was a rare spectacle to see the bishop clutching armfuls of silk to his bosom like a matron surprised at her bath, screaming at his men as his jewels showered to the ground, all the while battling to stay seated on his frantic charger.

It was time to leave.

"*Ride!*"

Jacques and I forced our horses through the bedlam, half-naked bodies tumbling from destriers all around us. We fled Saint-Julien-by-the-Stream at a gallop, the laughter of the villagers fading behind us.

XXXIX

There was only one place to go, really.

I knew Jacques wanted to speak to me, but I kept us riding at a gallop, heedless of our poor horses.

Outwardly, I was a model of righteous determination, with a show of clenched teeth and eyes narrowed in focus on the road ahead.

Within, my emotional state was spinning like a weathercock in a storm.

Was I angry? Goodness yes, I was *furious.* Was I confused? Yes again—utterly lost, in fact. Was I afraid? Most certainly.

Was I wounded?

Heartbroken. Almost unbearably.

The tender hope I had allowed to grow in my heart over the past weeks—against all good sense—had now been savagely uprooted. The hole it left was a ragged wound that ached with every breath.

As the fields and farmsteads thundered past on either side, I tried to conceal my inner discord from Jacques. This was made more difficult by Sarmodel's insistent (and quite shrill) objections in the back of my mind.

*Sebastian! Do not **dare** ignore me! Sebastian, you are fooling precisely nobody!* he said, as my conflicting passions spun and spun inside me. *Where are you going? Turn around immediately! We were just getting started!*

But Sarmodel—Antoine is Michael's puppet![1] *How is it possible?* I replied. Then terrible understanding came to me once again. *This is my fault! Because of what happened. Because of what I did. What he saw.*

Does it matter? Really? Sebastian, he is meat! Delightful meat, but still just meat. Did you think he would love you so very much, after a few months of frottage in the mountains, twenty years ago? I thought we resolved this last night. He growled impatiently. *Are we really not going back? They were disarmed—and naked! You love it when they're naked!*

But the things he said—he wanted to kill me!

***I** want to kill you!* he snapped. *Now either turn this horse around, or calm down. You are in an embarrassing state. And I will not be **teased** like this again, do you understand?*

I knew he was right. Regardless of how effectively I had stymied the bishop and the Archangel, I was taking us into possibly even greater danger. I would need to be thinking clearly.

---

1. "Puppet" is not precisely accurate. Antoine would not have been explicitly aware of Michael's presence at all. Angels are not permitted to take possession of a mortal host, or even to reveal themselves directly in the Mundane world—it's another one of those important prohibitions in the Covenant they signed with the Almighty. Michael and his brethren must rely on guiding their chosen with holy visions, voices and dreams, to preserve the gift of free will.

I slowed our reckless pace, allowing Jacques to ride up alongside me.

"Professor, where are we going?"

"We are going, sir, to see if we can remove the Beast's curse from your flesh, as I promised you. We may or may not succeed. You may or may not survive, even if we do," I answered. "After that, I do not know as—thanks to you—we are also now on the run from the barony's soldiers and the Bishop of Mende."

There was no indignation, no righteous rebuke from the young lord. He simply nodded. "Very well. Lead the way."

The way was closed.

I was not surprised. Cecile had warned me, and our path up the mountain had been marked by dispiriting signs. The lightning-split rowan had been taken over by a nest of beetles. The circle of toadstools was skewed and broken, trampled heedlessly by the creatures of the forest. We saw not one wild Spirit on the journey. In their place was a forlorn, disconcerting stillness. Where I remembered a singing ascent into the Fey realm, I had found only a procession of neglect and abandonment.

Where was Dayane, the lady of the leaping waters?

We had left our horses at the foot of the mountain, by the stream. Jacques was eager, impatient even, to begin the journey. He slipped under the musical enchantment of the Fey song just as easily as his father had. But the great symphonic instrument of the woods was uneven and faltering. It took most of my concentration just to maintain the melody.

I had led him beside the stream, just as I had led Antoine, up the secret ways I still remembered. This time there was no holding of hands, no childlike wonder as we ascended. Instead we held weapons—I kept my silver blade[2] at the ready, and Jacques carried his musket upright by his shoulder. We had arrived at last at Dayane's threshold, where the treetops swallowed the sun and the green gloaming lit the way.

And stretched across the path before us was an enormous silver spider's web. The silken threads glittered with dew, and the one who had woven them was nowhere in sight. In the Arcane realm, the web was a floating membrane of soft pink light: the barrier that protected Dayane's shrine. I could feel its resistance to our presence.

Twenty years previously, Antoine and I had stepped into the naiad's glade without impediment, but she was protecting her sanctuary now. I raised my arm just in time to stop Jacques from walking into the trap. He was barely aware of the world around him—he offered me only a questioning smile as I stopped him a hand's breadth from an unpleasant demise.

Can you feel her, Sarmodel?

Yes. She is hiding, but she is here.

I was relieved. I had feared that we would come all the way to Dayane's doorstep to find that she, like the forest Spirits, had disappeared.

I began to sing again, the same devotion song that had drawn the water nymph to me twenty years before. But this time I sang not only to adore her. This time, my poesy was filled with sorrow and great remorse, seeking not only her favor, but her forgiveness. I felt a stirring in the air around us as her awareness shifted toward me. The spider's web trembled as though plucked.

---

2. I replaced my wonderful Walloon silver just after the Red Winter. I opted for a more modern curved sabre style this time, similar to what would become known as the *briquet* of the Napoleonic Wars.

"My lady, please," I murmured. "Whatever wrong has been done to you, let me make amends."

But still the way did not open. I waited the space of a few breaths and then I felt the nymph's attention begin to withdraw.

Sarmodel. We need to get inside. Can you do it?

Hmm. We don't have a lot left after your performance in the village. It's going to smart.

Very well. Gently, now.

I felt his presence sharpen like a great tusk overhead. He thrust into the barrier once, and then again. He roared as the third plunge tore through the delicate Fey membrane and the spider's web was suddenly engulfed in scarlet fire. It disintegrated and fell away, revealing a dim opening choked with mountain salvias.

I paid the price immediately, a debilitating drop in my vital force. I was momentarily overcome with vertigo. I leaned on Jacques as the world slowly righted itself.

Thank . . . thank you, my love. I was suddenly ravenous.

"Come, sir," I said, tugging on Jacques's sleeve. "We have arrived."

"I am glad," he replied, his eyes faraway. Then his brow creased in sudden confusion. "Did we bring a gift for the lady? I do not wish her to think us rude."

"We did, sir."

I kindled the Violations on my silver blade. The surface began to swim with liquid heat. Then I parted the foliage carefully and we stepped through into the sacred glade.

I gagged immediately at the smell. Dayane's pool was not as I remembered.

By the Rift, said Sarmodel. *My love, be very careful.*

The gemstone-green pool was still clear and deep. The water nymph's cascade still fell in a glittering line onto the foaming granite slab. But Dayane's glade had become a slaughterhouse heap of animal bones and rotting flesh. Gone was the smell of fresh rain. The remains of every type of woodland creature were decomposing in the grass. My boots crunched on the corpses of martens and scrub fowl. The crawling, flyblown carcass of a boar lay at the water's edge. Its ragged hindquarters were half submerged, as though it had been dragged into the shallows before its violent end. All around us gaped the dead eyes of deer, wolves and rabbits.

"Will the wait be long, Professor?" asked Jacques dreamily. "I am growing hungry."

What has happened to her? I asked, looking around wide-eyed at the carnage. Some of the carcasses had been there for months, but others, like the boar, were relatively fresh. *Sarmodel, was it a mistake coming here?*

We'll soon see. Keep that brandy at the ready.

I took out the bag of offerings I had planned to dedicate to the water nymph. Within were a precious pouch of sugar, some tea and a handful of oats, along with a fine silver spoon engraved with a scallop-and-swan motif.[3] None of it would entice the mistress who now presided over this abattoir.

Fortunately, I had other options.

"My lord, come." I brought Jacques right to the edge of the water and bade him kneel. Disconcertingly, the water weeds beneath the surface flexed toward us like grasping hands.

Jacques complied like a marionette when I asked him to hold out his hand. He barely blinked when I pulled back his sleeve and

---

3. Yes, it was all stolen from the kitchens of the Baron d'Ocerne. Technically, I was still executing a contract on behalf of the château, so I felt quite entitled to a few of the family's resources.

sliced his forearm. His blood snaked down his wrist and began to drip from his fingertips into the water.

I did not sing. It was clear that Dayane would no longer respond to supplication. I took a deep breath.

"Dayane, attend!" I called across the still surface. "I have brought the price that was promised."

XL

At first there was only silence. Sarmodel shifted warily above me. Had I misjudged?

Then there was a deep gulping sound. The pool lurched and bubbled. A torrent of rotting detritus was sucked to the surface, releasing a rank, swampy stench into the air.

The naiad began to rise, ascending from the fouled water. I almost wept to see her.

I expected she would be changed; the state of her sanctuary was warning enough. But this . . .

Sarmodel coiled reflexively, rearing like an adder in my mind. *Sebastian, please—just this once, heed me. Kill her now!*

I . . . I . . . I could only stammer, agape, as Dayane emerged fully to stand on the surface of the pool.

I couldn't bear to look at her, but nor could I look away. I understood in that moment why Cecile had been unable to reach her mistress, and what had happened to the wild Spirits of the woods.

"Oh, Dayane. Oh no."

The water nymph's corruption was absolute. The down-covered horn buds on her forehead had grown into enormous, twisted antlers, spreading like the branches of a blighted tree over the pool. Her white body, which had once seemed to me like living ivory, was now disfigured with brown, fetid growths. With her hands she held her sagging, distended belly, bulging almost to her knees; Dayane's back stooped under the weight of it. Her hair—her beautiful green-black hair—once garlanded with water chestnut, was now matted with algae and clusters of tiny bones. No longer immune to the touch of the Mundane world, she dripped black mud into the water.

She raised her head and looked at me with something like desperation. Cruelly, her beautiful deep brown eyes were unchanged.

"Why? *Why* have you come?" she croaked. "What more do you want?" The water nymph's words were strangely impeded. Her jaw had grown too wide and muscular for easy speech, and her mouth too full of long teeth.

"I have . . . I have come to seek your mercy, Dayane, and one final boon if you will grant it," I managed to say. I still held my silver sword at the ready.

"I closed the way, Magician. I do not—ah!" Dayane groaned and her face twisted in a grimace as she clutched her bloated abdomen. "I wish to traffic no more with the world of men. Leave me, *please*." She collapsed to her knees with a moan as some terrible pain gripped her.

"Dayane, what has happened to you?" I asked softly. "Is this Avstamet's curse? Can we help you?"

"*Do not say his name!* I still hear his voice! He *speaks to me*!" she said, struggling to talk through her pain. "Oh, leave me! I must eat." She groped for the boar carcass, barely able to rise to her feet.

I could say no more, utterly horrified. Pity and revulsion

warred for dominance within me, both of them competing with the insidious suspicion that this was all my fault.

Sarmodel was not so afflicted. He assumed his most persuasive and ingratiating tone. *But we have brought you a gift, my sweet thing. Will you sing for us in return? Or tell us a story? The tale of your victory at the Lupercalia, perhaps?*

Privately, he hissed a warning. *Sebastian, she is beyond recovery. As soon as she is within reach, take her.*

Is there nothing we can do? Sarmodel, she may be the last of her kind.

And we may be the last of ours if you are not careful.

I nodded, swallowing. I glanced at Jacques, who was smiling in rapture, utterly enthralled by the corrupted nymph. He still held his arm over the pool, dripping blood into the water. Worryingly, he had put down his musket and was rubbing slowly at the front of his breeches with his other hand.

"A song? They came to hear me sing once. Kings and queens and great sorcerers." Dayane's voice was wistful. She rose unsteadily to her feet again, fighting the terrible weight of the antlers and her swollen belly. "I could sing for you. Yes. What is your gift? Is it something to eat?" The water nymph's eyes brightened. Her lips parted around her frightful teeth in hopeful anticipation. "I am always so hungry."

That is up to you, my darling. It is the life you were promised so many years ago—the price for your gracious assistance, replied my silken-tongued Guest. *The Baron d'Ocerne's firstborn.*

"My price?" Dayane looked suddenly stricken. She grasped the roots of her antlers as though to tear them free. "No! *No!* I was patient, for the stream is patient. Years I waited for my due and was *refused.* Years his voice was inside me, whispering and growing. Years I grew ever hungrier until I could bear it no longer. Each year I sent my handmaiden to collect the price, and each year I was denied. One final warning I gave to your young lover, Magician—I would have the boy when he reached his eighteenth birthday, or our bargain was forfeit. And again I was refused."

"So you cursed him," I said.

"I returned the Beast's gift to him, tenfold," Dayane hissed. "He who would not give me his son will live to see misery visited on *all* of his sons, and their sons, and theirs. Lords and masters? Savages and beasts, rather. The House of Avenel will show its true face with every new generation."

"Are you Lady Dayane? Can you help me?" Jacques interrupted suddenly. His eyes were half closed, his voice lazy and thick. His mouth worked soundlessly for a few seconds, as though it were jammed with words and he could not choose among them. "I killed my friends and ate their hearts," he said finally.

At first I thought that she had not heard him. But then she began to stagger toward us, her footfalls impossibly heavy on the surface of the water. Her eyes were not on Jacques, but on me. "Yes, I have a song for you, Magician. There is always a song at the end," she panted. "We will . . . weave rainbows—and we will *eat.* With patience, the stream will eat even the mountain."

I closed my eyes in dismay. Everything had turned to madness.

She came faster now, the mare's tail beneath her feet quivering.

"What is Mundane flesh but earth and water?" she mused, drooling.

"Dayane, I am sorry," I murmured.

I gathered myself and spoke the Crippling Yoke.

Only a few paces away from us, the water nymph stopped short, wrenched into a closing vise of Arcane facets. In seconds, she was bent and bound, held rigid with her arms outstretched, like a woman in the stocks. She screamed as the Yoke burned into her, searing flesh and anima both. She struggled like the Beast himself, her savage antlers tearing the air.

"No! Let me eat! Always I am deceived!" she sobbed.

"Please, Dayane, I do not want to kill you," I said, trying not to see my own brutality. In my mind, Sarmodel was coiling taut in readiness. "You must relent, I beg you. Surely there is something we can offer to earn your favor once more, you who are so full of favor. Something to ease your pain, to take away this curse you have held for too long?"

"It is too late!" Dayane began to sob, her tears as filthy as the mud that dripped from her skin. "I did not know what it was you gave me—*I did not know.* It took root within me and grew with each passing year, and now it is too late. I am the Water from the Mountain but I could not wash it away, not with rain, not with patience, not with blood. And now it is *become* me; I am the fountainhead and the stream, and every thirsty throat in Gévaudan will taste of it." She cried out again, the heartbroken wail of the betrayed. "Ask no more of me! Was it not enough? Did I not treat with you in good faith?"

"You did, Dayane. Always. Now please, this one last time, help me—*how can we be rid of it?* Please, you risk the return of the Warfather!"

Tighten the Yoke, Sebastian, urged Sarmodel. *Squeeze it out of her if you have to.*

I will not. This is already cruel beyond words.

Dayane subsided, crying desperately. "He is here already! Within me. Within the young lord. Within every soul who drinks the Water from the Mountain. The Beast has planted his seed, and he will have what he wants."

"Will the lady not help me, Professor?" asked Jacques languidly. "Can she cure me of this sickness?"

"I fear we have already asked too much of—"

"Yes!" Horribly, Dayane began to laugh between her sobs. "The remedy. It is a rite of the flesh," she said. "In flesh, it will be performed."

Sebastian.

I know.

I wished I could close my eyes for the final betrayal. My silver blade was light and sharp, and rippling with Violations. I prayed that it was also painless.

Her heart. Once, twice and thrice.

It was not anger but sorrow I saw in her eyes as she died. The luminous green pool suddenly dimmed and clouded. The waving mare's tail disappeared beneath a plume of silt. The eternal cascade faltered and stopped.

I covered my ears and screamed to hide Sarmodel's triumphant howl as he claimed her essence. I could not bear it.

Dayane's anima thundered into him like the rushing stream itself, filling us both with surging strength. My every cell and organ hummed with indescribable ecstasy. She left the mineral tang of snowmelt and an aftertaste of carrion in the back of my throat.

I wanted none of it.

"I am sorry," I said again, uselessly.

The Crippling Yoke still held the nymph's body as it began to dissolve. Her skin wept plasma and the monstrous antlers collapsed into ash. I dispelled the pitiless Arcane bonds, letting her fall into the depths of the pool.

Dayane, the Water from the Mountain, was no more.

XLI

Margeride Mountains
1766

The December nights belonged to the Beast.

Antoine and I felt increasingly alone as we tracked it farther north into the mountains, and then east, toward the border again. We were going in circles.

Most of the hunters had gone. It was not only because of the snow. The hounds were never the same after the massacre at Saint-Julien. Many had gone utterly mad, becoming feral killers that had to be put down. Entire packs had run off to join the wolves in the forests, and now they hunted their former masters through the wilds of Gévaudan.

Fear was a constant guest at the few campfires that remained.

Fear told the hunters of France that even with all their hounds and all their skill, they were no match for the thing they hunted. Fear whispered not that they would fail, but that they would die there in Gévaudan. So gradually, quietly, they left.

The Beast struck again and again, sometimes so close that we heard the screams. Once I was even close enough to feel the dizzying shift of his Incarnation, as though the ground had suddenly canted beneath me. He devoured travelers on the roads and shepherds in the fields. He pulled apart farmhouses like a bear breaking into a honeycomb, and in the morning the floors were slick with crimson ice.

I cannot say how many hearts Avstamet ate in those terrifying nights, but he never came for mine.

I do not doubt that he knew we were still there. It was possible that he was wary of us, after our encounter at Saint-Julien.

But it was more likely that he was simply dancing around us, as he had danced around the soldiers, the Church and the hunters for over a year. There was plenty of prey for him in Gévaudan—whole villages increasingly exposed and isolated as the winter advanced. He was restoring himself and building his strength. Perhaps he would come for us when he was ready.

In turn, we did our best to catch him first, but we were never quite fast enough. I did find a few critical clues about his identity. Once, close by the site of a fresh slaughter, I found his tracks in the snow. The Beast's footprints were filled with plasma, and they changed from one step to the next. Next to the farm gate, where the corpse of his last victim was not yet frozen into the ground, the impressions were monstrous paw prints, befitting the creature we had seen at Saint-Julien. Antoine rubbed nervously at the scar on his hand as we began to follow. The tracks changed as they moved onto the road, until they were human footprints we followed, and then the unmistakable tracks of horseshoes. On the roadside, I found a single, heavy pewter button.

"He had clothing ready here, and a horse," I said. My Guest was busy running his supernatural senses over both the trail and the button.

Woodsmoke. Traces of blood. I felt his shrug as a short ripple in my mind. *We would find the same anywhere in Gévaudan.*

"He rode away? On a horse?" asked Antoine. "My God, we could have passed him on the road and never known."

"Not quite. Look there." The horse's tracks left the road not far from us, disappearing into the woods. We followed them but lost the trail after hours of fruitless searching; whoever the Beast's host was, he knew how to disappear in the wilds.

"How?" demanded Antoine. He kicked at the snowpack in frustration. "*How* does he elude us every time? Is there any point anymore, Sebastian? Are we simply to wait for him to come and take us in our beds?"

"Come now. We have gained valuable knowledge," I replied.

"What do you mean?"

"First—we can confirm that we are looking for a man."[1] I held up the button. "This is from a gentleman's garment. I doubt he took the time to dress completely, so it's probably the fastener from something large like a greatcoat. And second—he is wealthy enough to own a decent horse. Look at the shoe prints and the gait. These are not the tracks of a farmer's nag."

Antoine seemed impressed with my sleuthing, though he was far from reassured. He raised his wine flask with a nervous smile and drank a long draft.

I smiled in return and kissed the wine from his lips. I was gradually allowing myself to believe that he was completely free of the Beast's curse. The wound was healed and he was back to his old self—no more strange moods or nocturnal wanderings. I wondered again what the price of Dayane's bargain would be, and if he even remembered it.

---

1. The Beast's male Incarnation was not necessarily a reflection of the gender of his host; for a Spirit, part of the appeal of living flesh is that it can be shaped.

"Have faith, my friend," I said to him. He only winked and made an obscene gesture in return.

In truth, I suspected that our efforts meant little. I feared that Avstamet was directing us like pawns in a great campaign. Footprints and fragments of clothing would not lead us to an ancient killer like the one we chased. We would meet him on his terms, and not before he was ready.

Antoine and I stayed in the woods as long as we could. Though the nights were cold and the game ever scarcer, we were loath to relinquish our solitude. Antoine's family would expect him to return to the château for the winter, and I doubted I would be welcome to stay there. So we prolonged our wandering, finding always another trail to follow. Each night, Antoine would light the fire with the "magic" words I had taught him and then I would tell him tales about other hunts and other monsters. He fell asleep in my arms, believing me to be the great hero of my stories, just as he believed in the magic of Sim Sala Bim. The mountains of Gévaudan had become a secluded world just for us, where I could live out a fond dream with my young lover. I was not ready to leave, not just yet.

Sarmodel humored me, partly because the object of our search was clearly still within range, and partly because he was being very well fed. Between the animals we killed and the regular harvest of my lovemaking with Antoine,[2] my Guest was receiving ample nourishment.

---

2. What we call "love" is a complicated and ultimately quite mysterious process of anima enrichment. The powerful energies exchanged between lovers—not to mention their various reproductive emissions—are therefore highly sought-after by Spirits and occult practitioners. You are likely beginning to understand why Sarmodel was so eager for me to pursue Antoine's affections.

But we could not pretend forever. There were other threats in Gévaudan besides the Beast, and they were already breaching the edges of our private domain.

We found ourselves early one morning enveloped in a choking cloud of smoke. We hurried to break camp and rode as fast as we dared in the snow, covering our mouths. Smoke by itself was no great anomaly on winter mornings, but this thick, stinging haze was not coming from a cozy hearth.

Burning bodies, Sarmodel informed me.

I called to Antoine and directed us upwind, toward the source of the smoke.

"A short diversion? I would like to know where this is coming from."

His gray eyes above the scarf were suspicious. "As would I. There have been too many fires in Gévaudan of late."

We had passed numerous blackened homesteads on our travels—whole farms razed to the stumps. Never once had we seen who was doing the burning.

It soon became clear where we were heading. Madame Pradels's orchards, which had yielded her prized yellow apples, were now a boiling inferno. The smoke was a shroud climbing the snowy mountainside, visible from the foothills for miles around.

Antoine swore. "The Pradels children are orphans since their mother was killed at Saint-Julien. They have seen trouble enough without this."

I didn't answer; my attention was on the indistinct figures moving around the edges of the flames.

I avoided the road and took us instead through the woods that bordered the Pradels farm on the southern side. It was the longer path, but it took us away from the smoke, and we would hopefully not be seen by the mysterious arsonists.

We left our horses concealed in the trees and took cover behind a woodpile.

A group of men was systematically setting fire to every apple tree on the Pradels land. The huge figure of the elder Enneval was there with his impressive military mustache, with the comparatively tiny Bauterne beside him. Nearby, with his back to us, was a large man watching them, mounted on an impressive charger. He wore a plain, shapeless woolen coat, a gray wig and a tricorne hat, in an ensemble that fairly screamed "incognito." The Lieutenant of the Hunt shouted orders to other men, who I assumed were recruits from Ocerne's standing army, or what remained of them. He stood beside a grim bonfire.

"Why?" Antoine demanded, whispering. "Why burn the farm? It makes no sense."

"Look closer."

Antoine squinted through the smoke and fire until he saw what I had noticed from the first. The pyre was built of bodies. The Beast had ended the poverty of Madame Pradels's many children by taking their hearts. The Master of the Hunt had piled them up with their livestock and burned them all together.

Bauterne approached the portly man on the horse.

"Antoine, please be quiet for a moment. I'm going to do something unholy."

"Of course," he said, smiling eagerly.

I spoke a Litany of Reaching, which Sarmodel granted with minimal complaint.

I ignored the sudden roaring of flames that filled my hearing, concentrating instead on the two men conversing on the other side of the orchard. My senses aligned after a few seconds and suddenly I could hear them clearly, as though they were standing right in front of me. More, I could feel the warmth of the fire around them and smell the burning bodies at their feet.

"—almost finished." Bauterne seemed weary and resigned. "The Beast left none of the children alive and the animals were crazed, just as they were on the other farms. The bodies have been consecrated and set to the flame, as you requested, Monseigneur."

"Bishop Fontaine of Mende. Interesting," I murmured.

"Mende? By the Christ, what is he still doing here?" Antoine whispered. "Is he the one who's been burning the farms?"

"It appears so," I replied.

I don't like this, Sebastian. The bishop and the Archangel's puppet meeting in secret? The Almighty is playing a very long game in Gévaudan, hissed my Guest.

Or Avstamet is playing them all. Now be quiet, I'm trying to listen.

"Your service remains invaluable, Lieutenant," said the bishop, on the far side of the orchard. His unmistakable voice was enough to dispel whatever anonymity his disguise afforded him. "It is not yet finished, however. The Beast's corruption cannot be allowed to spread."

"Another one, Monseigneur? Is this necessary?"

"Lord Bauterne, set it all to the flame. Store and stable, pasture and fold. We will raze this farm back to the bedrock, that it may flourish anew with the Lord's grace come springtime. Then we will move on to the next."

"And who will be left to till the soil, come springtime?" I murmured to myself.

Bauterne seemed troubled by the bishop's words. Bladed wings flickered in the smoke around him; the Archangel was no doubt offering some choice advice.

"If I may object, with respect, Monseigneur—surely we can—"

"You have pledged your very life to the pursuit of the Beast, Lieutenant, and to me as the hand of the Almighty in Gévaudan.

Will you falter now, at the last?" The bishop removed a glove and extended his hand, displaying his ecclesiastical signet.

Bauterne seemed about to object further, but then he stepped forward and kissed the ring, bowing his head.

"Have faith, Lieutenant, always. *Faith* will be rewarded," purred Fontaine. "Now, what is this other matter you wish to discuss? Quickly, if you please. I do not wish to be seen."

"Thank you, Monseigneur. Please, wait a moment." Bauterne called to the men and a makeshift travois was dragged over toward him. It was covered in a blanket that bucked and twitched. The men pulling it seemed eager to leave it behind.

"It is as I described, Monseigneur. The other hounds are scared of her, ever since the day at Saint-Julien. She eats and eats. This is an unnatural sickness," said Bauterne. He lifted the blanket on the travois and—thanks to the Litany—I received a face full of the stench it released. I began to gag, breaking my focus.

"What is it?" whispered Antoine, his hand on my shoulder. "Are you well?"

"Soeur," I answered, drawing a deep breath of comparatively clean air. "Bauterne has Soeur with him."

"The mastiff? I thought she died at Saint-Julien."

I held up a hand for patience and resumed my eavesdropping—taking shallow breaths this time.

"You are correct. This is an unholy affliction," said the bishop. He did not descend from his horse for a closer look.

Soeur was all but unrecognizable. The Lieutenant of the Hunt had bound her to the travois, and with good cause. The enormous hound had grown monstrous, her forequarters bulging with muscle and her form desperately misshapen. Her terrible injuries from her fight with the Beast were still in evidence, though they did not bleed. Soeur's hindquarters were limp—her back was certainly broken. But even in her shattered condition, the huntsman's favorite thrashed ferociously, spewing great ropes of foam from her muzzle.

It looks like your little meat-sheath was not the only one who received a gift from the Beast at Saint-Julien, said Sarmodel.

I remembered Soeur from that day, covered in the Beast's blood and plasma as he swatted her into the riverbed.

His very essence in the wound, Dayane had said.

The king's hunter regarded his stricken pack leader with sorrow. "I find myself tested to my limits, Monseigneur. I came to help these people, to do my duty as a servant of the throne and of the Church. But with all my skill and all the hunters in Gévaudan at my side, I can find only blind trails and fewmets, and this hellish Beast is laughing at us, I am sure. At every turn I seem only to make matters worse. The Gévaudanais welcomed me once; now they spurn me at the threshold, and nor do I blame them. These men I must work with—the Ennevals—they hate me still, though I have sought to uplift them with example and earnest instruction. They would rather see me thwarted than share a victory with me." He shook his head. "And now this. My Soeur. Can you help her, Monseigneur? If this is indeed the work of evil, is there not *something* you can do?" Bauterne seemed close to tears—for a moment, I pitied him. "You say faith is rewarded, and she has always been my most faithful, my dearest."

Fontaine, snared in his own words, smiled benignly. "I regret that I am no healer, my son. Nor can evil be cured with simple good intentions. If she is to endure this trial, then she must do so under the strength of her own spirit."

Bauterne was crestfallen. "Will you pray with me then? It would give me great comfort to know the Lord receives my prayers alongside yours."

The smile began to slide. The bishop was silent for an uncomfortably long time. "I will pray with you, if so you desire," he said at last.

Sarmodel snorted. *Oh, come! Prayer? The hound is a disastrous mess. Give her a swift death and bury her in salt.*

The bishop dismounted, no doubt to the great relief of his horse. The two men knelt together beside the snarling Soeur, their heads bowed. Michael's wings opened protectively above them, flashing more brightly than the flames of the bonfire and thrusting me abruptly back into my own surroundings. It seemed the realm of prayer was sacrosanct; the Archangel would not permit my intrusion any further.

"Come," I said to Antoine as my vision cleared. "We should leave before we are seen."

XLII

Ocerne, France
1785

"What now?" Jacques interrupted my narrative bluntly.

"Sir?"

We rode through the tracks and byways of Ocerne, heading east. We had so far managed to avoid the Bishop of Mende's men. The fields around us were little more than a rimy bog, a bleak reminder of the winter coming fast for Gévaudan.

I continued my tale more for my own relief than to satisfy my young companion's inquiries. He appeared to care little anymore, but I found I could not stop. After everything that had happened with Dayane, the story of the Red Winter was infinitely easier to bear than the silence.

"What now?" he repeated, frustration and despair dragging at the corners of his mouth. "There was no cure to be found with your . . . forest demon. What recourse is left to me now? And why do I not *remember*?"

"I will think of something, never fear. And it is better that you do not remember, believe me. I wish I were so blessed."

"Professor, I cannot return to Eloise with this illness in my flesh. I have killed another innocent, and I can already hear him again in my head—I am *hungry*, do you understand?"

"I do." I briefly inspected his teeth and his eyes; they would be first to show signs of the transformation. "You must eat properly, sir, or the hunger will return. You know this."

"Is this how it will be, then?" he demanded, his eyes hollow. He seemed half a corpse already. "Is this your only solution, you shameless mountebank? I must eat the hearts of cows and dogs and deer, every day until I die?"

I will admit that my nerves were ragged and my patience quite exhausted at the end of a very trying day. My response was not as compassionate as it might have been.

"Not at all, sir," I snapped. "Eventually, you will no longer be satisfied with such humble fare. As you have already discovered, you will become a beast that seeks out the hearts of your own kind, and you will come to enjoy it more than anything else in life." He looked at me in horror, but I found I had more to say. "The hunger you feel is not a matter of survival, you see, but of supremacy. It is your base nature taking hold, the animal soul of man that grows stronger by consuming his rivals and is never satisfied. It is the very Spirit of War, played out in your flesh. His voice will hound your every moment until you give yourself to him willingly, and you will become the Beast of Gévaudan reborn."

"I will kill myself," he said softly. Then he said it again, louder. "I will kill myself before that happens!"

"Not so," I countered, in full flight now—let the young lord have the whole truth if he wished! "Or you would have done so already. Have you forgotten your good friends, Gerard and Henri? Did you take your own life, after you killed them? No! You took refuge in delirium and subterfuge. And so it will be, young man.

So it is, always. You will kill and forget and dissemble until you go mad, or until someone like me is Contracted to uncover your secret and put you down."

He stared at me, wounded to the core. The only sound was the hoofbeats of our horses in the dirt.

Bravo! said Sarmodel, with delight. *I see your mood has improved immeasurably since this morning.*

Oh, be silent!

Jacques's lip curled in disdain. "God help us all, then. Someone like you?"

"Yes, sir. Just such an unholy degenerate."

"You are a terrible man, Sebastian Grave," he said, trembling, "but not because you are a witch. Whatever miracles you work, whatever good you wring from your misdeeds, you remain always the same loveless viper, consumed by your own self-regard. Little wonder my father wished nothing more to do with you."

"Would you prefer a fistfight, if this is to continue?"

After a tense moment of silence, Jacques laughed. It was a boy's laughter, bright and a little unsure. It was easy to forget that he was only nineteen. "No, Professor. No fighting. Though I would relish the chance to smother you in your sleep, if that were possible," he said.

I laughed with him this time.

"We are both men at the end of our endurance, I think," I said. "If it helps to set your mind at ease, know that this will all be over soon, one way or another."

I regretted my angry words. In truth, I was still deeply dismayed by our encounter with Dayane. In my selfishness, I had asked for her help; she had given it in good faith. And how was she repaid? A broken promise and the slow corruption of a curse she did not understand, and then the Crippling Yoke and death at my hand. I had seldom been more keenly aware of my own wretchedness.

Part of the trouble was that I felt *magnificent* in every other way. Dayane's anima suffused my every movement with a power and lightness that made me feel all but invincible. Sarmodel coiled drunkenly in my mind, basking like a lizard on a hot stone.

It was a dangerous state in which to plan our next steps.

"Where are we going, Professor?" Jacques asked, without petulance this time. "You are never without a plan."

I gave a long sigh. "I will do what I can to help you, sir. I found a cure for your condition once, and I can do so again. Do you trust me?"

"It is lunacy, but for some reason—yes, I do."

"Then come with me this one last time. I will tell you what happened at the Bow and Brace, and the truth of the Red Winter."

XLIII

Eastern Ocerne, France
1766

There were human finger bones in the fewmets. I also found a few cracked metacarpals.

I poked at the droppings for a minute or so; they were fresh, not more than half a day old.

"These were left by a wolf. It's eaten a hand—quite a large one," I called up to Antoine, who was sipping his wine in the saddle as usual. We were in the eastern steppes now, close to the place where we had been surprised by Bauterne and the Normans nearly a year ago. We had heard gunfire and awful screaming the previous night, and (with some help from Sarmodel) I had spent the morning trying to locate their source. The search had brought us to an old birch copse.

"Perhaps it belongs to him," Antoine answered, motioning with his flask.

It took me a moment to distinguish the body in the snowy underbrush. There were in fact two corpses there—the man lay against the carcass of his horse, their shattered rib cages gaping side by side.

"Did you know he was there this whole time?" I asked, using the slushy snow to clean the wolf shit off my gloves. It had been unseasonably warm the previous few days and the forest floor was turning muddy underfoot.

Antoine grinned down at me. "I didn't want to interrupt."

He dismounted and followed me to the grisly scene. The man was not long dead; it was certainly his screaming we had heard the night before. He was also easy to identify. His imposing stature and blond grenadier's mustache were unmistakable, the latter somehow still immaculately waxed and styled.

"Jean-Francois d'Enneval. I regret to say that I was never properly introduced to you or your father," I said, inclining my head politely to the corpse. "You found the Beast in the end, at least. Though I am surprised Lord Bauterne did not kill you first."

Enneval the Younger lay under a light covering of frost which was quickly disappearing in the morning sun. His mouth was fixed wide in a silent cry of surprise, gabled by the icy curls of his mustache. Below the waist, he was naked, and one of his legs was nigh twisted off; it did not bear thinking about how he had ended up so. Along with a great deal of blood, a search of his surroundings revealed a discharged musket and a congealed puddle of plasma.

"Where is his father?" Antoine wondered aloud. "They are never far apart."

"An excellent question." I pointed to a trail of hoofprints leading away from the copse, back toward the eastern road. Judging from their depth and spacing, the rider was moving at a furious pace. The tracks were also interspersed with heavy splashes of blood.

The younger Enneval's death was undoubtedly the Beast's handiwork. I suspected that his father had fled, suffering an injury of his own.

Confirming my analysis of the fewmets, one of Jean-Francois's hands had indeed been eaten, along with a reasonable portion of his exposed extremities. It was not surprising. During this, the leanest of winters, anything edible would be plundered by scavengers as soon as it hit the ground.

"Are you looting the corpse of the king's huntsman?" Antoine asked.

"I am *investigating,*" I corrected, pocketing Enneval's money pouch. I contemplated taking his handsome hunting knives as well, but concluded they would be too easily recognized.

"Well, when you are finished investigating, what do you want to do with him?"

"I do not think our latrine spade will suffice to dig him a grave, if that's what you mean. But I suppose it's not good to leave him here. We could burn the body, I suppose, but it may be too wet for that."

In fact, the steady sound of dripping filled the forest around us. It was warm enough that the trees were shedding their icicles. Antoine loosened the collar of his woolen greatcoat, raising his face to the sun with a smile.

"Antoine, where are we exactly?" I asked.

"Hmm. North of Château d'Ocerne, and quite a way east, I would say. If we go much farther, we will end up in Velay."

"Are there any villages nearby?"

"Not for miles."

"I thought as much. We need to find shelter, and soon."

He looked up at the clear sky, frowning. "I would never question your blasphemous powers of precognition, but are you certain? I have never seen a more perfect winter's morning. I would think the thaw had come early."

"Precisely."

He seemed dubious, but nonetheless we mounted our horses again in a hurry.

My misgivings were borne out within the hour. Clouds the color of gunpowder amassed over the mountains, growing thicker and darker with every passing minute. By the time we reached the eastern road, it was shiny with ice and we were riding into a stinging sleet. We reached a fork in the road as the day darkened further still.

"That way!" Antoine called over the wind.

I followed the line of his pointing hand. The sleet spattered against an elegant wooden shingle that swung madly in the gale. It directed us to a narrow but well-maintained road up the mountainside.

I recognized it, of course. I had been here once before, when I had first arrived in Gévaudan. I read the sign aloud, filled not with relief but with inexplicable dread.

The Bow and Brace.

ADDENDUM:

On the Madness of Gilles de Rais

Tiffauges, France
1440

There's a voice inside the head of Gilles de Rais, Marshal of France.

It's been there ever since he purchased the charred bone from Jehanne d'Arc's pyre, nine years ago. The voice belongs to her, his beloved Maiden, and she tells him secrets and mysteries he had never imagined.

Does he wonder what scandalous toys his neighbor keeps hidden in his garderobe? She knows. Does he want to know what his grandfather buried under the hearthstone? She can tell him. But she is terribly weak, and sad, and in great pain. Before she shares her secrets, he must send her something small, to keep her company in Paradise. At first, it's a rabbit, or a duck perhaps. Sometimes it's gold or precious stones, which she has him cast into the fire with a few strange words. When the flames die down, all that remains is a handful of thin white husks, like eggshells.

And then, for a little while, it's hundreds of jeweled silk costumes[1]

1. "Jehanne" must have been delighted with the thousands of fleas and scabies mites she received as a bonus.

and trinkets, from a grand mystery play performed in Jehanne's honor at Orleans.

She is very grateful, and she always keeps her promises. Dedications are all she requires. He must do it all in her name, and that's not so much to ask, is it?

At night, Gilles frocks up as the Archangel Michael, Jehanne's divine Messenger. He paints his face into a lion's mask and combs heated wax and royal-blue woad into his beard. He holds Jehanne's single surviving relic close to his heart. It's the head of her thigh bone, which used to sit so close to her virginal cooch, and he has polished it back to ivory whiteness. Gilles strokes it and listens to the Maiden's voice, which grows stronger all the time.

But there is more she can tell him, so much more. Jehanne always loved him, her dearest lieutenant, and she wants him to succeed her in greatness. She knows what his family are saying about him. She can teach him to whistle a melody that will make a woman barren. She knows words he can stamp into missives to make his enemies pluck out their own eyes. She knows . . . She knows . . .

It is getting harder to please her. Gilles's wealth is dwindling. His debts are growing and he is selling his estates to pay them. His family is snipping off his lines of credit. And his remaining creditors are disinclined to finance another season of his obscene stage spectacular.

I've been watching him for a long time. Gilles is growing desperate, and I fear that the next show he puts on is going to bring the house down.

I begin to wonder if the master will ever return.

The last corpse tumbled into the pit just as the moon was rising.

In the silvery light, the abandoned field was starkly lit and stippled with shale; it might have been the surface of the moon itself. Far from the Baron de Rais's stronghold and too rocky for the plow, it was abandoned and all but forgotten by the townsfolk. It was perfect for the evening's unsavory business.

A natural fissure in the craggy field was now filled with dozens of heartless bodies. Three men were already working to cover them with rubble and mud. A fourth man directed them, heavyset and mysterious in a black clerical cassock. In a year or so, the Baron de Rais planned to lay a foundation and build a brick chapel over the pit, dedicated to Jehanne d'Arc.

Livia watched the workers from the road, mounted on a gray palfrey and robed in glamers beneath a leafless tree. Had they looked in her direction, the men would perhaps have seen a pale deer, or a tall stone mottled with shadows. She held the reins with only one hand; the other arm she cradled close to her body.

"Quickly," called the fourth man in the field, the one in charge, who claimed to be a priest. The others did not trust him. His accent was foreign and his robes were unlike any holy vestments they had ever seen, but his tone of command was clear. "It must be done before dawn, or the baron will have your heads."

The working men only muttered in response. Paid to hide abominable acts, toiling in the dark under the direction of Gilles de Rais's strange associate, the men were uneasy and unwilling. The ground was only recently free of winter frost, and it was hard digging.

And the baron would have their heads anyway. Livia had made a careful body count and the total was three short of sixty.[2]

---

2. Sixty human hearts are quorum for Contracts with most Spirits of significance (at least on the downtown side of the Rift), since the time of Solomon. Note that I'm talking about serious contenders here, not bugaboo clowns like Krampus and Clauneck. And do not switch in pig or donkey organs and expect to open negotiations—they can always tell.

She turned to her second order of business. On a low branch beside her horse, a white goose perched. It bore strange markings—a black band around its slender neck and a black spot over one eye—and it appeared to be sleeping. In Livia's Arcane sight, it was not a goose at all, but a hook-beaked, winged serpent: a messenger follit.

The succubus chewed her lip thoughtfully. The activities in Château de Tiffauges were reaching their climax. The Spirit Avstamet was working his will on Gilles de Rais; so much was obvious. First the devotion play at Orleans, and now this flagrant harvest of the local peasants. He was gathering anima from every source he could find, masquerading as Jehanne and using her bone as a conduit for devotions made in her name.

But a nobleman—even a mad one—was not going to meet the needs of Mars ascendant. Gilles de Rais had begun spending his evenings with Francois Prelati, the strange Florentine priest-cum-sorcerer[3] who now directed the laborers in their work. In only a few months, the grand hearth at Château de Tiffauges was filled with the bones of children. The occult dabbling of a spoiled aristocrat had quickly become something far more dangerous.

And now this, at the eleventh hour: a message from the master. Livia had begun to fear that he had been unable to escape from Captain Renard after all. Now he might be too late.

Livia spoke a word of command and the goose awakened.

"I trust this message finds you well, Livia," said Sebastian's voice from its beak. He sounded weak, weary and very angry. "I apologize for my long silence, but I have been . . . detained

3. Pun intended.

by one Captain Renard. I believe you have met. We have much to talk about—your conspicuous absence not least of all. I am coming to find you, and then you are going to help me collect the relic from Gilles de Rais." There was a short pause. "Do not think about running. I have your hand."

Livia snorted. She had listened to the message several times since the goose had found her that afternoon. "Conspicuous absence"? Indeed! She shook back her cloak and held out her arm.

She nearly wept, as always, at the sight of her maimed wrist. The exposed stump was scarred and twisted, the result of desperate self-mutilation with hot shears. Naked in the moonlight, the scar shone like wax, and it was so very ugly. She invited the goose to perch on the ravaged stump; in spite of its size, the creature was almost weightless. Livia jostled her horse into an easy walk along the road.

An Arcane phrase brought a change over the follit. It stilled and sat expectantly, with its neck arched high. Livia took a moment to compose her thoughts.

"Meatbag," she began, "where are you? I am waiting for you at Tiffauges. Time is running short. You are going to miss Avstamet—again—if you take much longer. And you have my thanks for retrieving my hand. You may use it to find me when you get here. Until then, I'm sure there are many other ways it can be of service." She laughed heartily at her bawdy jest while the goose stared at her vacantly.

Livia sealed the message with an Admonition and raised her arm. "Now fly, straight to the master. And I apologize; he will likely wring your neck."

The messenger gave an ungracious honk and took to the air. It ascended against the moon, its white wings beating hard.

And then it descended again, not a hundred yards away,

where a familiar figure sat on horseback. Even from this distance, Livia could see the old one seething above him like a thunderhead. The goose alighted on his wrist.

"Well, shit," she muttered.

Her horse carried her inexorably toward him; there was no point in stalling now. As she entered the black aura of the old one, she heard the messenger Spirit speaking the final words of her message, in her own voice.

". . . Until then, I'm sure there are many other ways it can be of service."

Sebastian raised his eyebrows as the goose hunkered down to give full throat to Livia's laughter.

The succubus closed her eyes in chagrin and waited for the bird to finish. It seemed to go on for an age.

"Oh, meatbag," she murmured when it was finally over. "Just kill me. Is that really what I sound like?"

If I had flesh, succubus, that would be your final request, hissed the old one.

The master took the goose by the neck and flicked it like a dishrag. The follit discorporated into bright vapor with a choked guffaw.

"Livia." He kept his voice low, but his fury was clear. "I have traveled a long way to find you. I am very, very tired. I will ask you once: *Where have you been?*"

Livia widened her eyes disingenuously. "Why, I have been here, waiting for you, Dominus."

Impertinent slut! thundered the old one. *We were languishing in that henhouse of the Almighty for months!* Livia cringed beneath the boiling vortex of his form.

"I could not approach the abbey, as you well know!" she protested righteously. "You *commanded* me to stay away until I received word—right before you abandoned me at Rouen."

"Would it be the first time you disobeyed an order, Livia? I could have *died,*" hissed the master.

"Am I to obey or disobey, Dominus? Your terms are most unclear—and your Shackles quite unforgiving, with the weight of an extra two hundred years in them."

"You . . ." Sebastian raised his fists, trembling with rage. *"You . . ."*

Scathe her! She has more than earned it!

"You're hungry, aren't you?" Livia suggested. "I can tell. It always makes you irritable."

"You're *enjoying* this! All of it!" The master barely succeeded in restraining himself. "The disguises, the sneaking around, the guardsmen, the torture. From the beginning, it's all been a game to you, hasn't it?"

Behind them in the benighted field, the sorcerer Prelati drove a long knife into the first laborer's back. The man fell to the sod without a sound.

"A game?! I've got *no hand,* you ungrateful bastard!" Livia reared like a viper in the saddle. *"You left me* in the middle of a Holy Inquisition at Rouen, and you wonder that I didn't break my neck to come to your rescue! Did you know the good captain was already hunting me when you cast me adrift?"

"Was it perhaps because you left a dozen naked husks in the Rouen guardhouse?"

The second workman fell with his throat cut. His gurgling alerted the third, who barely had time to turn around before he was disemboweled.

"Oh, calm yourself! It was nine!"

"Nine?!"

"I don't remember—does it matter?"

Scathe her! *Do it now!!*

The sorcerer dragged the bodies to the edge of the partially filled pit. In the dark, he began the grisly work of cutting out their hearts.

The master gathered himself with a visible effort. "A thousand years. Is it possible that you're still the same spiteful, petulant child after *a thousand years*?" He pointed to the quiet butchery taking place in the field. "Now. Answer me! What is going on here? Does Gilles de Rais still have the relic?"

Steam still curled from the corners of her mouth, but Livia answered calmly. "He does. I believe he is attempting to lift Avstamet out of the Maiden's bone."

"A manifestation?" Sebastian scoffed. "The man is mad indeed if he thinks he can shift a Spirit like Avstamet."

"Maybe. He has help." Livia motioned to the murderous figure in the black cassock. "A sorcerer from Florence. Francois Prelati. He seems to be a competent practitioner, if a little reckless."

The master swore. "I know Prelati. He's more than competent. He was excommunicated some years ago for summoning a seraph."

"A seraph? What for?"

It may be the opportunity we need, my love, said the old one. *Summoning Barron will take time and concentration, on both sides. They will be distracted. We can dispose of the Madman and claim the Olympian as he is making the crossing.*

Sebastian was silent in thought for a few moments. "Yes. Yes, that could work. I will lay some Wards, get a few lesser Spirits onside. I might even be able to produce some quicksilver."

Don't forget, added the old one, *that Avstamet has agreed to treat with you—on the blood of Jehanne d'Arc, no less. If we cannot take him by force, you can invoke the Table.*[4]

"A last resort, but a good one." The master nodded decisively. "Risky, and the timing will be delicate, but it's nothing we can't manage with a little preparation."

"Excellent!" said Livia, clapping her hands. "Best get cracking. You have perhaps two hours until they start."

"They're doing it *tonight*?!"

The succubus clucked her tongue. "Tut-tut, my good citizen of Rome. Have you forgotten your *fasti*?"[5] She motioned to the benighted field. "Why do you think I am out here tonight, freezing my remaining fingers off? Don't you know what day it is?"

Sebastian did a quick mental calculus and then clenched his teeth. "The first of March. The day of his birth."

"And perhaps the day of his death, if you can manage it."

That was doubtful. Sebastian was in bad shape. He looked haggard, very thin and somehow smaller.

"I'm glad to see you finally got rid of Clauneck," Livia said. "Tell me—how did you escape from Renard?"

---

4. A Spirit can be called to account on any deal it makes, by any interested parties. The Table is the common name for the Sigil of Armistice under which such negotiations take place.

5. The *fasti* were the calendars of Rome, marking days permitted for business and religious observance. Each of the Olympians and their multitude of Arcane hangers-on had specific days devoted to them throughout the year, which were meticulously recorded by the city's bureaucrats. It was tedious, but it helped to curb squabbling among the pantheon and subsequent mortal bloodshed.

"The abbess took pity on me and shared her liquor."

Livia stared at him and then laughed. "Did anyone survive?"

The master did not smile. His eyes were haunted. "No, and I almost didn't either."

"Well, good and done." Livia attempted to fold her arms, failed and settled for placing them in her lap. "I am sorry I wasn't there to see Renard's last breath—I so wanted him for myself. Poor Michael must be tearing out his whiskers."

No doubt, said the old one. *And we'd best hurry before he finds us here.*

"Ha! If I know him, he'll be wringing his hands over at the abbey for quite some time. All those dead virgins—what a waste!" said Livia. "Now. Meatbag. You have something of mine?"

The master looked at her for a long moment, his eyes unfriendly. From his saddlebag he produced a twitching bundle, wrapped in dirty woolen cloth. He tossed it to the succubus, who snatched it from the air with a delighted cry.

"Oh! *Oh!*" She tore away the rags with her teeth and beheld her dismembered hand with tears in her eyes. Cooing like a new mother, she licked and nibbled at the stump and pressed the limb into place. There was a sizzle and a tremendous amount of smoke, followed by a dull, gristly pop.

"Are you finished?" asked Sebastian, waving his hand in front of his face.

"Oh, Dominus, thank you." Livia's voice was liquid with emotion. She flexed and wiggled her fingers, rubbing at the wrist with her other hand. There was barely a mark at the join.

"I suppose you're welcome. Please, try not to cut it off this time," he sighed.

Behind them, Prelati the sorcerer stood up from his work. He was holding a small, dripping sack and he glanced nervously at the moon as he mounted his horse. The master and the succubus both looked over as he headed for the château at a canter.

"Well, meatbag. It's time. Are you strong enough?"

We will have to be, answered the old one. *We will not get another chance like this.*

"I'm sure we can make it work," said the master, though he did not look at all sure. "Let's go. The first stages of the rite will take a few hours at least."

They whispered in conversation as they rode slowly after the sorcerer.

"You are pleased to see me, aren't you? Just a little bit?" asked Livia. "Admit it."

"Do you promise you won't try to kill me this time?"

"You know I wasn't serious about that."

"Do I?"

"Never mind."

PART FIVE

The Last Dinner at the Bow and Brace

XLIV

The Bow and Brace
Eastern Ocerne, France
1766

The Bow and Brace hunting lodge was a nobleman's playground, replete with luxuries and on a scale to rival a provincial castle. Two enormous fireplaces faced each other across the opulent grand salon. Chairs upholstered in velvet and satin were arranged around tables inlaid with chess and backgammon boards. The publican's astonishing collection of antiquities, weaponry and heirlooms was on display alongside the real trophies of his estate—the heads of deer, boars and wolves which covered the walls. There was even an enormous bear head glaring down at us with its twinkling glass eyes. It was all slightly grotesque (and quite morbid), particularly in comparison to the impoverished farmlands only a few miles away, but it was impossible not to be impressed.

As we entered, we were greeted by angry shouting from somewhere over our heads; someone on the floor above was dreadfully unhappy. It subsided immediately and Antoine gave me a shrug, with a mischievous smile.

Antoine barely seemed to notice the lavish surroundings; he

was a nobleman's son after all. We accepted glasses of warm brandy from the butler, who introduced himself as Gaspard and extended an invitation to enjoy the comforts of the grand salon until the publican arrived. Antoine finished his brandy in a gulp and then took mine, sipping it nonchalantly as he examined the publican's antiques. I browsed a bookshelf, selecting a hunting manual filled with delightful woodcuts.

We were not the only ones taking refuge at the lodge. As we dried ourselves by the fire, two more luckless travelers arrived on the doorstep.

The first was a young woman, finely dressed in a silver riding habit and teal hooded cape. The cape was a fashionable choice that had fared poorly in the storm; she left small green-blue puddles in her wake. "Messieurs," she said when she saw us, offering a gracious curtsy in spite of her bedraggled appearance. Antoine and I both bowed in return. The red-haired, middle-aged man who accompanied her had a harried aspect. He offered only a cursory greeting before taking the young lady upstairs.

Outside, the sleet had turned into fast-flying snow. The stormhead over the mountains was about to make good on its promise of a ferocious blizzard. I was, however, more concerned about the perils inside the lodge. Bauterne and the Ennevals had made it their home for the winter; we would be company most unwelcome at the dinner table.

While he could not turn us away—it would be a death sentence—Jean Chastel the publican was not afraid to show his displeasure. The tip of his elegant black cane rapped sharply across the Versailles parquet as he entered the grand salon, snapping orders to his staff.

"Have you come to the right establishment, young Lord Ocerne? You'll find no whores here," he said by way of greeting. The publican was handsomely dressed in a russet-colored ditto suit, trimmed with gold thread. His silver hair was neatly secured with a black bow and I was again struck by the taut power of his movements, even though he walked with some difficulty. His military bearing was unmistakable, well past the end of his career.

"I am glad to hear that, Monsieur Chastel. It was my intention to give the ladies of Gévaudan an evening of rest," replied Antoine glibly.

Chastel grunted, unamused. "I presume your father will be paying your account?" he asked bluntly.

"Of course, Monsieur Chastel. He bade me convey his regards."

"Did he indeed? He must be a man of remarkable foresight. You've not seen Château d'Ocerne for months by the look of you."

I smirked into my book as Antoine stuttered a reply. I found that I couldn't help but like the publican; there was something reassuring about his gruff manner and barbed conversation. But my levity was short-lived.

"Welcome back, Professor Grave. I did expect that I might see you again, given how much you enjoyed the amenities of my lodge the last time," said Chastel. His tone was mild but his steel-bright eyes were accusatory; I had the sudden irrational fear that there was still stolen silverware protruding from my pockets.

"I would have returned sooner, good sir, but we have been quite consumed with the hunt. I am looking forward to sleeping in a bed again after all this time," I replied carefully.

He looked us over with an appraising eye. "Very well. We have one remaining room for you—an expensive one. Gaspard will inform you when it is ready. My staff will see to your horses—"

He was interrupted by more muffled shouting from the floor above. He did not mention the disturbance, but the publican was more than a little irritated. He turned on his heel and limped back toward the dining hall. "We dine at eight. You will have time to make yourselves presentable. I suggest you take advantage of it."

After his fourth brandy, Antoine fell asleep in the cavernous armchair. There was nobody else in the grand salon, so I took the opportunity to do some snooping—something was definitely happening upstairs. A voice raised in displeasure within the opulent suites of the lodge was enough to rouse my suspicion.

I uttered a Litany of the Dusk and crept up the stairs, just another shadow in the vaulted hall. On an instinct, I drew my envenomed hunting knife very carefully as I ascended.

What are you doing? Are we going to kill someone? asked Sarmodel, his excitement palpable.

I'm not sure. I want to know where all the noise is coming from and I'm feeling cautious.

The upstairs gallery was exquisitely furnished and the walls were hung with an absolute bounty of religious paintings and tapestries. Directly in front of me was a pair of doors decorated with carved stags and gilded scrollwork—the Royal Suite. I counted eight other rooms in total. Thankfully, I didn't need to go opening doors to find the right chamber; I had only to follow the shouted obscenities that issued anew from a room at the end of the hallway.

I moved silently over the furs on the floor, still shrouded in the Litany. To an observer, it would have seemed that the lamps guttered briefly in a sudden draft.

I stopped outside the door and listened for a moment.

"He knew you were a dog-fucking bastard from the first!" snarled a man's voice from within. "Dog-fucking bastard! That's what he called you!"

The voice with its Norman accent could only belong to Enneval the Elder. Another familiar voice replied, in soothing tones.

"Sir, you are not yourself," said Bauterne with his urbane courtly inflection. "I fear your injury has taken a toll most—"

"Shut your arse-licking mouth! *Where is my son?!*" Enneval screamed.

I winced, chewing my lip. *Perhaps we should go.*

Sebastian, no! They're just warming up!

Sarmodel, if Bauterne is here, so is the Archangel.

Unless he decides to manifest,[1] *we can manage anything Michael pokes across the Rift.*

The decision was made for us a moment later.

"Who is there?" Bauterne's voice rose sharply and he jerked open the door.

This close to him, there was no hiding, even with magical assistance. My concealing shadows slipped away like a heavy cloak, and I was left looking into the weary eyes of the Lieutenant of the Hunt.

He did not seem surprised to see me. "Professor Grave. As though we required any additional troubles here." He raised an eyebrow at my drawn blade. "Are you going to stab me, sir?"

"My apologies, Lieutenant. We took shelter from the snowstorm and I heard a disturbance. I assumed the worst." I sheathed my knife with an apologetic smile. Behind Bauterne, the fire was roaring in the hearth. A pile of bloody bandages sat on the floor before it.

"I see. Your concern is unnecessary. Lord Enneval has suffered a grave injury and it has left him somewhat . . . confused. I am sure he did not intend any disturbance. I will see you at dinner, no doubt."

1. This was a joke—the Archangel has come to the flesh only once (ref. Luke 2:1–20) and we all know how that ended up.

He stood looking at me implacably and I turned to leave with a slight bow.

But then I turned again.

"Lieutenant, among other things, I am a physician. Though we are rivals in the hunt, I would gladly offer my services if you have need," I said.

Bauterne's first instinct was to refuse; he sucked in a breath to offer a swift retort.

There was an Arcane fluttering of wings behind his head; a gentle flicker of gold and malachite green. The Archangel's presence was soft—conciliatory, even.

Bauterne's angry refusal remained unsaid. His shoulders fell and for a moment he looked utterly defeated.

"Be assured, sir, that under ordinary circumstances I would not trust you with so much as a lame pup. But I am near the end of my endurance with the Norman, and I am not fool enough to believe there will be any other help coming for us tonight." He stepped aside with a nod of resignation. "Any assistance you can provide is welcome."

I stepped into Enneval's chamber in time for another flood of obscenities.

This time the vitriol was directed at me. "Ah! Professor Petticoat![2] Where is the young Lord Ocerne? Surely there is room for one more sodomite in here."

I gave a bland smile to cover my surprise. My private world with Antoine had obviously not been quite as private as I imagined.

"Monsieur Enneval. I understand you are unwell."

---

2. If I recall correctly, Enneval's exact words were "*Professeur Pipe,*" which amounts to a juvenile epithet related to oral sex, and a slur on my professionalism—both entirely uncalled for.

The Norman was sitting in the great wooden bed, his back propped up with pillows against the carved headboard. His flesh was a terrible gray color and hung from his huge frame like lumpy sackcloth. The lodge staff had swaddled him in cushions and blankets in an attempt to make him comfortable in his sitting position. Bandages were wound around his head, holding in place a thick wad of cloth on the back of his skull. His lush grenadier's mustache, always so carefully waxed and curled, was now bristly and unkempt, like barley straw. One glaring eye was a ghastly red, like fresh liver.

"Unwell" indeed. Not quite as unwell as his son, but it won't be long, said my Guest.

Sarmodel was correct; Enneval's anima was very gradually peeling off his body like mist. Without serious medical intervention, he would be dead within days.

"He has been shot, sir," said Bauterne, closing the door behind me. He was, as ever, dressed in his fine hunting attire of soft chamois britches and sturdy waistcoat with cabled silk galloons—all black, of course. "Though he begs to differ."

"Ah."

"*I told you* I was surprised by a boar and fell from my horse, you pompous cock! I will carve that smirk off your face with my knife," snarled Enneval.

"Indeed, but you are too weak to rise, as we have discussed many times," said Bauterne evenly.

"If you had allowed us to take our own hounds on the hunt, it would never have happened! As soon as Jean-Francois returns, he will tell you—*Ah! By the Lord!*" A spasm of terrible pain gripped the hunter. He attempted to clutch at his skull, but it seemed to cost him a dreadful effort just to lift his arms. His muscular limbs shook pitifully and, in the end, he simply rested his chin on his chest, panting. A small amount of clear fluid ran from his ear as he moved.

"Monsieur Enneval, if I had let you take your dogs, you would all be trapped in this blizzard by now. Your pack did not deserve to die because you cannot properly judge the weather." Bauterne shook his head. He seemed more disheartened than anything, or perhaps he was just worn down by Enneval's vicious fury.

I cleared my throat and spoke to the suffering man in the bed. "Monsieur Enneval, might I examine your wound? It appears to be causing you some pain. I may be able to help."

His head snapped up with sudden, furious energy and his whole body strained as he sought to lunge at me from the bed. Thankfully, he was too weak and too deeply engulfed in the cushions to do more than shift his weight. "Do not dare touch me, *anticoniste*![3] You may examine my knife with your liver!" he roared. Another trickle of watery liquid dripped from his ear.

I waited, smiling gently with my hands folded in front of me. It took only a few seconds for the Norman's agitation to exact its toll. His eyes fluttered and his heaving shoulders slumped. He sank back into the pillows, unconscious.

I immediately called for a manservant to fetch my medical kit from my valise. I asked Bauterne to support the Norman's bulk as I tipped him gently forward and tugged at the bandages around his head. I lifted away the clump of wool cloth and grimaced.

"You are correct, sir. It is a shot wound."

Even with the Norman's blond hair matted into the blood, it was easy to see the sizable hole in the back of his skull. It was

---

3. Yet another base insult from the Norman. This one implies an aversion to female genitalia, which is quite unearned in my case. I am partial to snails and oysters both.

undoubtedly made by a musket ball. As I unpacked the wadding from the wound, more clear liquid seeped out from beneath the clot.

"That was not in question. I suspect some violent dispute with another group of hunters, though he will admit to nothing." Bauterne seemed to find his task distasteful. "Professor, you offered to help. Are you able or not?"

Sebastian, this one—surely **this one** *is beyond help. I can see his thinking parts!*

I am inclined to agree. But I can't kill him with Bauterne watching.

I shook my head regretfully. "He will not recover, I am afraid. His violent temper and confusion are caused by damage to his brain, and it would take more skill than I have to repair it, even if I were able to remove the pellet. There is little I can do except ease his suffering."

Bauterne swore under his breath. "Then I will continue to pray for him, and I will thank you to take your leave."

"Of course, sir."

I replaced the crusted wadding with fresh, dry cloth and wound the bandages firmly around his head again. We returned the big man to his sitting position, arranging his limbs as comfortably as possible.

When we were finished, I took a small green glass bottle from my kit. I gave it to the lieutenant.

He closed his eyes briefly in forbearance. "Opium? You are indeed a physician of rare skill. I could have purchased this from any village in France."

"It is my own recipe, sir. Do not confuse it with some midwife's tonic." I held up a glass pipette, wrapped in soft leather. "Now listen. There are ten drops in a measure. Three measures will soften his pain and hopefully his tone. Four will grant him sleep. He will not awaken from five. Do you understand?"

"Of course."

"Repeat it."

"For the love of the Lord—I am not an idiot, sir!" Bauterne's lip curled.

"Then listen to me again. The Normans were indeed surprised in the woods, but not by a boar. Lord Enneval's son is not going to return. We found him this morning, killed by the Beast. There was no 'violent dispute'—it was his musket, fired by accident during his final struggle, which caused his father's injury." I showed him the pipette again. "I will ask once more—do you understand?"

Bauterne's sneer faded. He took the glass dropper from my hand, his eyes grave. "Three for relief. Four for sleep. Five for peace. I understand."

"Excellent. I will see you at dinner, sir."

XLV

The suite we had been given contained only one bedroom and only one bed, and the butler had apologized profusely when it became apparent that Antoine and I would have to share it. We had made a show of awkward acceptance and I resolved right away that we would put it to good use later that night.

I will not bore you with the afternoon's long and arduous toilette. Neither of us was traveling with appropriate dinner attire, and there was no question of us dining in our hunting clobber. The publican sent manservants to iron, fit and tailor a pair of simple gray ditto suits for us. They bore the marks of several prior alterations and I suspected that we would not be the last to make use of them. This laborious task was mixed with the interminable work—conducted by still more manservants—of bathing and shaving and fingernail-trimming and hair-styling.

Finally, just as the dinner bell was ringing, we were ready. I was, if not quite dashing, then at least respectable in my refashioned formalwear. I was not entirely prepared to see Antoine so changed, however. He winked at me in the mirror as he caught me staring. Smooth-cheeked and freshly groomed, he was utterly transformed from the pampered lordling I had met in the courtyard at Château d'Ocerne, back in the spring.

There was little danger he would again be mistaken for yet another frivolous young rake of the French nobility. There was something ***keener*** about him, a newly honed edge that had not been there before. Had so much changed in such a short space of time? Perhaps it was simply that I knew him better now, and I could see the determination behind the devilish spark in his eye, and the clear-sighted leader inside the irrepressible young libertine.

Yes indeed, I was hopelessly smitten.

"Sebastian, I am ***starving,***" said Antoine, following the last of the manservants through the open door. "I feel like I haven't eaten a decent meal in six months."

"As your personal chef for most of those months, I shall try not to take offense," I replied.

We nearly collided with a trio of footmen at the top of the stairs. They bore all the necessities for a sumptuous dinner service, carried carefully on silver trays. I noted with interest the lone glass chalice and the full, single set of silverware resting on the napery beside it. The food itself was covered in a silver dome, and it left a delectable aroma in its wake.

My curiosity turned into deep suspicion as the footmen took the meal to the gilded doors of the Royal Suite and then disappeared inside.

"One of our fellow guests will not be joining us for dinner, it seems," I remarked to Antoine.

"He must be very important or very rich. Probably both. The

Dauphin[1] himself has stayed in that room," he replied, his eyes narrowed.

"Whoever he is, he's remarkably concerned about his privacy. I am intrigued."

I closed my eyes for a moment.

Anything?

Sarmodel swiftly parsed the soft sounds and various airborne compounds in the hallway.

Fungus. Boiled bird. Roots. Animal fat. Some plants. Deer meat. Offal.

Delicious, thank you. Can you hear anything?

Voices. He's a man. I can't tell anything else, not with your ears. I interpreted a small mental spasm as a grimace. *There's also perfume. A lot of perfume.*

Interesting.

The dinner bell rang for the second time and Jean Chastel's cane rapped impatiently over the parquetry. We went downstairs to join our host at the grand table.

Dinner was a surprisingly enjoyable affair. There were twelve of us in total, though there were still many empty seats at the table. We were in any case far outnumbered by the staff, who hovered around us like mosquitoes, ready to respond to every cleared throat and cocked eyebrow.

Bauterne was the last to join us. Sarmodel hardened in my mind—a sensation like teeth set on edge—as the Archangel's wings unfurled above the table in a clear staking of territory.

---

1. Not an actual dolphin, the Dauphin of France was the title given to the heir apparent.

"Monsieur Enneval is unwell and sends his apologies," Bauterne said as he took his seat.

Monsieur Enneval's intermittent screaming from the upstairs suite did not sound at all apologetic.

He's still alive? For the love of—I thought I was quite explicit, I said to Sarmodel.

Perhaps we should take care of it ourselves, he suggested.

I hate to admit it, but you may be right.

The young lady we had met earlier introduced herself as Rosalie Mimet, the daughter of one of the barons of Velay. She was traveling to meet her cousin, a baronet somewhere to the west, to whom she was betrothed. Her forest-green gown with its stomacher of embroidered gold silk was no doubt intended for her presentation to him. The red-haired man who accompanied her was her uncle and chaperone, and he seemed to take the latter role very seriously. He seated himself purposefully between Antoine and Rosalie, the better to obstruct any attempts at conversation.

I noticed with some amusement that, while the other guests dined with the lodge's engraved silverware, my place had been set with tarnished pewter cutlery, no doubt from the staff kitchen. Jean Chastel glared at me from the head of the table, his eyes daring me to protest. I simply smiled and inclined my head.

Oh, I like him, chuckled Sarmodel.

You always like the military ones.

Sarmodel's olfactory portrait of the meal was (more or less) accurate. In spite of the winter dearth, Chastel's kitchen staff had produced a delectable banquet. We began with a duet of mushroom cream and pheasant bouillon, followed by roasted carrots and pumpkins, heavily buttered, with a juicy haunch of venison and sautéed liver. As I suspected, the choicest cuts had already been taken to the mysterious guest in the Royal Suite.

I don't remember the names of the remaining dinner guests. They seemed to me all different versions of the same young man—wealthy, educated, stylish and patently ill-suited to hunting. I suspected their noble parents had sent them to join the hunt for Gévaudan's Beast as a sort of Enlightenment gap year. With their labored wit and conspicuous aping of Versailles manners, they were like trained ornamental pets. I even marked them as such in my mind: Messieurs Dog, Ferret, Cat, Hare and Finch.

Bauterne surprised me throughout the meal by being consummately charming with the young nobles, who clearly idolized him. He entertained their questions and indulged them with a few stories of his exploits, some of which were even interesting. He was arrogant and condescending, but he did it with wit and passion. I saw for the first time the charismatic hero who had so fascinated the people of Gévaudan.

As the only woman at the table, Rosalie Mimet held court alongside Bauterne. Her exquisite etiquette and artful conversation were in the manner of a skilled performance.[2] She discussed her favorite Greek poetry with one young man and shared intriguing political insights with the next. Her uncle's duty as chaperone was no easy task; she had every man at the table in the palm of her hand before we even finished the soup.

There was nonetheless an ominous quality to the occasion. The heavy wooden window shutters, closed against the storm, thumped alarmingly in the gale. The shouted expletives from the upstairs

---

2. If this whole affair sounds like an elaborate pantomime, that's because in many ways, it was. The social tenets of the *ancien régime* were incredibly complex, and entire fortunes were built on reputation alone. Occasions like dinner parties were positively simmering with subtext, innuendo and petty pageantry, all delivered through discussions about fashion or philosophy.

suite continued to interrupt the conversation, the challenge for each guest being to demonstrate how staunchly they could certainly not hear anything untoward. As the meal finished with a course of wafers, cheese, candied ginger and brandy, Sarmodel *sharpened* in my mind.

Sebastian! Can you hear that?

I smiled politely as Monsieur Ferret recounted his (entirely fabricated) version of the Saint-Julien massacre.

You'll need to be more specific.

Sarmodel progressively suppressed my hearing, shutting out first the drivel in my immediate surroundings, then the rest of the dining room. I was left with the tapestry of environmental sounds which would otherwise have gone unremarked: the rushing of the storm, the hubbub of the kitchen and the faint, terrified howling of the dogs in the kennels outside.

And somewhere below us, howling of a very different kind.

I stiffened in my chair. In the cellar of the Bow and Brace, something *raged.*

Sarmodel. Is that what I think it is?

Oh yes.

I feigned great interest in the preposterous story being told at the dinner table, while redoubling my efforts to hear the muffled sounds coming from beneath the floor.

The animal's baying was very deep; it was much larger than an ordinary hound. Its hungering cries were punctuated with a piteous hacking and choking, hinting at some greater struggle.

Soeur. My God, Bauterne still has her. Has he lost his mind?

It would seem so, answered my Guest.

I listened to the pitiable sounds for a few moments longer. *I fear we've got a busy night ahead of us, my love. It's too dangerous to leave her down there—*

"—something to add, surely, Professor Grave?"

The sounds of the dining room returned in a rush.

Rosalie Mimet was looking at me, her mouth curved in a quizzical smile. The conversation around the table had stopped, and my fellow guests had turned expectantly in my direction.

"I beg your pardon, Mademoiselle, but I did not hear your question over the storm," I said.

Rosalie smiled charmingly. "Our companions—even the good lieutenant—have each said the Beast must be some unholy monster sent by the Devil himself. I must object. Such superstition surely has no place in serious discussions."

"Mademoiselle, the creature has killed ***hundreds***," interjected Monsieur Finch. "It cannot be any natural beast."

She shook her head. "I still assert that there must be another explanation. My question, Professor, was whether you, as a man of science, had something to offer the discussion." She raised an eyebrow, teasingly. "Or must we entertain, in seriousness, speculation about witchcraft and devilry?"

"Yes indeed, let us hear the words of the scientist!" said Chastel. There were two spots of color in his cheeks from the brandy and a hint of genuine amusement in his eyes.

I ignored Antoine's smirk and began one of my favorite monologues.[3]

"An excellent question, Mademoiselle. I have indeed slain monsters, and each was a monster in reputation only. Just as the products of science are often mistaken for supernatural phenomena, so

3. Maintaining the "man of science" façade was a necessary part of my survival for centuries. The patronizing half smile, the understanding nod, the aversion to layman's terms—it was all second nature to me by this point.

are ordinary beasts mistaken for fantastical creatures. I have found that with the application of reason and scientific principles—"

"How can you say so, sir?" I was fiercely interrupted by Bauterne. "*How?* You were at Saint-Julien. You saw what it is. The thing that murdered half the village—that decimated our packs—that creature was not a product of *reputation*." He turned to the young lady. "Mademoiselle, be assured that we will not be served by 'scientific principles' in this fight. The Lord Almighty is our only hope against such an abomination. And He fights alongside us, have no fear."

Rosalie looked thoughtful. "Though I do not share it, your faith is reassuring, sir," she said.

Looking around the table, I realized with no small degree of irritation that she was right. Bauterne's faith *was* reassuring, to everyone except me. The man's supreme confidence in the providence of the Divine put others at ease in his presence. It was no doubt why the Archangel had selected him.

I chose my words carefully.

"Perhaps the two might work together, then. There are any number of difficulties afflicting our brothers and sisters[4] in Gévaudan which the Lord Almighty has not yet seen fit to remedy," I replied. "A little assistance from the sciences might benefit us all, don't you agree, Monsieur Bauterne?"

As though to underline my point, Enneval the Elder unleashed a fresh flood of profanity from the room above.

Bauterne simply glared at me in silence while I laboriously cut a piece of cheese with my pewter knife.

"Perhaps a backgammon tournament in the grand salon to pass

---

4. Note that "Soeur" is the word for "sister," making this statement both very witty and exquisitely petty. I am still proud of it.

the evening?" suggested Monsieur Cat brightly, breaking the impasse. "We have the numbers to make it quite a competition!"

"A wonderful idea!" agreed Rosalie, rising from her seat, and we were all suddenly committed.

XLVI

I deliberately threw my first round of backgammon. This was not easy—I was matched against Monsieur Ferret, whose strategic skills were on par with his hunting prowess. Antoine did the same in his match against Monsieur Cat, and we excused ourselves from the competition. It was clear, in any case, that Rosalie Mimet was poised to conquer them all. Even the shrewd Bauterne struggled to match her.

Antoine and I fairly bolted upstairs, where we did indeed put the grand feather bed to good use.

"We've never shared a bed before," Antoine said languidly, as we lay together afterward. He had his head on my chest, with the warm length of his body resting deliciously against my side. "Not a proper ***bed***, I mean."

"I could certainly get used to it."

"You will," said Antoine. "I've been thinking."

We both looked up as the blizzard gusted mightily against the roof, causing the eaves to sob. The fire guttered momentarily and then surged back into life. I tried to stuff my misgivings further toward the back of my mind. The chamber was warm and cozy and it was ineffable pleasure just to lie there with Antoine. There was no need to think about the monster in the cellar, or the mortally wounded man screaming in the chamber down the hall, or the Beast about his murderous business somewhere, hidden by the night and the blizzard.

"I am scared to ask," I teased.

He nipped playfully at my throat. "When this is over, we will have need of men like you in Gévaudan. With the bishop torching the farms—may he burn along with them—and half the villagers killed or fled, the rebuilding will be difficult."

I smiled. "You would have me extend my stay when the hunt is finished? Provided we do not die, obviously."

"Precisely."

"Make me a convincing offer and I may consider it, Lord Ocerne."

He laughed. "Very well. I am to be married in the spring, and my father will be eager to start the work of restoring the farmlands. You could bring Madame Grave to Ocerne; we would host you at the château until you find a suitable residence of your own. And then, when we have the chance . . ." He raised his mouth and whispered erotic filth into my ear, liberally interspersed with brushes of his lips and tongue.

I laughed at the tickling sensation and rolled atop him, pinning his arms to the bed. "A baron's paramour?[1] Is that any sort of life for a respectable professor?"

---

1. No, I was not surprised or offended that Antoine did not propose a more exclusive arrangement; it was quite unthinkable at the time. Almost every marriage in the 1700s was a matter of practicality, and people usually indulged their true desires—homosexual or otherwise—discreetly and in their own time. For me, itinerant tomcat that I am, this arrangement was eminently suitable.

"Not at all. But for an abominable sorcerer? Yes indeed." He smirked at me, sighing as I leaned down and nuzzled my face against the side of his neck, the hair of his chest and the exposed, musky hollow under his arm.

"Well, as I am supposedly here at your invitation, what would you have me do, my lord? How should I turn my blasphemous powers to the benefit of Gévaudan? Will I be conjuring newborn lambs from rams' teeth? Or calling down the rain from blue skies? Shall I cause the fields to sprout sugarcane and cinnamon, that you may be both baron and trade prince?" I jested.

Just so we're absolutely clear, I will not be party to any of this, said Sarmodel. *Now, come—it's time to put some clothes on and take care of the business at—*

"Yes," Antoine sighed, looking up at me. "Yes. All of it. For as long as you will."

I stopped. My smile fell.

If there was a moment when I *knew*—when I knew I had taken things too far with Antoine and it would all end in disaster—it was then.

He was looking at me with love and desire, yes.

But he looked at me also with hope. I had shown him tricks and called them miracles, and now he imagined a future filled with them. He saw in me not only a lover, but a savior.

Hope. Of all my deceptions, it is always the worst.

"We shall see," I said, kissing him one more time. "Now sleep. With any luck, this storm will clear by morning and we can take our leave of Monsieur Chastel."

"'We shall see'? That's your answer?" His eyes narrowed. "You're up to something."

"What do you—"

"Sebastian. What devilish business do you have planned tonight, while I lie here sleeping?"

There was no point in denying it. "It's probably better that you don't know."

"You're going to see who's in the Royal Suite, aren't you?" he asked, his eyes sparkling.

"Yes," I said truthfully. I was fairly certain I knew who our mysterious neighbor was, but I planned to get confirmation.

"Let me come!"

"You have many great gifts, Antoine; stealth is not among them." I shook my head. "No, it's far less risky for me to go alone."

I rose from the bed and began to dress.

Antoine's eyes burned into me impishly, lingering on my skin as I began to button my breeches. "Sebastian. What else are you planning? A visit to Mademoiselle Mimet?"

"With her uncle in the next chamber?"

"Some dark ritual, then? Tell me!"

"Very well. A mercy killing. Perhaps two," I said gravely.

He looked as though he might laugh, and then his eyes widened. He sat up in the bed. "Enneval. My God, you're serious."

"I am. Now please, sleep."

"Sebastian, you can't just—Wait. Who else? Enneval and *who else*?"

"Soeur, Antoine. Soeur is here. Bauterne is keeping her in the cellar. If she escapes—as she surely will—the lieutenant's favorite will become a menace to rival the Beast."

"Sebastian, you can't, not alone!"

"I can, and it will not be the first time. Just pretend you don't know, please."

"It's *dangerous*, Sebastian—let me come—"

"Antoine. No. I will speak of it no more. Now—*please*—sleep." I kissed him on the forehead.

He said nothing more, but my young lover was not placated. After a short while, he began to snore gently. It was an endearing sham which I indulged for a few minutes. Antoine's anima was racing beneath his skin; he was certainly not sleeping.[2]

I took time to make sure I was prepared with pistols, ammunition and my poisoned hunting knife. Finally, I secured my brandy flask to my belt, and then I turned to Antoine one more time.

"Antoine, do not dare follow me. Try to get some sleep—real sleep—and when you wake in the morning, I will be there beside you again."

The snoring stopped abruptly and a spasm of irritation crossed his features. He opened his eyes. "Will you promise?"

"Will you?"

No promises were made, and I left him there in the grand feather bed.

---

2. In case you are wondering: no, I cannot force sleep on the unwilling, at least not without pharmacological help. The Litany of Rest only works on a subject who is already sleeping.

The Bishop of Mende was noisy even in his sleep. He huffed and snorted like a walrus, no doubt adrift in fond dreams of clerical overreach. He was slumped against the headboard, with a sheaf of papers by his right hand and an empty brandy balloon in his left. There was still venison grease around his mouth.

What are you doing holed away here, Your Eminence?

I briefly went through the bishop's correspondence. Some was exactly as I would have expected: tedious administrative matters from Mende. But the rest of the letters were *unusual.*

What do they say? asked Sarmodel as I flicked hurriedly through the pile.

Inventory of lands . . . request for title deeds . . . why would any of this interest a man of the cloth?

Who knows? And isn't he burning all the land around here anyway?

Yes. I put the letters down. *Yes, he is. I almost wish he were awake to explain.*

I stood over the bishop, shrouded in the Litany of the Dusk with my knife in my hand. The lavish chamber was uncomfortably warm, even with the snowstorm beating and sucking at the windows.

I had intended simply to confirm that it was indeed His Excellency hiding out in the Royal Suite—and to see what exactly he was up to. But being so close to him, watching his overfed body rise and fall with every brandy-soaked breath, was thought-provoking. Bare-headed, without his vestments and blowing raspberries in his sleep, he seemed much diminished and quite vulnerable. I wanted to kill him very badly.

Do it. You won't get a chance like this again, said Sarmodel.

You know, I'm really quite tempted.

He was right; this was truly a once-only opportunity. My personal antipathy for the man aside, killing the Bishop of Mende would lop a head off the ecclesiastical hydra in France. It would be a significant blow to the Almighty's operation which I would not again be in a position to deliver. I suspected it would also bring an end to the burning of Gévaudan's farms; the documents by the bishop's right hand raised all sorts of questions about his continuing presence in Ocerne.

And it would be so simple—there was enough feather bedding on hand to smother an ox.

But the bishop was not alone. In my Arcane senses, the shadow of the great lion stood resolutely on the wall behind him, and the Archangel's rose-scented breath filled the air.

Now, Michael and I often had competing interests, but I was not, technically speaking, his enemy. That would change if I decided to start murdering the clergy, particularly right under his nose. According to the tenets of the Covenant, I would be fair game for retribution, and it would be righteous.

I decided I really did not need the Lion of Judah stalking me alongside the Beast.

Oh, calm yourself, Michael, I sent to the menacing silhouette. *It was just a thought.*

I sheathed my knife, but I lingered a few moments longer in the Royal Suite. Before I took my leave, I collected the bishop's correspondence and threw it into the fire. I also pocketed every piece of jewelry I could find.

I received an unpleasant surprise when I returned to the long hallway.

Sarmodel.

Enneval's door, which had been closed when I entered the Royal Suite, was now standing open. I crept swiftly along the hall and peered around the doorframe.

Empty.

The fire still crackled cheerily in the hearth, but Monsieur Enneval the Elder was nowhere to be found. His great nest of pillows was scattered across the floor. It seemed the man's strength had returned somehow.

But he was supposed to be the easy one! Where did he go? I said to Sarmodel.

Find out, quickly, he answered. After some swearing, I uttered the Litany of the Hunt.

Enneval's trail went back along the corridor and then down the stairs. With my sharpened senses, I could still taste the rankness of his wound in the air; he must have walked right past the Royal Suite only minutes ago, while I was inside.

Where is he going? I demanded. *What can he possibly be doing?*

I hurried down the stairs, still shrouded in clinging darkness. Dozens of glass eyes glittered from the trophies on the walls, and

I detected the lingering traces of a half dozen people in the grand salon; the publican had been there recently, along with Bauterne. Enneval's trail was the freshest, but there was no sign of the man himself.

I followed the Norman's scent farther, through the dim dining room and then into the kitchen. Bauterne's scent—not nearly so fresh—went along the same route; Enneval had been following the lieutenant for some reason.

The door to the cellar was open.

Well. I suppose we were already going down there, said Sarmodel.

I don't like it, Sarmodel. He can't be up to anything good, following Bauterne like this. And they're both in there together—that's going to make it complicated.

Weren't we going to kill them both anyway?

Were we? That might be a little hard to explain in the morning, my love.

He grunted impatiently and I felt the Litany of the Hunt begin to soften. *Whatever you're doing, do it quickly. I can't keep this up all night.*

I swallowed my trepidation and stepped silently through the doorway. The stairs went down a long way, and there was faint light at the bottom. I descended as softly as falling ash.

The cellar was akin to a wide vaulted corridor, built of brick and polished stone. There were doors on both sides, leading to the lodge's wine stores and food pantries. All of them were closed, save for the last.

And it was within that last door that my business waited. From the open portal came the warm glow of lantern light, along with a terrible smell.

Rotting dog, Sarmodel confirmed.

The fetor from Soeur's corrupted body had only grown worse. My heightened senses made it almost unbearable.

Is this . . . is this a good idea? It's all become a little more complicated than I had planned, I said, covering my nose and mouth with a sleeve. The grand feather bed in my chamber—and the warm, handsome young man sleeping in it—were suddenly overwhelmingly appealing.

Don't lose your nerve now, Sarmodel replied. *Just get in there and—*

There was suddenly a flurry of muted sound from the open chamber—a sharp intake of breath, the susurrus of clothing and the scrape of boots across the floor. A terrible groaning.

I grimaced; some quiet violence was happening within.

I moved as fast as I dared along the corridor, skirting the pool of light that spilled from the doorway.

Enneval had indeed come after Bauterne. He had caught his prey unprepared, and the Lieutenant of the Hunt was at his mercy. The Norman had him pinned to the ground, his thick forearms pressing on his throat. Enneval was dressed only in his unwashed nightclothes, his bandages still holding the wad of wool against his ghastly wound. Though the big man was bereft of his strength and shaking uncontrollably, the sheer weight of him was enough to do his deadly work. The groaning I heard was Bauterne, trying to call out as the life was crushed from him.

Something stirred in the shadows at the back of the room. Chains clinked in the darkness, anchored to heavy iron rivets embedded in the wall. They secured something very large that spasmed restlessly beneath a thick blanket. Its form was indistinct, but the hulking mound was the source of the ghastly stench.

Soeur. The blanket rose and fell with her breathing, but she did not move to save her master. Somehow, she was sleeping through the mortal struggle happening not ten paces from her.

She's—Sarmodel, she's ***enormous,*** I said fearfully.

Not to worry, my love. There's enough poison on that knife to kill the Leviathan of Pontus.

"Who is too . . . too weak to rise now, Lord Bootblack?" growled Enneval the Elder, a long line of drool running into his bristling military mustache and falling onto Bauterne's reddening face. "Do you blacken your spindle as well, you little fop?" The words were thick, his tongue moving too slowly to form them properly. A crimson flower bloomed across his bandages.

I considered my options for a moment.

Bauterne could certainly use my assistance; he pummeled weakly at his assailant with his fists, which looked especially small in comparison to the Norman's massive shoulders. Enneval was also in dire extremity. He panted like a draft horse, dripping vital fluids from every orifice in his head. Neither of them would be alive much longer unless I acted. I crouched, holding the point of my envenomed blade low to the ground.

And I waited.

"I'm going to kill you, piss on your corpse and feed . . . feed you to that fucking monster," Enneval slurred. His shaking was only getting worse as he held Bauterne down, but he did not waver. I could only imagine what it was costing him to maintain his hold on the lieutenant—and the strength of the hatred that had fueled this murderous little excursion.

It only took a few seconds longer. Bauterne's eyes rolled back in his head and his struggles ceased. In almost precisely the same moment, Enneval reached the end of his endurance and collapsed, cheek to cheek with the lieutenant.

Sarmodel was ready, jaws wide open overhead. Anima gushed up and I felt him thrashing like a pennant in the wind as it surged into us. I shivered in delight; Enneval's anima was like heady nut liquor, with an enduring gamey quality like smoked meat. I felt immediately refreshed and wonderfully energized.

Well. Perhaps that wasn't quite so bad, I ventured. I stepped into the room, allowing the Litany of the Dusk to fall away.

Sarmodel fidgeted excitedly in my mind, with the Spiritual equivalent of an erection.

That one's still alive! He drew my attention to Bauterne, unconscious and trapped beneath Enneval's corpse.

Patience, my love. I glanced nervously overhead, expecting the gemstone gleam of Michael's presence at any moment. For the second time in ten minutes, I found myself forgoing a most satisfying murder for fear of the Archangel.

I turned my attention instead to Soeur's monstrous bulk at the back of the chamber, shifting my grip on my envenomed blade. Covered in the blanket as she was, I couldn't tell the best way to approach her for the killing stroke.

I also couldn't understand how she was still sleeping; a hound with her training should have been on her feet the moment anyone entered the room.

But then I realized what Bauterne had been doing down in the cellar. A metal bucket half filled with water sat near the sleeping hound, and next to it was the opium bottle I had given him only that afternoon. It was empty.

The lieutenant finally decided it was time to let go of his favorite, I remarked.

Why isn't she dead, then?

Look at the size of her—she'd need three times as much. What a waste.

Bauterne had intended to spend Soeur's last moments together with her. Her gilded collar lay on the floor beside him, and he had covered her in his own trail blanket.

I bent and lifted the edge of the woolen cloth with my free hand, carefully pulling the blanket off the gargantuan hound. It slid free and I stood for a moment in grim silence.

We had removed the Beast's eldritch infection from Antoine's flesh before it could take hold. In Soeur, restrained by her master and unable to satisfy her hunger, it had run its course.

She was easily as big as a horse now. Most of her brindled fur was gone, save for coarse black hair that grew thickly around her neck and formed a crest along her back. The poor hound's rib cage was a mighty drum wrapped in bands of sinew, and her forequarters were thickly cabled with muscle. Her skull had become both thicker and longer, and the part of her face that Avstamet had torn away still hung in a necrotic flap under her eye. Her muzzle was full of teeth grown unnaturally long; she would never properly close her jaws again.

Nor would she again join her packmates in the hunt. The Beast had crushed her spine and her back legs completely at Saint-Julien. While the affliction had transformed her flesh, it had not saved her hindquarters. They sat limp and gangrenous on the stone floor, the source of the stench that hung around her.

Sarmodel scrutinized her with particular interest. *Fascinating! She's—*

An absolute disgrace is what she is. How can Bauterne treat her like this? He should have killed her weeks ago, I said, shaking my head.

Well, hurry up. I want her.

Bauterne had secured Soeur with chains connected to a thick leather collar around her neck. Both the chains and the collar showed signs of repeated strain.

I took a careful step toward her.

And then I stopped.

What was that?

A choking sound was quickly stifled just outside the chamber, in the dark vault behind me. I caught a faint whiff of whiskey breath and postcoital sweat.

I straightened but did not turn around. "Antoine. What did I tell you?"

"Did you think I would let you go alone?" he whispered. "My God, the *smell*."

"Don't come in here!"

But he stepped into the room nonetheless, trying not to gag as he came to stand beside me. He was still in his nightclothes, though he was carrying his hunting musket. He looked at the sleeping bulk of Soeur and then the motionless hunters in their fatal embrace.

"Are they *dead*?" he asked, horrified.

"Not both of them."

He swore. "You can't just kill people, Sebastian! And why did you do it down here?"

"I didn't kill anyone! They were already here," I replied, "and Enneval was as good as dead anyway. Please, go back upstairs—there's no need for you to be here."

"But what are you going to do with them now?"

"I don't know yet—"

Sebastian! Quickly!

A low growl and an ominous clinking of chains silenced us both.

Soeur's opium-induced slumber had come to an end.

"Oh . . . oh Lord," Antoine stammered as the hound lifted her head, opening eyes as black as roe in the lamplight.

The attack took less than a second. Soeur awoke to the smell of blood and two intruders standing in her cell. The next moment she was in motion, launching at us with a roar.

The chains were—thankfully—not long enough and she was pulled short an arm's length from slaughtering us both. She strained against her bonds, raking at the floor with her grotesque forelegs, while her hindquarters flopped uselessly behind her.

I watched her movements carefully and lunged at her with my

knife, but she was too fast and the blade too short. I managed only to enrage her further, and nearly lost an arm to her snapping fangs.

I sheathed the knife and drew one of my pistols instead, scrambling to load it with my silver shot.

You should have brought the quicksilver! barked Sarmodel.

*It was supposed to be easy! They were **both** supposed to be easy!*

Antoine in this instance was far better prepared than I was; his weapon was loaded and ready. He knelt on the floor, took careful aim with his musket and filled the cellar with thunder.

Soeur screamed horrifically. The shot punched a bloody hole into her rib cage and covered the back wall with crimson spatter.

But she was not subdued; far from it.

"Sebastian, quickly," said Antoine, his eyes wide. Crumbs of masonry fell from the walls as Soeur renewed her struggles, heaving against her chains. "Sebastian!" The rivets were pulling free.

"Done!"

I raised my pistol at the raging hound. The rivets jerked one last time and then wrenched out of the brick.

Finally free, Soeur sprang for the kill.

My enchanted silver shot caught her in the shoulder. The ball shattered into a dozen fragments and the muscles of her torso were briefly (and beautifully) lit from within by a piercing blue radiance. Soeur screamed again, the force of the shot twisting her around. Though she stumbled, her momentum was powerful and she barreled right over the top of us.

Watch her!

In a second, the blighted hound crashed through the open doorway and out into the vaulted cellar. There she thrashed in agony as the Violations unspooled forcefully from the fragments of silver shot, making a wasp's nest of her flesh.

Well done, said Sarmodel.

I stepped forward, certain she would not recover.

But I had underestimated her strength.

With a pitiful sound, Soeur raised her head. She stood slowly and painfully on her two front legs, lifting the gangrenous flesh of her hindquarters clear off the ground. Her black, black eyes fixed on us again.

There wasn't time to reload. I crouched low with my knife, ready for her.

But we had proved a meal too dangerous. With a hunger-crazed snarl, Soeur bolted away from us, up the stairs.

ADDENDUM:

On the Spirit in the Maiden's Bone

Château de Tiffauges
Tiffauges, France
1440

And now we're down to the quick.

This part I remember clearly.

See us now—the master, the old one and me—as we approach the Madman's gates. We are on foot. Our horses have served their last and the old one is crackling with their anima. He is everywhere around us, like rats in the walls of the world.

It is dark. As we walk, I shed my beautiful corset, gown and chemise, and finally my shoes. My earlobes are throbbing with the weight of the Shackles and my Contract is a floating collar, ready to burn me at the slightest transgression. The master removes the earrings with a warning glare; I will need a measure of freedom if I am to be effective for the evening's business. He pockets the Shackles and draws his silver sword.

I step into the pool of torchlight before the gates, pushing my glamers ahead of me like smoke. The guards take notice and there is a lot of shouting.

But they're so confused! Why is there a naked woman here? What is that delicious scent? She must tell them her name! Does she know that they are in love with her?

They're already mine.

I close my eyes. This has been almost a decade coming.

Why am I suddenly so afraid? Is it because we're all likely to die tonight?

No, that's nothing new. My freshly reinstated hand is actually tingling a bit at the opportunity to get properly dirty again.

So, what's wrong? Is it the cold, or the memory of the deep, black touch of the demon Avstamet, who calls himself Barron and who was once Ares and Mars, curling inside me? Is that it?

I look at the master. He's frowning and muttering to the old one as we approach the gate, but every so often he glances at me.

And then I realize what's bothering me.

They're lying to me.

Call him Barron.

The cycles of the summoning rite pulsed through Château de Tiffauges like the heartbeat of a colossus.

Call him Ares.

Livia went first, entrancing the men of the château with her mere presence. They were drawn to her from every post and patrol. Distracted, aroused and unsure of themselves, their voices failed as they saw her. Those who came within reach died gratefully at her talons, their lifeblood splashing over her naked skin. The master and the old one followed with serpentine speed, dispatching the rest and consuming their anima under a shroud of Arcane silence.

Call him Mars.

"Excuse me!" hissed the succubus over her shoulder, tearing out the throat of a young guard. She let out a small whine of longing as the old one devoured the man's anima right in front of her. "Are you going leave any for me?"[1]

Your way takes too long. And we must be strong if we are going to win the Olympian. The Spirit's voice was heavy with satisfaction, and more than a little smug. The master was already reclaiming his magnificence, his mortal flesh thickly muscled and all but blazing with new life. Livia whimpered again as she saw him so delectably restored. She brushed her talons over her throbbing nipples; the temptation was almost too much to bear. *Keep moving, half-breed.*

The succubus gave a tiny, dry sob but strode ahead nonetheless.

The castle was strangely empty. Furnishings were spare and austere, and the walls were bare. Livia and her master carved a silent red path through the courtyard and the retainers' galleries, right to the doors of the great hall itself.

There they stopped. They could all feel the Arcane charge building on the other side.

The way is Warded, warned the old one.

The master nodded. He cast a handful of silvery ash into the air, murmuring quietly. The powder shimmered and sifted down, caught on a circular web of Arcane strands just in front of the doors. The barrier was gossamer-thin, but it seemed also unimaginably deep, yawning into a vastness beyond its own dimensions.

---

1. I cannot nourish myself by gobbling up hearts or released anima, just as I cannot draw sustenance from money (Clauneck), or fear (Kali), or stupidity (the Almighty), or any number of other mortal preoccupations. Succubi were created to exploit anima in a very specific, very powerful phase: the orgasm. I am quite literally made for it, and nothing else will do.

The master swore as he scanned the planes and angles of the Ward. "The Sudden Jaw. Prelati is as extravagant as ever." He looked at Livia. "Watch my back. I can unravel this, but it will take some time."

Livia watched, unimpressed, as he rummaged through his pockets. After a few moments, he produced a stick of chalk and a small silver mirror. He began to crawl along the floor, holding the mirror close to the stone. His voice rose and fell in whispered incantations.

The succubus snarled impatiently and strode over to the nearest dead guardsman.

"Livia, *don't you da—!*"

The corpse flew over the master's head and struck the glittering Ward with a purple flash. Triggered, the silver threads gripped the material world and then all aligned at once, converging impossibly to occupy a single, white-hot point.

"Oh," said Livia. This was quite bit more than she had expected.

"Down!" Sebastian leaped at her, enveloping her in his arms and bearing her to the ground.

Livia felt a vertiginous drag in the air as the dead soldier's matter imploded, collapsing the doorway and several inches of structural stone into a tiny, winking sphere. It vanished with a high *pop,* leaving a perfectly circular opening where the doors had been.

The master rested atop her for a moment longer, sheltering her from a hail of stone fragments.

"Livia, you reckless, stupid—are you hurt?"

"Not at all," she said. "Thank you, Dominus."

Their faces were perilously close together. He was positively singing with anima, a charging current that was more than just energy—it was *him*. Delicious, overcautious, frustrating, violent, magnificent *him*.

He lowered his face toward her, his lips parted and his breath coming faster.

Is now really the time? Get up, both of you!

Sebastian withdrew, standing up with a scowl. "Well, Livia." He helped her to her feet. "I'm sure we have their attention now."

"Have you ever raised a Spirit, meatbag? They're not watching the doors," she replied, stepping through the round opening.

Livia's assessment was correct. There were only two people inside the great hall, and they were paying absolutely no attention to the main doors.

On one side, the sorcerer Francois Prelati knelt in a triple Circle of ideograms. He was chanting, but Livia heard nothing. His voice was lost to the Mundane world, drowned in the waves of Arcane energy that thundered through the room, below mortal hearing.

Call him Barron.

Call him Ares.

Call him Mars.

On the other side of the hall, dressed in his theatrical white angel's robe, was Gilles de Rais. He was inside another protective Circle drawn on the floor, facing toward the center of the room. His ardor was palpable. He stood high on his toes and danced back and forth from one foot to the other. With one hand, he brandished his ceremonial rapier, waving it like a conductor's baton. With the other, he tugged and kneaded at the front of his robe. The Madman of Tiffauges was just outside the Arcane epicenter, and snatches of his voice came to the intruders in the doorway.

Gilles de Rais was singing. *"RISE, JEHANNE! RISE, FRANCE!"* he exulted. *"TO GLORY, TO GLORY IN GOD'S NAME!"*

In the center of the great hall, between the two men, was a veritable mountain of riches. It was suddenly very clear why the rest of the château had seemed so stark. Statues, priceless heirlooms, jewelry and piles of coins were heaped on the floor of the hall. The Marshal of France had spared nothing; among the treasures of his estates were his silks, his trophies, his weapons and his medals, ready to be consigned for the resurrection of his beloved Maiden. A third, much larger Arcane Circle surrounded the hoard, its sigils hewn into the stone floor and filled with molten silver—a Circle of Offerings.

And sitting atop the pile like a monstrous jewel was a great glass vessel, containing the sixty fresh, red hearts of the Madman's final harvest.

Sebastian took it all in at a glance, his face dark.

"Where is it?" he muttered.

Livia followed her master as he moved silently into the room. They hid behind one of the hall's mighty pillars; the eldritch charge in the room was quickly stripping away their Arcane concealment. Sebastian kindled the Violations on his silver blade with exquisite care, whispering slowly and softly, so close to the metal that his breath misted the surface. His eyes never left Prelati.

Livia could barely concentrate. Gilles de Rais was a fountain of lust, filling the air with his yearning—both for the Maiden and for Prelati. Every breath she took was ripe with the smell of him, mixing delectably with the scent of blood. It didn't help being so close to the master, with the anima of all those men boiling like magma just beneath his skin, and the lingering taste of his breath on her lips. She edged closer still, craving his heat.

Perish the thought, half-breed, warned the old one.

Livia stepped back, her eyes flashing.

She quickly realized what was wrong. The Maiden's relic—the centerpiece of the ritual—was nowhere to be seen. Had the Madman simply buried it among the rest of his fortune? It seemed unlikely.

The old one's presence sharpened. *Be ready,* he said. *The way is opening.*

The light changed.

Something shifted, like a hiccup in the natural order. The thumping subliminal pulse of the ritual cycled higher and higher until it was a single, crystal-pitched tone, resonating from the center of the room.

The sorcerer Prelati rose to his feet.

Livia exchanged a wide-eyed glance with the master and quickly covered her ears.

Prelati spoke a single word that shattered the air like a windowpane. Behind the pillar, the master crouched low and bit his sleeve to stop from screaming. The old one was buffeted like a tree in a hurricane.

The vessel of hearts burst into crimson flame. The glass did not crack so much as collapse, disintegrating all at once into glittering sand. Its cargo of flesh slithered down the mountain of riches, dousing the Madman's every treasure in molten scarlet fire.

All except one.

"It is time, supplicant," intoned Prelati. "The Spirit awaits release. Bring it forth."

Livia watched open-mouthed as Gilles de Rais stepped outside his protective Wards. She transitioned from incredulity to high anxiety as he then stepped inside the greater silver Circle.[2] Almost immediately, his anima began to rise off him like mist. He extended the ceremonial rapier and suddenly she understood.

"My lady!" sang the Marshal of France. He cast the rapier into the flames.

Sebastian and the old one swore in unison as they saw the polished bone pommel of its hilt.

"Rise!" boomed Prelati. "Take what is offered, for it is yours! Come to the flesh!"

Thick smoke was rising from the bonfire, and within its twisting plumes, a figure began to take shape.

"Yes! JEHANNE!" Rais was screaming now. Urine puddled between his feet. He raised his hands to the insubstantial figure. "FOR GLORY! *JEHANNE!*"

But Prelati called a different name.

"Come, Barron!" he boomed. "Come, Mars! Come, Ares! COME, AVSTAMET!"

The room seemed somehow to contract as the figure in the smoke *came forward.* Impressions flashed through Livia's mind as it drew nearer. A mouth rimmed with knives. A monstrous wolf, big enough to swallow the moon. It keened. It *strained.*

---

2. It is difficult to express just how many basic Arcane rules of self-preservation and common sense the Baron de Rais broke in those few steps. If you are ever dealing with a practitioner who encourages you to position *yourself* inside the Circle of Offerings, get your money back.

Livia struggled to keep her balance as the laws of matter began to stretch for its unspeakable birth.

"My lady . . . Jehanne?" Gilles de Rais was mad, but even he could see that the presence above the conflagration was not the Maid of Orleans. He turned to his sorcerous lover. "What . . . what have you done, Francois?"

"What you Contracted me to do, my darling," answered Prelati, all of his focus on the rising conflagration. He disdained to even look at the nobleman. "I have raised the Spirit in the relic, and now it will be made flesh."

"But . . . Jehanne! Where is she?!"

Now! Quickly, kill them! the old one crowed. *Half-breed, take the cretin. We will handle the sorcerer. Barron is ours!*

"Finally!" Livia ran out from behind the pillar, followed closely by the master. She spun her glamers thicker and thicker, ready to unleash them upon the stricken Gilles. The master stalked across the floor with his silver blade flashing at the ready. Above him, the old one gathered his form into a pillar of Arcane flame so intense it began to arc into the Mundane spectrum, projecting frightful silhouettes onto the walls.

Come Barron! he screamed, with the hunger of millennia. *I am here for your immortal essence!*

The great presence taking form in the Circle was indistinct, but Livia felt its attention alight on them like the heat of a star. It emitted a pulse of *something*—part sound, part sensation, part intention—which resolved into words in her mind.

COME, THEN.

But they were all to be disappointed.

Livia was lifted from her feet as the great hall shook once again. The back wall exploded inward, showering all of them with debris.

She landed in a tangle of limbs next to Sebastian.

"There they are!" The man's voice was familiar, but in her dazed state, she couldn't quite place it. Livia sat up, blinking and rubbing the back of her skull. "The abomination has led us true! Take them all! Find the relic! In the name of the Archangel!"

A wide section of the far wall had been destroyed, leaving a crumbling hole. Over the rubble charged the men of the Rouen Guard, their voices raised in psalms of devotion. Behind them came Captain Renard himself, brandishing his silver cross idol; Livia could feel its hateful, bruising presence even from the other side of the hall. And finally, secured by a chain to the captain's belt, came a hunched, misshapen figure.

"*What?!*" Springing to her feet, Livia whirled on the master. He had the grace to look ashamed. "Renard?! And *Clauneck*? You didn't kill them?!"

"I was barely alive myself!" snapped Sebastian. "I escaped, I took what I could find and I fled!"

Behind them, the sorcerer Prelati snarled as he struggled to his feet. From his robes he produced a long knife and a globe of quicksilver. The latter he cast into the group of oncoming guardsmen. It exploded with a wet, heavy boom, dismembering some and blinding others. Then he sliced the knife across the palms of his hands, smearing his face with the blood and invoking a terrible name.[3] Filled with unholy strength, he discarded the blade and tore at his assailants with his bare hands.

The white-haired Captain Renard strode forward into the

---

3. Which you are better off not knowing. Using your own blood to attract a Spirit is a zero-sum game—this sort of parasite will be helpful to you only in the very, very short term.

chaos, yanking Clauneck behind him. The demon had become a lumpy, inhuman thing, barely contained by the shapeless dress and cloak. She seemed defeated, her face turned to the ground and her hair hanging in ragged clumps.

The captain's strange golden eyes found them. His face was suddenly transfigured in victory, and Livia thought she might swoon from her desire for him. "Yes! Sebastian Grave—I have come for you!" he exulted. Above him, immaterial jeweled wings unfurled in the sign of the Archangel.

Again, Livia was assailed by a wave of male lust; Captain Renard was extremely glad to see them. She whimpered as an exquisite tingling began to climb her tail.

"You used my own demon to find me? Captain, this is why you should never take Arcane advice from an angel." Smiling, Sebastian rose to his feet. "Clauneck—attend!"

The miserable creature gave a helpless moan and raised her face to look at them. Sebastian breathed a low, vile curse.

"See your ungodly work undone, witch!" called Renard. The light of the Archangel intensified around him, shining painfully from the silver cross. "I have broken your hold on her, and she serves the Almighty now!"

The coin in Clauneck's forehead was gone, leaving a round, red welt in its place. The demon's eyes were huge and utterly dark, their golden glitter all but extinguished.

"He's Unshackled her," the master murmured, disbelieving. "What kind of idiot—"

"What kind of *idiot* didn't dismiss her?" Livia demanded. "She must be feral by now!"

Clauneck, attend! You know who I am. Do not dare disobey! The old one's voice crackled with the menace of the Rift.

Clauneck simply hunched where she stood.

But now something else had attracted the abomination's attention. Clauneck's wide mouth fell open. She drew deep breaths and then let out a bellow of naked, desperate desire.

"GOLD!"

Clauneck's black gaze alighted on the pile of riches in the center of the room, now blazing with crimson fire. Heedless of her manacles and of the colossal figure coalescing in the smoke, she heaved herself toward the conflagration with inhuman strength.

Captain Renard was dragged from his feet with a startled cry as the demon's chain snapped taut and broke. The silver cross was jarred from his hand, and he was suddenly defenseless.

Livia felt the last of her self-control fall away like old skin. In its place settled single-minded clarity. She faintly registered the rampaging abomination in the Circle, shoving great fistfuls of burning treasure into its bag-like mouth. Not far away was the blood-smeared horror of Prelati, tearing apart a guardsman with his hands and teeth. And closer still was the master with his crackling sword, now beset by five of Renard's men—difficult odds even with the old one's help.

But it all seemed so unimportant as she beheld Captain Renard, exposed and winded on the ground.

With a moan, she launched herself across the room, gliding improbably through the altered air. Her glamers struck the captain in an overwhelming torrent, and he gasped at his sudden, painful arousal.

"My darling!" Livia landed atop him and kissed him deeply, piercing his lips with her fangs. "Do you want me?" she whispered in his ear, smiling wickedly.

The captain was beyond speech. He nodded slowly, with tears in his eyes.

Faintly, somewhere in the distance, Livia could hear someone shouting her name, yelling strange words like "half-breed" and "Archangel" and "Scathing." Her earlobes tingled with the phantom presence of the Shackles. But she was utterly lost in the warmth of the man between her thighs and the limpid devotion in his beautiful golden eyes.

She tore Renard's clothes open with two powerful swipes. They cried out together as she impaled herself on his aching member.

And then . . . and then it was just the two of them, joined as one, in a liquid, writhing, golden cocoon that smelled of sweat and roses and sulfur.

It lasted only a few seconds.[4] Livia felt the captain's anima quicken and change, igniting with pleasure. He burst into crippling ecstasy that poured into her, and then she too was afire.

She caressed his handsome face as it began to shrink and tighten, frozen forever in his final grimace of pleasure. His body shriveled beneath her until it was little but bones and feathery chaff, crowned with a tuft of striking white hair.

"Yes, my darling," she murmured. "Oh, how you love me."

And then the world came thundering back down around her. The voices in the room seemed all to be screaming at once.

"Get off him, Livia*!"*

You have defied me for the last time, succubus!

"Come, Barron!"

"My lady Jehanne! Where are you?!"

And then over them all rose an enraged, primeval roar.

"GOLD!"

A nightmarish, hulking thing burst through the pile of

---

4. No surprises there.

riches. The Madman's fortune pelted the walls as Clauneck's uncontrolled flesh convulsed through its final transformation. Gilles de Rais was thrown from the Circle, and with him the bone-handled rapier.

Above them, the figure in the smoke faltered. The world slipped, and then slipped again, subsiding back toward its natural locus.

"No!" Prelati snarled, breaking a man over his knee like a dry branch. He lunged after the rapier. "Gilles—my love, quickly! The relic! Before he—before the Maiden is lost to us!"

But Gilles de Rais was defeated. He lay on the ground, his eyes streaming in silent suffering. He did not resist as Renard's men secured him with chains and began to drag him toward the hole in the wall, their voices raised in desperate prayer.

Clauneck's rags fell away as she rose, monstrous, over the smoldering pile. Like a gargantuan gray toad she squatted, her swollen abdomen covered in a multitude of gulping mouths. A dozen limbs scooped coins into her insatiable gullet, and every mouth screamed, *"GOLD! GOLD!"*

Sebastian, the Olympian is fading! Invoke the Table! The old one was shrill with desperation. *Half-breed! Get the relic!*

Livia stood up, feeling the room groan as the laws of the material world were reinstated. It was not a gentle transition. The walls around them made a terrible dry snapping sound and were suddenly mapped with cracks.

"Meatbag, he's gone!" she said. Energized from her meal, she was quick and strong, dispatching the master's assailants with her talons. "We'll never get him back now! It's time to go."

BE SILENT! boomed the old one. *We cannot leave! Sebastian, find the relic and return it to the Circle! Throw in the succubus too! Avstamet can still be raised!*

The back corner of the room collapsed with a sound like thunder.

Go! I will protect us!

"No, you won't!" Livia stepped in front of Sebastian, taking his face in her hands. "Look at me! Dominus!" Tentatively, gently, without fangs or glamers, she leaned forward and gave him the kiss he had denied himself earlier.

"This is certain death, meatbag. You know it is," she said. He looked at her with wide eyes and nodded.

"I'm sorry, my love," he said to the old one. "If we stay, we will all die. Come, Livia."

No! NO! the old one screamed. He clawed ineffectually at the walls, trying to drag the master back toward the Circle. The great presence over the flames was a bare shadow now, but it was watching them with a terrible hatred. *Barron—Avstamet! I am coming back for you!*

The old one's howling was enough to draw even Clauneck's attention. The abomination looked up with her huge eyes, now completely filled with gold. Heedless of the crimson flames consuming her hide, she settled like a hen on the remaining riches.

Finally satisfied, she watched them flee as the great hall crashed down around her.

XLIX

The Bow and Brace
Eastern Ocerne, France
1766

A blast of frigid air greeted us at the top of the cellar stairs. The door to the rear courtyard had been smashed out of its frame and the blizzard was roaring into the kitchen.

Soeur had left a trail of blood and reeking detritus across the floor and out into the night. Outside, I could faintly hear the baying of dogs.

"She's gone after the hounds," I muttered.

At the same time, I heard movement and voices from upstairs; our activities in the cellar had been audible enough to wake some of our fellow guests.

I pulled Antoine back through the dining room and into the grand salon, out of the screaming wind.

"Antoine, go upstairs and tell everyone . . . tell them the Beast is here and that they need to be as quiet as possible and stay in their rooms. The hounds aren't going to satisfy her for long."

"And then what?"

"Find the publican and tell him what happened."

"What about you? Are you going after her?"

"Of course. No, you can't come with me."

He looked at me, wide-eyed with fear and excitement and—yes—with lust. "Very well—on one condition," he said. He pulled me close and kissed me so hard I could taste blood. "Promise me you're going to stay. Afterward, if we don't die. Sugarcane and cinnamon, just like you said."

And then he laughed. Standing there, shaking with adrenaline, splashed in hound's blood with a monster on the loose and a snowstorm pouring into the building, he laughed.

I can't really describe what I felt in that moment. I wanted to laugh with him, fuck him and devour him alive, all at once.

"Sugarcane and cinnamon. I promise," I said, my voice trembling.

Oh, Sebastian, said Sarmodel, with profound disdain.

The voices upstairs grew louder. Antoine kissed me once more and then took the staircase at a run.

I was once again alone in the grand salon, under the twinkling eyes of Jean Chastel's trophies.

Sometimes, when disaster comes, I am taken by surprise, along with everyone else.

But sometimes I get a warning. Sometimes, there's a signal that my immortality is about to be tested in earnest, and the hourglass is either going to turn over once again or run out forever. It may be a clear sign—a portentous comet, or an army massing on the horizon.

Or it may be something small. Something ordinary, out of place.

Something as prosaic as the publican's cane, leaning on the scrolled corner of a backgammon table. He must have left it there, on his way to somewhere else.

Sebastian! Sarmodel's presence brittled, like a windowpane poised to shatter.

I approached the table, my heartbeat surging with each step. Every sound was amplified in the empty salon; the great fireplaces crackled on either side of me and the snowstorm moaned through the portico outside. I had the strange sensation of floating, as though my feet weren't touching the floor.

Is that . . . ?

The handle of the publican's cane shone in the firelight, but it was not cast from silver like the heel. It was a knob of ivory, rounded but not completely spherical, worn smooth by Jean Chastel's strong left hand.

No, not ivory. Not quite.

A bone.

The firelight showed black stains in the creases and hollows, as though it had, many years ago, been burned.

I forgot all about Antoine and Soeur and the massacre she was perpetrating in the kennels.

I picked up the cane, my hands trembling. It had been removed from its original setting, as the handle of Gilles de Rais's ceremonial rapier, but I knew what it was immediately. We had chased it across the continent during the Hundred Years' War. We had searched for it for years in the rubble of Château de Tiffauges.

The head of the femur of Saint Jehanne d'Arc.

Her only surviving relic, and the vessel that had housed her demon during the centuries since she had been burned.

Until very recently.

Empty, hissed Sarmodel.

Naturally.

The absence of the Spirit in the relic only confirmed what we already knew: Avstamet had abandoned his vessel in favor of a willing host.[1]

And now it appeared that we knew who that host was.

*He's **here**.*

I was paralyzed at the thought. He had been here the whole time, in the one place in Gévaudan I had been avoiding. And we had sat across from him at dinner, eating his food and listening to his war stories.

The front door handle turned with a clank. My mind was sprinting in so many different directions that all I could do was watch in a daze as the elaborate door swung open.

Jean Chastel came inside slowly, accompanied by whirling snow and a frigid wind. He wore a thick, steel-gray greatcoat, flocked with snowflakes and hay. The smell of blood and horses filled my nostrils sickeningly.

Chastel closed the door shakily and turned to face me.

His face was a scarlet horror.

"For . . . forgive me, Professor Grave," he slurred through blood-smeared lips. He seemed confused and embarrassed to find me there. "I was not expecting company at this hour."

"Not at all, Monsieur Chastel," I murmured automatically.

The horses. He's killed the horses.

---

1. Avstamet's decision to find a new host in Gévaudan was a matter of practicality. Jehanne d'Arc's bone was no longer attracting the anima it once had; there were few devotions being made to the Maid of Orleans three hundred years after her death, and no gullible Gilles de Rais to heap glories upon her. It's not so surprising that Avstamet took a more hands-on approach to his resurgence the second time around—or that he was looking for different ways to keep his anima in circulation.

Even without the blizzard, we were all now trapped at the Bow and Brace.

"I must apologize. Sometimes I am . . . so *hungry*." He retched on the last word, disgorging a mouthful of crimson vomit down the front of his coat. He wiped his brow with a shaking hand; in spite of the cold, the publican seemed to be sweating copiously.

Plasma.

I slowly drew my blade, resting the cane gently on the corner of the table again.

In my mind's eye, Sarmodel was hurriedly constructing the Word he had taught me, the one that caused the unsettling flickering in my mind.

"Do not trouble yourself, sir," I said, taking a step back.

"Please, return . . . return to your chamber, Professor," said Chastel with difficulty. He covered his eyes with his hands, shaking his head. "Please. He wants to *have* you."

I felt the world begin to tilt.

Sarmodel, he's coming!

The light in the grand salon suddenly burned with impossible, screaming colors—the fires flickered violet and rose madder, and the glass eyes of the trophies flared white like stars. The choking odor of sulfur rose around us.

"No—*no*!" shouted Chastel, clutching at his head. "Not again! I have *eaten*! Leave me—ah!"

His words were cut off by a violent convulsion. His spine snapped taut like a pennant in a sudden wind. In the altered air, I felt something enormous approaching us—a Spiritual colossus surfacing from the vastness between worlds, grazing the thin shell of our Mundane reality. I took a step forward, my knife raised.

Not yet—let him come! This is our chance! Sarmodel's voice seemed to come from high above me.

Again and again the publican seized, his body racked from end to end. Plasma wept from his skin and pattered to the floor like rain. It was an unnerving spectacle made worse by the man's utter silence; Jean Chastel endured his agony without even the agency to scream.

Finally, with a sound like snapping branches, his joints came apart.

Chastel's greatcoat fell to the floor. Beneath it, he was naked and covered in horse blood, though his body could barely be considered human any longer. In my Arcane sight, anima poured into him like a torrent of lava; he was little more than a bladder held over the fountainhead. Chastel's skin split like a squeezed plum and plasma boiled from the openings, building itself into terrible new flesh.

Strong, muscular limbs and deadly claws. A powerful jaw full of fangs. The whipping tail and mane of black fur. With Avstamet's vast reserves of anima, the transformation took only a few moments.

The Beast rose to his feet before us.

Ready, Sarmodel? I asked silently.

Always, my love.

Avstamet shook himself like a hound emerging from a puddle and then reared to his full height, standing on his hind legs. His near-human face bore an expression that could only be called a leer. His voice resonated ***within*** me, like notes plucked at the base of my spine.

"So, you have found me, Magician. What a hunt we have had."

L

I did not waste time on a reply.

Now!

Sarmodel came forward in a dizzying surge. I tasted hot metal and sour bile as my bones filled with lightning.

Quick as thought, I bounded onto the backgammon table and then launched myself across the salon, leaving a trail of steam.

Avstamet did not anticipate such a direct attack. After our encounter at Saint-Julien, he no doubt expected more Arcane badinage or an attempt at the Crippling Yoke.

Not this time. His face registered annoyance—if not quite surprise—as I peppered his torso with a dozen knife wounds in less than a second. He swatted me aside with a snarl, sending me crashing onto the staircase. I felt my ribs crack as I landed, and the envenomed blade was knocked spinning from my hand.

The Beast examined his injuries, barely visible beneath the thick fur of his coat. "Cease your idiocy. A knife? Where are all your tricks and vapors?" he asked evenly. Then he smiled as he saw plasma beginning to flow from the wounds. "The Mother of Ants![1] A priest's concoction. Again, you surprise me!"

In my mind, Sarmodel's dreadful Word was taking shape. I lay there panting, steam cascading down the stairs below me.

Avstamet continued in his regal Latin. "Take care with your next words, Magician. Though you have vexed me, I do not wish to kill you."

"You—you don't?" I tensed warily in my vulnerable position.

"No, but I will not hesitate if you test me further. You have ***troubled*** me since our last meeting, Sebastian Grave—you should mark your singular privilege among men, to so occupy the attention of a god. Have you not wondered, oh marvelous freak, why I have not come for you? Have you never questioned, as you groveled in the snow with your mortal acolyte,[2] why I have not yet taken your strangely twinned heart?"

"I would not presume to guess, my lord," I wheezed. The amphisbaena venom was working in earnest now; the flesh around the Beast's wounds was dissolving into seeping jelly. If the dose was sufficient—and I couldn't know that for certain—I would only need to wait a short while longer.

"Scheme if you must, Magician—do you believe I cannot see the maelstrom in your mind? But first you will listen to me, and before you answer, remember that it is *you* who struck the first

---

1. Another name for the amphisbaena, the two-headed serpent whose venom was now burning through the Beast's blood. The toxin would break down his borrowed flesh into plasma and impede his efforts to reconstruct it.

2. This was a reference to Antoine. In Imperial Rome, the most favored priests were granted the power to draw on the anima of the faithful. Acolytes were the feeding stock so appointed to each priest. The comparison was not a comfortable one.

blow." He looked above my head, at Sarmodel's unknowable form. "And *you,* old one—you are patient, I will grant you that. What a wretched union you have made. I wonder . . . how many forbidden names would I find in your long, long history? How long have you been waiting for your master to relinquish his exquisite anima? How much longer will you endure it?"

So many questions, my lord! Do you wish to Contract for the Truth again? Shall we lay out the Table? asked Sarmodel. But my Guest's scorn lacked its usual bite. He paused in his crafting of the Word; it turned like a half-cut jewel in my mind.

Sarmodel, what are you doing?

Let us listen for a moment.

The Beast's awful gaze returned to me. "Truth! No indeed. I have thought long on the last Truth you gave me. To *know not what you are.*" He shook his terrible head in pity. "I believe that you alone—*you,* disgraceful abomination—may be the only creature in existence who remembers the world as I do, and yet you skulk among the cattle and live as one of them. So, tell me. With no Contract between us, no Table—tell me *why.*"

"Why?"

He nodded, his human eyes regarding me with fascination. "Why do you so degrade yourselves? You belong to this Mundane midden no more than I. This new world, this mortal domain without living gods—it is a fallow field waiting for the plow. Why have you not taken it for yourselves? Why do you allow this Almighty to enjoy the fruits of the world *we* made—when surely you see that He will never awaken? You knew the glory of the empire we built, the age of heroes and conquest. You have time and power. What prevents you from building it anew in your image?"

The ancient god of war was sincere, his gaze relentless.

Again, I felt the crushing force of his will, compelling me to answer.

I took a shuddering breath. "I lived as a god for a time, my lord, many centuries ago. It ended as it always does," I replied. "Men are not meant for such power."

Oh please, you weren't even trying! objected Sarmodel. *My lord Avstamet, this one is not a natural leader.*

I beg your pardon?

Avstamet looked at us both for a long moment, his wounds weeping. A thin line of plasma dripped from the corner of his mouth. He seemed to be weighing up options in his mind, and I was fairly certain that several of them involved devouring me.

"Serve, then," he said finally.

"Serve?"

"I will not countenance a rival, but a general must have his lieutenants. This new world is strange to me, and I admit there is much I do not yet understand. In this regard you are useful to me, and I reward my faithful well—remember my most favored in Rome, and you will know I speak the truth." His lips pulled up in a smile full of violent promise. "And I have learned new ways to distinguish my flock—and to ensure I will never again be left to languish in some mortal relic. Did your young charge know the gift I gave him? A splinter of godhood; did he enjoy it? He would have, in time. In time, he would have wanted ever more, and I would have filled him to splitting. A great pity that you squandered it out of cowardice—and be assured that the Water from the Mountain will be chastised for her presumption in opposing my will. Yes, Magician, I have magnificent designs for this new age of men, and you may yet sit beside me."

He pointed one clawed finger at my chest, right over my heart.

"But first you must relinquish your mortal folly and submit. Submit and *serve*, be my right hand in a new empire, and I promise you every earthly delight. No longer will you hide among the ***phlam*** like some half-breed parasite. We will take the fight to the Almighty and his angels; Michael will be but the first of your thralls, if so you desire. I promise you dominion over men—and for you, old one, a favored seat in a new pantheon. More, I promise you *purpose* that you will never know in this listless morass. What better test of a man than *war*? What better way to answer the question you could not? Serve me, and *know yourself* once more."

There were few surprises in Avstamet's pitch; it was what I would have expected from any Spirit of comparable vintage. I was ready to cast the Warfather's bargain back in his teeth. I opened my mouth and drew breath to voice my denial.

Except.

Except, I was also . . . intrigued.

I want to tell you that I was resolute before the Warfather's temptation. I would like to say that any offer Avstamet made was immaterial in the face of the horrors he had committed in Gévaudan.

But the thing is, I *did* remember.

I remembered the Roman Empire and its great temples, and the priests with their mysteries and divine boons. I had been one of them for a time, with Sarmodel as my patron in the service of a magnificent Spiritual regime we thought would never fall. There had been monsters and abominations and bloody wars and terrible disasters, but there were also Incarnate gods and great heroes and breathtaking miracles. I had a place there—a purpose—and it was glorious. We had been *alive*.

Purpose.

Of all the things the Warfather might have used to tempt me, it was the most powerful.

And all it would cost me was a measure of freedom. . . .

I will admit that the thought of the Archangel Michael bound to me in service was also quite appealing.

My immediate, instinctive refusal went unspoken.

Well. What do you think? I asked Sarmodel.

He could be lying—there's no Contract in play, he answered.

But what if he's not?

Hmm. High Priest Sebastian Grave, vanguard of a new Roman Empire. Sarmodel said the words speculatively, as though trying them out. He churned slowly in my mind. *It would be a nice change of pace from Professor Petticoat.*

And so?

He was silent for a moment. I could feel him weighing up the risks and benefits on both sides of the choice.

He set the Tartaric Word spinning again in my mind and it crystallized into terrible sequence.

The choice is yours. But if you're going to refuse, do it with this.

LI

I honestly don't know what answer I would have given. I don't know what answer I would give today, offered the same choice.

I suppose it doesn't matter; I never got the chance.

"Sebastian, stay down!"

The Beast looked up with a snarl as Antoine's voice broke the silence in the grand salon.

Something smooth flashed through the air, like a glass bottle filled with moonlight.

A quicksilver globe.

It smashed on the floor right beneath the Beast with a heavy, wet explosion, stripping chunks of flesh from his legs. Avstamet roared and recoiled, collapsing against the wall. Two more globes followed, obliterating swaths of Versailles parquet as well as the mighty front door.

Well, that settles it, I suppose, said Sarmodel, not without some regret. *Go!*

I covered my mouth against the fumes and sprang to my feet, leaping down the stairs in a blur.

"Cover your ears, Antoine!" I called over my shoulder.

And then I drew a deep, deep breath.

The Word was an Arcane nightmare, a manifest crisis of energy and matter that would cast a shadow if I spoke it in the daylight. The Tartaric syllables blasted my mind and pulled the air from my lungs.

I had little fuel to give the Word—Enneval's anima was consumed in an instant, and the sweet liquor of my lovemaking with Antoine burned with the briefest flame.

In my Arcane vision, a point of terrible stillness settled in the air between Avstamet and me. It was tiny, no greater than one of the snowflakes that flew through the night outside.

But it was enough.

For a moment, it was as though all of the life had been drawn from the room. There was no sound and the firelight was suddenly cold. The Beast glared his rage at me across what seemed a cosmic void.

And then the world collapsed.

The windows and their wooden shutters were sucked into the grand salon, the blizzard pouring in behind them. The fireplaces coughed explosively into the room, spraying the publican's priceless collection with burning embers.

At the dreadful center was the Beast. He seemed to *skew* somehow, his form distending like clay as plasma erupted from his wounds. His eyes bulged from his skull as the forces I had set in motion first pulled him upright and then crushed him to the floor.

I was not immune.

As the final syllable left my lips, I felt a terrible crack. There was a red explosion in my head.

I cried out and fell to my knees, clutching at my face.

Sarmodel! My mouth! I spat bloody fragments of my teeth onto the floor. My jaw had snapped like a wishbone. The pounding in my head told me I had also likely fractured my skull. ***Help me!***

It can be fixed! It can all be fixed! he barked. I felt him frantically scraping at my mind, erasing the last traces of the Word; it would be dangerous to hold it even in memory. ***Finish him! Quickly!***

Yes. Yes!

I nodded. I did my best to ignore the pulpy ruins of my mouth and the astonishing pain in my head.

I drew my pistols, relying heavily on Sarmodel's strength; with his help, my hands flickered like hummingbirds through the movements of loading and priming the weapons.

It was still too slow.

Avstamet was already on his feet, his ravaged flesh striving to repair itself.

But the amphisbaena venom had done its work. His healing was sluggish, and his blood flowed freely. Where Avstamet would normally have shrugged off all but the gravest injury to his mortal vessel, he was now vulnerable.

And he knew it.

The Beast took one look at the pistols in my hands and then bolted through the shattered doorway, out into the night. I went after him, lumbering across the burning floor as Sarmodel's boons began to falter.

At that moment, the sound of screaming reached us from the rooms at the back of the lodge.

I stopped in the doorway.

Oh.

I had forgotten all about Soeur. She had found her way into the servants' quarters, it seemed.

What a night of monsters it was for the good people at the Bow and Brace.

I turned around and saw Antoine at the top of the stairs. Gathered behind him were Mademoiselle Mimet, her uncle and several of the young hunters. And behind ***them*** was the unmistakable bulk of the Bishop of Mende. They all had the same wide, disbelieving eyes, their terror naked on their faces.

From the courtyard, I could hear with dreadful clarity the slaughter taking place in the servants' quarters.

In my pounding head, two singular thoughts circled each other, like bubbles rising slowly to the surface. The first was how curious it was to see all the guests gathered there together in their nightclothes, when I had specifically instructed Antoine to keep them in their rooms.

The second was that they would assuredly all be dead soon.

Around me in the grand salon, the publican's beautiful furnishings were burning heartily, a bonfire fanned by the wind now rushing into the room. The staircase was already ablaze; the rest of the building would go up like brushwood. Even without the imminent peril of Soeur, it would be certain death to remain inside the lodge now.

And *outside.*

Outside were the Beast and the blizzard. What hope did they have?

Someone was saying my name.

"Sebastian! ***Sebastian!*** You can't go out there!" Antoine shouted down at me, as the fire began to roar up the staircase.

The others joined him in desperate protest.

"Professor! What is happening?" shouted Rosalie Mimet. "You can't leave us here!"

"Is it the Beast? Where is Lord Bauterne?" demanded the Bishop of Mende.

"Come, sir!"

"You must help us!"

"Please!"

Their wailing merged into a gibbering cacophony and I held up a hand for silence. The terrified nobles stared down at me while death closed in on every side. There was no way to reach them.

Sarmodel's voice was like a hand on the back of my neck.

Come, my love. No more foolishness. This is our last chance.

I know.

I held my swollen jaw and called up the stairs, as coherently as I could.

"Find a way out! Antoine, get everyone into the courtyard! Stay away from Soeur, if you can—I will return!"

He didn't like it, but he nodded. "We will find a way."

Michael! I called silently.

There was no response, but I detected the flicker of green facets and the flash of golden blades through the flames.

Save them, Michael, I sent. *Give me time. You have missed your chance, and your Chosen is out of contention—this victory will be mine. But if you love your Father's creation as you say, then* **do something** *to save them. I will take care of Avstamet.*

Then I stepped out into the darkness.

LII

Beyond the lights of the lodge, the darkness was complete. All of Sarmodel's tricks had fallen away, spent, and I was left with only my human senses as I lurched through the blizzard after the Beast.

That's far enough, said my Guest.

I stopped, panting wetly, and glanced back at the Bow and Brace. I took the flask of brandy from my belt and removed the stopper.

They . . . they won't see?

What does it matter? They'll be dead before morning.

I froze there for a moment, staring at the open flask in my hand. My fingers were so cold I could barely feel it.

Do it, Sebastian. Quickly!

I paused a heartbeat longer.

Do you love me? I asked.

I felt Sarmodel's tendrils curl through me like a new layer of nerves. He twined around the impenetrable center of my being, the impossibly deep core of anima in which the many years of my life were distilled like honey. He pressed hard against my immortal soul, like a claw dimpling the surface of a throbbing vein.

Oh yes, my love. He said my name—my True name—and it was like a hot kiss over my heart. ***Forever and ever, world without end.***

I closed my eyes and drank the flask dry.

The brandy burned like wildfire across the rubble of my teeth. I swallowed it in desperate gulps and waited.

In moments, it began to affect me, filling my blood with fire. My vision clouded. My limbs were heavy. I fell to my knees in the snow.

Seconds later I felt the alcohol dissolving my centers of reason and will, a delightful release that seemed to tip the world on its head. The core of my being—that sacred, inviolate vault housing my soul—was thrown open.

And, sensing freedom at hand, he came to me.

The mandrill. The painted baboon. He loped through the darkness toward me, untroubled by the blizzard. His yellow grin was murder and mirth in equal measure.

Do you love me?

He came so close that I could smell his musky stench. Our eyes were level and he placed his forehead against mine, staring into me with tenderness and hunger.

And then, just for a moment, I caught a glimpse of him. This was the real face of the demon who shared my body. Not the baboon with its garish visage, nor the man-child, nor the bodiless companion and sometime mentor I knew. His Truth was far, far worse and it blackened my mind. Even now it is like a hole burned through my memory.

I could not resist him. I was beginning to drift, my gaze losing focus. His smile grew. Then his fingers were in my broken mouth, pulling it wider and wider until I was nothing but an open bag of meat, and he climbed up inside me.

For a second I was utterly still, victim to an awful paralysis. But then I felt my limbs begin to stir under the direction of a new master.

Sarmodel was a Guest no longer, and he put his new body to use.

What rapture.

What mind-breaking anguish.

Unlike the publican, I was permitted to scream during the transformation.

LIII

I was the spectator now.

Unable to control my own body, I seemed to float somehow within myself. I could only watch through Sarmodel's eyes as we stalked the Beast over the snow.

I have never properly seen what we become when Sarmodel takes control of my flesh. From my limited perspective, it seems a monstrous multiplicity of me, an abomination sculpted from man meat. I know it has more than four limbs. I know my skull and my sternum become great bulwarks of bone, and my ribs double in number around a heart grown immense.

I know it is powerful and it consumes a little more of my essence for every moment it remains in this world.

Through the snow-filled forest we ran, a demon in a coat of human flesh. The snow boiled into steam where we stepped, and the creatures of the forest fell dead in our wake. There was no real word to describe our rippling, many-limbed gait, galloping over the snow and leaping through the trees with equal grace.

The forest thrashed around us as we ascended. The Beast was easy to follow with Sarmodel's supernatural senses, though our quarry was moving at fantastic speed. He was leading us higher up the mountainside, right up into the maw of the snowstorm.

Sarmodel, be careful, please, I whimpered. It shocked me to hear how small and hollow my voice was.

His laughter bubbled around me. *How is it, then, to be the prisoner? How does it feel to be trapped in flesh that does not obey?*

We bounded over ravines and crashed heedlessly through thickets and snowdrifts alike. The scent rising from Avstamet's blood trail grew stronger and stronger; we were gaining on him. Filled with the heat of Sarmodel's essence, my body was hungry in every possible way. My belly growled and my manhood throbbed hard against it like an iron bar. Sarmodel drank greedily from my anima and we surged ahead with ever more power.

And there he was.

At the highest edge of the forest, where the trees gave way to barren stone and snow, Avstamet had reached a crevasse he could not cross. He paced the brink, looking for a way down.

But he could go no farther. The warm days that had incubated the snowstorm had also melted the high snows, and the canyon was filled with thundering white water. In his weakened condition, the Spirit would risk killing his vessel in such a flood.

Our quarry was cornered.

Sarmodel wasted no time. With a powerful bound, he leaped for the Beast's throat.

The fight was terrible; two abominations locked in mortal struggle. Their cries challenged the blizzard itself.

Great sagas have been written about such battles between gods and monsters. None of them capture the savagery of a contest in which the flesh is just another resource to expend.

Gobbets of meat were torn away with every blow. Sarmodel hooked his many claws into the Beast's wounds and stripped the skin from his torso like a furred apron. I screamed into the ether as Avstamet raked his way into my abdomen and began to unspool my innards onto the snow. There were no rules of engagement and no taboos—they blinded and crippled and violated each other without compunction. Each was simply intent on devouring the other body and soul, and they set about it.

Even in his extremity, Avstamet was formidable. He outmatched us in size and strength, and he had ample experience operating a body in the Mundane world. But he had suffered grave injuries already, and Sarmodel was fast and fearless. He made no effort to evade Avstamet's blows; with my millennia of anima at his disposal, he could repair our flesh as soon as it was damaged. I screamed in terror each time a mortal blow was struck to my altered body, only to see the wound flood with plasma and the tissue regenerate in seconds.

The Beast was not so blessed, thanks to the venom running through his veins. Where his flesh was torn, his blood flowed.[1] While Sarmodel attacked ever more vigorously, the Beast grew slower and heavier in his movements.

It could not last forever.

I began to feel a hot prickling, as of a numb limb regaining sensation. It started at the base of my spine and then sent spasms shooting through me.

Sarmodel, hurry! It's wearing off! I said. The spasms gripped

---

1. I can only image the horror of Jean Chastel, who was no doubt in a similar position to me, watching helplessly as his body was possessed by one nightmare creature and torn to pieces by another.

harder and I detected the flicker of a response when I tried to move my eyes. My body was beginning to return to me.

*No! Not yet! **Not yet!***

The Beast was standing upright, his shredded torso exposed, and Sarmodel took his chance. Rearing like a mongoose, he leaped high, gripping onto his foe with his hind claws. Anima surged into his arms and he brought his bunched fists down like a hammer on Avstamet's bloody chest.

The Beast's rib cage collapsed under the blow. He made a terrible wet grunting sound, staggering to his haunches. Sarmodel howled in triumph as he clawed through the shattered bones for the Warfather's heart.

But Avstamet was not yet defeated. With his remaining strength, he gripped us in his hands and kicked us away with a roar.

We hit the ground and skidded in the snow. Sarmodel sprang back to his feet immediately and charged at our enemy.

And then he stumbled. Once. Twice.

His gait began to weave.

He was losing control.

He is mine. He is mine.

Sarmodel was not speaking to me; I'm not sure he knew he was saying the words at all. He continued his advance, first running and then limping and finally shambling toward the Beast.

But Avstamet was in no state to face him again. Blood poured in a cascade from his broken body, far more than could ever have been contained within it; we had pierced his heart after all. His ancient anima swirled within the vital fluid like nectar.

"You. I . . . do not understand . . ." He looked at the blood and then back at us, his terrible face stricken. His voice cut through the snowstorm. "How can you bear it? How do you endure this perpetual, aimless pasture?" he demanded, panting. "How can you refuse the promise of empire? I would return this world to life, uplift the race of men from this indolence and bring them to glory once more—and you *refuse*?"

"Your time has passed, Warfather," answered Sarmodel through my mouth, and not without regret. "There will be no glory, no empire—not under your name. But I will take what you have to offer, yes indeed. This hunt is over, and I claim the victor's prize. What is yours will be mine. I will take it all, beginning with your heart."

Avstamet looked at us not with anger, but with pity.

"You are not worthy of it."

He stepped back and fell into the roaring crevasse.

LIV

I know Sarmodel would have leaped after him, with no regard for the body he inhabited. The violent current pounding through the canyon below was of no consequence.

But his control was waning quickly, and he could barely stay on his feet. The spasms I had felt were increasing in strength, like reflex points rapped with a knuckle. Even as Sarmodel faded, I was returning to myself.

Oh, but he resisted. I felt him clinging to my centers of consciousness like a child refusing to relinquish the reins after a pony ride. I could feel his hunger and his desperation as my own. He began to drag us toward the edge, a low growl rolling in our chest.

Sarmodel.

Sebastian, we must go after him! Please!

With a mental heave, I forced him out. I felt him shoot up above me, billowing like a storm cloud, as I settled back into my familiar position of control.

Well, perhaps not entirely familiar.

The monstrous body Sarmodel had created would take time to revert, and for now it was mine.

Hurry! ***Hurry!*** he fretted above me. He was weak and depleted after his excursion into the flesh, but his passion was palpable.

I tested my powerful limbs. Already droplets of plasma were condensing on the skin of my extremities; soon the tissue would begin to dissolve, but until then . . .

Until then I had the upper hand. The Beast was broken. His heart was mine for the taking. Saliva squirted into my mouth at the thought, and a deeper, more carnal compulsion stirred in my loins.

After the transformation and the chase, my body was in need of replenishment. I was *starving.*

The water roared below me. I could not see any sign of the Beast. It would be almost certain death to follow him into the flood. But my hunger was stronger than my reason; I was already looking for footholds on the cliffs.

Yes, Sebastian! We will never be hungry again, said Sarmodel. *Go! If you want that empire, you can build it yourself. We will be a power in this world, a rival to the Archangel himself.*

. . . Michael!

I shook my head. The desperate red lust in my mind gave way to a moment of clear thought. In a rush I remembered the looming disaster I had left behind at the Bow and Brace.

I spun around and looked back down the slope. Even without benefit of my preternatural sight, I could see the whirling pillar of flame shining on the mountainside. The lodge was utterly ablaze.

Leave them! They're already dead! said Sarmodel.

We don't know that! Antoine is still in there! I looked down into the crevasse and then back to the lodge.

Finish the hunt! Don't you want to feed?

But . . . Antoine. I told him I would return.

*You **will** return—with the heart of a god beating inside you! You may ride back on a comet and rebuild that lodge from marzipan and moonbeams if you want to, but **you need to move now!***

I do. Yes.

My body was crying out for sustenance. The hunger was a kind of madness, growing to obscure my every other thought.

I think, ironically, that it was the fire that saved me. Looking at the distant glow, I saw not the peril it represented. Rather I saw Antoine's face squinting in concentration over a hundred campfires, and his careful enunciation of the nonsense words I had taught him.

Sim Sala Bim.

I pulled away from the brink with an anguished whimper.

I can't, Sarmodel. I'm sorry.

I closed my mind to his howling. I gathered all of my remaining strength—both physical and mental—and fled back down the mountain.

I remember little of what happened next.

There are a few moments of clear recollection I can piece together. I remember the courtyard roaring with flames and the huddle of terrified faces at its center, surrounded by corpses. There were perhaps twenty of them still alive. What did they fear most between the fire, the storm and the slaughter, I wonder.

I remember the horrifying abomination circling them. Soeur was stalking around the group on her misshapen forelimbs, dripping red from muzzle to tail. I recall that the sound of breaking glass punctuated the screaming—the constant, many-throated screaming from every corner of the lodge, like a high chorus above the roaring of the storm.

A small figure faced Soeur in the courtyard, dressed all in black but also shining with gold and emerald radiance. It could only be Bauterne; the Archangel had decided to lend his aid after all. He held the ravening hound at bay with a long ceremonial spear, no doubt taken from the publican's collection.

I remember the miasma of intoxicating aromas that washed over me as I descended on the courtyard. Blood. Smoke. Fear, and its various organic companions; sweat, urine, tears. Blood. Wine. The sour tang of Soeur's gangrenous flesh. ***Blood.***

Worse than the memories, however, are the parts I can only imagine.

I can picture the survivors' fresh horror at the naked abomination suddenly appearing in the midst of the chaos; at the carnage as it tore apart the monster that had once been the lieutenant's favorite.

Then a pause, perhaps, as the creature cast about, looking for something, or someone.

How much did they see, those few survivors, and how much did they understand? How far had my body reverted? Did they recognize the eloquent Professor Grave, who had sparred so nimbly with Bauterne over dinner, in this new monster's face?

The next is a memory I would gladly replace with ignorant speculation.

"Abomination!"

Bauterne lunged with the spear, the Archangel's radiance whirling around him. Verses of scripture flew from his lips as he struck at me again and again.

I snatched at the spear with one of my limbs and flicked it away. Unable or unwilling to release it, Bauterne was flung across the courtyard into a pile of burning rubble.

The rest were silent now. The onlookers only cowered as my gaze returned to them.

I believe that was the point at which I truly went mad.

It had grown too much to bear, you see. The smell of blood and freshly killed meat was more than I could stand.

I began to eat.

LV

"Sebastian?"

Antoine's voice roused me from my orgy of bloodlust.

I found myself on my knees, dazed and disoriented. I was hunched atop a warm, mutilated body, pinning it to the ground with my hands. It had been half devoured. In my state of confusion, I could not imagine the creature that could have caused such dreadful injuries.

I wondered for a second at my own nakedness. I marveled at the sticky film of blood that covered me. Around me, the snow was a sludgy mess of plasma and body fluids, strewn with dismembered corpses.

Before me stood Antoine and the last group of survivors he had managed to rescue from the flames: the steward, the Bishop of Mende and a number of the lodge staff. I gathered they had just climbed down a length of knotted curtains from a shattered window.

But it is my young lover's face that remains imprinted in my memory, the image unsoftened by the passage of centuries. I had never seen him wear such an expression of dismay and revulsion; he was like a different person.

"Antoine!" I rasped, my voice barely human. I worked my mouth, spitting unspeakable gore onto the ground. "Help me, please!"

"Sebastian . . . what . . ." he breathed.

I was distracted by a whimpering cry. The body beneath me heaved weakly, still alive somehow in spite of its mortal wounds. In the light of the conflagration, Rosalie Mimet's chaperone looked up at me, his wide eyes staring from a mask of blood.

"Release him, monster!" shouted the bishop. He strode forward and shoved me solidly in the chest with his boot. "We will put you to the flame!"

I collapsed back into the red slush, my strength gone. I could feel the world beginning to darken. My body had resumed its natural form and it was time to pay the price for Sarmodel's abuses; the long sleep was coming for me.

"Antoine . . . don't . . ."

But it was not my lover's face I saw as my senses faded.

Instead, it was the grave, beautiful visage of the Lion of Judah.

They came to me in my delirium—the mandrill and the Lion both.

"Where is Avstamet?" demanded the Archangel, his eyes burning like suns as he towered over my mother's humble table. "The Warfather cannot be permitted to return to the world!"

"He is gone—lost to us both!" shrieked the baboon, standing on my shoulders. As ever, I was a child in my father's house, chained to the floor and crying with hunger.

The Lion roared and the sound shook the world. "I surrendered my chance to claim the Warfather's heart—yes, abandoned it gladly at your request, because I would save at least a few of those lives endangered on this hunt. And you, despicable creature—not only have you squandered the chance I afforded you; you have returned to slaughter those you left in my safekeeping!"

"I'm sorry," I sobbed, "I didn't know!"

The Archangel looked at me in silence for a long moment. "Lariel, look upon the wretchedness you perpetuate. What joy can there be in this for you? What victory can you claim from this misery?"

"Only the chance to see you thwarted once again, Great Prince, and it has been worth every moment," sneered the mandrill.

"A blaggard's empty retort, Lariel. Your failure reveals you for what you are—a gormless pretender playing at greatness. What hope did you have of claiming a Spirit like Avstamet? You are nothing more than another Arcane parasite, living far too long with only its own emptiness to fill."

"Leave us!" screamed the mandrill, incensed. "You will get nothing more from us, Michael! Return to the side of your silent, sleeping Almighty, and comfort yourself with fables of his return."

The Archangel lowered his great head and looked directly into my streaming eyes. "So I will, Lariel. Such is the nature of love, and faith, and service." Then he slammed one of his paws onto the table with sudden violence, dragging his golden claws across the wood. Five deep gouges were left in its path. "But know that I will return. This prison cannot protect you forever, and I am ever ready to reconcile you with my Lord and Father. Remember that in the humbling days to come."

He left me in the dark, with the mandrill panting on my back.

LVII

I was told by a manservant that they took me back to Château d'Ocerne at Antoine's insistence. I received no confirmation of this from Antoine himself; he refused my requests to speak to him, though the care I received must have been provided under his instructions.

I lay for days in a twilight of muttering voices and muted sensations. My physical wounds healed rapidly, though it cost me pounds of my own tissue. My transformation had been fueled by the very bedrock of my being and the damage showed; though I returned to wholeness, I looked a walking corpse.

Sarmodel barely spoke to me for the entire time. His resources were as depleted as mine. He was distant, injured and brooding; I had no desire to disturb his solitude.

I believe I saw Antoine only once, though it may well have been a hallucination. He was standing at the end of my bed, watching me as I groaned and spasmed in the sheets. His face was stricken and his fists were clenched by his sides.

"It was *you*. You were *eating them*," he said.

I fought to rouse myself properly, to speak in my own defense—*you are still alive because of me!*—but when I finally managed to sit up, I found the room was empty.

There were no more visits from Antoine, real or imagined. Servants came and went with food and water and linens, locking the door behind them each time. They spoke little to me, but I came to understand I was something in between a guest and a prisoner, partly, I think, because they didn't know what to do with me. I waited for either the bailiff to come and charge me, or perhaps the bishop to barrel in with Michael screeching overhead, but it seemed I was simply to be kept out of sight for now. It mattered little; I was utterly defeated. I hadn't the energy to do anything but wait. Slowly, slowly, I came back to life.

I rose from my bed for the first time to investigate some faint fanfare from the courtyard. The herald's voice rang out in an announcement I could not discern. I crossed the floor with difficulty—my joints *screamed* with every flexion—and pulled back the curtains.

The Ocernes had hidden me away high on the third floor to convalesce, so I had a commanding view of the courtyard from my window. Lord and Lady Ocerne were once more arrayed in their finery on the landing before the great doors, surrounded by their retinue. Antoine was with them, as were the bailiff and a handful of other nobles. In the wintry courtyard, it was a dire, threadbare reenactment of our assignment ceremony.

The herald spoke again as the Bishop of Mende emerged from the château, moving slowly to stand beside Antoine. The clergyman had not escaped the massacre unharmed—he looked absolutely dreadful. Aside from his pronounced limp, one arm was cradled in a sling and half of his face was completely covered in bandages.

I opened the icy window a fraction to better hear the proceedings.

"*. . . the selfsame Beast, which has been the scourge of Gévaudan these many months, now slain by Lord Francois Antoine de Bauterne, Gun-Bearer to the King and Lieutenant of the Hunt.*"

Bauterne limped into the courtyard through the main gates. His battered face was almost as black as his clothing, his nose swollen like a mushroom and his eyes bloodshot. Behind him came a flat wagon bearing a great mound of rotting flesh.

Soeur. The hound's carcass had been reconstructed imperfectly for display, but there was no mistaking her blighted form. It was disintegrating slowly thanks to the extreme cold, but tendrils of plasma were already beginning to drip from the wagon.[1] Though she had done her violent best to kill me, I felt only profound pity for her. The proud mastiff was to be paraded before the king as the very Beast she had come to hunt.

Bauterne bowed his head to receive the thanks of the lord and lady, and then it was Bishop Fontaine's turn.

"And so ends the terror of Gévaudan, by the grace of the Lord and His Majesty Louis XV, King of France and of Navarre!" he announced with characteristic bombast. "Return now to Versailles with your trophy and the blessing of our Holy Father, and claim your bounty."

The speech went on but I had heard enough. My legs were beginning to tremble from the effort of standing and I was painfully cold. I closed the window with a final glance at Bauterne. The

---

1. The specimen was completely unrecognizable by the time it made it back to Versailles for presentation to the king. Bauterne still received his prize, but there remained a (very convenient) level of mystery around what the Beast actually was.

lieutenant did not seem to be enjoying his triumph. His head was bowed and his swollen eyes were closed. Around his wrist I spied the glimmer of gold; the gilded chain collar once worn by his favorite hound.

I returned to my bed and called for food. It was time to hasten my recovery.

The second time I arose was for another commotion in the courtyard. Several weeks must have passed since my first look outside; the ice was gone and the first spikes of green growth were showing on the boughs around the estate.

I was stronger this time. I stood at the window with a cup of lemon tea in hand, watching the bustle in the courtyard. The château staff were all gathering as though to receive a visiting dignitary. Antoine stood in the center of the thoroughfare, flanked by his mother and father, with the Bishop of Mende and his retinue to one side.

Fontaine's convalescence was obviously nearing its end. He had donned his choir dress of purple and white, presumably to lead a service for the people of the château. His wounds had mostly healed, though bandages still covered the burned half of his face. Antoine looked thin and tired. He was dressed in the sable-trimmed, honey-colored velvet waistcoat that had first caught my eye, back when I had first signed my name in the ledger in the courtyard, right where he was standing.

Antoine, you are impossible! Have you no fear?

Of you? Yes. From the first.

The courtyard continued to fill as people filed in from every corner of the château. They hurriedly adjusted wigs and waistcoats, assembling behind the noble family to face the front gate.

A few minutes passed in tense silence. I stared at Antoine, willing him to look up at me. Lady Ocerne was leaning toward her son, her mouth moving in a constant stream of speech near his ear. Antoine was unmoved; he might as well have been made of wax.

And as the herald announced their important guest, he looked for reassurance not to his parents, but rather to the Bishop of Mende.

"Baron Jean-Michel Voltours d'Apcher!"

A fine horse-drawn carriage appeared at the gates, decorated with the red castle of Apcher. The driver stopped it in front of Antoine and his family, and a valet stepped forward to open the door.

The Baron d'Apcher alighted and went down the line of very important people, greeting and genuflecting as appropriate. Antoine did his part with impeccable etiquette and not a trace of humanity.

"*Lady Ninette Voltours d'Apcher!*" announced the herald, and I felt an unwelcome stirring in the hollow cage of my chest.

So this was Antoine's betrothed.

Ninette stepped delicately down from the carriage, with the aid of the valet. She was dressed in a beautiful gown of cornflower blue, with a rose-pink stomacher and a sable-lined cloak. She was smiling nervously and her round face was beautifully painted with cosmetics. She could not have been more than fifteen years old.

She's a child, I said to Sarmodel. It was the first time we'd spoken in weeks.

He roused himself disinterestedly and gave a cursory inspection of the scene. *So? They're all children, Sebastian.*

Antoine greeted his intended bride nervously. He gave the flicker of a smile as he took her hand, and showed some genuine warmth as they conversed.

Yes, I suppose they are.

I raised my hand to close the window and noticed I wasn't the only one watching from the fringes. Cecile, the young herbalist from Saint-Julien, stood in the crowd just inside the gatehouse, her pale blond hair sticking out like dry sedge. The hagstone, Dayane's boon, winked across the courtyard like a coin catching the sun. Antoine's debts were already beginning to return.

I drew the curtains; I couldn't watch any more.

That evening, the butler brought me a set of fine traveling clothes and a message from the Baron d'Ocerne: in recognition of my service to the barony, a small sum had been set aside for me along with a horse, available at my earliest convenience. It seemed my time at Château d'Ocerne had come to a close.

Banishment is better than execution, I suppose, I said, reaching out to Sarmodel.

Is it? Leave me be.

I left as soon as I was dressed, taking the long eastern road through the mountains. Sarmodel said nothing and I was glad. I cared not for company or conversation. I felt hollowed out—corroded from within by an aching of my very spirit.

It was the last I saw of Gévaudan for twenty years.

PART SIX

The Spirit of War

LVIII

Saint-Julien-by-the-Stream
1785

"You're sending me back to the château? Professor, I don't understand," said Jacques.

We stood at the crossroads near Saint-Julien, where we had passed the funeral procession for the pig farmer and his family only the previous day. I had told the story of the Bow and Brace as we descended from Dayane's pool and out of the mountains. Now the day was growing late. It was overcast and gusting, and the roadside puddles were crusted with a brownish rime.

"I need to you to deliver a message to your father—and only to him."

"But—you will not come with me?"

"No, sir. I do not believe Antoine would countenance my presence. You must understand why by now."

"After what you have told me . . ." Jacques had listened wide-eyed to my confessions of murder and cannibalism over the course of the day. He was shaken, though he tried his best to hide it. "Professor, if your story is true, then everything my father has told us about the Red Winter is a lie." He shook his head. "And I have dragged you back here, when the source of our troubles was always within the château walls. I feel a fool. Worse—a child."

"I chose to come, young sir. And we have all played our part. I have certainly earned your father's enmity."

"No. If my father condemns you, then he must also condemn me," he said. "After what I have done—the people I have killed in Gévaudan. And Gerard, Henri. Cecile."

"And there will be more." I took a deep breath. "Which is why this will be your last night at the château."

"My last . . . ?"

"Yes. Until I have found another way to get rid of what ails you, now that Lady Dayane is gone. Take the opportunity to say goodbye to your family, at least for a time. You said yourself your hunger is getting worse, and there is no telling how soon it might return. Find me here again in the morning; we will be leaving Gévaudan."

"So I must leave my family. My home. It seems this curse will never end."

Oh—really? said Sarmodel. *Come back in three thousand years and we will discuss never-ending curses.*

"It will, and we will find the way. But not here. Not with your father and the bishop pulling the barony apart to find you."

Jacques seemed to gather himself. "Very well. What is your message? I will take it to him."

I told him what I wished to say and then I sent him on his way. I laid a hand on his shoulder with a final warning. "Young sir. Say as much or as little as you wish to your wife and mother, but do not speak to Bishop Fontaine of Mende—not of me, nor of leaving."

"You have my word."

I watched him for a few minutes as he took his horse slowly

along the high road to the château. Even in the gray autumn light, the castle was magnificent, glowing like a filigreed pearl at the top of the rise.

Sebastian, you are a fool. He's going to get home and sing like a nightingale. You'll have the bishop and his soldiers after you by sundown.

I don't think so. And we have run out of options, I am afraid.

We have not. There is a very simple solution to all of this, and it's right inside that brandy flask on your hip.

We can't just kill them all, Sarmodel.

Why do you always say that? Of course we can!

I waited until Jacques was too far to see clearly, wishing for a moment that I could call him back, if only to have some company on the road. Then I turned my horse down the eastern fork, away from Saint-Julien.

I waited in what had once been the grand salon of the Bow and Brace.

The hunting lodge had never been rebuilt. Jean Chastel had no surviving family, and so the land had returned to the Baron d'Ocerne. Neither the baron nor his son had seen fit to restore the burned wreckage.

The bones of the building still stood, but the majority had either been destroyed in the fire or succumbed to the patient, consuming embrace of the forest. The walls of the ground floor were still upright and mostly intact; there was even a hoard of blackened silver cutlery in the remains of the dining room. The two great brick fireplaces now faced each other across a nodding carpet of ferns.

I wondered if Jacques had made it safely to the château. I wondered if the voice in his head was already returning.

It hardly mattered now. If he delivered my message as I requested, then we would all be on a new course by the end of the night. And if not . . .

If not, then it was probably too late for Jacques anyway.

I took some time to prepare. I went back down the road a short way and took a small bird skull from my pocket. Using the tip of the beak, I drew a simple Ward in the soil. Then I returned to the lodge and lit a fire in one of the hearths. I rolled a pair of fallen stones into place as makeshift seats, facing the flames. I had no idea how long I would need to wait, so I made myself comfortable, watching the fire as the sun fell through the trees. As dusk turned into darkness, I roasted a squash in the coals and ate it with a little soft cheese and bread. I wished uselessly that there were some way for me to check my appearance properly. It had been necessary to discard some of my clothing after my bloody encounter with Jacques in the mountains, and my remaining attire was shabby and mismatched.

Really, Sebastian? Is this the time for vanity? said Sarmodel.

I know, I know! It's pathetic, but I can't help it.

Try to focus, please. We are going to need—

He was interrupted by a distinctive whistling call from the bird skull in my pocket.

Someone had crossed my Ward on the road. I tensed, waiting for the skull to sing again, but it seemed my instructions had been followed; my visitor had come alone.

I rose to my feet in anticipation of his arrival, holding my hands at my sides where I could reach my weapons easily. My heart was a fist thumping the inside of my rib cage and my face was uncomfortably flushed.

The slow rhythm of horseshoes on the road grew louder as he approached. He stopped well outside the light of the fire, another tall shadow among the trees.

"I am here. Speak."

I could barely make him out, but I knew it was him. The way he leaned back in the saddle. The proud set of his shoulders. Even the slight tilt of his head. It was all the same.

Do you remember the trout in the stream? The day under the bridge, when you were wounded and you looked at me like a wonder, like a miracle?

"Antoine, please come and sit."

He stiffened. "I've done as you asked. I have come to find you here—to this place, of all the evil remnants you might have chosen." His voice was shaking with emotion. "Put your weapons away—I am alone, as you requested. Believe me when I say I am here for Jacques's sake alone. Tell me what you want."

"Sit with me, Antoine. We have things to discuss and you well know it. I have traveled halfway across the continent at your son's behest—do you think I mean you harm?"

His breath clouded the air as he stared at me in silence. "Sebastian, what good can come of you being here?" he asked finally. "What can we possibly have to discuss?"

He had said my name. It was a small thing, but it gave me hope.

"I promised Jacques I would help Gévaudan and so I will. But first there are things you must know." I motioned behind me to the two stones before the fireplace.

I thought he would leave. He said nothing and continued to stare at me from the darkness.

And then he dismounted with a swift, terse movement. He secured his horse to a tree and walked stiffly toward me. Every step and gesture was tightly controlled, as though it were costing him some great internal toll. As he came into the light, a heavy pectoral cross flashed on his breast. It was no doubt on loan from the bishop, though it was not the same bejeweled confection Fontaine had been wearing at Saint-Julien.

He sat on a stone seat and looked directly ahead, into the flames. The shadow of the Lion stretched long on the ground behind him; Michael was making his presence known.

Sarmodel shifted apprehensively in my mind. *I hope you know what you are doing, Sebastian.*

So do I.

"There—I am sitting."

"Thank you." I sat across from him, looking at the face of the man I had loved so many years before. In the firelight he seemed to be the Antoine I remembered again, his hair burnished to its youthful golden blond, and I saw a shadow of the irreverent, daring thinker I had known. "Antoine, I understand you must hate me. I don't blame you for that, and you may be assured that I will soon be gone. But I wanted to talk to you one more time."

He grimaced and swore, screwing his eyes shut in frustration. "Just tell me what you want and begone."

"Antoine, I am taking Jacques with me."

He gave a tiny, furious shake of his head, though he still would not look at me. "Never."

"I mean him no harm—you have seen he is not my prisoner and I would not take him against his will."

"I would rather see him dead," he spat, his eyes fixed on the fire.

"Then so you will, I fear. Antoine, Jacques is—"

"The Beast. I know."

"You *know*?" I stared at him.

"He is my son, Sebastian, living under my roof. Do you think I did not notice when he began disappearing? When he was sickly and starving for days, and then suddenly hale the next morning, always after the news of a fresh kill in the village?"

"And you have allowed him to go on this way? *For a year?*"

"Allowed? *Allowed?*" He turned to look at me for the first time, full of rage. "What should I have done? Killed him? Locked him away?"

"You should have sent for me, as soon as you knew. Can you not see he is getting worse?"

"You? It is your fault he suffers under this curse to begin with! You and Cecile and that demon in the mountains; I would not give him up, so she has taken him from me anyway. Him and his children, and theirs, and theirs. My line, forever blighted." He gripped the pectoral cross tightly. "No, Sebastian, I would not have sent for you if the Lord himself had demanded it. I would sooner never have met you."

"Then why did you keep my letters, Antoine?" I asked sharply. "If you hated me so much, why keep them at all? You certainly never replied."

He opened his mouth but did not respond. He simply looked at me, his eyes shining and his face golden in the light of the fire.

I heaved a breath and looked away from him. "It doesn't matter now." I tossed an old bough laden with pine cones into the hearth. They crackled and snapped like gunpowder. "Antoine, I can still help Jacques. I will take him back to my home in Corvano, where he can do no more harm to the people of Gévaudan or the ones he loves. I will find a way to remove this curse from him, and then I will bring him home. Please trust me."

"Trust you? This is your fault—all of it!" Again he raised his fists in restrained violence. "I trusted you to help us twenty years ago, and what happened? I stayed behind to save the innocent and you returned to murder them all. And then you . . . you devoured them, you monster! I would say it was lunacy if I had not seen it with my own eyes. You *ate* them—the nobles, the hunters, the butler." He seemed unable to go on.

Uh—if I may, objected Sarmodel lightly. *Not the butler. That was Soeur.*

"I am not . . . I am not always a monster, Antoine," I said with difficulty. Now it was I who struggled to meet his gaze. "But there are no wonders without horrors; no miracles without sacrifice. No great deeds without payment. And how many more has Jacques killed? How many have you allowed to be murdered and devoured, for the sake of someone you love?"

We looked at each other in the firelight, as we had on so many nights during the Red Winter. Something in Antoine softened. His shoulders slumped and the brittle rod of his spine relaxed.

"Sebastian, you should not have returned to Gévaudan. I do not want your help. Why can't you see that?"

"Because I want to make amends. You may hate me for the rest of your life, but I must at least try," I said. "Let me take Jacques, with your blessing."

"Sebastian, it is too late. I have found another way," he answered.

"Another way?"

"The Bishop of Mende. When Jacques disappeared, I went to him and confessed my misdeeds during the Red Winter—you, Dayane, the Beast, all of it. He has agreed to come to Gévaudan to remove the curse, that Jacques may be cured and my line restored."

"What has he promised you—the rite of exorcism?" I shook my head. "This is another devil's bargain, whether you realize it or not, Antoine. Has the bishop named his price yet?"

He leaned forward suddenly and took my hands, his eyes staring into me. I couldn't speak, stunned by his sudden intimacy.

Antoine's eyes brimmed. He leaned closer and closer to me. Close enough that I could smell the lavender scent of his clothing.

Close enough to kiss me.

"He has."

Sebastian! Sarmodel was suddenly coiled and bristling in my mind. *Run!*

In the same moment, the bird skull in my pocket shrieked its alarm—once, then twice, then a half dozen times. The sound of rapid hoofbeats came soon after.

I turned to see Bishop Fontaine crest the top of the road on horseback, followed by the guardsmen of Mende. His voice rang out just as Antoine closed steel manacles around my wrists.

Of course.

A trap.

"You are undone, witch! Your crimes have been witnessed and your trial awaits at Château d'Ocerne. You will not speak again until your words can be judged before the Lord Almighty."

Disbelieving, I looked down at the chains now binding me. Their design was unusual but very familiar.

The Choking Braid.

"I'm sorry," said Antoine, turning away from me. "I cannot trust you and there is no other way. They will not harm you, I promise."

Antoine spoke to me one more time before the soldiers bound me and tied me to the saddle of my horse. His eyes were full of sorrow, but not regret. He wiped his tears with his fingertips and drew a ragged breath.

"You signed a contract to serve my family in destroying the Beast. You will serve us one last time."

LIX

I was surprisingly calm during the journey. They had tied me backward in the saddle so I would not easily be able to ride away, even if I managed to free myself.

Antoine rode ahead with Fontaine, while I rode under guard at the rear. In my Arcane sight, the Archangel's wings floated triumphantly above my former lover, plumes streaming.[1]

The soldiers around me were in high spirits discussing what violent demise might be in store for me. They seemed to be good friends and their banter was lively and engaging. Would I be burned in the traditional way? Or dragged behind a horse and drowned in the sea? Perhaps the bishop would have me closed inside a barrel of caltrops and rolled down the mountainside? Was a crucifixion out of the question? I gathered this expedition had turned out to be far more exciting than their usual duties.

---

1. The Angelic Host are all shameless gloaters. I suppose it's hard to be gracious when Divine supremacy is your *raison d'être.*

The men were also unfortunately quite alert, and my bonds were very secure. Escape was unlikely.

Sarmodel? Any suggestions?

I could feel him thinking briefly. *The barrel, if it were up to me.*

Please, I need your help or we're both going to die.

It's hardly our first witch trial. You must know the script by now.

I think somehow this one might be different, and they have witnesses—that always makes it harder. Plus . . . well, my options are limited with this damned thing around my wrists.

True. And how did that get there?

I know. My fault. Again.

The Choking Braid was like a fist in my throat. If I even began to formulate a spell, my tongue caught and my gullet swelled shut. Sarmodel was likewise closed off from me, as though someone had dammed up my anima. I stopped trying after the third time; whoever had crafted the chains knew what they were doing. I would need to wait for Antoine to speak the words to release me.

Can you help at all? I asked.

Let's see.

Gradually, gradually, like collecting the dew, Sarmodel was able to gather enough energy to brighten my vision and ease my discomfort a little, without provoking the Braid.

Thank you, my love.

It's not much, but it will have to do for now, said my Guest grudgingly.

I was distracted by thoughts of Antoine. Our conversation at the ruins of the Bow and Brace disturbed me. It was hard to see him as he was now; hard and suspicious, clinging to the only faith he trusted. I found I couldn't hate him, even if he had called for my death.

Antoine, Cecile, Dayane, Michael—this new trouble had

brought them all into my path again, and there was unfinished business everywhere I looked. Antoine's terrible bargain with Dayane. The Beast. The curse of the ancient Spirit Avstamet, driving his violent madness across the land. And driving Jacques to unspeakable acts with a hunger that was only growing.

Now Antoine had made a new bargain, with the Bishop of Mende and Archangel Michael himself, and this time it was my life to be taken in payment. There was, I could admit, something quite poetic about it.

We passed several groups of villagers on the road, all on foot and all heading toward Saint-Julien as we were. They exchanged frightened glances as we left them behind, clearly unnerved at the sight of our armed and mounted company. None of the others in our retinue seemed to pay them any attention; they were just peasants on the road.

But after the third such group, it began to bother me.

Another half dozen men, walking the road together at night. Why are there so many of them? I wondered to Sarmodel.

Probably for safety, my love. I understand there have been some animal attacks in the area.

My misgivings grew as we went through Saint-Julien's main square. The fountain gurgled across from the gallows, now creaking drowsily with the weight of a half dozen freshly hanged bodies. Coraxes were clustered all over the corpses like engorged ticks.

I wondered briefly at the sudden spree of executions. But then I remembered the chaos of the square earlier that morning—had it really been less than a day?—and the coarse laughter that had followed us as we fled. The bishop had clearly returned to answer his humiliation, in the most brutal terms. Now it was the soldiers of Mende who laughed as their lanterns revealed the swollen tongues and purple faces of the victims.

My captors remarked on the sport they had made of chasing down the villagers. From what I could gather, the unfortunates hanging from the beam were those who had helped themselves to the bishop's fallen jewelry. They had been singled out by their fellow villagers with the use of torture, and each was marked for their crime before they died. A finger was pulled off for every golden link found in their possession, and an eye spooned out for any precious gems. The men bragged that all the missing pieces had been recovered before noon.

An optimal result, I remarked uneasily to Sarmodel.

We headed up the high road toward the château. From my rear-facing position, and with Sarmodel's assistance, I had ample opportunity to observe the panorama as we ascended.

There was movement all around the benighted village. I had a magnificent view of the surrounding countryside, and everywhere I saw them—little groups of people, traveling by night. They were all on foot, and they were all heading toward Saint-Julien.

My captors were absorbed in conversation and blinded by the light of their own lamps; they had noticed nothing. I contemplated drawing their attention to the strange crowd converging on the town behind them, perhaps as a diversion.

But there was no point.

The soldiers of Mende would see nothing because there were no lights in Saint-Julien. No windows were lit, and no lamps illuminated the streets.

And of all the dozens of people making their way into the village, not one of them carried a lantern.

LX

My strange calm persisted as we rode into the château courtyard. I was not unduly ruffled as they dragged me from my horse. I made no protest even when they stripped off my outer clothing, with a few gratuitous fondles.

I had done this all before, you see.

It's ended this way many, many times. Too often, my best efforts to help people with their troubles earn me only their suspicion. Friends, colleagues and benefactors—and yes, lovers—find they are suddenly not quite so comfortable with a warlock by their side once the terms of a Contract have been met. A witch trial is a wonderful way for them to absolve themselves of any Arcane dealings—and to avoid disbursing any rewards I am owed at the same time.

Bound, beaten, neutralized, betrayed and put on trial by Michael and the Almighty, said Sarmodel. *You know, I have been wondering how this could possibly be worse, but I am at a loss.*

Thank you, Sarmodel. That's enough.

Do you remember, back in Corvano, when I recommended we feed the boy to the succubus? I'm sure you do. This is exactly the situation I was trying to avoid.

It's a witch trial. As you said, we've done it before.

Of course, the prospect was a little daunting, as always. But it was not a surprise. I found I was even grateful for the speedy turnaround; generally, I would languish in a cell for days before the proceedings began.

Not this time.

Antoine spoke to me again before it began.

The guards left me in only my undershirt and breeches, without benefit of even my belt or boots. My hair had come loose and I must have looked quite the scarecrow. He stood over me, looking at me with genuine pity in my shameful state.

"This is the only way," he said, his fist wrapped around the pectoral cross. "If you wish to help Jacques, then do not resist—the bishop has promised me you will not be harmed."

"Do you really believe that?"

"I do. I have confessed and given him stewardship of my soul. My heart is glad for it. I suggest you do the same."

He nodded for the soldiers to take me inside. He looked not at all like a man with a glad heart.

The sumptuous parlor of Château d'Ocerne had been transformed into a makeshift ecclesiastical court. A lectern and a brazier stood before the grand western windows, flanked by Fontaine's soldiers.

To my surprise, I was not the only prisoner at the trial.

Lorette was there too, kneeling on the marble floor. Her wrists were bound in front of her, bloody from the coarse ropes they had used to tie her. Her face was bruised, the left eye swollen and streaming. She looked at me with barely controlled fear as the guards dragged me across the floor.

Our "witness." The bishop is in an inquisitorial mood, it seems, I said.

A single row of seats had been arranged to the left, providing a gallery for the official witnesses to the proceedings: the bailiff, Père Arnaud and a few of the local noblemen.

To the right was the seat of the Baron d'Ocerne, with his wife and son on either side of him. Antoine made the required genuflections and took his place, the Archangel's wings resting like a feathered mantle on his shoulders.

Jacques was on his feet the second I arrived.

"Professor! This is not my doing, I swear it!" The boy looked as though he were ready to set himself on fire, clammy with sweat and fidgeting like a schoolboy. "They . . . they said they would hurt her if I tried to reach you!"

He pointed to Lorette and I suddenly understood.

Oh no. Jacques, how could you be so careless?

The guards had deprived the girl of her pinafore and she was dressed only in her rough chemise. Without her voluminous skirts, Lorette's condition was very much apparent. She held her hands protectively in front of her belly, but there was no disguising it. Jacques stared at her wild-eyed, but she would not meet his gaze; this was clearly the first he knew of the matter, too.

"Sit down, Jacques!" said Antoine. "None need be harmed, you will see."

She is carrying the young lord's child. You know what that means, said Sarmodel.

I do.

We were all in for an eventful evening.

Almost everyone's here, I said. *They'll be starting soon. If you've got any advice, now is the time.*

*Oh, **now** is the time? Not twenty years ago, when you had the chance to prevent all this?*

Never mind, then.

*Do **you** have a plan?*

I chewed my lip. *I wish Livia were here.*

I'm going to pretend you didn't say that.

When Bishop Fontaine finally arrived, he was announced not by the usual fanfare, but by the clunking of armored boots across the floor. The soldiers moved into position around the room, guarding the various entrances to the chamber.

Then came Fontaine himself, no longer in his choir dress but rather in his silken bishop's vestments. A number of the château's attendants followed him, carrying various goods which they placed on the floor before the lectern. I recognized my confiscated belongings, including my physician's valise, my weapons, my flask of Armagnac and the pouches of herbs Cecile had given me.

The leather bag containing my money was absent from the pile. It was only a small portion of the sum I had locked away in my trunk, but it still rankled.

*Sarmodel, they took my **money**. I haven't even been convicted yet!*

We'll take it from their corpses, don't worry. Just get your hands on that brandy and I'll show them a real unholy misdeed.

That . . . may be our only option.

I eyed the silver flask, only a few paces away at the bishop's feet. It was, as always, a last resort, but I could think of no other way to overcome the Choking Braid. My odds of reaching it were slim, but the alternatives were all very unpleasant.

"Children of God!" said Fontaine, raising his gold-tipped crosier above the lectern. His beautiful voice filled the dim parlor like song; the volume was entirely excessive for such a small gathering.

"You are the true flock, come to witness the most miserable of tragedies and the grandest of triumphs: the scourging of a soul, and its return to the light of righteousness. We begin with the words taught to us by our Holy Father . . ."

The trial commenced—as ever—with a lot of bastardized Latin.[1] The prayers lasted almost half an hour. Edicts and holy proclamations took us well past bedtime. Finally, the bishop got around to the case against me. The bailiff picked up his quill with a glad sigh.

". . . Professor Sebastian Grave of Larnaca, brought here to answer charges of witchcraft and sorcery; for the affliction of these lands with the creature known as the Beast; and for the murder of Mademoiselle Cecile Desmarais."

Oh—really? Cecile?

Lorette simply closed her eyes in quiet fury. Her fists clenched within the binding manacles. What else had they made her confess?

The bailiff's quill scratched frantically at the ledger, trying to keep up with the bishop's litany of sins.

". . . and Mademoiselle Lorette Desmarais, come as a witness to the murder of her mother, and to confess her own crimes of witchcraft, abortion and infanticide."

There were cries of shock from the gathered officials.

Lorette's head snapped up suddenly, her lips pulling back in a sneer. "Oh, yes, my lords—weep and curse! As though not one of you had ever sent a maidservant to the *sage-femme* with money for pennyroyal tea!"

---

1. The bishop was, unsurprisingly, a staunch traditionalist. His chosen liturgy for the trial was a particularly laborious order of proceedings that I hadn't seen since the 1600s.

"You will be silent until you are asked to speak," said the bishop, his voice somehow still rich with compassion. The guard standing above Lorette swatted her much-abused face with the back of his hand. She grunted and collapsed to the floor.

"Monseigneur!" protested Jacques, rising to his feet. "No more! This is disgraceful—Lorette, I am sorry!" Jacques interjected again. The young man gripped Antoine's shoulder. "Father! You said she would not be harmed! Will you allow this under your roof?"

"Sit down, Jacques," said Antoine softly. "Please be calm. She must be here and this *must* be done, you will see. It will be over soon."

"Have faith, young sir," said the bishop sternly. "This is what it means to be lord."

Jacques sat down reluctantly, flushed with rage and wet with sweat. The Mende soldier placed the toe of his boot on Lorette's neck and drew his rapier, pressing it into the soft hollow beneath her chin.

"Speak again, witch, and I'll make you a new mouth," said the guard. Lorette began to cry, but she said nothing more. She met my gaze and I shook my head very slightly; best she ended her valiant protest there. Jacques would not be able to save her if she tested the bishop's patience again.

"Is it an accident, then, that the people of Gévaudan are again being taken by some hellish monster, and again we find this 'professor' here?" Bishop Fontaine went on. "No. See the face of a man unnaturally immune to age. See the evidence of his own arcana, which lay bare the nature of his unholy work." He motioned to the pile of goods on the floor. I tried not to look too obviously at the glinting silver flask of brandy.

Père Arnaud splashed my possessions[2] with holy water and moaned tunefully over them. The bailiff's scribbling only intensified.

"And finally, the testimony of a witness. The young woman before us has sworn under the sight of our Lord that she saw Professor Grave call forth the Beast from a whirlwind, and thence commanded it to kill the midwife of Saint-Julien," the bishop continued. There was more murmuring from the officials and quiet sobbing from Lorette.

"Further, the witness has confessed that she, her mother and the accused dealt with the Beast on numerous occasions, calling it by the names of the Devil—Lucifer, Satan and Beelzebub—and that she carries his very child in her womb," said Fontaine.

*By the Rift—**Lucifer? Again?!*** fumed Sarmodel. *Sebastian, I give up! Are we never to get any of the credit for anything?*

We are being framed, Sarmodel. Are the names important?

". . . offering it the blood of their neighbors in exchange for their sorcerous powers."

I shrugged. It was as likely a version of events as any other; the truth was no less outrageous.

"What have you to say in your defense, Sebastian Grave of Larnaca? Know that even one of these crimes warrants a sentence of death. In the face of this evidence, will you offer your confession?" asked Fontaine, hefting the gold-tipped crosier in my direction.

---

2. It is not lost on me that there was actually nothing explicitly Arcane in the "arcana" the soldiers of Mende had gathered. My sword was (to Mundane eyes) quite ornate but otherwise unremarkable. My valise contained very ordinary medical tools, and the herbs were available in every village in the realm. My true Arcane supplies—which would have been far more damning—were still sitting in my locked trunk in the guest room upstairs.

From every side, they stared back—guards, nobles and clergy. The only ones not looking at me were Antoine and Jacques, who were in that moment uncanny in their resemblance, with their eyes downcast and jaws clenched. The Choking Braid was cold around my wrists, and the brandy flask was tantalizingly close.

"I will, Monseigneur."

It was time.

Immediately, the Archangel's wings flexed high over Antoine's shoulders. Michael had been waiting for me to say those words for over a thousand years.

Sarmodel stirred in my mind, suddenly distracted. There was a faint sound from outside, like voices raised in greeting.

Are we ready? I asked.

We'll have to be, he answered.

"Come! Speak, and be received by the Lord! Will you now confess?" pressed the bishop. Michael's radiance began to grow, suffusing me with a reassuring warmth.

"Very well, Your Excellency. My crimes are many, but I wish to say only one thing," I said. I raised my voice so they could all hear me.

"Listen carefully: Everyone in this room is about to die. Your only chance to survive is to release me and do exactly as I say—and quickly."

LXI

The scratching of the bailiff's quill stopped abruptly.

There was no hymn song or scandalized muttering. Even Lorette was silent. The expectant eyes shifted slowly from me to the bishop.

"A threat?" asked Fontaine, his voice full of condescension. "*This* is your response to the clemency we have shown?" He shook his head in pity. "Offered a chance to redeem yourself, you answer with the promise of violence. Truly, I had not expected such depravity, even from one such as you."

"It was not a threat and I do not speak idly. If you would live through the night, get these chains off me right now," I said. I turned to the noble family. "Antoine—Lord Ocerne—*look at me,* for God's sake! Do you believe I am lying?"

"You have abused the grace offered to you, and I will hear no more," announced the bishop. He nodded to the Mende guardsman standing over me.

"Wait—!"

The room somersaulted around me as the man delivered an armored knee to the side of my head.

Did that hurt? asked Sarmodel dryly as I hit the floor. *Sebastian, they're not listening to you.*

I know. I know.

I lay there on the marble, waiting for the spinning to stop. It took me a few moments to realize that the roaring I heard was not all in my head.

The sounds of some loud commotion intruded on the parlor from outside in the courtyard. The faint voices I had heard before were now crying out in alarm, and a series of deep shocks kicked through the floor beneath me.

I raised myself slowly back to my knees.

"I warned you; it is already beginning," I said.

Nobles, officials, clergy, soldiers—they were all afraid now. They looked to the bishop and then back to the doors. They started as one as the unmistakable sounds of gunfire reached us.

"No! *No!* The witch has called the Beast to his side!" stammered Père Arnaud suddenly, his eyes wide in (entirely mistaken) revelation. "Monseigneur, we must—"

"No, you cretin, I have not called the Beast," I snapped. "The death you can hear coming for us walked straight up the high road, just as we did."

"*My lord!*" shouted a new voice.

The main doors were suddenly thrown open and Dimitri the butler burst in. His waistcoat was splashed with blood and his powdered wig sat askew on his scalp. The old man slammed the doors closed behind him and fumbled desperately at the keys on his belt.

"Don't let them in!" he screamed, violently thrusting a key into the lock. He turned it so hard that the stem broke.

"Who?" demanded Antoine, rising to his feet. "Dimitri, who is there?!"

The old butler turned around to face us. His eyes were wild. "Everyone, my lord! *Everyone!* They've gone mad!"

"Everyone? Everyone what? I don't understand!" Antoine shouted over the confusion. "Dimitri?"

Outside, the great cacophony grew suddenly louder. The butler fled to the back of the chamber with a whimper.

"Soldiers of Mende, make sure nobody else comes through the doors—we are under attack!" barked Fontaine. The bishop wasn't taking any chances.

Everyone was suddenly on their feet. There were three entrances into the parlor in grand baroque style, and in minutes there were about a half dozen soldiers at each, methodically stacking furniture in front of the doors.

I predicted they would buy us ten minutes at most.

Lorette and I were not left unattended; Antoine stood over us and took the ends of my chains in one fist, his dueling sword in the other. The girl sat up slowly, a red boot print standing out on the skin of her neck. Like everyone else, she was watching the doors. But unlike the others, she did not look afraid. She was no longer crying, either. If anything, she seemed positively breathless with expectation.

"But we will be trapped in here!" said Lady Ocerne, watching the soldiers slide a heavy sideboard across the northern entrance. "Antoine, what is happening?"

The bishop raised his crosier and called again for calm, but there were too many people trying to speak at once.

"My lord Ocerne!"

"Is it the Beast?"

"Monseigneur!"

They all subsided into silence as the hubbub outside grew closer and louder—the unmistakable song of a mob in a killing rage. Then the doors to the grand salon suddenly *boomed.*

Inside, the bailiff and the pastor cried out in unison. Their immaculate harmony would have been comedic in other circumstances.

The doors shook again.

"Soldiers of Mende—brace those doors! Everyone else, get back!" called Antoine. Half of the soldiers began desperately loading their pistols; the rest stood ready with their military blades. The nobles and officials gathered in a terrified knot behind the bishop. Behind them, the great western windows with their beautiful English glass showed only darkness outside.

Antoine looked down at me suspiciously, his fist around the bishop's pectoral cross. "What is going on, Sebastian? What have you done?!"

"Me? You think this is *my* doing?" I protested.

"He does!" interjected Lorette. She was looking at Antoine incredulously. "My lord Ocerne, if you have not foreseen what is coming for you, then you deserve it all the more."

"Foreseen *what*? *Tell me what you mean!*" Antoine almost screamed.

"War, my lord," she replied bleakly.

LXII

The doors boomed again, but they held. The voices outside swelled and then, ominously, fell silent.

"War?!" demanded Antoine. "What war?!"

I swallowed, my throat suddenly very dry. "In the simplest terms: the people of Gévaudan are coming to kill you, Antoine—you and the bishop who has bankrupted and fleeced them. They have been planning this for some time. If I had to guess, I would say that your ruthless punishment of the people in Saint-Julien today was the final affront."

"Kill me?" Antoine gaped. He seemed unable to comprehend what I was saying.

The bishop was much faster to grasp what was happening. "Rebellion!" he said incredulously. He was flushed and panting, the burned side of his face livid and waxy.

"Father, I warned you of this!" snapped Jacques. "How many concessions did you refuse? How many petitions?"

"Do you not see how we live? Did you think we would allow

you to steal the food from our plates forever?" demanded Lorette. "Did you believe we would work your fields and raise your flocks and want nothing for ourselves?"

"Our own people?" demanded Antoine. "This is not war—this is treason! Jacques, my son, please tell me you are not involved in this! These people are traitors to France. They are *criminals*!"

"They are *hungry,* Father! They cannot feed their families, and now they are here for yours," Jacques fumed, wiping gelatinous sweat from his brow. He motioned to the soldiers now barricading the doors. "How did you let it get to this?"

Antoine turned to Lorette, the Archangel's bladed plumes quivering about him. "You did this!" he accused. "You have been a crow on the eaves of this house your entire life!"

"Me?" scoffed Lorette. "I struck the spark, but the tinder is all yours, my lord. You will lay the blame anywhere but at your own feet."

"Be quiet, everyone! Lady Ocerne is correct: we are trapped in here," I said. "They are going to break through the main doors and slaughter us like weasels in a burrow—or burn us alive, more likely. We have as long as it takes them to find gunpowder." I held up the manacles of the Choking Braid. "Antoine, I can save you—say the words and release me, *please*."

"No! Do not be tempted, Lord Ocerne," admonished Bishop Fontaine. "You know the price of my intervention. The professor will be brought to justice, or there will be no salvation for you and yours."

"Look at me, Antoine." I reached up and took his face in my hands, ignoring the protests of his wife. "Do you really want me to die here? The truth."

He did not open his eyes. But nor could he hide the tears on his face.

"No, God help me, I cannot say I want you to die. But nor can I forgive you for what you did. I *remember* what . . . what you are . . . and that is why I cannot release you, no matter what you promise. I must keep faith with my Lord, though it may cost me my life," he said, his hand still wrapped tightly around the pectoral cross.

"Then so it will—and not your life alone, I fear!" I answered angrily. "Think of your wife and your son, who are about to die thanks to your pride!"

Antoine seemed to waver, though he said nothing. He opened his eyes and looked to his family, standing fearfully behind the bishop.

"Stay true, Lord Ocerne. Do not be deceived. He is in league with the Beast himself; every word is an invitation to corruption," warned the bishop.

"Antoine, believe me when I tell you this can all be set to rights, but we must get out of here right now. The Beast's curse has spread through every living thing in your lands—it is in the very water you drink, thanks to Dayane—and now it will bear fruit. This uprising—this *war*—is his lifeblood and his ultimate gift, and you have all helped him bring it about. And now this massacre will be his victory feast, unless you do something to stop it." I held up my manacles once again. "Say the words, *please*."

The doors shook again. Time was very nearly up for us all.

"Your tongue is knotted with your lies! Do you think to accuse us of these depravities? Would you lay the work of the Beast at our feet?" demanded Fontaine.

I met the bishop's eyes and he flinched as though I had slapped him. "Tell me, Monseigneur—when the animals turned to savagery, was it the Beast who razed the farms and brought the families of Gévaudan to the brink of starvation? Was it the Beast who then bought their land for a handful of chaff? And what of you, Lord Ocerne?" I asked, turning to the man I had loved. "What exquisite hospitality I have enjoyed in your home—to eat at your table is truly to experience the riches of Ocerne. Shall we pretend it was the Beast, then, who claimed the cream of Gévaudan's harvest and sent the rest to Versailles and Mende? No. That was your doing."

"Mine?" protested Antoine. "These were the edicts of king and Church—was I to betray France herself? Should I have reneged on my duty as baron and committed treason on their behalf?"

This time, it was Lorette who answered. "Look at you! You are beyond absurdity—pigs, all of you! Can you even imagine that the people about to kill you all might have their reasons? Duty, Lord Ocerne? *Duty?* Do you believe the Gévaudanais will see duty when they find Lady Ocerne in her satin and the bishop in his jewels? Will they understand that you were forced to fill the château with marble and stained glass? Will they?" She challenged them with her upthrust chin. "I think not. I think they have had enough of being told who and what to believe, and of the 'edicts of king and Church.'"

"Antoine, you know she is right," I said. "I think that, in their extremity, your people have looked at their lot and reasoned for themselves on its merits. I would say—in the words of a young man I once admired—that they have *dared to know.* And they are less than delighted with the knowledge they have gained."

It was too much for the bishop. Gone was the placid, understanding smile. He drew himself up, full of fury, and leveled the crosier at me like a sword.

But he never voiced his final condemnation.

A loud metallic thud from the main doors startled us all. I recognized the sound immediately.

"Petard!"[1] I yelled, dropping to the floor.

The explosion was devastating in the confines of the parlor.

The armored soldiers were at least partially protected, kneeling as they were behind their barricades. But over their heads, metal fragments and yard-long splinters flew in a deadly fusillade.

The bishop was strafed where he stood, his expression of righteous rage forever obliterated by the twisted remains of the door handle. Père Arnaud and the bailiff fell alongside him, punctured in a dozen places. The Archangel's wings flashed, and the dead men were immediately engulfed by the white corona of the Almighty's radiance.

And Antoine . . .

Antoine was standing over me, facing away from the doors.

Antoine dropped to his knees in front of me, his face white with shock.

The shrapnel had hit him in the back like grapeshot. His vest was soaked with crimson in seconds.

"Antoine!" Lady Ocerne screamed.

"Professor, take him, quickly—Ah!" said Jacques, clutching at his head.

Dust and smoke billowed through the room and engulfed us. The soldiers of Mende had taken some losses, but they were bet-

1. A ridiculously dangerous explosive device used to break through defenses during a siege. It was essentially a bell-shaped chamber full of gunpowder, with the open end placed against the obstructing door/wall by means of a brace. It is remembered for two reasons. First, the name "petard" is derived from the Latin verb for "flatulate"; and second, the role of petardier was often a once-only appointment, for obvious reasons.

ter armed and returned righteous fire of their own to the mob of villagers outside the door. I scrambled to drag Antoine behind the bailiff's enormous upturned bureau—no easy task, manacled as I was. Lady Ocerne did her best to help, but she was shaking so badly she could barely grip his shirt.

We cowered behind the surface of the stout desk. We sat Antoine upright between us, provoking a cry of pain as we leaned him back against the wood. We had left a wide wet trail of his blood on the floor.

"I am sorry," Antoine rasped. "Sebastian—the girl . . . don't . . ."

"No, stop," said Lady Ocerne, placing her hand over his mouth and shaking her head. Her eyes were wide and her trembling fingers pressed hard into his lips. "Stop. Stop." It seemed to be the only thing she could say.

"Lorette!" called Jacques. Crawling low to the floor, he risked the cross fire to retrieve his father's dueling sword where it had fallen. He used it to slice through Lorette's bonds and pulled her back to relative safety behind the bureau with us.

"Stay down. Are you hurt?" he asked, taking her face in his hands. She stiffened, her mouth twisting as he rested his fingertips on the swell of her belly. "Why didn't you tell me? How long have you known?"

Lorette gave a cold shrug. "Some months now."

"Some months? Did you know before I—before we spoke?"

"Before you tried to buy me off with an expensive bauble? Does it matter, Jacques? You made it clear where your future lies," she said. Her voice was calm, but there was terrible pain in her eyes.

"My wife—"

"I have not forgotten."

"Jacques," I interrupted, my chains rattling as I gripped his shoulder. "We must find a way out or Antoine is going to—"

I do not know if I finished the sentence; the air was suddenly full of fire and thunder.

The second explosion blasted through the barricades completely. The majestic windows behind us shattered outward in a cascade of glittering shards. The soldiers of Mende were scattered—many of them in pieces—and the rebels were finally inside.

"It is time, Jacques," said Lorette, as the air once again filled with smoke. She had taken Antoine's sword for herself. She stood over us in her chemise, pointing the blade directly at her former lover. "Time to choose. Come with me now. Or die with them."

"Jacques, she cannot leave!" I snapped, tugging impotently against my chains. "The child—your child—will bear the same curse you do. That's why your father brought her here!"

"Lorette, please! You must reason with them!" Jacques begged, his hands raised in surrender. He was shaking noticeably, his face drawn in terrible concentration. The smell of the blood all around him must have been maddening. "Please! You owe me at least that much!"

Lorette was incensed. "I owe you *nothing*!" she snarled, lunging at him with the sword. The blow was weak and clumsy; the tip snagged in Jacques's waistcoat and she nearly jarred the weapon out of her hand. But it was enough to scratch him, and what poured out of the young lord's wound was not blood but thick yellow plasma.

"Wait!" I called.

But Lorette was gone, running toward the barricades without a backward glance. She knew where her true safety lay.

Jacques straightened slowly, his skin beginning to steam. His eyes were full of fear.

"No . . . no! *Get away! I cannot stop it!*"

The rebellion had brought scores of people to the château.

They were all there; young and old, men and women. The common people of Gévaudan had nothing to lose, and nobody was denied their chance to fight.

They beat down the remains of the barricade with triumphant savagery. They surged into the parlor, their hands filled with iron and fire.

"Justice!" chorused the mob. "Equality!" they called, and "Freedom!"

The Gévaudanais were no longer colorless; their dun attire and gray skin were splashed liberally with red. Their thin, dirty faces were transformed in the passion of their uprising. Bodies weak with hunger were suddenly galvanized with rage. Eyes once flat with despair now shone with terrible hope. Where once all had been bleak, there was now a chance for freedom and glory.

It was a desperate chance, bought with violence and blood, but it held more promise than their lives had known for twenty years. They were so very *alive.*

This, then, was the Warfather's promise and his gift.

But they were not greeted by the cowering noble family they had come to murder.

Instead, a young man thrashed in agony there on the marble floor, his skin dripping yellow ichor as he tore at his own clothing. Even the ringleaders balked at the sight, faltering in their brave song. His mother knelt at his side, screaming as she tried to calm him, fouling her exquisite gown with dirt, plasma and blood as she cried, *Jacques! Jacques! Jacques!*

The change took only moments, and then she said no more.

LXIII

Shall I describe, one final time, a great slaughter?

Shall I give the account of yet more bloodshed in this already blood-drenched story of the Beast of Gévaudan?

I find I haven't the heart for it.

I will tell you first that there were almost none left living in the parlor of Château d'Ocerne afterward; be clear that there is no hope in what there is left to say.

I will tell you that the rebels had dragged prisoners with them from the château apartments, among them Jacques's dear Eloise.

I will allow you to imagine for yourself the horror of Jacques, in his bestial form, devouring his family. His mother. His own wife. You can conjure your own picture of the starving villagers who assailed him with farming tools and antiquated weapons, and the awful wounds suffered on both sides.

And I will tell you that I fled, dragging Antoine with me to the back of the room while they were all distracted with the horror of it.

I thought only of getting him away while I could. Tendrils of anima were rippling up and away from him, starting always around his heart. Michael's presence began to soften, now surrounding Antoine's head with gentle white light. It was beginning.

Antoine was dying.

"Antoine," I said, close to his ear. "Antoine, I need to get these chains off! I can help you, but you must release me! Please! What are the words?"

He looked at me bitterly, his breath coming shorter and shorter. "Why, Sebastian? Do we not both deserve this?"

I looked into his eyes, despairing. "Antoine, please. We are going to die!"

"Do you believe I wish to survive after what I have done? This ruin I have brought on my own house? My own family?" He coughed, a dreadful, sticky sound.

"Antoine—" The room shook again with the roar of gunpowder and one of the doorways collapsed. Jacques roared; horrifyingly, I could recognize his voice in the sound.

Hurry up, Sebastian! ***That*** *one is nearly out of villagers and* ***this*** *one is not going to last much longer!*

Antoine gripped me suddenly by the shoulder. The radiance around his head was growing brighter and *deeper.*

"Promise me! If I release you, promise me you will find a way to cure Jacques!"

"I . . . I will, Antoine. If it takes me the rest of my life. I promise."

And still he hesitated. "But how can I trust you again?" he rasped. "I feel I have placed my trust always in the wrong place. First in miracles and magic. Then the bishop and the Lord Almighty. Either way, a massacre."

"Then one more time, I beg you. No magic. No Almighty. No bargains." I placed my hand on his chest, feeling his heart like a frightened bird under my palm. "Just me. If you ever loved me, trust me now."

He is going!

"I . . ." Antoine's voice failed and his eyes began to close.

"No. No! Antoine, not like this!"

Mercy! I called to the Archangel above me. *Mercy, Michael! I wish to treat with you!*

Wh-what?! balked Sarmodel. He hissed in disdain. *Oh, Sebastian, you are* ***disgusting****!*

I ignored him and instead opened my heart to the Archangel's implacable gaze, letting the Grand General see my pain and my shame and my fear—all of it. I hid nothing and allowed him inside the wordless desperation I felt.

I promise payment in kind, whatever you will, I pleaded. *But I beg mercy. For Antoine. Keep him here, just a little while longer. Give this one thing to me, please.*

There was no answer—there could be no answer in the Mundane world—but the Archangel's Divine radiance brightened once more. Beneath my hands rose a sudden thrumming vibration in Antoine's chest, as though a fire had been vigorously fanned, or a vessel filled with rushing water.

Antoine opened his eyes.

Thank you, Michael.

On my palm appeared a shining white sigil, traced in lines of Divine fire.

The Contract of Obligation. And at its center, the symbol of the lion.

The Archangel would claim his price when he was ready, it seemed.

"Sebastian," said Antoine. He was lucid once more.

"The key, Antoine!" I held up my Shackles, and this time he did not refuse.

With a sluggish nod, he placed his hand on the Shackles.

"Sim Sala Bim," he said.

The chains fell away immediately and I threw them aside.

Finally!

The fist in my throat was gone. Sarmodel came forward in a rush and my veins were filled with molten silver.

I looked back only once.

Jacques . . .

The young man was a frenzied monster, bleeding from so many wounds that he seemed to wear a glistening red skin. The remaining villagers were no match for him, but the creature was almost spent. His shining, tarry black eyes met mine with flat hatred, and I know that if he had found the strength, he would certainly have taken me as his next victim.

*By the Rift—**move,** Sebastian!*

I collected Antoine in my arms and sprang through the shattered western window, out into the night.

And then I ran, fast enough and far enough that even the Beast would not find me.

I set him down by the stream as the sun was coming up.

It was the same stream where he had once caught a fine silver trout in his drawers; the stream where I can see him still, his body dripping water and shining like polished wood in the fading light.

Antoine's anima was lifting off him in sheets now. But Michael's gift was still strong enough to keep him breathing, and as he opened his eyes, he smiled.

"Sebastian," he said. He seemed confused, but he finally saw me; I don't know how else to describe it. For the first time since my return, he was *there with me.* "I feared I had lost you."

"No, Antoine. I'm here," I said. I took him in my arms and kissed the blood from his lips, heedless. "I'm here, at your service, always."

"It's a strange thing . . . at the Bow and Brace . . . did you know I wanted to go with you, when you went after the Beast? I have always thought it might have been *different.*" He looked at me with wonder, as he had that time under the bridge at Saint-Julien-by-the-Stream, as though he were seeing the face of the world for the first time. "How did I let you go alone?"

"You're here now," I said, choking. "It doesn't matter. You're here." I rubbed my face against his, feeling the warmth of his breath, the rough tickle of his stubble, and the soft pressure of his lips on my temple. I whispered the words over and over into the hollow of his shoulder.

You're here. You're here. You're here.

"How? How are you still so young? Surely a lifetime has passed since I saw you." He kissed me and touched his fingertips to my face. "Is it magic? There was always magic with you." Tears rose in his eyes. "What happened? We were going to . . . together . . ."

"Antoine, it doesn't matter," I said. "*Please.* I don't want to talk. Rest now."

"I am tired, in truth. Will you light the fire? I tried using the words after you left, but they never worked again. Sim Sala Bim. Another one of your tricks," he said with that sardonic smile. He tried to pull me closer. "Please, Sebastian, stay with me. It's cold."

"I will say the words," I said. "Do not worry, Antoine. Sleep. I won't leave you."

"Thank you," he said. "I am . . . glad of you. Did I ever tell you that?" Then he looked at me, smiling one last time. "Will you give me an answer, now at the last?"

"An answer to what?"

"Will you tell me who you are?"

"Antoine. No," I said. I found I could not look at him. "I still don't know, and I fear I never will. I have lived so long, and yet I feel I am still the child I once was. There have been too many years, too many lifetimes of mistakes; looking back I can barely see myself."

"Then I will tell you what I see. You are the man who brought my son home safely, when he was already half a monster. You are the man who followed me to the riverbed, and the one I kissed under the maple. You are the man who came to find me in the dark when I was losing myself. You are the man who bargained with a monster—twice—to save my life. You are the man I wanted to rebuild Gévaudan with—sugarcane and cinnamon, remember?"

"Antoine, I . . ." *I lied to you, and I ruined you, and you are dying because of me.*

He was breathing in shallow gulps and he was suddenly confused again. Michael's gift was fading. "There was a bargain with *her*—the Lady in the Water, wasn't there? Did we do something wrong? I have felt that something . . . went wrong."

"I know, Antoine. I'm sorry. It was my fault, all of it," I said. "God, I'm so sorry." I shared his last breath and sobbed, struggling to speak. "But I loved you, always, even when you wanted to kill me. That never changed. I loved you."

But Antoine was gone. His body was warm, but the divine current of his anima was leaving, gathering all at once into a brilliant mist that began to rise . . . *away*. . . .

Michael was there waiting, building the Almighty's light around Antoine like a rising flood.

I closed my eyes and, against all reason, followed him across the divide.

LXIV

The darkness was all but absolute.

A single light held back the shadows, a pained and trembling wisp hovering above my open hand.

The Archangel leaned into the frail light. The lion's face was a ghastly mask, looking down from overhead.

"This one is in my charge, Sebastian Grave of Larnaca. He cast aside the false tenets of his youth, and devoted his life to serving the Almighty. In death, he will Commune."

The magnificent beast's half-human paw stretched out for the glimmering light, ready to carry it away. But then it stopped, uncertain.

"Just take him, damn you," I sobbed, lowering my face. "If this is the price you demand for allowing me to share his last moments, then I despise you. But I will not fight you."

But another hand appeared from the darkness, covered in stinking, ragged fur. It also yearned for the beautiful light, hovering just within my reach.

"Why so coy, Michael?" came the voice of the baboon. "Take it, if the claim is yours."

The Archangel did not reply to the mocking voice in the darkness. The silence grew long, and I feared I would go mad there, stuck in between waking and sleeping.

But then a tiny thing fell, flashing through the air, down into nothing. It sang like crystal.

A tear from the eye of the Archangel.

His breath was a rush of divine perfume over my face as he lifted the shimmering wisp gently from my palm. "I could take this one; it is my right. He followed the Sacraments, even unto his death. The pathway he chose led always to the Almighty's door. And you are indeed in my debt. But . . ."

I drank in the hovering light with my gaze. In its flickering, sleeping form I could *feel* Antoine. His laugh. His curious eyes. His surprise as the trout slapped him—*one-two!*—with its silver tail.

"But *what*?" I demanded brokenly. "Take him if you must! Do it, and leave me! I cannot bear it."

The silence was heavy.

"I . . . will not. Not unless it is also your will," he said finally. "There is so little mercy in the world, and there are so few worthy of it. But I would allow you to exercise that Divine gift which so uplifts mankind, and which you have so abused. I would give you *choice*—you, Sebastian Grave, most wretched and most wondrous of men."

"You're not . . . you're not going to take him?" I asked.

"If so you will, then so I shall," answered Michael gently. "I will take him to the Almighty and you may consider our Contract fulfilled. He will know infinite peace, infinite love, infinite—"

"Infinite *shit*," interrupted the baboon. I could not see him, but

I felt his other hand alight reassuringly on my shoulder. "He will be erased like an eddy in the ocean, and the Almighty will add another dimple to his burgeoning rump. Sebastian, this one is *ours.* We have earned it. How many have loved you like Antoine did? To the very end, he wanted to be with you—he chose *you* over the Almighty!" The glee in his voice seemed an affront to this quiet place.

"He did. He *did.* He loved me." I said the words almost in disbelief. The realization was like the soothing of a long-standing ache; a balm over a place in my soul I had rubbed raw with questions.

The Archangel hesitated before speaking. "You overstate your claim, Lariel. You held a place *alongside* his Lord and God, it is true. In his final moments, his heart was clouded, and so I have met you here." He gave a rose-scented sigh. "It says much of the fickleness of men that they die so, their love sincerely divided between their immortal God and the impermanent things of the world."

"But you take them all anyway, Great Prince," said the baboon. "You and Azrael and the rest of the Host. Do you not?"

"Only one love is eternal, Lariel," said the Archangel, with patience. "All other ground is sinking sand."

"One eternal love, and one eternal lie," mocked the voice from the darkness. "You have said it yourself—man was given *choice,* and yet you would have them all follow blindly where you lead, unto death. When the Almighty awakens, will he thank you for the millions you have hoodwinked into his sleeping maw?"

"You are a tiresome thing, Lariel. Must you always answer charity with scorn; compassion with ridicule?" The lion showed his teeth, but did not rise to the bait. Instead, he turned to me. "Mark me, Sebastian Grave, and mark the honor you are afforded. Take him with you, if you will, and add him to the many souls who so amplify your own; he would join them as gladly as he would the faithful in Paradise."

"Yes, Sebastian!" Another matted paw emerged from the shadows, beckoning. Suddenly there were three, then four, then a dozen of the baboon's hands surrounding me in the darkness, all reaching, imploring, reasoning. "Do not consign him to the oblivion of the Almighty! Come, I will take him. You may have him with you, always. Antoine will be *part of us*."

The dancing, quivering light waited. The beautiful face of the Archangel bowed in compassion. The hand of the baboon squeezed my shoulder in camaraderie.

And then I saw the long muscles of Antoine's forearms kneading as he secured the straps of his saddle. I saw his fingertips stained with walnut juice. I saw him laughing madly as the timber wolf carried him off the bridge at Saint-Julien-by-the-Stream. I saw the hollow below his jaw, where he liked to be kissed. I saw him naked and breathing hard in the shelter of the maple, his hair tangled with leaves and his eyes full of pleasure and wonder.

"Can you give him what was taken, Michael?" I asked. "Give him back the life he deserved? Without . . . without me, without any of us, I don't care. Can he live again?"

The Lion of Judah was silent a moment. Then he shook his head gravely. "You know that is not within my power. Only the Almighty has ever dared such a miracle, and the world was changed forever."

"Then the choice is not mine," I said. Tenderly, I scooped the light from his paw. "Or yours."

"Sebastian, wait! Think on it!" The baboon babbled desperately in my ear. "Do not—NO!"

With a cry like dying, I cast Antoine's anima far out into the infinite blackness.

It blazed liked a meteor for only a moment, and then it fell apart, dissolving into bright mist. Whatever Antoine had been, whatever delicate energetic configuration and spiritual circuitry had made the man he was, sublimed in an instant. He would return to the eternal cycle of matter and energy, dispersed to become a million new children of Creation.

And he was lost to me forever.

"So mercy is answered. Your debt stands," intoned the Archangel. "Say Grace."

LXV

I returned to Château d'Ocerne only once. I walked back that same day, to collect my belongings, knowing I wouldn't have the chance again. There were bodies everywhere—the rebels had been fast and thorough—and a few looters did their best to hide when they saw me. Much of the building was ruined by fire or explosion, but I managed to recover my wagon, my horse and my trunk (still undamaged and unopened thanks to my exceptional Wards). In the Arcane spectrum, Michael's Contract of Obligation burned brightly on my palm the whole time; the Archangel was not going to let me forget my debts anytime soon.

I found Jacques sleeping in the noble family's private quarters.

He had somehow made his way back to his own bed. I watched him as he lay there, naked and covered in blood like a newborn. He had managed to survive, in spite of his many wounds, thanks to the number of hearts he had eaten.

Sebastian. You know what I'm going to say.

I should kill him. I know.

But I didn't. I couldn't.

"Jacques, wake up." I sat on the side of the bed, shaking him gently.

"Professor?" He was groggy. And then he sat upright in a shot, his eyes wild. "They are coming! The villagers have come for us!"

I placed a calming hand on his shoulder. "Slowly, slowly. We are safe for now."

His confusion was clear as he took in the familiar surrounds of his bedroom and then his own nakedness, and the sticky film of blood and plasma that covered him. Realization came faster this time.

"Again?" he asked with resignation.

"I'm afraid so. There is much to explain, but right now we must leave, Jacques."

"Leave?"

"Can you stand? Here, I can help you."

He glared at me with familiar fire. It was oddly comforting. "I will manage alone, or not at all."

"As you will. But make haste. I do not know how much you remember, but it would be best for us to be gone from Château d'Ocerne—and Gévaudan—as quickly as possible. Have no fear, there is still room in my wagon to hide an ill-tempered Occitan nobleman."

"But what of my family? What of Eloise?" he insisted.

"They are . . . gone, Jacques. I am sorry. The rebels left none alive. There will be time to mourn them once we are away from here, I promise, but we must *leave.*"

Jacques said nothing; he only closed his eyes and nodded. He packed very little, but he pocketed the little cameo, Lorette's likeness in amber and ivory, with its jet-studded silver setting.

And what exactly are we supposed to do with him? Am I to have any say in this at all? demanded Sarmodel.

Not this time.

I ensured Jacques did not see inside the parlor as I helped him make his painful way out into the courtyard. I spoke the Pyric Word as soon as we were over the threshold, knowing the looters would certainly not be taking the trouble to bury anyone. The flames kindled in the closest bodies and then quickly began to spread.

"Do not look back, Jacques."

We met nobody on the high road. I decided to bypass Saint-Julien-by-the-Stream, now terribly quiet. I do not know how many of the villagers were lost in the attack, but I doubted that those remaining would be amenable to hungry travelers looking to shop.

"Where are we going, Professor?" asked Jacques despondently from the wagon as we turned along the eastward road.

"We must address each other more familiarly now, Jacques. There can be no young Lord Ocerne and Professor Grave traveling through France, not for a time."

"What am I to call you then?"

"Call me Sebastian. Pretend that we are friends."

"I would rather pretend that we had never met. But very well. Sebastian—where are we going?"

"We are going back to Corvano, that I may find a proper cure for your affliction. I promised your father I would, and I owe it to him. I owe it to you." I ran my fingers across the glimmering mark on my palm. "And I have other debts to pay. In the meantime, stay away from my horse."

We said little else for the rest of the day, and Jacques slept for most of it. I passed the time by making a mental list of the things he would need; the beginnings of a new regime of care for his unique condition. The first item was a long bath.

It was close to sundown when I saw the bird.

A beautiful white goose came gliding along the breeze. I watched it warily, noticing as it drew closer the striking black markings around its throat and wings.

Oh, by the Rift, what now? groaned Sarmodel.

I raised my arm as the goose approached, and it alighted on my wrist without a sound. In spite of its size, it had barely any weight at all. In my Arcane sight, it was a winged serpent with a wicked hooked beak and a frighteningly vacant stare. Its feathers were singed, as though it had escaped from a fire.

Full of trepidation, I spoke the word of command.

"Meatbag! I trust you are well!" said Livia's voice from its beak. There was a worrying level of tension in her tone, not alleviated by the trill of forced laughter that followed. "Where are you, I wonder? I understand you're busy, but you may want to—" The goose made a dreadful sound as something inhuman roared over Livia's voice. "You *may want to* consider returning as soon as you can. There have been some . . . developments here at home and I—"

I reached up and broke the creature's neck with a sharp twist. The follit discorporated into a mist of anima without a sound of protest.

I was so very tired and it had been quite a trying day. I indulged in a tiny sob.

"Professor—Sebastian? Who was that?" asked Jacques drowsily from the cart. "Did I hear a woman just now?"

"It was my housekeeper," I answered automatically, wiping my eyes.

"Mademoiselle Livia?"

"The very same."

He was groggy and still half asleep. "I am sorry, I did not see her. Please convey my regards."

"I will, Jacques. Go back to sleep."

My draft horse farted in mild surprise as I jostled her into a canter.

I told you, said Sarmodel, as he settled his coils within my mind. *Sebastian, I told you this was a bad idea, from the very beginning! One day, perhaps you will listen.*

Yes, my love, I answered wearily. *Perhaps one day.*

AFTERWORD

When you have lived as long as I have, it is hard to know when one story finishes and the next begins. There is always more to tell.

But no, this was Antoine's story in many ways, and it doesn't feel right to move on without him. Even spending time with his memory has been a comfort, and I pray that I have honored it, and him.

And I think I will leave Jacques like this for now—how I like to remember him. A young man, deeply troubled, impossibly stubborn and cursed. But still hopeful, I think. And perhaps a friend, at a time when I had so few.

Writing this down has taken me far longer than I would have thought, and I have been in Europe for months. It is time to put it to rest for now and return to my home in New York. I have learned not to spend too long living in memories, and I am starting to miss the excitement of life in the shining glass canyons of Manhattan.

Livia also updates me on the state of my inbox every week or so; the current count is over fifteen thousand.

It is time to go home.

While the story of the Red Winter is done for now, I am taking Lorette's cameo home with me. I am going to leave it unrestored; I have decided the blemishes of the past are sometimes worth keeping. It certainly has another story in it—perhaps one I will write down someday.

I do not know where Lorette went after the massacre at Château d'Ocerne. I know she did not stay in Gévaudan.

I did meet her again—her and her daughter—but that was many, many years later. You can be assured that Michael got his pound of flesh as well; the Contract of Obligation was completed on his terms, at the most inopportune time, as ever.

Nor do I know what was made of the uprising in Gévaudan—it certainly does not appear in any historical account, save this one. But I believe that it was the beginning—the true beginning—of the far more famous Revolution.

The French Revolution. The violent redress delivered by the poor for the many injustices they suffered. Liberty, Equality and Fraternity are what they fought for. But shorn of its slogans and its justifications—however valid—it was no different to every other war: they fought over wealth and territory, and tens of thousands died. The victors took the wealth and the power, and then killed hundreds of thousands more trying to hold on to it.

And so on, and so on.

So, if you have any questions about the fate of Avstamet the Warfather, be assured he was only getting started in Gévaudan, and he got exactly what he wanted in the end. Look to the decades following the Revolution that spread the many passions of war from France across the entire continent. Look to the crippling of the Church, and the censuring of the Almighty's agents. Look further still, to the armies of Napoleon marching under the eagle-crested standards of Rome in their conquest of a new empire.

Yes, I believe the seeds Avstamet planted in Gévaudan bore fruit for generations. Just look around now. The Spirit of War is eating very well these days, I think.

Call him Ares. Call him Mars. Call him Avstamet.

Or call him the Beast, as did the good people of Gévaudan, before they marched into his jaws, singing Liberty, Equality, Fraternity.

Sebastian Grave

Florence

2013

ACKNOWLEDGMENTS

It's a little embarrassing to admit it's taken nearly a quarter of my life to get *The Red Winter* out. It's a mountain I could never have climbed on my own, and I'm indebted to so many people for reaching this point.

First up, all my love goes to my mum, Jude, and my sister, Meg. The book is dedicated to you for a reason. I wouldn't have got any of this done without your love and support, always, even all the way back when I was a six-year-old writing about cannibal werewolves and black magic. I'm a better speller now, but my influences have changed not at all.

Bottomless, eternal thanks to my editor, Ali Fisher, for giving *The Red Winter* a home at Tor: you have quite literally made my dreams come true. Thank you for believing in the book and taking a chance on a complete unknown from the other side of the world. I owe huge thanks to the rest of the Tor team as well, in particular to Dianna Vega, Will Hinton and Dakota Griffin. I've come to appreciate the amount of work, detail and logistical skill that goes into producing a book, and I'm so grateful for the care and dedication that you've all put into bringing it to life.

I have been incredibly lucky at so many points, and none more so than in finding my agent, Christabel McKinley. Yours was the "yes" that completely changed my life. You have been such a champion for my book and I couldn't have asked for a better guide/sounding board/cheerleader when I needed one most. Thank you for all of your kind advice, patience and tireless advocacy—I promise I won't need hand-holding forever.

Decades of gratitude to Euan, Kimmy, Justine, Jeffrey and the Darlington-Boston Wiltshire-Cohens, who have known me longer and better than almost anyone, and who have nourished my soul with questionable charades, costume parties and toilet humor. I'm so lucky to have you all in my life.

I think if there was a point when it could have gone either way, it was when I gave my first few chapters (or more) to a few gracious friends for review. I am admittedly not much of a self-starter and your words of encouragement gave me the boost I needed to get it done. So, a very special thanks to Aimee, Nita, Eric, Max and Phil C., and also to my UK crew—Shaun M., Julia and Cam R.

Editing that first draft was a daunting job and I owe so much to my dedicated early readers, Jonathan PH and Alex Dook, who gave me the feedback I needed to make a start. It would be remiss of me not to mention Sarah and Nadia from Scary Movie Club here as well—thank you for years of quality scares and tech support. Especially big thanks to my manuscript doctor, Liz Monument, for helping me to get it all in sensible working order, trimmed down (ha!) and market-ready. I'm also indebted to Doug Whyte at UWA for his assistance with some of the Latin phrases—I hope I have avoided disgracing myself.

A particularly massive thank-you to my found family here in

Melbourne, who read this hefty, excessively footnoted beast and somehow made me feel like a genius. To Dr. Brent, who knows what it's like to put years and years and *years* into a big piece of writing: here's to many more *Dead Cells* Sundays and evenings spent torching terrible movies. To Luke: let's never forget where we came from—coffee and donuts are on me now. And to Mitchell: I hope you're enjoying Glitterwolves in its ultimate form, and I'll try to put more old-timey filth in the next one.

I owe a special debt to Marie, the Batch crew and the team at Goodies for letting me occupy a corner of your café for the last several years. This book was largely fuelled by your incomparable coffee, toasted cheese scones and poached eggs, and I think it's better for it.

Alongside the gratitude, some apologies. First, I beg the forgiveness of any historians or language experts, particularly those who specialize in Joan of Arc or pre-revolutionary France. I've taken a lot of liberties and doubtless made a lot of mistakes, but always in the spirit of a good story, so please don't come for me. Second, to everyone who's had to deal with me trying out an elevator pitch, soliciting feedback or just losing my mind over THE BOOK for the last ten years: I'm sorry, it won't happen again (it will).

And finally, to every reader who has chosen to join me in this dark little history for a while: my sincerest, most heartfelt thanks. This story and these characters have lived in my head for so long that it feels a bit like sharing my journal. For those who found friends here: Sebastian, Sarmodel and Livia have plenty more adventures in them, and I hope you'll come along for the next one.

ABOUT THE AUTHOR

CAMERON SULLIVAN was born in Perth, Western Australia. He grew up with the dark fantasy and horror icons of the eighties and went on to study classics and creative writing at the University of Western Australia. After several years working and studying in Italy and the UK, he returned to Australia and settled in Melbourne, which is the best place for Australians who actually enjoy the winter. He will easily lose a weekend to a good book, a new recipe or games of any kind.